SURRENDER AT SEA . . .

"Come on now, drink up like a good sailor," said Black Patch. Fancy took a good swig.

The counterpane slipped from her shoulders and Black Patch's good eye fixed itself on the smooth skin of her arms. Slowly and lightly he caressed her and she, eyes glazed slightly from the potent drink, nestled closer to him until he could feel the length of her body.

And then all her resistance gave way. Her free hand came up and explored his chest, feeling his powerful heart beat. His skin, warm and still smelling faintly of the river, excited her and she craved his body on hers. His caressing hands moved to her breasts, and then she was in his arms . . .

Sweet Fire

Kate Fairfax

PUBLISHED IN ENGLAND AS *WILD HONEY*

C

CHARTER BOOKS, NEW YORK

This Charter Book contains the complete
text of the original paperback edition.
It has been completely reset in a typeface
designed for easy reading, and was printed
from new film.

SWEET FIRE
Published in England as *Wild Honey*
A Charter Book/published by arrangement with
Macdonald and Company (Publishers) Ltd.

PRINTING HISTORY
Macdonald Futura edition/1981
Charter edition/April 1983

ISBN: 0-441-79119-0

Charter Books are published by Charter Communications, Inc.
200 Madison Avenue, New York, N.Y. 10016
PRINTED IN THE UNITED STATES OF AMERICA

CHAPTER ONE

Fanny crouched lower in the thicket, her heart beating fast and her eyes nearly starting out of her head. She could hear the low moans and the thrashings about in the undergrowth and her curiosity was nearly her undoing. She trod on a twig and there was a loud snap.

"What was that?" The thin dark face of the young gypsy girl that Fanny had seen knocking at the doors in the village popped up from the luscious grass of the thicket.

"'Tis nothing. A rabbit perhaps. I'll take a look at the traps after we've done." A large brown hand came up and pulled the gypsy wench down on to the grass again.

Fanny held her breath, and the giggling started again. She bit her lip. She would have dearly liked to watch what was really going on. Oh, she guessed! But that wasn't the same as seeing it properly.

There was a flurry of arms and legs, and Fanny saw a slim brown leg and foot raise itself. What could the couple be up to now? She bit her nails in an agony of frustration. It would have pleased her to go home and tell Billy she had actually *seen* someone fornicating! Of course, her brother would never believe her; he never believed anything she said. He was going on eighteen, and she had just had her fourteenth birthday—that is, if the old cat who looked after them both was speaking the truth. But then, Aunt Beamish was given to telling many different tales when she'd been drinking old Farmer Milton's ale.

Anyway, she'd nearly seen what all the girls whispered about, hadn't she? She could always use her imag-

1

ination and fill in the extra bits herself. Would the young
gypsy girl and the broad dark youth come there again?
She would come again on her day off—next Sunday,
that was—and perhaps the next time . . . aye, she'd
make certain she was in a better position to see. . . .

The girl stood up and stretched. Fanny looked at her
with interest. She wondered if there would be anything
about her to give her away, any sign by which the village
would know that she had been fornicating with the
young gypsy boy in the wood. . . . But the girl looked
happy and showed no sign of guilt. The old vicar must be
wrong. He said hellfire would belch and thunder roar if
females walked in the wood with the young men of the
village. Or was that only for the villagers? Perhaps two
gypsies did not count. They were not of the village, but
just passing through.

For years Fanny had stood watch during the hot summer months, waiting for the gypsies to return to the old
campsite. And for years she had dreamed of young Caleb Neyn who was so different from the village youths.
He was taller, broader and blacker than those clumsy
clods who gawked and whistled after her. She wished
she too was a gypsy.

But now, here he was with this dirty thin slut. Plainly,
whatever Caleb had been doing to her, she had enjoyed
it. Her giggles had made it plain. She envied the slut and
could have spat in her eye!

As the girl stretched, Fanny could see that except for
a torn skirt that showed brown bare leg through the slit,
she was wearing only a skimpy blouse, which was none
too clean. She had the untamed look of the wild. Her
blue-black hair was uncombed and hung raggedly down
to her waist. Gold earrings hung nearly to her shoulders,
and as she twisted a red handkerchief around her brow,
Fanny saw the smooth brown skin of her waist.

Caleb's hand came up and stroked that skin and then
slipped underneath her blouse. Fanny could see he was
fondling her breasts. The girl made a purring sound like
a well-fed cat. That's just what she is, thought Fanny

viciously—a black cat! But the girl laughed and moved away.

"Tomorrow, Caleb. Come tomorrow. I must sell some lace and pegs to these miserable gaujé, or I shall not eat tonight."

"Not so fast. Not 'miserable.' The gaujé in these parts are our friends. The Neyns have always gone out of their way to be friends with the villagers. But you Fingos are strangers here—this is your first visit to these parts. So tell your father and brothers to take only what is necessary."

"Pah! They will take no notice of you! Father has the nimblest set of fingers in the business. What he wants, he takes. And let no man try to stop him!"

Caleb laughed. "You forget, he has not met the Neyn family yet. We have ruled these parts for generations, and several other tribes have come and gone again. Our word is law!"

"Then try telling my father that!" She smiled down at him mockingly. "And if Father knew that Savina Fingo was no longer a virgin, he would doctor you like he does the young colts!"

"He would have to tie me down first," Caleb snarled. "Don't underestimate me, Savina. There are other women."

Savina frowned and looked anxious.

"I'll come tomorrow, Caleb. I have no quarrel with you."

"Very well. I'll be waiting. Now run along and sell your pegs."

Picking up a woven willow basket, the girl ran swiftly off through the wood. Caleb lay propped up on one hand, a grass stalk between his teeth. He watched her go, then turned his head and looked at the spot where Fanny was hiding.

"You can come out now, whoever you are. And if you don't show yourself by the time I count three, I'll choke you with this rabbit wire!"

Fanny gulped and for a moment could not move or

speak. Then she stood up and moved forward.

"It's me—Fanny. Don't choke me, Caleb, please!"

Caleb looked up at her and laughed.

"Fanny Bickler. I might have known it. You came like a cow smelling water. What do you want? Or can I guess?" He considered Fanny's dark skinny look and was plainly not impressed. "Go on now, go home. You're too young for love. Come back next year when you've got a bit of a bosom."

Fanny shrank back, blushing.

"I know there's not much of me . . ."

"Well? What are you waiting for? Get home before you're missed."

Fanny stood, twisting the toe of her broad, clumsy shoe with its big steel buckle. There was something she *had* to know.

"First tell me what it's like!"

Caleb cocked a quizzical eyebrow.

"That's a very unbecoming thing to ask a fellow! Why do you want to know?"

"Well—Nellie Simms is always talking about it . . . and Thomas Pye is always on about it. He wants me to, but I don't know. Vicar talks about hellfire, and I'm afraid. Are you frightened of hellfire?"

Caleb laughed and shook his head, and Fanny smiled. Caleb sounded like such a warm person, and so full of humor. Not like her dried up Aunt Beamish, or that horrible old man she worked for, Farmer Joshua Raybold, and his vinegary daughter Rebecca. She took heart and spoke again.

"I've watched you for the past four years, Caleb Neyn. I look for your coming, and I've watched you leave. Where do you go from here?"

"Oh, we roam all through Sussex and Kent, Dorset and Hampshire. We wander the lanes, and in certain parts we are welcome and stay some time. Other places we avoid because we are warned off. We sell our tinware and mend pots and pans and tell fortunes and sell pegs and ribbons. We know who buys and who has no truck with us. We get by."

"And are there other girls like me waiting to see you?" she said jealously.

"There are a few," he said with a shrug. "It depends what you are waiting for."

"I'm not sure what I'm waiting for." She raised her shoulders and shrugged. "You are so different. You've traveled and seen things. Tell me, have you seen King Charles or any of his mistresses?"

"Yes, once. It was just after he was crowned. A great to-do that was. He was in Dover awaiting his queen. She had just come off the ship from Portugal and she was weak and seasick. The King lay at Dover until she recovered, and he attended the Fair. My mother told his fortune, pretending she did not know who he was. . . . He gave her a gold piece."

"What did she tell him?" Fanny asked breathlessly.

"That he would never be beheaded like his father before him."

"Then what did he do?"

"He laughed and chucked her under the chin and kissed her. He said it was the best news he ever heard."

"Could she tell me my fortune?"

Caleb looked at her narrowly.

"Why do you want to know your fortune? Anybody can tell what your fortune will be. You'll beget some brat in a hurry, wed the first poor fellow who will confess to being the father, and work yourself to the bone for the rest of your life. What more do you want to know?"

"I don't want that kind of life. Surely there is something better? I want to leave Gilbourne and Sussex, and travel. They say London is the place to prosper. I want to go there."

"You've got some uppity ideas for a village wench. What do you do?"

"Me and Billy were brought up by Aunt Beamish. She's housekeeper at the big house, and I work for Farmer Raybold and his daughter, Miss Rebecca. I'm their maid of all work, and two more miserable people I've yet to meet!"

"I know old Raybold. A skinflint and a miser. He once caught me snaring rabbits. I was only a little lad then, and he kicked my arse. I've not forgotten. I've had many a pheasant from his woods since then."

"So it's you who pinches his pheasants! He's raring mad about that. Someday he'll find you out and then it'll be deporting for you!"

"He'll have to catch me first. I wager I could show him a clean pair of heels any day. I can even creep up on a fox. I know what I'm doing."

Fanny looked at him with admiration. His dirty sweat-stained shirt was open down to the waist and the brown hairy chest did things to her that she had never dreamed of before. She wanted to stretch out a hand and run her fingers through the tightly curled hair and to kiss the side of his neck.

Caleb's black eyes took in her emotion-charged form and he smiled. He knew the effect of his bare torso on impressionable young wenches! His hand ran up her bare leg, and she shivered. He pulled her down beside him and kissed her. Fanny felt the blood rise within her.

But suddenly Caleb pushed her from him in disgust.

"Phew! You smell like rotten cats! When did you wash last?"

Fanny sat up angrily.

"I had a bath at Easter! I don't smell too bad. Thomas Pye says he likes my smell!"

"Then he's got no taste! Do you want to know what love is like, Fanny Bickler?"

"Yes, I must know! Nellie Simms is the only girl in the village . . ."

"Oho! The village whore, eh?"

"She doesn't do it for money, if that's what you mean."

"More fool her, then. But I expect she likes presents?"

"Well . . . she told me that Ned Higgins once gave her some cherry ribbons. Good as Lady Letitia's, they were."

"And you think the Lady Letitia is the finest lady in these parts?"

"Aunt Beamish says so, and she should know!"

"Enough of this senseless talking. Will you swim in the river with me?"

"What! And get wet? Not likely."

He shrugged and stood up." Then I'll be going. I'll not bed a wench who stinks and is crawling with lice! I can pick and choose my women, you know."

"Wait! Please don't go, Caleb. I want—I want you, Caleb. I *love* you, do you hear!"

"Aw, get yourself home. The church bell's stopped ringing. You should be at your prayers by now."

"I'll not be missed, I promise you. Aunt Beamish stays with the family all day on Sundays. There's only Billy in the cottage. I'm supposed to clean the cottage on Sundays, but sometimes I don't. Aunt will only give me a beating, and then I can do it before I go to work up at Fellside. I can stay . . . if you want me to."

"Only if you come swimming."

"Then I'll try it. I've never been in the river before. Is it very cold?"

"A little. But it sends your blood pounding through your veins and makes you feel alive. And when the sun beats down on your back everything takes on an extra beauty. The fields, the sky and all growing things. Do you like trees, Fanny Bickler?"

"I never thought of them. I suppose I like them. Why?"

"If you have never lain under a tree and watched the blue sky peeping through the leaves and felt all was well with your world, you have never lived."

"And do you feel like that?" she said breathlessly.

"Often. After tickling a trout, wrestling with my friends, or after making love. Aye, that is the best time."

"Then perhaps I shall feel the same way today."

Caleb gave a great shout of laughter. "Methinks it is I who will be seduced! You are a very precocious child.

How old are you, Fanny?"

She thrust out her chin. "Fifteen. Old enough to marry, if I had a dowry!"

"So! You don't look fifteen! Too small and skinny. But I like your eyes. Come on, Fanny and watch me dive into the water off Devil's Rock, and then you can jump in and I'll catch you."

They walked through the wood until they came to the river, Caleb moving like a great black cat and Fanny watching his lithe gait in anticipation of what was to come. Then he stripped naked, throwing down his tattered pants and shirt in a heap under a tree. Hesitantly, Fanny took off her shirt and old tattered shift. Her jacket came next. And then she, too, was naked. They faced each other. Fanny, small-boned and slim as a boy, with her long dark hair hanging in rats tails down her back. And he, broad and strong and proud in his male arrogance.

Fanny's violet-blue eyes darkened and opened wide at the huge proportions of him.

"Are all men like you?" She moved forward to touch him, but he stood back, frowning.

"You'll not entice me like that, wench! I may be only a gypsy, but we set much store on cleanliness. And that boy's body of yours is not for enticing a man. See, you're crawling. Come on, get in the water first and clean yourself."

He dived in and swam underwater for a while before coming to the surface, while Fanny anxiously waited for him to reappear. Then, spluttering and laughing, he came up by a huge black rock at the water's edge.

"Come on in and I'll catch you."

She drew back, looking like a startled wood nymph.

"I am afraid. The water ripples and rushes so."

"It is fresh and clean. Look, the bottom is sandy. The water is so clear you can see right down to the bottom. Come on. Think what we shall do afterward!"

Spurred on by the thought of lovemaking, Fanny took a deep breath, and screamed as she hit the water. The cold seized her and, panicking, she grabbed Caleb and endeavored to wind herself around him.

He cursed, and taking a good grip of her hair, doused her, holding her so that her head was just clear of the water. She gasped and spluttered, but he held her so until she quieted down.

"Little fool! You should have trusted me."

"It is so co-cold."

"Then jump about and splash in it while I find you a bunch of soapwort to clean yourself with."

"Soapwort?"

"A herb that lathers up like soap. Wash your hair with it, too. Make yourself sweet and clean and then . . ."

"Yes?"

"I shall teach you what love is."

Later, dry and warm, Fanny shook out her long hair in the sun and marveled how smooth her skin felt, swearing that from this day on she would keep her body and hair sweet-smelling and clean. She looked at her reflection in the clear water and liked what she saw. The dark smiling girl with the small breasts and narrow waist had an ethereal look.

Then she piled her shiny hair on top of her head and turned to Caleb, who was lying under a tree.

"Do I look older, Caleb?"

He nodded lazily.

"Then love me, Caleb Neyn, and teach me. I want to know what love means."

He stretched out a lazy arm. "Come here then, my keen and eager young bitch. You'll not rest until you get it."

He buried his head between her small breasts and took a deep breath.

"You smell much better, to be sure. I do believe you hold an attraction for me." He kissed her neck and then her mouth, and her arms entwined themselves around him.

"Oh, Caleb, I *do* love you. I want to please you in every way."

"Hold on then, my young spark, or all will be over.

Take your time and relax!"

They locked together in another embrace, and Fanny squirmed underneath him. He tapped her lightly on the buttocks, and she lay still.

"God's teeth," he muttered, "I never knew a virgin so keen and eager to be ravished!"

"Oh, Caleb, Caleb, my body *aches* for you! I want you—please take me, Caleb, and put my body to rest!"

Caleb did not answer. His hands caressed her expertly, noting her responses. Then they came together with a force that seemed to shake the very ground beneath them.

Fanny cried out in sudden pain, then felt herself being lifted on a wave of ecstasy. She clung to him. And then it was all over, and they lay together, spent and exhausted.

For a long while there was a silence between them, and then Caleb stirred and went down to the river where he doused his sweaty head. Languid and at ease now, Fanny lay in the long grass watching him, a fond smile curving her lips.

"I love you, Caleb Neyn, and I always will! You are my man, and I am your woman." A sudden thought made her sit up and rest herself on one hand. "Is there anyone else who loves you as I do? Come on, tell me."

Caleb shrugged. "Better than some, and worse. One swallow doesn't make a summer, m'dear! Cheer up, though, everyone has to begin sometime." He laughed at her crestfallen face.

"I thought it was wonderful, after . . ."

He nodded in understanding.

"Of course, the first time. A little discomfort. Never to be experienced again."

"No? Then what about a second time?"

He shook her playfully and stroked her cheek. "Never thrust your favors on a man. Let him make the first move. Besides, I am no love machine. I have heard of such—but not I. Remember Savina?"

"But . . . don't you want to, Caleb? Is that what you

mean? Are you tired of me already?"

Caleb's mouth twitched, and he sat up to pull on his pants. He ran brown hands through tousled wet curls.

"Ask me that tonight or tomorrow and I could show . . ." He pulled her into his arms and kissed her, forcing her mouth open. "There. That will do to go along with. You know, Fanny Bickler, you are a witch. If it hadn't been for Savina, I would have taken you again."

"Oh, Caleb!" She pressed her trembling young body to him. "I want to be yours! If only I could run away with you and live the life of a gypsy!"

"You wouldn't like it, Fanny. Gilbourne is our most welcome place. Many villages will not have us camping within miles. Then we starve and have to move on, and then it's poaching all the way and the danger of being hung for stealing. No Fanny, a gypsy life is rough. You are better off in a house."

"When will I see you again?" It was a cry from the heart.

"Whenever you will. I shall pass this way every morning."

"I start work at the half-hour after five. I leave the cottage at five. Is that too early?"

"Not at all. We gypsies are up before dawn, setting our traps and making the rounds before the gamekeepers." He showed his large even white teeth in a grin. "And now, I have an added lure. I'll meet you under this tree."

"Oh, Caleb, I cannot wait for tomorrow."

"Well, you will just have to have patience." He pulled on his shirt and, leaving it open, bent down and kissed her again. "Now, run along home, or someone will be wondering about us."

"Caleb, should I confess at church? Is this really a sin, this wonderful feeling?"

"No. How could it be? 'Tis as natural as breathing. Keep it a secret, just between the two of us." He turned away and, whistling, started off through the undergrowth. He turned just as he came to a hedge.

"I'll bring you some herbs tomorrow. My mother is an expert on such matters."

"Herbs? What should I want herbs for?"

"Do you want a baby, then?"

Fanny was startled and showed it. "Do you think I'm having a baby now? Aunt Beamish would kill me."

"No, I don't think so. I was careful, but you are a passionrouser—or you *will* be, when I teach you all the tricks!" He laughed at Fanny's look of curiosity.

"Caleb, stop! What tricks?"

"I'll show you some of them tomorrow. Now go home." He bounded away, and Fanny watched until he disappeared.

She smoothed her bodice and adjusted her skirt, and then, peeping into the water, studied her reflection. Was she changed? The reflection was of the same Fanny, but there was a rosy glow about her now—yes, she looked happy!

She hastened home and found her brother Billy chopping and piling logs for the winter. He was a quiet stolid youth without too much imagination.

"Where have you been?" he asked, as he watched her approach.

"Never you mind, Billy Bickler. I've been looking for wild strawberries, if you want to know."

"And where are they then? I can't see a bowl of strawberries."

"I ate what I found. I was hungry."

"Huh! Are you sure? You weren't with that Thomas Pye then?"

"What? Thomas Pye? He stinks. I'd not go with him!"

"Oh, hark at you! Talking like a fine lady now." He peered into her face. "You're looking different. Have you been washing yourself?"

Fanny looked flustered. "No. I fell in the river, if you must know."

"And your clothes not wet? Do you take me for a fool, Fanny? You've been in the river with nothing on.

Who with, Fanny? You wouldn't dare go in by yourself."

"It's none of your business, Billy," she said sharply. "I'm old enough to look after myself, like Nellie and Betsy-Ann."

"You don't believe all that claptrap they talk, do you? You're no more than a child, Fanny, so don't go messing about with the boys . . ."

"You mean it's all lies, what they talk about? They're only pretending?"

"Aye, they boast a lot, especially that Nellie."

"But Nellie swore on the Bible."

"Nellie's a liar, then, I should know."

Fanny gulped and turned slightly pink. Her main reason for wanting to be deflowered in the first place was to be able to boast to Nellie Simms!

"You mean you want to . . . with Nellie?" Fanny was more diverted than scandalized. Billy turned brick red. He nodded awkwardly.

"We was messing about, kissing and the like, in the wood. She was out sticking and I stopped to help her. I was kissing her and got the idea. She screamed and yelled like a mad thing. Frightened her stiff, I did." He grinned at the recollection. "She frightened me, too. I didn't know how to quiet her. Got me flummoxed, she did. I was in a rare sweat. I thought I would have to marry her, and Aunt Beamish would have gone wild."

"Why didn't you tell me about it? I think it was most mean of you, Billy. I am your sister, remember. We should stick together about these things."

"What? You must think I'm daft or something. A fellow doesn't want that kind of thing talked about."

"But I mean about Nellie. I don't know how she dares talk so."

"Well, no one in their right mind would believe Nellie. If she had done it as many times as she *says* she's done it, there'd be a baby by now. It stands to reason."

"Has there always to be a baby, Billy?"

Billy looked at her narrowly. "Why? Why do you want to know? You haven't been messing about with someone else, have you?"

"Of course not, you fool. Now I'm going to do some cleaning."

With that, Fanny flounced into the cottage, inwardly swearing that she would get even with Nellie. And yet she was glad—oh, so very glad—she and Caleb had loved each other. But a baby! Her heart lurched. For an instant she pictured herself standing with a bundle in her arms and Aunt Beamish pointing to the road, with the snow falling in huge flakes all around her. Then she picked up a broom and got down to the cleaning. Aunt Beamish should have no cause to complain.

Although Billy had jolted and frightened her with his views on love-making and babies, Fanny was up sharp at half-past four and was early on the Monday morning for her tryst with Caleb. She was sitting in a dream, listening to the early morning chorus of the birds, when he arrived whistling and swinging two rabbits in his hand. He dropped them down beside her, and then lowered himself to her side.

"Have you washed?"

She nodded, trembling at the sight of him. Suddenly she was shy and needed reassurance. "Do you love me a little bit?"

For answer, he pulled her over so that she rested on his legs.

"Would I be here otherwise?" The answer seemed to satisfy her. She snuggled in against him, arching her back, and reached up for his kiss. It was as satisfying as she had remembered. His hand unbuttoned her bodice, and her nipples stiffened and became two thrusting points. She moaned with happiness and turned to him, hot and ready.

This time there had been no Savina, and his appetite for love was keen. He took her again and again until she moaned with exhaustion. Her lips and bosom were bruised with his insatiable passion.

And yet she would not give in. Her responses were as wild and eager as his. And even when exhausted, she tried to match his loving. He laughed exultantly. He knew he could play this girl like a man playing his favorite harp.

Finally, even he was slaked and free of passion. He lay back, mopping his forehead and smelling of fresh sweat. For a long while they lay, replete and satisfied. And then he stroked her forehead.

"Tomorrow morning? Same time?"

She nodded, too lazy to speak.

"Then you must be off to your work, remember? You must not keep Mistress Raybold waiting."

Fanny suddenly started up in alarm.

"God's teeth! I had forgotten . . ." She quickly adjusted her clothing.

"Yes. You must run. The sun is high. And, Fanny—here are the herbs. Make a hot tea of them every morning and drink some, morning and night."

"What are they? Do they stop babies?"

Caleb laughed. "I cannot tell you what they are. It is my mother's secret, but it works. Never forget to take it twice a day."

"You will keep giving me some?"

"Yes. There's enough there for several weeks. Six spoonfuls and enough boiling water to fill a mug."

"Then I'll take it." She stuffed it into the pocket of her skirt. "What if I forget?"

"Then you will have a baby. Would you want that?"

Fanny shook her head slowly. "No. Not if *you* didn't want a baby, Caleb. Otherwise I should love to have your child. I love you, Caleb." Her eyes were big in her small young face.

"It isn't love, Fanny. You think you love me because I thrill your body. You want me as I want you, but do not call it love. You could feel this way about many men, just as I do about many women. That is lust, Fanny, not love."

"Not with me, Caleb. I couldn't let any other man do

what you do. I should die if you ever left me."

"I must leave soon, Fanny. The tribe is talking about moving on a little sooner this year. 'Tis nearly the end of July and we are going in September instead of October."

Fanny gave a cry. "But why? Why go so much sooner?"

"Because one of my brothers is wanted for sheep stealing and he is even now in hiding somewhere in Dorset. If we can get to Plymouth in good time, we can catch a friend who plies his boat from Polperro to France and get the lad away."

"But you will come back?" Fanny could not keep the anguish out of her voice.

"Of course. Do we not always return in the spring?"

"But how will I ever live through the winter without you? Oh, Caleb, take me with you." She collapsed in his arms, sobbing.

Caleb's face took on a tight, steely look. He rubbed her dark hair with a gentle hand and sighed.

"You knew how it would be, Fanny. I cannot take you with me when we move on."

"But why? Why? Surely if you love me . . . I would sell pegs or learn to tell fortunes. I only want to be with you."

He shook his head. "I could never marry you, Fanny. You are a *gaujo,* and gypsies who marry such are shunned and must leave the tribe. It is a worse punishment than death for a gypsy! Besides, our children would be *posh-rats*! You know what that means?"

She recoiled and shook her head.

"Half-bloods! Neither one thing nor the other, and shunned by all. No gypsy will trust a posh-rat . . . and *gaujé* look down on half-breeds of any kind. So you see, it is hopeless."

But Fanny sank to her knees and held him around his legs, her face streaming with tears. She clung to him in a fever of apprehension.

"But think what we mean to each other! You *do* love

me? Oh, Caleb, we could go away, just you and I."

"Stop it, Fanny. How can you talk like that when I have just explained? A gypsy's family comes before all others! A gypsy family must cling together and be loyal otherwise all must perish." He pushed her away in sudden irritation. "If you can't control yourself, get back to your own village—and stay there."

She looked at him now with anger in her eyes.

"It's that Savina Fingo, isn't it? You are making your family your excuse. And she's a gypsy, so it's all right to have her!"

"I told you the truth. Leave Savina out of this. She's a good girl and I could marry her tomorrow."

"Then why don't you?" spat Fanny. "Or don't you love her either? How many silly females do you lie with?"

Caleb made a sudden violent movement, and Fanny felt his rough hand slap her cheek. She staggered and looked at him with horror.

"You hit me!" She cowered back, her hand on her cheek.

"You asked for it! Jealousy will get you nowhere. A gypsy goes his own way and answers to no woman. What I do is my affair. Remember it!"

Fanny stared at him for a long moment, then turned and ran away through the wood.

Several days passed. When Fanny left the cottage to go to Fellside, she would cast a glance towards the road leading to the wood, half expecting Caleb to be waiting for her. But he did not come.

She knew the gypsies were still at their campsite because several of the men were working temporarily for Farmer Raybold. Fanny would stand and watch them haymaking, and sometimes she would hear Caleb's name mentioned, but he never came looking for work.

At night her body ached for him. She would toss and turn, then rouse herself at five o'clock and force herself to walk the two miles to Fellside to light fires and cook breakfast for Mistress Rebecca and old Joshua Raybold.

Mistress Rebecca noticed the dark shadows around Fanny's eyes.

"You are not sickening for something, Fanny?" she asked suspiciously. "You are very thin and white. There is nothing you ought to tell me, is there?"

Fanny looked puzzled.

"Tell you? I don't know what you mean."

"Come now, Fanny. You are not a child any longer. I mean, are you with child?"

Fanny felt an insane desire to laugh and scream, and then fear hit her.

"No, no. Nothing like that. I'm not sleeping well, that's all."

"I hope so. I don't want a girl who can't cope with her duties. I should have to look elsewhere."

"Oh, no, Mistress Rebecca. I am well enough, I assure you. 'Tis but a passing thing."

"Well, see that you get your rest. You get up at five, you say, to be here on time?"

"Yes, Mistress."

"And you leave here at eight. Then you must be in bed by nine to do me justice. See that you get to your bed early enough."

"Yes, Mistress, I will. You will have no further cause to doubt me."

"Very well, Fanny. Now go and black lead the parlor fireplace, and make sure you use plenty of lime for the hearthstone. And after that . . ."

The days dragged on. Fanny's hands were red and worn with constant use of hot water and washing soda. There were beds to attend to, carpets to sweep, butter to make, sticks to be gathered and hens to be fed. And then came the special days when the great oaken barrel was rolled out and the washing done, and the ironing and pleating of shirts and petticoats and ruffs and aprons and lacy hose and kerchiefs. Later came the day for making weak beer for the men in the hayfield, and the days she helped with the bread making and the mutton pasties and head cheese and black puddings. . . .

And all the while she wondered. Was she already with child? She examined her thin young body for signs, but there were none. She felt no queasiness, and her small breasts were no different from usual. And then one morning she knew she was childless. That bitch Rebecca had frightened her for nothing! She was so elated that for once she smiled and even skipped as she made her way to the farm.

There was still no sign of Caleb. It was as if he had disappeared into thin air. She was piqued. Who was he sniffing after now? Surely he wasn't always with that dark gypsy girl Savina? Fanny vowed that if she ever met her in the lane, she would scratch her eyes out.

Then, during the second week, she gave in to the urge to seek him out. She found him lounging under their tree, and he looked up at her with no surprise.

"So you came at last! You took your time. Sit down beside me and tell me what you have been doing."

She dropped down beside him and put her head on his shoulder. "I've missed you! I wanted to come before, but I thought you were still angry with me."

"I am. But I knew you would want me soon! You do, don't you?"

"Oh, Caleb, you know I do! This wanting has made me ill. I have a hunger . . ."

Caleb's arm tightened about her and she fell silent. Her arm crept around his neck. He muttered something low and gentle in the Romany tongue, and she strained and stretched to him.

"Oh, Caleb," she moaned. "Take me, thrill me again with your loving! I want to feel your caresses." Her hands caressed him in turn. . . .

So for the next two months they met, while Fanny turned a blind eye to his philandering ways and tried not to think of the parting that was drawing near. She was happy in her work, and Rebecca eyed her suspiciously.

The narrow face of the spinster showed jealousy of a young girl just blossoming and she deliberately made life hard for Fanny.

"Fanny, polish those pewter platters again! Last night's food is still stuck . . . Fanny, bring more logs for the parlor fire. I am chilled . . . Fetch water from the well . . . Carry buttermilk for the pigs . . . Heat my bath water . . . Empty the tub. . . ." It went on and on—and all for four pounds a year and her food!

But when she was tired at the end of a long day, there was always the thought of seeing Caleb the next morning to comfort her before her daily drudgery began anew.

As she blossomed and filled, her aging master, Joshua Raybold, began to take notice of her. He became solicitous in asking after her health. His little eyes in their puckered folds gleamed with a desire far beyond his years. It had been a long time since Rebecca's mother died, and he had scarce looked at a woman since. But Fanny's youthful burgeoning had awakened his lost desires. He wanted her.

Fanny laughed at his crude fumblings. At first she was incredulous. Surely a man of his years should be preparing himself to meet his Maker, not thinking of fornication! But a tweak here and a caress there made it quite clear to Fanny where his desires lay.

One day he caught her in the still room.

"Ah, Fanny, there you be. I have looked all over for you. Can you bring another pitcher of cold beer to the field?" He put his head close to hers. "And bring it by way of the wood. I have a mind—"

He stopped short. Rebecca was just coming through the doorway.

"I was just asking Fanny to bring another pitcher of beer to the field. The men need it on such a hot day."

"Aye, and it'll all disappear down those gypsy throats! I never knew such drinkers! A dirty slovenly lot, they are too! I'll bring it myself and see that they do not take too long to drink it. If Fanny comes to the field"—she looked Fanny up and down—"the good

Lord knows when they shall start again!"

"Aye, you're right as usual, daughter. And there's one thing certain, they start work again quickly enough when they see you coming!" He chuckled and turned away, giving Fanny a meaningful look. "The wood!" he whispered as he walked out.

Rebecca scowled after him.

"What was he muttering about? Someone has to keep the men working. They're a lazy lot of scoundrels when they've a mind to be!"

Fanny pulled a face behind her back. Dried up old stick! Bet she's never had a man in her life! Grinning, she went on stirring the last of the gooseberries to make conserve for the winter. . .

It was a piqued Farmer Raybold who went to bed that night. Fanny told Billy about him when they were both in their hard, narrow trundle beds in the room under the eaves.

"And you really think he would lie with you, sister? I thought he was too old. He must be sixty-five, if he's a day."

"Sixty-seven—I heard him tell that vinegary bitch one day, when he was whining on about having a cold. She wanted him up and out of the house, and he accused her of wanting his death. Do you think she'll ever marry?"

Billy sniggered. "Not her. I've half a mind to go up there and do something for her."

"Billy! You wouldn't!" Fanny was quite shocked. "She's old enough to be our mother!"

"If she paid me plenty, I'd go! I wouldn't mind marrying her to get the farm. It's quite an idea. I'll have to think about it."

"Billy, you're not eighteen yet! You've plenty of time to think of marriage. Why throw yourself away on a woman nearly forty?"

"It was just a joke. But the more I think about it . . . how many young females are there with her kind of money? I don't want to be a farm laborer all my life."

"Well, I think it's a stupid idea."

"What else is there for me? I nearly got dragged into this Dutch war, didn't I? It was only Sir Timothy who got me off. I wish King Charles to Hell sometimes. We were better off under Cromwell."

"Billy, don't ever say such a thing! If anybody heard you . . . I hope you don't talk wild like that when you go down to the inn?"

"Nay, I'm not that stupid. What I say to you I know you'll not repeat. I trust you, Fanny. You're my only kin, barring Aunt Beamish—and she's kin I could do without."

"Now you're being ungrateful. Where would we be, but for her? She's kind, even if she's not loving. She does her duty by us, you'll allow."

"Aye—her duty, that's all."

Billy spoke bitterly about the woman who housed them. To be sure, she got back every penny she had ever laid out. She took Billy's wages from Sir Timothy Gilbourne himself, and Billy was fed and clothed on cast-offs from the big house. She collected Fanny's money, too, quarterly from Mistress Rebecca; and Fanny's clothes were castoff as well—old Quaker clothes too old-fashioned for the Gilbourne women to wear.

Fanny lay silent in her bed. All Billy had said was true. She thought of her early life, with no parents to comfort her and remembered her aunt's venomous references to her mother.

She could vaguely remember her tired pretty mother. Aunt Beamish's much younger sister had been feckless enough to marry a sailor who had gone back to sea once too often, leaving behind a wife and small son and un-born daughter—Fanny. She had died when Fanny was four, after living in Aunt Beamish's cottage and becoming her drudge. A wraith of a woman, anxious and uncomplaining, her whole life centered around her two noisy children and in keeping them quiet and obedient so that Aunt Beamish would not grumble and punish. Fanny had to admit it: she hated the woman who so reluctantly did her duty by her sister's children. She would leave Gilbourne tomorrow without a pang . . . if only there was a way of keeping in touch with Billy.

"Billy," she said softly. "Promise me, whatever happens to us, we'll keep in touch and help each other if need be. Promise, for the sake of our poor mother."

"Aye, I promise, sis. But what could ever happen to the likes of us? We'll be here in Gilbourne for the rest of our lives. We have no money to go anywhere else." He spoke bitterly.

"I don't know. But I *do* know I'm not stopping here for ever. . . ."

"It's that gypsy boy, isn't it? You haven't fooled me, Fanny. I've watched you stealing away early on a morning to meet him!"

"That's not true . . ."

"Don't lie—at least, not to me. I followed you one morning to see for myself. How you come not to have a baby I'll never know. Perhaps you're the barren kind!"

"Billy, you'll not tell Aunt, or anyone else?"

"What do you take me for? Of course I won't. But how do you do it? Is that gypsy boy giving you some potion?"

"Stop calling him that 'gypsy boy'." He's got a name. Well, yes, if you must know, he gets herbs from his mother."

"That's interesting. Can you get me some?"

Fanny sat up in bed and peered through the moonlight that streamed over Billy's bed. "What?" She laughed. "Herbs are no good for you, Billy-boy."

"I didn't mean for me, silly. I have a fancy for Jane Broughton and she says she loves me, but is afraid . . ."

"What! That horse-faced girl up at the big house! Kitchenmaid, isn't she?"

"What if she is? She's a nice girl . . ."

"I thought you had your mind on Mistress Rebecca?"

"I have, but I'd want somebody young to dally with, wouldn't I? She'd be too old for love-making, wouldn't she?"

"Not if she takes after her father. The old goat nipped

my bottom till it was black today."

"Why didn't you stop him?"

"And lose my job? Besides, it amuses me to see him aroused. He goes through agony. It makes me laugh."

"You're a cold-hearted bitch, Fanny. Do you know how a man suffers, them times?"

"No, and I don't care!"

"Well, don't overdo it, Fanny. He could kill you if you got him in a frenzy."

"What! Him? You must be teasing me. He's too crippled up with gout to harm me. I could stamp on his foot and run!"

"Well, I'm warning you. By the way, do women of forty fornicate?"

"How do I know? Why don't you try her and see?" She laughed under the thin bedclothes and snuggled down to sleep.

CHAPTER TWO

Her meetings with Caleb were the highlight of Fanny's day, her sole reason for living. By now she had become used to swimming naked in the river and was proficient in deep water. Caleb showed her the correct way to tickle a trout, and they watched the birds nesting while Caleb patiently taught her their names. She also learned how to find her own herbs and dry them. Caleb told her that pig lard mixed with elderflower made a good ointment for chilblains and rough hands. So when the next Raybold pig was killed, Fanny smuggled away some of the lard and tried it for herself.

Being with Caleb on his own ground opened her eyes to sights and happenings she had never dreamed of. When he imitated a blackbird, she delighted in his delicate rendering and shared his pleasure when a bird answered his call. And above all, she enjoyed him when they made love.

But all too soon it was at an end. One morning he came early under their tree. He carried no traps, and he was quiet and withdrawn. The first leaves were beginning to flutter down and the early morning air was chilly. Fanny shivered. She knew by his look that their parting was near.

She sat down beside him, silent and watchful. He did not speak, but put an arm about her. For a while they sat, and then he sighed and buried his face in her thin bosom.

"You witch! I never dreamed it would be so hard to part. What have you done to me, Fanny Bickler?"

"Then you *do* love me?" breathed Fanny, suddenly joyful and incredulous. He nodded, muffled by her warm skin. She stroked the curls, which never failed to arouse her.

"When do you leave?"

"Today . . . after noon. And we shall be traveling fast."

She sighed. This was the news she had dreaded for the past weeks.

"And you will return?"

"Aye. As usual, in the early spring."

"Promise me that you will return."

"I've told you—in the early spring."

"Swear then, an oath."

"If it pleases you. I swear."

Fanny relaxed. "Then forget this parting for a short while, and love me as you have never loved me before. I want to remember you in an ecstasy that will serve me until you return. Oh, Caleb, never was a man so well loved and well served. Remember me, when you meet all those fine city ladies who will tempt you. No gypsy girl or woman of quality could feel more gentle toward you than I. Remember this in the days of our parting."

She twined herself around him and gave him her open mouth to kiss, and then, as never before, she plied all the tricks he had taught her, and her whole body sang to his playing. Time passed and the sun rose high. Still they lay together and aroused each other time after time. Then at last Caleb lay back spent, and Fanny stretched out beside him quietly. They dozed, content, all urges satisfied.

Then Caleb blew in her ear. She stirred, and her fingers automatically pulled him to her.

"No, no. Don't go yet. Please stay a while longer."

"I must go. I shall be needed to help pack the *vardo*. There's man's work to be done."

"You'll not forget me? You will come back?"

"Of course. How could I forget you? You have wound yourself around my heart—and I did not wish it.

Oh, that you were a gypsy!"

She clung to him in sudden tears.

"I can't bear to see you go. I shall follow you and sleep in the hedges. I need not come near the gypsy camp. You could visit me . . ."

"Silly wench! How could you ever sleep out? You are not used to it. And in all weather. No, it is not to be considered."

"Caleb, I can't let you go." Her hold tightened, and he clasped her to him and kissed her for the last time. Swiftly, while her eyes were shut, he slid out of her grasp and on to his feet. He walked with fast gait until he came to the edge of the clearing. She watched him go, and when he raised his arm in a last farewell, she turned away, blinded by tears.

For a long while she lay sobbing, too spent to worry about being late at Fellside. Nothing mattered any longer. Caleb was gone!

Slowly she dressed and dried her eyes, and made her way to the Raybolds'. Mistress Rebecca would have had to light the fires and make her own breakfast this morning. Serve her right, thought Fanny resentfully. What right had she to someone else's services? She didn't know how to make a man happy. Why should she be privileged just because her father had a farm and money? It wasn't fair!

But the mood of rebellion left her when she reached Fellside. Rebecca Raybold's eyes were blazing with anger.

"And where the devil do you think you have been? Do you realize it is long gone eight of the clock? Lazy stick-a-bed! If it wasn't for the fact your aunt has already received this quarter's money, I would send you packing! I'll not have you coming here after half-past five."

"I'm sorry, Mistress Raybold. Billy was sick, and . . ."

"Billy, sick! Never! I saw him myself riding past the gate on Sir Timothy's business. That's a downright lie, and I hope you beg for forgiveness in church on Sunday.

By the way, I have not seen you in church for the last few weeks. Pray don't tell me you are one of the Devil's disciples!"

Fanny was shocked. She knew she was a sinner, but a Devil's disciple! That was too much.

"I-I'll be in church on Sunday, Mistress. I'll work late to make up for today if you like."

"And for several days," said Mistress Rebecca grimly. "I'll not have a slovenly servant in my house."

So the dreary round went on. But now there was no meeting with Caleb to look forward to. The next morning she went to Fellside by way of the gypsy campsite, but found it bare and blackened with dead campfires and the scufflings of many feet. She poked among the debris in the forlorn hope of finding something of Caleb's but there was nothing. Only stinking rags and a pile of chicken and rabbit bones. All trace of Caleb Neyn and his family were gone. Soon even the rubbish left would be overgrown by weeds, and she would have only her memories.

As September turned into October, Joshua Raybold became bolder. The time had come for harvesting. Now that the gypsies had gone, all the available men from the village were called in to help.

Joshua grumbled about the gypsies going sooner than usual.

"To get out of some hard work, no doubt. They would rather steal a shilling than earn it doing honest work!"

Fanny held her tongue.

Tempting Joshua was becoming a game, and Fanny played it without mercy. Once, when he had caught her feeding a young calf with new milk and tried to kiss her, she had threatened to scream for Mistress Rebecca and had seen his old face turn pale. He was frightened of his own daughter! The knowledge made Fanny's lip curl with contempt. But all that did not stop her from giving the old man tantalizing glimpses of soiled white petticoat.

One Sunday morning Aunt Beamish roused her early.

"Come, my girl. There'll be no Sunday work for you here today. You are to come up to the big house with me. Lady Letitia is ill again. She has never fully recovered after that last miscarriage. The poor lady is in such a state of weakness, I am frightened for her."

"What's that?" Fanny lay looking up at her aunt, her mind still dreaming of Caleb.

"Lady Letitia, sleepyhead. The other servants are going to church and they have the rest of the day to themselves. Sir Timothy is driving to Tunbridge Wells to take the waters. I shall be alone with her, and I have a mind she should have the doctor."

"Make Billy go with you, then. He can run faster than me."

"What an idea! Nobody wants a boy hanging around at such a time. No, you will be far more useful. You can help in the sick room."

"But I've had no experience, Aunt. I should make a poor nurse!"

"Then all the more reason you should learn! Dress quickly, child. We must leave immediately."

Fanny looked at the tall bony woman who had taken the place of her mother. Her back was ramrod straight, and her pursed lips told more than words. Lady Letitia was Aunt Beamish's life. For her, Aunt Beamish was all heart; any love and compassion she felt was kept for her alone. Silently Fanny dressed and made herself ready.

She had never been encouraged to go to the big house. This was Aunt Beamish's other life. Fanny had called there a few times with messages or a basket of berries for the cook, so the kitchen was no mystery to her. But the other rooms—Fanny gasped at the comfort and opulence of them.

With clumsy feet, she followed her aunt to Lady

Letitia's private apartments. Her head swiveled from
side to side to take in the ornaments and pictures, the
carpets and the wonderful small tables and chaise
lounges. Aunt Beamish saw her wonderment.

"Watch your step, child," she said sharply. "You
should have slipped off your shoes. I hope you cleaned
them before you stepped into the house?"

"Of course, Aunt. As you always taught us to."

"Good. Now speak to Lady Letitia when spoken to,
not before. Well, what are you looking frightened for?"

"I'm frightened of her, Aunt. I would much rather
help you in the kitchen."

"Nonsense! Lady Letitia is kindness itself. Come,
walk into the room behind me. I shall tell her who you
are. There is no need to be afraid."

"Very well, Aunt."

Fanny followed her aunt into the darkened bedroom.
The curtains were drawn and the sickly smell of candle
wax pervaded the room. That, and something else. Fan-
ny recognized it as the smell of sickness and ill health.
She remembered when old Nanny Tomlin had died and
Nellie Simms dared her to go in and view the body. Was
Lady Letitia going to die?

Slowly she stepped forward to the four-poster bed.
The curtains were drawn back and under the feather
coverlet Fanny could see a thin white face and a mass of
golden hair. She stood silent, mindful of her aunt's instructions, eyes down and gripping her apron tightly. A
slim white hand flickered and on impulse Fanny looked
up at the sick woman. Aunt Beamish was bringing water
to rub her down with. But to Fanny's amazement she
was watching Fanny. She smiled wearily and Fanny
smiled back.

"Now then, m'lady, can Fanny and I make you more
comfortable? This is Fanny, my niece. You have heard
me speak of her."

Lady Letitia tried to sit up. "Hello, Fanny. Come to
help me?"

Fanny jumped forward and tried clumsily to help.

"Not that way, Fanny. Hold her in the small of her

back. There now, m'lady, if we can but wash you and comb your hair . . .?"

Lady Letitia sighed as if it was all too much effort.

"Thank you. You are indeed kind. Is Sir Timothy gone?"

"Yes, m'lady. He went before we arrived."

Lady Letitia sighed again and her fretful hands plucked at the bed sheet.

"He never came to say goodbye."

"Perhaps he did not want to disturb you, m'lady."

The lady laughed bitterly. "Oh, Beamish, how you can keep up the charade is beyond me! You know he does not care, and holds no consideration for me. I wish I were dead!"

Fanny looked with shock at the woman who was not so many years older than herself. Then she looked at her aunt and saw tears in her eyes. That was more of a shock than what Lady Letitia had said. Dumbly she held cloths and towels, and then went to fetch Lady Letitia's silver brush and mirror from the vast dressing chest.

"There," said Aunt Beamish as she fussed over her." You will feel better after your toilet. Now lie easy, and I shall bring you some hot chocolate to revive you. Stay here, Fanny, and put the basin and towels outside the bedroom door."

Fanny did all that was required, and then came and stood patiently, waiting for any further commands.

Lady Letitia lay and watched her for a minute or so and then said in a quavering voice. "Come nearer, Fanny and let us talk. Why have I never seen you before?"

Fanny shrugged and stepped nearer.

"Perhaps Aunt Beamish thought it was not seemly."

"More likely that she did not trust Sir Timothy."

Fanny started and then blushed.

"Oh, you needn't be embarrassed. I know Sir Timothy's ways," Lady Letitia went on. "It is no secret that he married me for my money—and to get an heir. He thinks a child of his whose grandfather is a Duke will be of value to him. He sets much store by wealth and position. He also wants to cut a figure with King Charles.

His intention is to rent a house in London and become a
member of the London society. But, at present, it would
not be seemly to do so, while I am ill. My father's family
and friends would take it as an affront if he went alone.
So he wants to present me with our child before he does
so. That way he will have more prestige."

"M'lady, I think you talk too much," said Fanny nervously. "If Sir Timothy knew."

"But you will not tell him, will you, Fanny? I know
you are a good girl. Your aunt assured me."

"Of course I won't tell him. I am truly sorry you have
lost the baby. If I could only help in any small way . . ."

Lady Letitia took her hand and squeezed it. It felt like
a fluttery bird, helpless and without strength.

"You help me by letting me talk to you. You do not
know what it is like to live here with no one to talk to. I
am glad Beamish brought you." She lay back, gasping,
and just then Aunt Beamish came back into the room
with the chocolate.

"Now then, m'lady, I hope you haven't tired yourself
out." She looked at Fanny in annoyance. "Has Fanny
been a nuisance to you? I'll send her away."

"No. Please let her stay, Beamish. I find her company
comforting."

Aunt Beamish looked suspiciously at Fanny, but
made no comment. With a certain disapproval she
watched while Letitia drank her chocolate. Then she
motioned Fanny outside the bedroom door.

"I trust you will not tire Lady Letitia, but if you do
stay with her, be sure to let me know if there is any
change, and one of us will go for Doctor Byng."

"Very well, Aunt, but what should I look out for? She
seems well enough."

Her aunt tutted impatiently and then sighed.

"Surely you must know! If she complains of bleeding
or appears to faint, or otherwise cries out for help. Sit
quietly by her bed and watch . . . and if you fail me, I'll
give you the hiding of your life!"

Fanny drew back, impressed by the threat. She entered the sickroom again, and after seeing that Lady

Letitia appeared to be dozing, she sat quietly on a low stool.

Lady Letitia lay most of the time with her eyes closed, but whether she slept Fanny could not decide. Once, while Fanny made up the fire with logs, the lady stirred, opened her eyes and smiled fleetingly at Fanny, then turned her head to the wall.

And so Fanny spent a quiet Sunday, very different from the Sundays she was used to—with plenty of time to think about Caleb. It was now three weeks since she had watched him walk away from her, and the memory of him was still sharp and keen. The sharp hurt of parting was still with her, and she wondered where he was. Had he found another *gaujo*, or was it Savina who took up his time and his love . . .? Her imagination was working overtime. What if Caleb was ever caught stealing? Shuddering at such a painful thought she crept near the big bed to study the Lady Letitia.

How strange to think of her lying there, with all the money and beauty anyone could wish for and yet so unhappy. Fanny came to the conclusion that Lady Letitia pined for her husband, or at least was hurt by his coldness. Poor girl, she thought pitifully—wanting a child so desperately to make her husband happy, and losing it each time as fast as it was conceived! It made Fanny think for the first time that position counted for little compared to the blessing of good health. She studied Lady Letitia's face through the oval mirror opposite the bed. In repose it was white and gaunt. Lines stretched from mouth to chin, and the droop of her mouth was that of a disillusioned child. But Fanny was only vaguely aware of all this. She only knew that she was sorry for this girl, this lady who was the daughter of a Duke . . . and whom Aunt Beamish loved like her own child.

Then Aunt Beamish bustled in with a silver tray laden with good strong broth and some slices of chicken. The smell of it made Fanny realize she was hungry, too.

"Come, m'lady, it is time for your luncheon. Fanny, bring that table nearer and place it to m'lady's convenience. Now, m'lady, cook's made this broth for you spe-

cial, like. Take a few spoonfuls to please Beamish,
m'lady."

"Oh no! I can't eat anything, Beamish. I just want to
be left quiet. I like Fanny about me. She doesn't fidget.
But food—the thought nauseates me."

"But you must eat, m'lady! You will never gain
strength otherwise."

"Gain strength for what?" She gave Beamish a bitter
smile. "For all this to happen again? I can't bear the loss
of another . . ." Her voice sank to a whisper. "Dear
God, how I want to die!"

Fanny looked at her aunt with shock. It was a sacri-
lege to wish for death. She had been taught that trials
and tributions were sent by God to test both men and
women . . . and that no one was too humble for God,
who knew best. . . .

Aunt Beamish burst into tears and cast herself down
by the big bed. Lady Letitia's hand came out and
stroked the gray head.

"Dear Beamish, you have been like a mother to me
and now I have shocked you. Please stop crying. It will
do you no good, and does nothing for me. And look . . .
Fanny is shocked too. See to her."

Aunt Beamish snuffled into her handkerchief, and
then turned round viciously.

"What are you gawking at, girl? Haven't you ever
seen me cry before? Get you down to the kitchen and
make a posset of ale and eggs and lemon. Maybe you
will take a hot drink, m'lady?"

"Please don't speak harshly to Fanny, Beamish. She
is not to blame. Yes, Fanny can make me a posset. Perhaps that might give me the will to prepare myself for
another ordeal."

Fanny heard her aunt's outcry as she closed the door.

"M'lady, don't talk that way. Why not go home to
your father?"

Fanny strained to hear her answer, but the oaken
door muffled the reply. Thoughtfully she went down to
the kitchen.

All during the winter of 1661 Fanny visited the big

house on Sundays, and a certain friendship grew up between herself and Lady Letitia Gilbourne. Soon Fanny, who at first had stood in some awe of the lady, found herself looking forward to her weekly visits.

She also gave Lady Letitia a new interest. Sir Timothy left her alone so much, that to the ailing girl Fanny was like a breath of fresh air. She taught her to read a little and write her name, and Fanny, for her part, lapped up learning like a kitten lapping up milk. She watched Lady Letitia closely, and tried to emulate her manners and mode of speech. At night, in the bedroom of their cottage, Fanny would show Billy how Lady Letitia walked, how she held her fan, how she ate. And though she and Billy would have a good laugh, each time Fanny felt a sneaking pang of guilt. She was beginning to feel ashamed of her own lack of manners and polish. But there was one thing she always felt superior about, and that was her healthy animal strength, her ability to love. She knew that when the time came she would have no trouble producing healthy babies.

Lady Letitia was now giving Fanny her castoff clothes. The lady had lost much weight during her illness, and small as Fanny was, Lady Letitia was smaller and thinner still. Instead of the grays and blacks of the Quakers, Fanny now wore the richer fabrics and colors of the Royalists.

Rebecca Raybold watched the change with jealousy and asked innumerable questions about Lady Letitia and the big house, unable to understand the interest shown by Lady Letitia in her serving girl. But Fanny just smiled and went on with her work.

She also continued to side-step the advances of Joshua Raybold, whose desires were inflamed by her young girlish clothes—the sprigged muslins and the turned back skirts that showed lacy petticoat. One morning he caught Fanny kneading bread in the kitchen, up to the elbows in flour.

"So, I've found you alone at last, Fanny, m'dear. Come on now, give me a kiss. You are getting too bonny by far. What about it?"

"Mr. Raybold, sir, if I may be so bold as to speak my mind, I think you are only teasing me. Either that, or you are a foolish old man. Mistress Rebecca would not like to hear you talk so!"

"Why so prim all of a sudden, Fanny? You have enjoyed my attentions these past few weeks. I gave you a whole shilling last week for a fondle of your charms. Is a kiss so very different?"

"Sir. I have been to church since then . . ."

"You didn't confess to the vicar, did you?" he cut in hastily, wiping his sweaty forehead with a voluminous handkerchief.

"No. Should I have done?" she said innocently. "I will next time, if you like."

"No, no, no. You mistake me. You need not talk to the vicar. This is between you and me only."

Fanny saw the look of fear on Raybold's face, and could hardly help laughing.

"What is only between me and you, sir? She turned limpid eyes on him. "I know a respectable man like you—a man old enough to be my grandfather—would mean me no harm."

Joshua Raybold coughed. He was torn between honest virtue and the role of passionate lover. His feelings won. He seized her by the arm, immediately covering himself in flour.

"You little devil!" he hissed. "You know well what I want. Will you warm my bed at night and be a comfort to me? I will pay you double what you earn now."

Standing behind her, he squeezed, and stroked her breasts. Vaguely she wondered why it was all so different from when Caleb caressed them. Caleb . . . dear God, send him back to me!

She looked over her shoulder with a saucy look.

"Well, I never! Do you take me for a fool, Mr. Raybold? Aunt Beamish takes all my money. You have an arrangement with her."

"Ah, but this is different. This is a secret arrangement. The money will go into your hand this time.

Now, how about it? It is a generous offer." His eyes, in their baggy folds of skin, gleamed with anticipation.

"Aw, go on, sir! I'm not good enough for you. If 'tis marriage you are asking of me . . ."

The old man gasped and drew back.

"Nay, wench, 'tis not marriage. I want you for a mistress."

Fanny laughed inside, knowing all too well what he was after but enjoying the sport while it lasted.

She feigned alarm, and her eyes widened.

"Then you had better unhand me, Mr. Raybold. For one moment I weakened. As a wife, maybe"—she sighed—"but as a mistress—never!"

Swinging away from her, Mr. Raybold stamped with his gouty foot and then gave a roar.

"You damned wench, flaunting yourself and showing me your ankles and your petticoats! You Devil's daughter, tempting me—'tis all your fault! A pox on you and all women!" He stormed away, shaking his head and limping.

Fanny's laughter followed him. She had suddenly discovered something—a power over men! Other men, that is—but not over Caleb. Her power would never tame him.

She counted the days to Easter, the surest time for the gypsies to return. She had visited the campsite throughout the winter, and the scene was always changing. Sometimes the wind blew the debris, and there was an air of desolation about it. Then, when the snow came down, the clearing took on a beautiful timeless look. And on days like this one, after a rain, it was bare and the branches of the trees held their black skeleton arms up to a leaden sky. It was all so very different from those idyllic mornings with the warm sun beating down on their naked bodies.

She paced the clearing for a few minutes and then decided to walk home by their tree. It would be at least another six weeks before the gaily painted caravans would come creaking through the village, pulled by the piebald ponies.

She was now well turned fifteen, and had grown a little. Her figure had blossomed, and the gown passed on to her by Lady Letitia emphasized the curve of her bosom. She had enveloped herself in a warm old woolen cloak of deep blue, and the hood was well pulled down to protect her from the wind. She was no longer the little shy orphan of the village, and her learning had given her more poise.

The walk was quiet and restful. It was Sunday again, and she was on her way to the big house. Sunday was still the day she loved best, but now it was for seeing Lady Letitia, not Caleb.

She turned, now in a hurry to be gone. There was no future in fretting after Caleb. He would come when promised. She firmly believed that.

And then he was there.

She stood, unable to believe her eyes. Caleb! Her own beloved man! Tall, dark and broad, he stood like some king of the forest, his crisp black curly hair longer than she remembered, and with a fuzz of dark hair at his throat. The strong planes of his face looked thinner than before, but his eyes were the same—black, merry, teasing and searching. He held out a hand to her and her full lips twitched to a smile. Her pulses leaped.

"Caleb! What are you doing here? The caravans—there was no sign."

He shook his head.

"I came on ahead." Suddenly he coughed and leaned up against their tree. "I couldn't . . ." He stopped and spat. With horror, Fanny saw that he had coughed up blood.

"Caleb, what happened? You're hurt. Are the soldiers after you?"

He shook his head. She ran to him and tried to hold him upright.

"I must help you. Let me see where you're hurt." She opened his vest and saw the wound in his breast. "You must lie down and let me bind it."

His arms went around her, and he sighed.

"Oh Fanny, I've wanted you so. . . ." He buried his head in her hair and Fanny's heart thumped with happiness and fear. Caleb had come back! She cradled him in her arms, and they clung together for a wild moment. When she drew back her new gown and cloak were covered in blood.

"Your wound! I must bind it."

"'Tis nothing, only a knife wound. It only opened again because I was in such a hurry."

"To come to me?" she asked tenderly.

"No. To get away from those damned Fingos! Fanny, Savina's brothers are after me."

"Why? Why are her brothers after you? She drew away from him, suddenly fearful.

"Because I've got to marry her. She's with child. It's either marriage . . . or my hide!"

"Caleb!" The cry was from the heart. "Damn you, Caleb Neyn, for a lecher and a rogue! I love you, and I have kept myself faithful for you! And this is my reward for loving out of wedlock. I never want to see you again!"

She turned to run headlong, but Caleb's arm shot out and he held her.

"Wait! I love you, Fanny, but I told you I could not marry a *gaujo*. I never persuaded you by offering marriage."

"No. It was my own fault. I wanted you."

"And you seduced me! The only woman ever to do so. I love you, Fanny. I want you now."

His arms explored her body, and she felt him tremble. She closed her eyes against him, and let his hands speak for him. She felt him undo the laces of her corset, and she stood helpless in his grasp. That familiar warmth crept through her body and as she stood, shivering and naked before him, she knew she wanted him as much as he wanted her.

He wrapped her tenderly in her cloak and laid her down under their tree, and then he pressed her warm body to him and the whole of Heaven exploded. Despite the cold of winter, their brows were beaded with sweat.

Fanny had entered into Paradise. The exquisite rendering of flesh, and the rapture of submission to his passion drove every other thought from her mind. Indeed, the world dwindled to mere feeling and thrilling, endless, rising passions. They were alone in a universe of their own. Time meant nothing.

Her love-making was as demanding as his. She was as a tigress to his tiger. She rent and tore him and bit and her sharp teeth left marks that would remind him. He, in turn, bruised and used her unmercifully. It was as if they loved and hated each other and wanted the other to suffer. Until at last, exhausted, they lay in each other's arms.

It was Fanny who stirred first.

"And now you must go and marry that gypsy wench of yours!" Her tone was contemptuous. "And I hope you remember our loving for all time. Whoever you lie with, she will never love you as I do. I hope I haunt you for the rest of your life."

She stood up, ignoring the fresh blood running down his shirt, and touched him with her foot. He looked up at her, laughing, and grasped the foot that had spurned him.

"If you haunt me, Fanny Bickler, I have made mighty certain that I will haunt you!"

She tried to free her foot but he held on grimly.

"What do you mean by that?" Suddenly a finger of fear touched her spine.

"Are you still taking your herbs?"

The stunned look on her face was answer enough. He let go her ankle, and she fled through the copse to the road, his laughter following her.

CHAPTER THREE

It was in the middle of April when the gaily painted *vardos* of the Neyns and Fingos clattered through the village. Now there were ten or more caravans and nearly twenty ponies and foals. Fanny, along with several other children and old women, stared after the trundling procession. Already several of the village women were seeking out their pots and pans to be mended. Fanny had just delivered a basket of butter and gooseberry conserve to the vicarage for the new curate who was taking over part of the vicar's duties. Idly she wondered if Mistress Rebecca had any ideas in that direction.

But now she shaded her eyes from the sun's glare and watched the *vardos* pass. Then she recognized the van of Caleb's mother and the one following behind. Caleb sat well forward, reins slack in his hands, staring morosely ahead, while Savina, swollen belly swaying as the *vardo* wheels lurched over the ruts, clung to his arm. There was the air of the wild about her. Her hooked nose and flashing eyes gave her the look of a predatory bird, and she gazed down from the cart with haughty disdain. Greasy black hair plaited in two thick braids hung down each side of her weathered brown cheeks. Fanny noted with some satisfaction that her skin was already parched and wrinkled. A bright red scarf fluttered at her neck, hiding a half-bared bosom which was already filling with milk. How different she looked from the skinny creature who had made love with Caleb under the trees! Their eyes met as the *vardo* passed. Fanny grounded her teeth together and stared at the other girl, but Savina smiled triumphantly and one hand patted her stomach.

Fanny turned away with a sudden nausea and fled from the scene, her eyes clouded with tears. Running behind the nearest house she doubled up and vomited, feeling the world spin giddily round and round her. For a long time she lay in a feverish sweat, not moving for fear of bringing the sickness upon her again. Savina's smile of triumph danced maddeningly before her eyes, taunting her and seeming to mock her plight.

A sudden thought sent a stab of fear down her spine. This was not the first time she had been sick—she, who was never sick in her life. Could it be that . . .? In a flash the terrible truth dawned on her. There could be no other explanation.

She was with child!

Faintness threatened to overcome her again and trembling she sat down in the hedges and pulled her shawl closer around her. A voice called out in the field behind her and she remembered that old Tom and her brother Billy were working there for Sir Timothy. She crouched low, not wanting to be seen. She must think.

She still loved Caleb, and her body had responded to the sight of him, but his fondness for other women made her gall rise. She could have killed him. And to think her faithfulness had got her into this mess!

She tried to calculate her times. Yes, now she thought of it, there had been nothing since she had lain with him in the middle of February. She thought of abortion, but the memory of Rose Culley made her shiver. Rose had gone to the old woman who lived outside the village and had come back in severe pain. She had died three days later, screaming for mercy from Heaven. No, Fanny couldn't face that. It would be a sin to get rid of Caleb's child. There must be some other way.

And then the solution came to her in a flash. She would marry Joshua Raybold! The old lecher would be easy enough to handle. For a long time now, Fanny knew that given the right encouragement, Joshua would do more than make her his mistress. And it would serve that bitch Rebecca right if he did!

Much cheered at the thought, she moved on to Fellside. No better time than the present to get matters under way. She closed her mind to Caleb. He belonged to Savina. Let them both rot!

Mistress Rebecca was waiting for her when she returned.

"Well? Did you see the new curate? Did he take kindly to the basket of provisions?"

"I didn't see him. I left the basket with Mistress Lawson. I just went round to the back door and gave it to the housekeeper with your compliments."

"Stupid girl! You should have asked for Mr. Shelton."

"Why so? I never have before!"

"Because . . . Oh, never mind! Get on with your work." She turned away biting her lip.

Fanny smiled behind her back: so the old pinch-penny *was* after the curate! So much the better. It would be that much easier to handle the old man if Rebecca was out of the way.

"I could take him a message, though, personal like. He might come and see you then." Rebecca turned eagerly.

"Do you think so?" Then the light went from her eyes. "No. There's no reason to ask him to call. It would not be seemly. I saw him on Sunday. He gave a fine sermon, so fiery and full of Christianity. He is a fine man."

"And our next vicar, I should well think. He will need a wife, no doubt."

"Yes, yes. He will need a wife." She frowned. "What are you suggesting? I think you are being too familiar."

"Sorry, Mistress Rebecca. But I thought . . . well, there are other farmers' daughters who will set their caps at him. I only wanted to help."

"I don't need your help, Fanny, thank you." Rebecca pursed her lips and moved sedately away.

Later in the day she called Fanny to her.

"Fanny, are you free for an hour? How is your work going?"

"There's nothing that will spoil, Mistress. I can polish

afterward if there's something special you want doing."

"Could you go down to the village for me with a message for the curate?"

Her face was blank as she looked at Fanny. Fanny smiled to herself. So the hint of rivals was doing its work! She felt a strange sense of power at her ability to sway people, but kept her eyes down to hide the heady feeling of triumph.

"Yes, Mistress. I'll go now."

Slowly, Rebecca gave her a note sealed with wax. Fanny would have dearly loved to read what was there, but Rebecca now knew that Fanny could read and had taken no chances.

Fanny looked with interest at the new curate when he came to greet her in the hall of the vicarage. He was short and inclined to fat, and his round moon face held little humor. Fanny found him pompous and condescending. He opened the missive, studied it for a few moments and then, scratching his chin, said in a booming voice as if speaking in church, "Tell Mistress Raybold that I shall wait on her tomorrow at noon. Is she so very unwell? Her note conveys some urgency. 'To wrestle with a devil,' she says. Does she often have these humors?"

Fanny thought fast and looked up at him innocently.

"I don't rightly know what you mean, sir. Mistress Raybold is usually the soul of light and goodness and a powerful good prayer. If she says she is disturbed, then disturbed she must be."

The curate nodded gravely.

"Then I shall endeavor to give her all the spiritual comfort I can. Please tell her to worry no longer."

Fanny bobbed respectfully.

"That I will, sir, and I know she will be happy to see you tomorrow!"

She sped back to Fellside, laughing heartily. She could see the time coming when both Rebecca and Joshua would want her to take over the running of Fellside. Mistress of Fellside! It was not a bad position for an orphaned village girl!

That night she told Billy all about the curate and Rebecca.

"Those two would be well suited, Billy. Both have that mean look about them. But it leaves me wide open . . . for the position of mistress of Fellside. What do you think about that?" She giggled under the bedclothes.

There was a long silence, and Fanny raised her head.

"Are you asleep, Billy?"

He grunted.

"Then why don't you say something? Don't you like the idea of me being mistress of Fellside?"

"I thought you hated the old man. Why the change of tune? You laughed at him only a few weeks ago."

"Well, I changed my mind. A woman has a right to, you know."

Billy snorted.

"Woman! You're nobbut a bairn!"

"I'm coming up sixteen. Many a wench is wedded and bedded by the time she is fifteen. They say King Charles likes his mistresses young. I wish I could be one of them."

"Fanny! That's lewd talk!" Then a thought struck him. "Has old Raybold been a-messing about with you?"

"Him? I wouldn't let him touch me with a hayfork!"

"But you'd have to if you wedded him! Have you thought of that?"

"Yes, and it's the bit I don't like. But I could think of something."

"You're getting into deep water, Fanny. Forget it."

"I've got to marry, Billy." Fanny's voice was suddenly tense.

"What do you mean—*got* to?" Suddenly he sat up in bed. "It's that damned gypsy, isn't it? You are going to have his brat! And you're going to foist it on old Joshua." He started to laugh and wiped his eyes. "You've got some nerve to try that, I've got to hand it to you, sis, you've got a man's nerve!"

"I don't know what's so funny. I must do the best I can for myself—and the bairn."

"You must have known that gypsies don't marry other than their own kind. You were playing with fire. What happened? Didn't those herbs work?"

"I wasn't taking them when it happened. I'll know better in the future." Her voice had an edge to it.

There was a pause and then Billy said softly, "So that's why you want the curate and Rebecca to marry."

"What of it? It would solve many problems for both of us."

"But not for me. I had plans for Rebecca Raybold, remember?"

"But, Billy, I thought you were fooling me. You say so many things. I didn't realize you were serious."

"I'm serious all right. I want the farm."

"Well, you can't have it. It would come to me after he was gone."

"You bitch! You'd stand in the way of your own brother?"

"Yes—in this case. I want what I can get."

"But we promised to help each other . . ."

"Don't shout, Aunt Beamish might hear. Yes, we promised to stand together. But in this case, as a wife—"

"Look, if Rebecca Raybold is like a bitch on heat . . . *I'm* going to be the one, and you go ahead and marry old Joshua if you like. There should be plenty for us both."

"And what about my child . . . and Joshua's?"

There was silence for a moment, and then Billy got out of his narrow bed and came and stood beside her.

"Fanny, you've got to promise now that there'll be a dividing fifty-fifty, and I get the farm. I need it more than you. You can take what money there'll be, and most likely you'll marry again. I want land of my own."

"Always providing Joshua dies soon, and you can marry Mistress Rebecca. What if she doesn't like you, Billie Bickler? What then?"

He laughed, but the laugh was more of a growl.

"Then it would have to be rape! A struggling woman always rouses me. It would be easy, and then she'd marry me out of shame."

"You'd go as far as that?"

"Yes, Fanny. We're both made from the same mold.
We'll both get what we go after!"

Fanny lay awake a long time that night, hearing Billy's
voice repeat that sentence over and over again: *"We'll
both get what we go after."* But as she tossed and turned,
she knew drearily that it wasn't true. She could never
get what she wanted—to lie in Caleb Neyn's arms and
know that she had the right to be there . . .

The next day she watched for the curate. Rebecca had
already ordered the best bottle of Madeira to be on
hand and some freshly made macaroon biscuits. Fanny
had to give her credit for knowing how to conduct herself in polite society. After she announced him, she
stood outside the door with her ear to the keyhole. But
the voices were low and muted. Fanny stared at the
door, wondering what excuse she could make to walk in.
But even her courage failed her. She could have kicked
the door in vexation.

In the meantime old Joshua had come into the house
for a jug of small beer. It was time to put her own plan
into operation. She smiled sweetly at him and told him
she would draw the beer herself from the barrel while he
could rest and turn the spit for her while she was away.

The old man was surprised at her sudden affability,
and his hand trembled as he turned the pork over the
fire. Fanny came back with the jug of beer and set it
down beside him, taking care he saw the small swell of
her bosom. She had hurriedly tucked a few sprigs of
rosemary between her breasts, hoping that her warmth
would bring out the scent—thank goodness she had
been using rosemary to stuff the pork.

He motioned for one of the pewter pots on the dresser
and slopped beer into it, his eyes still dwelling on Fanny's charms. He quaffed half the contents of the tankard
and then wiped his mouth on the back of his hand.

He sat for a while and Fanny went on making the
stuffing. Now and again she passed before him, hoping

the scent of the rosemary would tickle his senses and
that he would make a move before she had to start on
the onions. Then he spoke.

"Fanny, have you thought any more about my offer?"

She stopped her mixing, looked at him and smiled.

"Oh, I've thought much about your offer, Mr.
Raybold, and I am honored. But I am a good girl, Mr.
Raybold. 'Tis marriage or nothing for me. I should like
to wed some nice caring man, and age would not come
into it."

"I'm not out for a wife, Fanny. But I have a deep regard for you, and I should look after you."

"And what about your children, Mr. Raybold?
Would you be willing for them to be bastards?"

He blinked as if about to say something, then changed
his mind.

"Would you be willing to have children, Fanny?"

Fanny came over to him and gazed on the dirty earth-
stained face, noticing with a tremor of disgust that he
smelled more of pig than of man. But she did not falter.
It must be done.

"Bless you, Mr. Raybold. Of course I should want my
husband's children. And a fine upstanding man like
yourself would make a splendid father!" She watched
him puff himself up, and he smirked and cleared his
throat.

"Give me a kiss, Fanny, and I'll think about it."

Fanny bent slowly, giving him a fine view of her bosom, and gave him a chaste peck on the forehead.

"I can't do any better than that, Mr. Raybold. A good
girl like me has to be careful. Aunt Beamish would not
like to think I kissed my employer."

He gave a cackle of laughter.

"So Mistress Beamish wouldn't like it, eh? And she
Farmer Milton's doxie, and has been these last dozen
years, ever since Mistress Milton took to her bed!"

Fanny's eyes went round with amazement. She knew
that her aunt sometimes called at Farmer Milton's
house, and occasionally came home slightly tipsy after-
wards. But she had always thought it was poor Maud

Milton she had been calling on, not the farmer himself!
Her evident surprise made Joshua laugh.

"Eh, but she was a fine woman, was Alice Beamish.
Threw herself away on that scoundrel of a coachman
who up and left her. If it hadn't been for her sister and
you two brats she would be a lonely woman today. Let
me kiss you, Fanny, I want to feel the goods and see if
they are worth buying!"

"Well, if you put it that way, Mr. Raybold. One kiss
just to feel the quality, shall we say?" She sat on his knee
and felt the hard bony hand go around her waist, nip-
ping and hurting.

"Got yer! You little devil!"

His mouth sought hers and she struggled. His breath
smelled as bad as his teeth looked, and she was hard put
not to vomit. She stiffened herself and he took his time.
Then he let her go and, gasping, he stood up and
laughed.

"You're a fine hot wench! It's marriage, if you want
it. Otherwise you'll be turned out of my house. I'll set it
about that you're wanton and that I turned you out to
protect myself."

Fanny glared at him, uneasily aware of the growing
burden in her belly. She gritted her teeth. This was going to be harder to bear than she had thought. Her ideas
and dreams of marriage to Raybold were one thing; the
reality was different. But she must go on.

"I'll marry you, Joshua Raybold, and promise to
make you a good wife!"

CHAPTER FOUR

Lady Letitia was with child again. Fanny suspected she would be brought to bed a month after herself, but as yet no one suspected her own condition. Lady Letitia lay white and pale on her chaise longue, to her husband's great disgust.

"I never knew such a milkweed as yourself! Where the blood of Dukes has gone to, God alone knows. If you fail me this time, madam . . ." His voice sank to a whisper and Fanny was hard put to hear the rest.

It was Sunday again, but this week Sir Timothy had not made his usual ride into Tunbridge Wells. Fanny had long ago decided that Sir Timothy visited another woman there, but she kept her thoughts to herself.

It was not often that Sir Timothy was at home, and she rarely came in contact with him. But now all the household was aware of him. The atmosphere was altogether different when he was around. Cook did not sing at her work, and the little maid of all work who uncomplainingly carried coal and wood up two flights of stairs crept about the house, looking frightened and pale.

Fanny had quizzed her about Sir Timothy that morning and Betsy had frowned.

"He's got wandery hands, and it would be one-two-three-bang if he could get away with it!"

Fanny had nodded. She too had that feeling.

So now standing outside Lady Letitia's chamber, she listened avidly for further disclosures. She already knew of the deep rift between the couple and that Lady Letitia dreaded his morning visits which invariably left her more anxious than ever about the child she was carrying. It was not surprising that the unhappy girl dare not risk going for a walk or driving in her carriage or even climbing the stairs. The fact that she lived the life of an invalid only angered her husband the more.

Hearing Lady Letitia scream, Fanny opened the door with a rush and bounced into the room, a silver tray with hot chocolate in her hand.

"You called, m'lady?" Her tone was bland, but to Sir Timothy her look was mocking. He did not pay her good wages to be insolent!

"And who the devil are you? What gives you the right to burst in here before the bell rope has been pulled?"

Fanny eyed him steadily.

"I thought m'lady called. I help out my Aunt Beamish on Sundays. I was bringing m'lady her usual hot chocolate. Can I help you, m'lady?" She walked over to the day bed and put down the tray on a small table. "Can I shake up your pillows, m'lady?"

She looked at Lady Letitia and smiled, noticing with anger that the pale cheek was red, as if she had just suffered a slap. She adjusted the pillows and Lady Letitia's hand went up and covered the mark.

"Thank you, Fanny, you are very kind. That will be all now. I can manage while Sir Timothy is with me." Her lip trembled, and Fanny was hard put not to turn around and tell the handsome devil some home truths.

"Very well, m'lady. I'll remain within earshot, and if you want me . . ."

Sir Timothy cut her short.

"You'll do no such thing! Get yourself down to the kitchen. I want no eavesdroppers about when I talk to my wife."

"Please Fanny. Do as he says. . . ." came the small voice from the day bed.

"Very well, m'lady."

Fanny marched to the door. But Sir Timothy was quicker. He held the door open for her, and she saw his quickening look of interest.

"You're an attractive child when roused," he mut-

tered under his breath. "God's teeth! To think you have
been coming here and I didn't know it." One finger
traced the line of her bosom. "I must remember to be at
home on Sundays in future . . ." His smile was charming and altered his whole face. Now Fanny could see
why Lady Letitia was so unhappy. Possibly the poor
lady loved this bully of a man.

It was the first time she had surveyed him closely. He
was older in years than her first impression of him, and
much more aggressive. Crisp black curls surrounded a
face thin and lean with the hooded brown eyes of a
hawk. He was as dark as Caleb, but with a lofty disdain-
ful look nurtured by generations of blue-blooded
breeding.

His sensuous lips parted as his fingers made contact.
Fanny drew herself up boldly and gave him a scornful
look.

"I come here to service m'lady and no other!" she
said, and slipped through the door, much to the gentleman's chagrin. But it was a thoughtful Sir Timothy who
went back and dispassionately looked down at his lady
wife.

"Drink that chocolate and then get dressed. I mean to
take you driving. The doctor says you need fresh air and
exercise. I intend to see you get it."

"But—"

"Do as I say, and don't ring for your maid. I'm quite
capable of buttoning a woman into her clothes myself.
God knows, I've had plenty of practice."

He saw the hurt on her face and smiled grimly. "Why
the sour look? I have made few enough demands on
you. All I ask is a son, and you fail me again and again!
A son, Letitia—and you will not have to endure me
again!"

"But you do not understand. I want your baby too."
Lady Letitia looked with anxious eyes at her husband.
"I love you, Timothy, as any wife should. It is only that I
find you . . ." She stopped, searching for words.

"Too earthy? Well, madam, love me or not, you have
a fine way of showing it! I cannot abide your gentle pi-

ous ways. Bedding you is like ravishing a nun at the altar!"

Letitia gasped with shock and shrank back horrified at Sir Timothy's blasphemy.

"I am sorry," she choked. "It is the way I was brought up. My mother . . ."

"Pah! Your mother wasn't a flesh and blood woman, she was a saint. Gad! When I think of the women I could have married!"

He strode up and down the room in a rage of frustration.

"Come, get off that day bed and change your shift, and try and act like a lady. We are going to call on the Belmonts."

"But I am not well enough!"

"Nonsense! You must take your place in society. And when our son is born, he will take his place with us!"

A little later Fanny was surprised to see Lady Letitia dressed in her best velvets and a smart blue hat on her fair curls, being helped down the stairs by Sir Timothy.

"Don't stand gawking, girl. Find Meadows and tell him to send the coach to the front. We are driving to Belmont Park!"

Now that there was no Lady Letitia to watch over, Fanny had time to talk to Aunt Beamish. They took a luncheon in the housekeeper's own sitting room, and Aunt Beamish stared across the table.

"You are going to marry Joshua Raybold? And without him consulting me, or Billy? I can't believe it! Are you marrying him for his money, child? Remember Rebecca. She will fight for her share. Or is it something else, Fanny?" Aunt Beamish looked hard at her. "You look a trifle peaked. Have you and he . . ."

Fanny stuck out her chin and said bluntly;

"No, aunt. He's never touched me. Not that he didn't try . . . but I said marriage or nothing."

Aunt Beamish nodded approvingly.

"Good girl. I see I brought you up right and proper." Then she stopped and frowned. "But . . ."

"Yes, I am with child . . ."

Aunt Beamish threw down her napkin and screamed. "God in Heaven! Whose child?"

"Caleb Neyn's." She looked proudly at her aunt, asking no sympathy.

"Caleb Neyn's! That tricksy no-good gypsy? You slut! You dirty fornicating little slut. After all I've done for you! How will I ever live it down?"

Fanny's quiet reply stopped her dead in her track.

"What right have you to talk? I know you warm Farmer Milton's bed, and have done these last twelve years! Is it so different?" Aunt Beamish did not answer. Fanny went on. "If you keep mum about this, who's to know it isn't Joshua's child?"

"But the time—anyone will know, if they can add on their fingers!"

"Not if you tell them the baby is born before its time. You can blame that on its aged father." She laughed and looked consideringly at her aunt. "Otherwise it could get out about Farmer Milton."

Aunt Beamish looked hard at her.

"You devil! I never knew I reared a cuckoo. There's bad blood in you from that sailor father of yours, but I suppose being married is something. I see I have little choice!"

And so, early one morning, she walked to the church with her aunt and Billy and found Joshua Raybold and Rebecca waiting. And she became Mrs. Joshua Raybold, and stepmother of Rebecca.

Outside the church a small crowd had gathered and gave the couple a faint cheer as they emerged. The curate had taken the ceremony, and while Fanny was inviting him back to Fellside for the wedding breakfast, Sir Timothy drew up on horseback. He looked long and hard at Fanny with a raised eyebrow. She smiled and he doffed his hat.

"Good morning to you all. I see that a wedding has taken place. May I offer my felicitations and wish you every happiness?"

Joshua cleared his throat awkwardly, Fanny bobbed a curtsy, and Sir Timothy rode on.

Taking her unfamiliarly clean husband by the arm, Fanny climbed into the waiting carriage and the others climbed on behind. She saw that Billy was losing no time in being a little more familiar with Rebecca now the knot was tied. He touched Rebecca by accident, and she flinched. Billy smiled and muttered his apologies, and Fanny grinned to herself. If Rebecca was really looking for a man, the curate would never get a look in. As it was, he seemed to take no special interest in Rebecca and remained distantly polite.

The wedding feast was simple, and after the toasts in ale and wine were given, the curate made his departure, taking Aunt Beamish with him. No so Billy. He stayed on to talk, and soon Fanny overheard him inviting Rebecca to walk in the garden.

But now she had to face up to her own situation. The guests were departing, and Joshua looked at her in a new familiar way. She felt his eyes undressing her and knew that it would not be long before the moment she was dreading would arrive.

So she was surprised when he said in a sharp voice.

"Well? What are you standing there for? Get out of that finery and get back to work. Feasting is all very well, but it makes no money. It makes a man lazy and a woman fat." He grinned suddenly. "Eh, you're a fine-looking wench, Mrs. Raybold. Plenty of time to find out how you bed later!"

Fanny, pleased at the respite, ran from the room. Gasping, she ran into the big main bedroom that until today had been Rebecca's. Now her clothes chest had been removed to a small room under the eaves. Joshua's own room had been left as it was. Rebecca had sulked, but old Joshua had had his way. Fanny looked at the huge four-poster with its heavy feather quilt. Could she stand sleeping in that bed night after night? She doubted it, for she knew instinctively that Joshua would want the heavy red curtins drawn while she preferred fresh air and freedom.

Biting her lip, she changed her gown. And as she smoothed her undershift and fastened her white calico bodice she looked at her figure in the cracked dressing mirror. Blast Caleb and his love-making! Already there was a suspicion of thickness to her waist. She would not be in this position now if he had stayed away. But it had been her fault. She was honest with herself. She had wanted him after she knew about Savina. Now she must pay the price!

Her old lilac dress seemed stale and musty after the pretty wedding gown of pale blue, one of Lady Letitia's gowns that she had altered slightly. But her heart lifted suddenly. There was always the possibility of duping Joshua. She could make sure he was drunk by the time they went to bed. It would be easy to persuade him that he had done his duty next morning. He would be too proud to admit failure, especially if she aired it abroad what a good husband he was!

So she was careful with the late dinner. She made a syllabub, recklessly emptying a bottle of Madeira into it, and also prepared a huge punch bowl of mulled ale. Joshua was partial to mulled ale, so she squeezed a much prized lemon into it, and added a bottle of brandy for luck.

Joshua, home from the fields, came in and sniffed.

"A fine smell, Fanny. Are we to eat well tonight, then?"

"Of course Joshua. Is it not fitting for our first night as husband and wife?"

"I thought the wedding feast would have been enough frippery for one day. I'm not having a lot of extravagance now we are wed, remember that!"

"Oh, Joshua, just this once. Why it's all ready now. A boiled ham, a nice round of beef and salad stuffs, and then a pair of pigeons with sage and onions, and a custard done just as you like it. And to follow, your favorite syllabub. There's mulled ale to celebrate with, too."

Joshua smiled at her.

"All for my benefit, eh? Then I forgive the extravagance this once. When do we eat? And where is Rebecca? There's been no trouble between you?"

"Oh, no! Whatever gave you that idea?" she said innocently. "Rebecca knows just where she stands with me."

"Good." He rubbed his hands together. "Well? What are you waiting for? Get the victuals on the table."

"You must wash first, Joshua. I'll not have you coming to table in all your muck!"

"Well, I never! Rebecca fed me straight from the field. You know my ways, wench, so no silly notions."

"I'm your wife now, Joshua, not your servant. You'll wash!"

She glared at him, and he glared back. Then he coughed and muttered, "Well, I suppose there's no harm in eating with clean hands." But to assert his authority again, he said sharply, "Where's Rebecca then? Why is she not here to help you?"

"She's in the parlor with Billy. They walked together for a long while, then they went into the parlor and have been there ever since."

"What? And you left them alone? Disgraceful goings on! You had no business to allow it! I'll go and give them a piece of my mind!"

"I didn't think there was any harm in it. She's not a young girl to be watched and protected. She's old enough to be his mother," said Fanny, and shrugged her shoulders.

"That's as may be, but she should still not be alone with a man for so long. I'll stop whatever's going on."

He marched out of the huge flagged kitchen and Fanny heard him give a great bellow. She held her breath and listened. Surely Billy had not asserted himself so soon? But the door shut behind Joshua, so Fanny busied herself with the meal. She laid out huge bowls of bread and used the best pewter platters for the food. She found a silver salt cellar inside the dresser and, looking around, found other treasures, including a teakettle and some fine china. The first Mrs. Raybold must have had good taste. She made up her mind to look through all his chests and cupboards at the first opportunity. Now she was mistress of Fellside, she planned to make the most of it!

Joshua stormed back into the kitchen.

"The very idea! Your brother is like a tomcat, and my daughter is acting like a bitch in heat!" A sly look came into his eyes. "How would it be if Billy married Rebecca? I never thought to see her married. It would dispose of her comfortably and I should have another pair of hands on the farm, I know Billy is a good worker."

"Billy might have other ideas." Fanny's quick brain had followed Billy's devious plotting. He was using Joshua to force Rebecca . . . She could have laughed aloud.

"Then he should have thought of that before he started fornicating in my parlor."

"Billy wouldn't do that! Not in the parlor, I mean," said Fanny, much shocked.

"If I hadn't walked in, God knows what would have happened! I'll have a word with the boy."

"Billy will do as he pleases."

"He'll do as I and Rebecca tell him, and no nonsense."

"Then go and wash, Joshua. This food will not wait forever."

Grumbling, Joshua stumped out to the horse trough in the yard to sluice off the sweat and muck. When he came back and sat down, the clumsy deal table had taken on a festive air again. A brown pitcher holding bluebells and small wild jonquils was set in the middle among the gleaming pewter. A carving chair stood at the end, and in front of it a huge dish of beef for Joshua to carve. At the other end Fanny took her place in the second armchair and made ready to carve the boiled ham. Two wooden benches ran along each side of the table, usually shared by the farmworkers. Tonight there would only be Rebecca and Billy. Tomorrow they would be back to their usual numbers.

The dresser held the other dishes, all ready for Fanny to serve. The meal was ready. Sharpening her knife,

Fanny waited for Joshua to begin. He cut into the succulent meat and, after she watched the first blood drip from his knife, she started on her boiled ham. At that moment the door opened, and Rebecca entered with Billy close behind. Her usually neatly drawn-back hair was slightly ruffled. She gave Fanny one quick look, and her face darkened.

Fanny looked at her and smiled.

"I'm sitting here from now on, Rebecca. You may have my seat on the bench. Billy, will you sit opposite Rebecca?"

The plates were filled and the bread passed, and Joshua filled all the pewter mugs with ale.

"Now, can we start and forget all the frills? I'm starving."

"Not before you've said a grace!" said Fanny implacably. "From now on, we're going to live like they do up at the big house!"

They all stared at Fanny, and Billy's jaw dropped in admiration.

"You are getting quite uppity now, Fanny," he said waspishly. "Remember you are married to a yeoman farmer, not the squire of the village."

"He'll not let me forget that!" said Fanny with distaste, as she watched her new husband eating noisily. "And talking of marriage . . ."

Joshua pricked his ears and stopped eating.

"Ah yes, while my mind's clear," he said between mouthfuls. "Billy Bickler, are your intentions honorable as regards this daughter of mine?"

Rebecca blushed with embarrassment.

"Father! Must you talk—"

"Aye, we must! Now, young fellow, how about it?"

Billy gave Fanny a look, and she, under cover of carving more ham, grinned slyly at him. She had started the discussion. Let him carry on from there!

"I'll marry her if you make it worth my while!" Billy put another forkful of meat into his mouth, apparently unconcerned by the rudeness of his reply.

Rebecca flushed angrily.

"I'm not a parcel or an animal to be bought and sold!" she said sharply.

"You were eager enough in the parlor," leered Billy.

Rebecca coughed and looked anxious.

"Yes, well . . . I was carried away. Need we speak about that?"

Fanny laughed out loud. So Joshua had been too late! Billy had known how to persuade her. Now that she considered, Rebecca did appear somewhat different— like a flower that had bloomed overnight! In that case, old Rebecca would not let Billy go. It was now simply a matter of satisfying Billy's greed—and her own!

"You can work for me, Billy Bickler, and become the son I never had. You shall have the farm, if you promise to look after Rebecca properly, and be a good husband to her."

"And what about me?" Fanny broke in. "Have you forgotten you have a wife who might bear you a son!"

Billy looked at her and frowned. He could smell trouble.

"You, bear me a son?" Joshua's face showed his astonishment, and he coughed and tried to hide the fact. "Ah well, of course you might have children. I didn't think of that."

"You're not too old, Joshua," said Fanny in honeyed tones. "I'm looking forward to having your son or daughter," she went on. "You do want children?"

"Of course, of course!" He suddenly looked pleased. "Fanny, do you really think. . .?"

"Why not? You're a fine figure of a man."

She looked him over dispassionately, and could have laughed at his shrunken, round-shouldered body. If ever she saw anyone with one foot in the grave . . . Plainly the old fool would believe anything!

"Well, then, Billy could have the farm, and I have money tucked away that would keep you and your family. How about that?" He looked at Fanny. "You would not want to farm this place on your own?"

"I might. I could marry again!" She watched Billy's glowering look and then laughed. "I'm only teasing. Billy would be better here. I should want to live in a town house in Tunbridge Wells!"

"You talk as if Mr. Raybold is at death's door," said Billy sourly. "In my opinion you could live for years yet, sir, God willing!" He cast Fanny a mocking look. "In the meantime, if Rebecca and I marry," and he took her unresistant hand, "she and I could live in the village in that house of Tyler's that has just become empty."

Fanny was furious. The house was the second best in the village. It belonged to Sir Timothy and had been the trader's house until recently, when he was moved into a new stone-built house in the Park. The house in the village had three acres of land with it, and pig houses and an orchard. Billy and Rebecca would be far more comfortable there than her, and less lonely. She bit her lip.

"Well, daughter? What do you say? There's not many men offered for you. I should take him if I were you, and thank God on your knees."

"There's no need to take that attitude, father, I was only waiting for the right man . . ."

"*Any* man, more like," said Joshua truculently. Already he was on his third mug of mulled ale.

Rebecca glared at him and then at Fanny, as if daring Fanny to speak. She turned to Billy.

"I'll take your offer, Billy, on condition you take my advice on business matters. After all, I am older than you."

"You'll marry me, and leave me to look after your affairs. I'm young, but I'll not be told what to do. Understood?"

Rebecca sighed and gave way.

"Yes, Billy. I understand."

So now the celebrations really began. Joshua and Billy toasted each other, and Rebecca started to giggle. Her hair came loose from its confining net and she looked younger and more attractive—or so Billy thought at least. Fanny watched with distaste as he fondled Rebecca, rather too brazenly, but Rebecca obviously loved it.

Fanny looked from Billy to Joshua and had the heart to envy Rebecca. At least she had years of ardent love-making in front of her. What had she? An unwanted child from her lover, and years stretching ahead when most probably she would have to nurse an ailing husband. Fanny took a deep breath and wondered where Caleb was at this moment. Perhaps some day they could come to some arrangement. The gypsies always returned each spring. Perhaps they would meet under their tree . . .

But right now, her main concern was to keep Joshua's mug filled up. Billy, on shaky legs, left to go outside in the yard to relieve himself. She followed, needing the same relief. He caught her as she was pulling up her skirts.

"Hey, what's this, sis? I notice you keep filling up the old man's mug. Can't you face your wedding night?" He grinned in understanding. "I don't blame you. It was a hard bargain just to get your brat a name!"

She pushed him roughly aside.

"What about yourself? Won't you find it hard?"

"Not as hard as I thought. She's got something. And then there's always Betsy and Polly and Mary to fall back on." He showed his even white teeth in a wolfish grin. "I'd marry Joshua himself to get my hands on this farm."

"You're drunk," said Fanny tersely, and walked back into the kitchen.

She found Joshua singing a vulgar song of the tavern and Rebecca half asleep. She poured herself a half mug of brandy.

"Ah, there you are, my little dove, my bonny bride! Shall we go to our love nest and truly become man and wife?"

"Not yet, Joshua. See, Billy is not mindful of going yet awhile, are you, Billy?"

Billy gave her a fuddled look and shook his head.

"No, the night's young and we've much to celebrate

yet! Come on, Joshua, old man. Let's drink to the future?"

"Aye, one more drink and then I've a mind to lay with my wife." Joshua turned and leered at Fanny, his head wobbling drunkenly on his shoulders. She swiftly filled his mug with brandy. That should quiet the old devil, she thought.

He and Billy clashed their mugs together, spilling most of Joshua's. Fanny cursed her brother for a clumsy fool. And then Billy laughed and picked up the sleeping Rebecca and carried her away upstairs, and Fanny's head started to swim. The brandy was taking effect. To hell with Billy and Rebecca. They could look after themselves! She reeled, and the ground seemed to rock as she made her way to the wooden staircase. To hell with the clearing away. The dishes and food could wait! She clutched the stair rail. Joshua was nowhere in sight. With luck he might collapse outside and sleep in the yard all night. But she was in no state to worry about him. To hell with him, too!

But as she fell into the big bed, Joshua came in, banging the door shut behind him, and lurched across to the bed.

"And now, my pretty little dove, we're all alone." He hiccupped, and there was a gush of foul air. Fanny sat up with a jerk, her head clearing for a moment.

"What do you want?" she said thickly.

But without a word Joshua fell upon her, his hands seeking and tearing at her shift.

The assault on her person disgusted her, but Fanny was too drunk to care what was happening, and her husband's fumblings and frustrated ravings merely made her giggle. Eventually Joshua lay back exhausted, with Fanny lying supine and uncaring beside him.

"You're not a bit of help!" he raved. "Come on— help me! Kiss me! Rouse the passion that's been in me all night!" But she only giggled and lay still. Until at last, he collapsed on top of her in a snoring heap.

She lay motionless and then pushed him off her. Gasping with the effort, she rolled free of him and

slipped out of bed, feeling soiled and degraded by his at-
tempts at love-making. She crept downstairs in bare
feet, found enough warm water in the old black kettle to
half fill a bowl and washed herself all over. Then clean
again, she tidied all away, stacking the dirty dishes in the
flat brown sink. She broomed the stone flags and
mopped up several pools of beer. The kitchen smelt like
an alehouse and now that the effects of the brandy were
wearing off, she wrinkled her nose in distaste. She
opened the kitchen door and saw that the night was
over. Over the horizon the first streaks of dawn were
visible.

Then she remembered Billy. Had he gone home or
was he still here? She crept upstairs and opened her old
bedroom door and looked in. She smiled to herself and
closed the door quietly. Rebecca was snoring gently,
and she and Billy lay entwined in each other's arms.
Both were stark naked.

Fanny walked outside and took great gulps of fresh
air. Her head ached and she still felt queasy after the
drunken night. She would clear her head and then creep
back to bed. She still had to convince Joshua that he had
been a success. She laughed. It had been quite a night.
Her own wedding might not have been consummated,
but Rebecca's betrothal certainly had!

When she went back to the big bedroom, she drew the
bed curtain and looked down at her sleeping husband.
Her heart cried out for Caleb. Joshua was sprawled on
his back, gap-toothed mouth slack, and with deep rhyth-
mic snores coming from way down in his chest. A thin
dribble of saliva oozed from the corner of his lips and every now and again his tongue moved around his mouth
as if he was enjoying her. She felt revolted and trapped,
like some wild animal. She must have been mad to marry this sorry hunk of meat—and submit to his lusts! But
now, she forced herself to lie beside him. For this one
morning he must wake up beside her, and believe that
he had had his way. Henceforward she would insist on
separate rooms. She would make an excuse of her preg-
nancy. She would become prey to many humors, and if

he really thought the child was his, he would respect her wishes.

The waiting beside his sweating, stinking body felt like an eternity. Each time he moved, it was as if stale beer gushed from the pores of his skin. Then suddenly he turned, and one old claw fastened itself about her waist. She pushed him from her, and he awakened and groaned. Sighing with relief she moved and sat up in bed.

"Wake up, Joshua. It's nigh on milking time. The cows are lowing and their udders will be a-paining them. Joshua!" She shook him and he blinked and opened his eyes, only to shut them again. "Joshua! Are you awake?"

"Wha's that? Wha's tha' you say?" From his halting, slurred speech Fanny knew he was still drunk.

"Get up, man, and put your head in the horse trough! I've got to get your breakfast. What about some home-fed fat bacon?" Joshua groaned again.

"No breakfast for me . . . not yet awhile. Get me some ale. I could drink the horse trough dry."

"Get up yourself and fetch it. You wore me out last night."

"What? You get me that ale or I'll take my belt to you."

Fanny stroked his arm, and smiled seductively.

"Oh, what a masterful man you are, to be sure. You were like a boar pig last night . . . and me a-brimming and a-groaning like a sow! You must get your own ale and your own breakfast. I'm quite bruised with your passion. My! You do make a lovely husband!"

"Wha', me? Wha' did I do? I don't remember much about it." He nursed his sore head and moaned as his eyes strained to focus on Fanny. "Gor, my head's fit to drop off my shoulders. Wha' did we drink las' night?"

"You drank nearly all the mulled ale yourself and a bottle of brandy. And you drank another bottle in bed while you were making love. In between bouts, you might say."

"In between bouts? What do you mean? Speak up,

Mrs. Raybold. I don't remember . . ."

"Oh, Joshua, you great big tease! Of course you remember how you made love! You told me you had never known such love before. Am I to take it that it was all a fabrication?"

Joshua scratched his head and looked uncomfortable.

"Well, I dunno . . ."

"Oh, Joshua, don't break my heart! Say that you meant all you said—how I was the best female you had ever been with and how you loved me better than anyone else in the world!"

Joshua's eyes were staring.

"I said all that?"

Fanny nodded. "And all the things you *did*! I never knew such a man! If I had only known before . . ."

"What did I do, Fanny? Tell me quick." Joshua licked his lips. "Did I . . .?"

"Yes, Joshua, three times. I thought you would kill yourself. Does your back ache, Joshua?"

"Aye, it does now I think about it."

"Then I'll rub it for you with aromatic oils like a good wife should."

"Eh, you're a good wife, Fanny. I remember now! I was as good as when I was a lad! I didn't think I could somehow. It was you that wrought the miracle. Perhaps we might have a child yet."

"I hope so, Joshua. But now, we'll have to be careful. No bouncing round the bed—it could harm me if you've put one in there!"

"You mean . . .?" Joshua looked pleased and overawed. "Gor, I didn't realize I'd been all that good. I wish I remembered it all. You'll have to tell me all about it."

Fanny lowered her eyes and looked away.

"Tush! That wouldn't be seemly. I must not think vulgar thoughts. Of course, I may not become a mother, but you certainly did your job well! I must admire you for it. You were in a Heaven of your own. And if you become a father after last night's work, you will be a lucky man indeed!"

Joshua pulled on his trousers and his voluminous shirt and leather vest.

"Fanny, from now on it's no hard work for you. We'll find some wench to come and do your duties. I'll not have my wife risk the loss of my child, if it's God's will that we should have one. Gor, after all these years! Wait until I tell old Milton and Jim Bletcheley. They're both younger than me and haven't been able to get bairns for years!"

"You tell them I say there's no one better at getting bairns! I'll tell 'em myself if you want me to. So there!"

"Very kindly of you, Fanny. I knew you would not let me down." He patted her on the shoulder. "Now lie still and rest. I'll rouse Rebecca and she can get your breakfast!"

Fanny snuggled down and smiled to herself. If she was any judge, Rebecca was going to be caught any minute now!

The roar came ten minutes later. By the splashing, Joshua had spent some time at the horse trough and now had his wits about him. Fanny guessed there would be another wedding before long.

And so it came about that another wedding took place a month afterward. The happy couple moved into the Tyler house with sundry bundles and parcels that had belonged to Rebecca's mother. At first Fanny looked on with jealousy at all Rebecca carried away; but soon she comforted herself with the thought that her loss was her brother's gain.

At Fellside a fourteen-year-old wench, a tall rawboned piece by the name of Sarah, came to work and clean, and Fanny, who was expert in such matters, kept her busy from morning until night and delighted in keeping the poor girl scurrying from one job to another. She derived pleasure from watching her work and kept a stern lookout for any slipshod ways, until the poor girl came to dread her gimlet eyes. She would stand watching for hours up to her elbows in soapsuds, while

Sarah used the heavy stick to beat the clothes in the oaken tub. Fanny took a malicious delight in seeing the expression on the girl's face when she complained they were not clean enough and ordered her to start again.

But soon she tired of this sport and started to go back to the big house to see Aunt Beamish and Lady Letitia. She had never thought she would miss Rebecca, but she did. And so she found relief in woman's talk with her aunt and the other servants, and listening to the frail Lady Letitia.

Sometimes she heard Sir Timothy raising his voice in the distance, but nowadays he rarely visted his wife—and never when Fanny was present. She watched and listened, and began to understand things that had puzzled her in the past. She learned about managing a large house and staff. She knew she was ignorant, but she was willing to learn—and learn fast. Joshua would not live forever, and she was preparing herself for the day she moved into her own house in Tunbridge Wells.

Now the child was quickening within her. She found that when she was excited or tired the child kicked all the more. And as time went on she blossomed and grew more beautiful and her hair shone with health and cleanliness, for Fanny never forgot Caleb's lessons during their love-making.

She had now persuaded Joshua that it was better for him to sleep away from her. She told him of a dream she had had, in which he had overtaxed himself and died in the middle of a bout of passion. And then, counting up the months on her fingers, she knew the time was right to tell him of the coming child.

"See!" She told him, "I knew it all the time! I was sure you had made me with child! Now you can boast to all those old men about how young you really are!"

"Fanny! You're sure now, girl? I don't want to be the laughingstock of the inn, you know. We'd better wait and be certain."

Fanny shrugged her shoulders.

"As you wish, but I'm quite sure I'm not mistaken."

"When Fanny, when?"

The old man's eyes glistened with pleasure. Fanny did some quick sums in her head, and added on a couple of months. He would think her full-term baby was born before its time!

"Oh, about the middle of January."

She prayed she did not look too full in front. She had tried to hold herself in with laces, but lately she had had to let out some tucks.

"Eh, you're a grand lass! I must remember to buy you a new bonnet when I go to town!"

"A bonnet! What would I do with a bonnet? I could do with a new gown."

"A new gown! But that would cost money."

"And what of it? You must see that your wife does you credit. I could do with a new cloak as well, and some shoes."

"Oh dear me! I never thought having a wife would be so expensive!"

"Do I not keep you comfortable? And cleaner than you've ever been?"

"Aye, all that . . . and more. But I wish for less cleanliness and a little more of that which I don't remember. Fanny, can't you find it in your heart to let me come to you in your own room. I promise to be very careful with you. I would buy you an extra gown."

"Joshua! How can you think of such a thing at a time like this! Think of the child. You might influence him to evil and fornication! Besides which, the exitement might kill you. You know the dream I had. Would you want me to give birth as a widow, without a husband to protect me in my hour of need?"

Joshua drew back, downcast.

"Nay, you're a good wife, none better, and I'll not be the one to put you at risk. You'll not be a widow before you're brought to bed!"

Fanny squeezed his arm to show her appreciation.

"You're a good man, Joshua Raybold, and you'll get your reward in Heaven!"

Joshua sighed and went back to work.

CHAPTER FIVE

Sir Timothy Gilbourne was furious that the promising young Billy Bickler had left him to get married and work for that old upstart, Joshua Raybold. But thinking of Mrs. Raybold delayed any act of reprisal. He wanted Fanny Raybold's gratitude. Some day it might be useful to him. There was something about Fanny that quickened his pulse.

Now, from his dining room window, he watched her walk up the driveway. He was fully aware of her visits to his ailing wife, but at the moment it pleased him to ignore her.

He frowned when he saw how blooming she looked. Why could his own wife not blossom as Fanny did? It was as if she was proud to carry that dirty old man's child! He wondered what Letitia's thoughts were. For the first time he imagined Letitia's agony, losing so many children and now waiting patiently to see if she could carry this one. He clenched his fists. He hardly dare think of a child of his own. Perhaps someone somewhere had laid a curse on him. There were so many people willing to do him harm. He had turned forty and could think of several occasions on which he had given some man or woman the right and cause to curse him . . .

But if only Letitia managed to give him a son! He would light candles and humor her by going to church, and his life would be changed. His honor as a Gilbourne and a father would command respect. He would turn over a new leaf for the sake of his son.

He stood, scratching his scalp under his long glossy periwig, and eyed Fanny. And yet, if he could only have Fanny discreetly . . . He turned his thoughts firmly from her. He must avoid her at all costs!

Fanny, unaware of Sir Timothy's admiring eyes, slipped in the side door and quickly climbed the stairs to Lady Letitia's room. She had with her a basket and fresh herbs she had gathered to help the invalid. Among them was a fresh supply of wild raspberry leaves with which to make a tisane. Fanny had already brought raspberry leaves and told her the gypsies always drank the tea to relieve the muscles before childbirth. But Lady Letitia had only laughed. She did not really think she would carry the child for the full term, so why drink the putrid stuff?

Fanny was worried. If she loved any other woman it was the gentle Lady Letitia, who needed love and protection so badly. And Aunt Beamish had told her she was at her wit's end to find food that would tempt her appetite.

"Cook tries all manner of recipes, but nothing is acceptable. She either wrinkles up her nose or is sick. I very much doubt—"

"It is Sir Timothy's fault," said Fanny furiously. "He keeps her in such a state of tension. If he would only go away—"

"Hush! Someone may hear you." Aunt Beamish spoke uneasily.

"Oh, so now he's got spies, has he?"

"The new chambermaid—he engaged her last time he was in Tunbridge Wells. A superior piece, if ever I saw one. A proper townie who shrieks when she sees a cow!"

"You don't think . . .?"

Aunt Beamish nodded. Fanny pursed her lips.

"So! The old devil brings his common mistresses to the house now! I hope poor Lady Letitia doesn't become aware of it!"

"M'lady has too innocent a mind to think of him bringing his women here. She does not particularly like

Rosy Meldrum but she tolerates her because Sir Timothy particularly asked her to be kind to her. He gave her some sad story about finding her on the streets and being worried about her moral welfare."

"He probably spoke the truth about finding her on the streets, but her moral welfare! Huh, I doubt if her moral welfare would worry him. Why, he's . . ." Fanny stopped dead. There was no need to alarm Aunt Beamish with tales about Sir Timothy's amorous attentions to her in the past.

Aunt Beamish did not seem to notice the slip, and busied herself with the tea tray.

"There, run upstairs with this. She looks forward to seeing you."

But now she stood outside the bedroom door with the herbs. Had m'lady taken them? She knocked and waited, then entered after a faint voice called "come." She was shocked at the change in the lady. The light was dim for the heavy curtains were nearly full drawn over the window, and the room smelled close and stuffy.

"How are you today, m'lady?"

Lady Letitia stirred fretfully.

"Oh, 'tis you, Fanny. I thought it was . . ." She stopped, and Fanny knew she had steeled herself, thinking it was Sir Timothy.

"I've brought you some more herbs. You will have used the last, I hope?"

M'lady's head moved from side to side.

"You should never have bothered. I feel so ill, I might die."

"Come, m'lady, you are no way near dying."

Fanny took a deep breath. Somehow she must shock this frail girl into bestirring herself. Aunt Beamish pandered to her, and her husband was indifferent.

"You will never be well unless you live a healthy life, and for a start you want some fresh air!"

Purposefully she strode to the window and pulled back the curtains, letting a stream of sunlight into the room. Then she threw the windows wide open, and the breeze moved the curtains. Lady Letitia gave a little scream.

"What are you doing? Do you want to kill me? I thought you were my friend."

Fanny moved back to the bedside.

"Believe me, m'lady, I am your friend. Fresh air will not hurt you. Come, sit up and take your tisane, and then I will help you to dress. If you sat by the window . . ."

"No!" Lady Letitia cowered under the silken covers. "I don't *want* to be well! You don't understand. I want to die with this baby!"

Fanny stared at her, shock and fear prickling her spine.

"You can't mean what you say, m'lady. Think how pleased Sir Timothy will be if you give him a son!"

"But what if it is a girl, or I lose it when it is born!" she whispered. "I cannot endure the thought much longer. I have pondered ways of doing away with myself, but I am too afraid even to do that. I am a failure! I should never have been born."

Fanny went down on her knees at the bedside.

"I never knew you felt so badly. I knew you weren't happy. Forgive me, m'lady, for mentioning this, but I had no way of knowing."

Letitia held out her hand to Fanny.

"Dear Fanny, you have been a great help to me. If only I was as well as you, and had your courage to hope and love the child kicking inside me. Instead I feel he is alien—that I don't feel like a mother. Help me, Fanny! Help me in spite of myself!" She clung to Fanny and their tears mingled together.

Fanny made up her mind to help the Lady Letitia. She ignored the demands of her own household and elevated Sarah to be cook and housekeeper, much to Joshua's noisy indignation.

So Fanny became a constant visitor at the big house, and Sir Timothy found himself waiting eagerly for her arrival. She was gaining weight steadily now and her bosom had increased, giving her figure a pleasing roundness. She wore her cloak to hide her swollen condition, and at times, when her cloak slipped, Sir Timothy's blood stirred at the titilating sight. He was becoming increasingly irritated with Rosy, who was putting on airs and graces and constantly bickering with the other servants. He wished Fanny would come to her lying-in; he had the feeling that she might welcome his attentions. There was something about her eyes that spurred him on to hope. He licked his lips. Fanny was young enough to be an entertaining lover . . .

Fanny, unaware of these thoughts, decided to call in at Tyler cottage on her way home to see Rebecca. Billy puzzled her, and she wanted to find out from Rebecca if all was well.

Billy had become Joshua's right-hand man, and the old man sang his praises frequently. Billy was slow, but his love was land, and now that Fellside was within his grasp he was contented. But there was something wrong somewhere, for Billy had been evasive when she asked after Rebecca.

She found Rebecca much changed. She was blooming and happy, and greeted Fanny with a broad smile.

"Come in, come in. This is indeed a surprise! I understood you were too busy at the big house to visit me. Sit down and I'll order Mary to bring us some tea."

Fanny sat down and looked around. It was the first time she had visited the woman who was now her stepdaughter, and her sister-in-law, and she was curious. She found the parlor comfortable, and Rebecca's taste showed. She wondered how Billy fitted into this house, for she remembered him to be as rough and ready as old Joshua.

Rebecca soon put her straight on Billy's account. With a triumphant smirk, she said, "I want you to be the first to know. I'm with child!"

Fanny looked at her in disbelief.

"You! A child?"

"Yes. Why not? I'm not that old! And I'm young

enough to have several more, Doctor Byng tells me."

"But I thought . . ."

"Yes, what did you think, Fanny?"

Fanny looked uncomfortable.

"Well, I hardly thought of a child at your time of life. Do you think it wise?"

"I am well—better than m'lady up at Gilbourne House! I am only thirty-eight. Billy has no complaints. Indeed, he complains I am too demanding! But I was determined to have at least one child!"

"You are very blunt, Rebecca. So you are determined to give your father a grandchild? Perhaps you expect him to provide for your child, too?" said Fanny silkily.

"Of course, he will! This child of yours . . ." She looked at Fanny in a hard and calculating manner. "Is he my father's? I somehow had the impression . . ."

"Yes?"

Now it was Rebecca's turn to appear uncomfortable. Her courage left her when she saw the blaze in Fanny's eyes.

"I'm sorry," she mumbled. "It was just that . . . my father seemed past marriage, and all that it implies."

Fanny smiled sweetly.

"We all get shocks. I thought you, too, were past marriage—and all that it implies. But I was wrong seemingly."

Rebecca flushed angrily.

"There is a world of difference between myself and my father!"

"True. But it is a well-known fact that a man can be a father late in life. With a woman it is different."

She gathered her basket and her reticule together, and carefully placed the cup and saucer on the side table.

"Thank you for the tea, and I hope and wish for every happiness for you. I will tell Billy you have told me your news."

"It is well. Strange, though, that my passion outstrips Billy's. I was beginning to doubt Billy's stamina." She gave a self-satisfied smile. "But there. They do say better tunes are played on old fiddles!" Abruptly her face changed, and she looked vicious for a moment. "Too many people talked of Billy marrying an old woman for her money, and I know Billy talked that way too. But I married Billy for love. And I mean to see I get it!"

Fanny considered her carefully, and what she saw made her think. Clearly love and the marriage bed had done wonders for the vinegary spinster of Fellside. Now she was warm and passionate and young-looking! Fanny nodded her goodbyes and walked away, deep in thought. To remain young with old Joshua, it would be essential for her to find a lover—a man who would rival Caleb Neyn, a man to whip up her passions. Yet she knew of no one in the village who appealed to her. The face of Sir Timothy swam before her eyes. The handsome, cold Sir Timothy was the only other person to arouse her interest. What would his love-making be like? He was so different to Caleb, who was a wild man of the fields, a free spirit. Sir Timothy was an aristocrat. Would his love-making excel even Caleb's?

Then she drew herself up short. She was thinking sinful thoughts about Lady Letitia's husband! Whatever she did, she could never bring herself to do anything to hurt that lady. She, who was like a poor fluttering dove. No. A woman like Lady Letitia needed protection from the harsh world.

She was pensive as she walked back along the narrow winding lane. It was a long time since those golden mornings when she had run so eagerly to meet Caleb. She looked about her. It was near this spot that her heart had filled with anticipation for her first glimpse of him.

Then her heart fluttered in her breast, for there stood Caleb, under their tree, calm and casual, watching her from under a battered old hat. He grinned, and Fanny was transported back in time to last summer . . .

"Hello, Fanny, and how are you?" He lounged forward, broad shoulders well set back, eyes flashing mischievously, and took her in his arms, as if there had been no separation. But Fanny moved back.

"Oho! So you are becoming a little more choosy." He grabbed her, and as his mouth closed firmly over hers, she felt again the familiar thrill envelop her whole body, lifting her toward an ecstasy that she had all but forgotten. She clung to him, all vague notions of repulsing him gone. His hands wandered over her body and when he felt the swollen belly, she felt his shock. He put her aside.

"What's this?" he growled. "I heard rumor that you had married old Raybold. So it's true! You married an old man. You couldn't wait! You married him for his money."

Stung, Fanny's hand came up in a sharp blow to his cheek.

"You were marrying Savina. How is she, by the way? Did she give you the son you wanted? The full-blooded son that I wasn't good enough to bear you?"

"She gave me a daughter," he said sullenly. "We didn't suit and she went back to the Fingos a month after the birth. My mother looks after the brat!"

"And so now you come running to me, now your passion is not sated with her! Well, you're wrong, Caleb Neyn—I can live without you."

"Not by the way you kissed me, Fanny. You wanted me in that moment. Does the old man satisfy your lust? I see he has done his duty by you!" She laughed bitterly, but something kept her silent. Her revenge on him would be the sweeter if her child was a son! His son would be a posh-rat, a half-blood! Something even he had been contemptuous of. Let him sweat. He would have to make do with his full-blood gypsy daughter! The thought of the gypsy regarding himself as of better birth had always stung her . . .

She moved away, but she was clumsy. Her foot caught in a root, and she would have fallen but for Caleb's timely assistance. His arm closed about her, and she felt it tighten cruelly.

"I want to love you," he breathed into her ear. His heart was pounding and her own blood leapt to his. Why not? Why not seize the moment? He would soon be gone for the winter and she would be alone, except for that odious old man.

Her heart sang. She turned to him, and their bodies and lips clung together.

"The baby! You'll not hurt the child?"

"Nay! I'll be gentle. The child will take no hurt from me. I want you, Fanny, I want you now!" He drew her down under their tree, and the months of separation melted away to nothing as their bodies met and became one.

They lay in close communion. He buried his head in her bosom and groaned aloud.

"If only I had taken you away with me! We could have made a life together! But I wanted you *and* my family— there are so many taboos amongst the gypsies. Savina was never right for me. She wanted her way . . . and the Fingos' way. To her, the Fingos were the only gypsies. When passion faded away, she chose the Fingos instead of the Neyns. I could never forgive her for that!"

Fanny sat up with difficulty.

"You mean that if Savina had chosen to become a true Neyn, she would still have been your wife?"

"Of course. She was a true gypsy, wasn't she? A fit mother for my sons. If she had stayed, there would have been other children."

Fanny rolled onto her knees and then struggled upright. She took a deep breath.

"You bastard! You can talk like that just after—" She couldn't bring herself to say the word "love." Caleb scrambled up, belting his moleskin trousers. He looked puzzled.

"Why do you say that? I loved you well, didn't I? I was gentle and considerate. Are you jealous of Savina?"

Fanny whirled round him in a fury.

"Why should I be? First you tell me the marriage did not work and lead me to believe you did not love her.

And then you say you love me. Now you say that had Savina chosen to be a Neyn, you would have been happy to have other children by her!"

"Well, she is my wife—it would be a wifely duty!"

"But you must love her if you want to give her other children!"

"What has love to do with it? She is my wife—nothing more. I would give her children because it is my duty to my family to breed. Love is what I feel for you, even though you are a *gaujo*!"

"You mean—you love me, and not your wife?"

"Love? What is this talk of love? My body cries out for your body, and your body answers. If that is not love, what is?"

"But the vicar calls that lust. He preaches that there is another love . . ."

"Pah! What does the vicar know? A wishy-washy love of the mind! What ecstasy will that give you?"

Fanny looked at him doubtfully, suddenly tempted to tell him whose child she was carrying. But again she fought the impulse back. Some wild notion that gypsies killed unwanted babies flashed through her mind. She wanted and needed this child who kicked so vigorously in her womb! A protective instinct rose within her. She would fight the world to keep her baby!

"I must go now, Joshua will be expecting me. It is time for our evening meal."

She was gasping suddenly. She had just this moment realized the meaning of real motherhood. Until now, the child had been a burden to her, an idea, a nuisance—something that made her body ugly and clumsy. Now the lump had taken on a character of its own. She was sure it would be a boy; she would call him William, after her brother . . .

"You'll come tomorrow? I'll see you again?" cried Caleb.

She nodded. Yes, her flesh would not allow her to keep away.

"One more kiss then, and I shall let you go home to

that detestable old man."

"Are you jealous, Caleb?"

Caleb frowned.

"Why should I, a strong man, be jealous of a skinny old man with one foot in the grave?"

"Because I will share his bed tonight," she lied.

He laughed, a deep laugh full of amusement.

"That bed cannot see much action, for if you used him as you use me he would be dead by now." He kissed her and there was a wild promise in the kiss. "Tomorrow at this time." He turned into the wood and, laughing loud enough to frighten the birds, he strode away, confident in his masculinity.

Fanny watched him go, biting her lip. Now that he was gone from her, she could resist him. She resented his authority over her. She made her mind up to avoid the lonely woodland road in future. Caleb could sing like a tomcat for his love! Her greatest worry was that Caleb would realize that her baby was due earlier than she had indicated. She prayed to God to make the gypsies start on their winter pilgrimage early this year, for she knew that gypsies had been known to steal children. If it pleased Caleb to do so, it would not be beyond him to steal the child—if he knew it was his!

She set her shoulders back. There would be no more meetings with Caleb until after her lying-in and until the child was christened as a Raybold. It all sounded so easy. Just avoid Caleb and wait until the last *vardo* had left the campsite . . . But she had forgotten Caleb's determination and her own bodily needs.

For two days she resisted his lure. Her visits to the big house were made earlier and she arrived home early. Then on the third morning she found Caleb at the door of the farm, asking to see Joshua.

There he stood, a wide grin showing his even white teeth, as he looked her up and down.

"Mr. Raybold in, ma'am?" he asked, for Sarah's benefit. The wench looked mesmerized at his giant figure. "Tell your fortune, ma'am, while I'm here?" He winked and Fanny pursed hard lips.

"Mr. Raybold is in the cow pasture. He'll not be in until noon."

Caleb leaned against the door, putting a foot across the threshold at the same time.

"Well now, that is interesting. Can I come in and wait?"

Fanny heard Sarah suck in her breath.

"Indeed you cannot!" Fanny snapped. "Please get on your way. Sarah and I have work to do!"

Caleb laughed.

"Can it not wait? I am sure this wench would like her fortune told, wouldn't you, my young beauty?" He chucked Sarah under the chin, and she gave a little scream and ducked behind her mistress.

Fanny was angry and showed it.

"And what might you want with Mr. Raybold?"

Caleb leered at her.

"Do you want the wench listening in on this conversation?"

Fanny looked helplessly from him to Sarah.

"Sarah, you go and see to the milk churns in the still room. I'll be with you in just a few minutes."

"Yes." She bobbed a curtsy and, staring at Caleb with big sheep's eyes, she ran off.

"There! You've frightened the poor girl to death! What do you mean by coming here like this?"

"You promised to meet me, Fanny, and I waited and you did not come. I want you, Fanny, and I want you now!"

"You must be mad! I can't come now. What would Sarah think if I walked off with a gypsy?" The scorn in her voice flicked Caleb on the raw. He gripped her arm and turned her to face him.

"You promised to come to me. Why didn't you?" His black eyes held hers and she felt like a rabbit mesmerized by a snake.

"I-I . . . couldn't come."

"You lie. You didn't *want* to come. Why?"

"I told you the truth. I couldn't come. Joshua wanted me . . ."

He pushed her away roughly.

"I can tell by your eyes you're lying. You went early to the big house to avoid meeting me at the set time. I'm not a fool. *Why*? And don't think up any more lies. I want the truth!"

"Because I don't want to see you any more, that's why. Isn't that enough? What can we hope for, you and I? Whatever happens between us, we can never hope to be together! Can't you see, it will only lead to heartbreak? You're leaving Gilbourne soon, and we shall have to suffer the parting all over again. Is all this worth it?"

"But I shall return again in the spring. Don't you want to see me again?"

Fanny groaned.

"Are you going to haunt me every spring? Will there be no peace for either of us?"

"We love each other, Fanny. Can you deny that? Our paths are destined to cross—"

"What makes you say that, Caleb?" Suddenly Fanny was fearful.

"There is a bond between us, no matter how you fight it. My mother told my fortune. She says my future will be held in the hands of the *gaujé* wench. That we should both go far and yet come together, and that someone of the name of Charles will hold us fast willy-nilly. Who is this Charles, Fanny?"

Fanny looked back at him in puzzlement.

"Nay, Caleb, you'll not deceive me with your riddles. The only Charles I have heard of is his Majesty King Charles, and he is the last Charles to hold the likes of us together! Your mother is a fraud—she must be playing some game of her own!"

"Not my mother. She has the gift . . . and what she saw in the crystal she did not like. She spoke the truth."

Fanny shrugged.

"Well, you must look for this Charles yourself. Now go, and please . . . please, leave me be."

She tried to remove herself from his grasp, but his grip tightened.

"Not until you kiss me. And only then if you want me to . . ."

His broad body leant over hers and she could smell the stale sweat of him, and something else—the animal odor of the male who desired his woman. As he kissed her, her body gave her away and her arms crept around his neck.

For a moment or two she wrestled with her conscience, but the struggle was short-lived. She gave in to a wildness of spirit. If only she had a husband like Caleb! They clung together and Caleb started to tremble.

"Where can we go? he whispered into her hair.

"The loft over the stable," she breathed. "We'll not be disturbed there."

"Come then, and be my woman. You know you belong to me." So saying, he took her by the hand and led her unresistingly away.

They met every day after that beneath their tree in the wood, and it was not until late in October, when the harvest was in, that the colorful *vardos* left that year.

Fanny cried when the bitter day came, and she took a walk towards the gypsy encampment, where nothing remained but the black ashes of their fires. Now she could only wait for his return in the spring, and this time she was fearful. For when he came there would be a child, a child who would resemble him. So she pined for him, dreaded his return, hated and loved him, and could do nothing but wait for the winter mists to come and for the birth of their child. . . .

She didn't really believe it when the pains started. She told Joshua it was only colic and the eating of fat pork. But then the pains worsened, and she sent a frightened Sarah for her Aunt Beamish and the village lying-in woman.

She was like a young animal in her pain. She snarled at Joshua, who was fussing and getting in the way. She directed him to boil water and find fresh linen, and she saw the old hands tremble in their eagerness to help in the birth of his son.

Fanny was sure it would be a boy. And sure enough,

after hours and hours of labor, the slim narrow body gave up its young—a dark fuzzy-haired boy with a very red face. He yawned and raised clenched hands to his mouth, which moved greedily to find sustenance. And when he came in contact with the arched protruding nipple, he clamped on and fed with gusto.

Fanny looked down at him with a strange satisfaction. He was hers entirely! She had carried him, been sick for him, and forced her tired body at the end to give him life. He was hers and no one would ever take him from her!

Then weakly she passed him to Aunt Beamish.

"Show him to Joshua, and tell him he is before his time and must be kept here in my room for a few weeks until he gathers strength. He is to be called William, after my brother . . ."

"Why your brother? Joshua will want him called after himself. It is only fair, Fanny. He is to be the boy's father."

"I want him to be called William, Aunt Beamish. They were my pains that brought him forth, so I am naming him—William!"

And William he was. For hours Joshua looked at him with a mixture of delight and incredulity, before rushing out to boast of his prowess to all his old cronies. Indeed, for the first month after the child's birth he rarely came home sober, and it was the usual thing for Fanny to have the unenviable task of undressing him and putting him to bed.

Fanny was soon up and about after her confinement. She was like a young heifer. Birth had been a natural process, and now, full of milk, she gloried in motherhood. But to Joshua she was still an invalid with an ailing child.

She was careful now to allow Joshua only an odd peep at the child, when he asked after it she always shook her head.

"If he is to live through this severe winter, he must be cosseted and kept away from all draughts and cold. A child born before its time is always at risk. Wait until the

warm days of spring . . . then you may take him abroad
and show him off.''

Even Rebecca and Billy were discouraged from
viewing him. Since he was always smothered up in
shawls, there was very little to see anyway. And so it was
only Sarah and Aunt Beamish who actually saw how fast
he was growing.

Letitia asked often about him, and Aunt Beamish
told her the same story—that the child was delicate. She
shook her head over the news. She always expected
Fanny to have a robust child. It did not seem fair.

But her own time was drawing near. In spite of several setbacks, this child was fighting for its life. She lay in
her room, waiting and hoping. She knew that if she
could bear this child naturally, the credit would be Fanny's. She had been a repeated visitor, and for the last
few weeks had never missed. Truly a loyal friend, Fanny
had kept up her courage. So now if she failed, she would
fail both Fanny and her husband . . .

The day after Fanny's boy was christened, Lady
Letitia's son was born. It was Christmas Eve and the
bells were ringing for midnight mass when the news
reached the village that a boy had been born in
Gilbourne House. And on Christmas morning Billy
came up to Fellside to tell Fanny.

At once she put on her cloak and made her way down
to the village towards Gilbourne House. She must see
Lady Letitia and wish her well. She was happy as she
walked. A great weight was off all their minds, for both
she and Aunt Beamish had feared for Lady Letitia's life.

But a surprise awaited her. A white-faced Aunt
Beamish took her in to see m'lady. She was laid with her
face turned to the wall. Fanny knelt down beside her
and took her hand in hers.

"M'lady, what is it? You have a fine son, m'lady. You
can be proud of him." She looked down at the cot beside
the huge four-poster and gazed at the small red-faced
scrap who lay there so quietly. His hair was fine and
black, a smaller edition of her own William.

"Take him away! I don't want to see him! I hate

him—and his father!" She sobbed and stuffed a handkerchief into her mouth to stifle the rising hysteria.

"But, m'lady—"

"Fanny, I don't want to be reminded. He hurt me so! I never ever want another little monster! Fanny, don't ever let Sir Timothy come into this room again!"

"But m'lady, I cannot refuse to allow your husband into your room! It would hardly be fitting—"

"Fanny, you must! Promise me you'll tell him to keep away. Tell him I commanded you!" She clung to Fanny's hand, and tears of weakness ran down her face. "I'll kill myself if he comes to me again! I promise you."

Fanny turned to Aunt Beamish, who was standing silently in the doorway.

"What can we do? We cannot tell Sir Timothy."

"There is no need. I heard it all." And from behind Aunt Beamish stepped a peculiarly ashen Sir Timothy. "The woman's mad! What shall we do with the child?"

Aunt Beamish swallowed and faltered.

"I've tried to reason with her ever since the child was born. She'll not put him to the breast. He'll die if he doesn't start sucking soon. He's weak already."

"Then force her, Mistress Beamish. My wife must be forced to feed him," said Sir Timothy harshly.

"But we cannot do that! She will not even hold the child." Aunt Beamish's voice was trembling with fear and alarm.

"Tie her down and pinion her arms. There are ways. Hogtie her and use her like an animal!"

Fanny's blood boiled and she stood up straight.

"You inhuman monster! Do you know what she has endured for the sake of this son of yours? Do you have the least notion of what it means for a delicate-natured lady like her to give birth? She is suffering from shock. She will come about later."

Sir Timothy looked at her coolly. Her bitter words rolled off him like water off a duck's back.

"I care not what you think of me, madam. All my concern is for my son. I want him alive! Are you prepared to suckle him?" Fanny looked at him with shock. "I understand your own son is sickly. Can you feed two?"

Fanny looked from him to Aunt Beamish, who slightly shook her head. For a long moment there was a deathly silence in the room, and then Fanny looked Sir Timothy in the eyes.

"Yes, I'll suckle your son, Sir Timothy."

"Good. Then take him away and bring him back in six months' time. I'll pay you well and not forget this night's work!"

He looked meaningly in her eyes, and Fanny knew in that moment that she had Sir Timothy where she wanted him.

"And his name, Sir Timothy?"

"Call him Charles—after my father."

And so Charles Gilbourne went to Fellside, and the two children were laid side by side. Although they could almost have passed for twins, William was the most robust. Charles lay quietly, day after day, giving Fanny little enough trouble; but somehow she knew that he was never destined to live long in the world—that he was only a visitor.

CHAPTER SIX

Fanny agonized over little Charles Gilbourne. She loved him because he was Letitia's child, and she nursed him devotedly. But in spite of all her efforts, Charles did not thrive. It was as if he knew he lacked the will to live, and took the easiest way out. He lay all day and night with his small hands curled, and only opened sleepy eyes when he was washed and changed.

But William was growing apace, and Fanny was proud of her strong noisy boy. There was now a marked difference in the babies. Both were dark, but that was as far as the likeness went. William had the broad frame of peasant-gypsy stock, with well defined features. Charles was small-boned like his mother, with his father's darkness of skin and hair; but he was small and did not grow.

Fanny's mind often wandered to the fate of Letitia's child. She looked down at Baby Charles and then at her own son, and her eyes clouded. Supposing Charles died? She shuddered at Letitia's fate. Even now, there was not much hope for the gentle girl who was wasting away upstairs in her overheated room at the big house. But if her baby died now, Sir Timothy would abandon her completely to his servants and then all Letitia's suffering and supreme effort would be wasted. Fanny swore that she would not let that happen.

So she showed Charles to her husband and told him he was sickly, and Joshua, who had never been allowed to see much of his son, was deceived. He was already used to the idea of having fathered a sickly child. After all, hadn't he been born before his time?

One morning, Fanny came downstairs, hollow-eyed. She was holding a dead child in her arms.

Joshua was resigned and sad. He took one look at the child and then walked outside to his barn, there to weep out his old heart and put away any ideas of raising a son. He was too old and tired to hope for another . . .

And so William Raybold went to his resting place, and a new Charles Gilbourne, strong and lusty, grew apace.

Fanny endured the commiserations of the villagers with fortitude. Many admired her courage and comforted her by saying most women lost a child or two and assuring her she would have others to take the dead child's place. Fanny merely smiled quietly and passed on. Only Sarah and Aunt Beamish knew of the deception, and Fanny felt sure that Sarah in her new role as housekeeper could be trusted, and that Aunt Beamish would never reveal the truth. Lady Letitia was Aunt Beamish's reason for living, the child she never had, and nothing would be allowed to hurt her. Fanny knew this, and felt no pangs of jealousy, even though her aunt had shown no love for her and Billy.

Privately she gloried in the fact that her son and Caleb's would one day become Sir Charles Gilbourne, and own the parklands and several farms and an estate in the north belonging to his dukely grandfather. It thrilled her to think that her son would be a man of consequence.

The weeks passed and no inquiry or summons came from the big house. It was as if young Charles Gilbourne had been forgotten. But Aunt Beamish told Fanny that Sir Timothy was spending more time with King Charles in London. And Lady Letitia would not hear any news of her child. She did not ask for him to be brought to her. So Fanny had the pleasure of watching the boy grow and look on her as his mother. . . .

The weeks passed and then the early spring flowers appeared. Soon the first pale green buds on the trees blossomed forth, and Fanny's thoughts turned to Caleb. The clatter of creaking caravans and the clash of swinging kettles and pans would soon be heard along the lanes. Would Caleb be changed? And would that devastating attraction still be alive between them? She hoped not. She must fight herself and him, and keep him at bay. She put out of her mind those wild ecstatic hours together. He was a blight on her life and made her restless, and there was no future in their love. They would never make a life together . . . Why, *why*? Why did she still desire him, yearn for him, hunger after him?

And then the unforeseen happened. Rebecca had just had her baby, a girl, and Joshua had been down to the village to celebrate the birth of his first grandchild. On his way back he fell into a slithery wet ditch. It had rained heavily that night, and the next morning when Fanny had got up to rouse him for the milking, she found his room empty and his bed undisturbed. Worried by his absence, she raised the alarm. The two lads who helped with the milking were sent along the road to the village to look for him, and they came back to Fellside with Joshua's dripping body laid out on a gate. He had drowned in his cups.

So that spring of '63 saw many changes. Rebecca came home with Billy and her new daughter, and Billy took over the farm. Fanny packed her bags and, taking all Joshua's spare money retired to Aunt Beamish's cottage with Charles.

Her idea of a house in Tunbridge Wells had been set aside. Now all she wanted was to remain beside her son. So one morning, hearing that Sir Timothy had returned from London, she boldly set out to see him, taking the child with her. It was time Sir Timothy should meet his son and pay her for her loyalty and competence.

He watched her walk up the driveway, admiring her straight back and easy walk. Even though burdened with the child, she had a wild proudness about her which caught his interest again. Curious how her own child had died and Letitia's had lived! But there must be something tenacious about a highborn child. He put it all down to blood and breeding, and thought no more of the matter.

He received her in the library. Knowing the time had

come to recognize his son, he held out his arms without a word. She placed the boy firmly in them and looked him straight in the eyes.

"I did what you asked. I made a fine boy of him. You will be proud of him some day!"

He looked down on the sleeping child. He was pleased he took after him for coloring. All the Gilbournes had dark curly hair. He could see nothing of Letitia in the child, and was thankful. There was a weakness in the Duke of Lanbridge's line, probably due to inbreeding or some such. He was pleased to see that Charles was a Gilbourne through and through.

"You've done well. I'll pay you as I promised." Fanny gave a quick bob and Sir Timothy's eyes gleamed. "Is there anything I can do for you? I heard of the death of your child and the passing of Joshua Raybold. A monstrous tragic thing to happen."

"It is the Lord's will," said Fanny piously, and dropped her dark eyes demurely. Then she raised them and gazed at Sir Timothy with an alluring and inviting air. "There is something you could do for me, Sir Timothy." She stopped and they stared at one another. He licked his lips, his mouth suddenly dry with anticipation.

"Yes? What is it?"

She smiled, now the mistress of the situation.

"I would like to live here with your son. He regards me as his mother. Is that being unreasonable?"

Sir Timothy put the boy back into her arms.

"No. I do not find that unreasonable. You are his mother in all except birth. You suckled him and cared for him. Who better to look after his wants? You may have a suite of rooms near me, so that I can see my son more often." He looked deeply into her eyes. "Does that arrangement suit you?"

"Quite well, Sir Timothy. It will be most convenient."

He took her hand in his, and kissed it.

"You do me honor, mother of my child," he murmured softly.

So Fanny packed her meager bags and moved into the spacious suite next to Sir Timothy's. It was in the opposite wing to Lady Letitia's and as that lady never ventured forth from her room, it made no difference to her. Only Aunt Beamish disapproved. She thought it outrageous that her niece should become the mistress of her employer. But Fanny only smiled and bid Sarah, who came with her as personal maid, fetch Aunt Beamish a glass of the best Madeira.

As Aunt Beamish sipped the Madeira she gradually relaxed and resigned herself to the situation. Perhaps, after all, it would be better for her beloved lady. . . . She motioned Sarah out of the room.

"Fanny, I trust you're not getting ideas above your station? If anything happens to Lady Letitia—which God forbid"—she crossed herself as she spoke—"you'll not get any ideas of marrying him? If he takes another wife she will be a gentlewoman, mark my words!"

Fanny shrugged indifferently.

"I don't care. He can marry whom he pleases. Nobody knows better than I what a precarious life a mistress has! I've heard the villagers talk about the most notorious mistresses of all, the King's whores: but *they* manage to come about, and so will I!"

"But, Fanny, is that what you want? What about young Charles?"

"What about him? He is well cared for and holds a position against the world. Some day . . ." Her eyes held a dreamy look. She could see her son kneeling before the King, handsome and aristocratic. That would show Caleb what she was capable of! A pity he would never know who Charles really was. It would be worth his anger to seek him out one day and tell him the truth, just to see his face!

She sighed and came back to Aunt Beamish's question. "What are you trying to tell me?"

Aunt Beamish moved uneasily, setting down the wine glass with care.

"Have you thought of your position if Sir Timothy *did* marry again? You would be cast aside and parted from

Charles. Have you thought of that?"

Fanny looked at her in amazement.

"Sir Timothy cast me off? Are you mad? While Charles needs me, Sir Timothy would never think of it—for the child's sake."

"But what if he found out about Charles? What then?"

"How would he find out? You would never reveal the truth?"

"No, but he looks like you."

Fanny raced to her mirror and viewed herself from all angles.

"God's teeth! I never thought of that! Do you think he really does take after me?"

"Who can tell, yet? But you must be prepared."

Fanny looked sullen and confused.

"Then I must make certain he *does* marry me! That way, if he does find out, I can cajole him. No man would want the world to know he had been duped! Stop worrying, Aunt! Let us worry if the need arises!"

So she proceeded to unpack her belongings and make herself comfortable. She reveled in the large opulent rooms, and could not resist stroking the rich fabrics and handling the delicate china. The situation was beyond her wildest dreams. But *marry* Sir Timothy? This was a new thought. Well, why not? She was pretty enough, and she had picked up many pretty manners from Lady Letitia and could even read and write a little now. Why not aim at being the next Lady Gilbourne?

Sarah helped her to survey her few clothes, but Fanny cast them all on one side. They were far too old and dowdy for the mistress of Sir Timothy.

"Here, Sarah, take these for yourself. I shall keep the gown I am wearing and one other. Sir Timothy will buy me a complete new wardrobe before I am much older."

Sarah grinned.

"Oh, miss, you talk like a lady now! I want this, and I want that! And you do stick out your chin and sound so haughty like . . ."

"Hold your tongue, Sarah! It doesn't become you to talk so!"

But Sarah only laughed and, gathering up the discarded clothes, giggled and left the room.

Sir Timothy came later to see how she was settling in. The child was in his wooden cot by the fire in her sitting room. He looked down at him and then at Fanny.

"He is a fine boy. You have done well. Now come and sit by me and tell me what you want."

He took her arm and drew her down beside him. Her heart pounded. This was the first time they had ever really been alone together. Fanny was a little uncertain of herself. Sir Timothy was so very different from her wild gypsy boy. She felt childish and inexperienced in front of this man of the world, who must have known many women who were expert in the arts of love. She bit her lip.

Sir Timothy ran his hand up her arm and watched her, smiling softly. He felt her quiver, and, turning her head, he ran an exploratory finger round the contours of her cheek.

"And so you blush! Are you frightened of me, Fanny?"

Fanny gulped.

"No . . . I don't think so. Should I be?"

"I hope . . . a little. But I don't like submissive women. They bore me. Will you bore me, Fanny?" He bent his head and kissed her lightly on her dimpled elbow.

"No-no . . . I hope not, Sir Timothy."

"Call me Timothy, in private." He fondled her arm and then his hand strayed to her bodice, and Fanny heard his breath come faster. She herself was trembling, but whether it was fear or anticipation she could not determine.

Then, somehow, she was in his arms. His kiss surprised her. It was exciting and pleasant. For some reason she had thought no man could stir her like Caleb did. Now she knew she was wrong. Sir Timothy was an expert on kissing, and she gave back kiss for kiss with good measure . . .

Sir Timothy paused and mopped his brow, then took off his periwig. The short cropped hair underneath was dark and grizzled at the temples. It reminded Fanny that he was no young boy, like Caleb. Her pulses quickened. She had a mind to find out what Sir Timothy was really like! She turned her back to him.

"Will you loosen my gown, Timothy?"

He laughed and ran his lips along the back of her bare neck.

"Not yet, my sweet little savage! Tonight after a sumptuous meal, wine and the glow of lamps—after we have had time to dally a while and get to know each other. I'm not a stud who wants a quick jump. You must learn to be a proper mistress to a man. To pander to his wishes and learn what pleases him; to know when to talk and when to listen; when to be relaxing and when to excite. Then, and only then, will you be a valued mistress." His lips ran down her spine and she tingled at his touch.

"But Timothy . . ."

He pursed his lips and shook his head.

"I must leave you now. My bailiff wants to see me. He is waiting in the library. I hope I leave you wanting me."

"Timothy," she said with a little gasp. "How could it be otherwise?"

He smiled a devilish smile. "That is how a good little mistress should be. Now, prepare yourself. Have a herb bath and use all those sweet-smelling oils I brought from Paris. The bergamot oil is particularly seductive. Try it, my dear. It is one of my favorites. And one of the King's favorites, too . . ."

He left her, and she was crestfallen and disappointed. She was eager to find out what kind of lover he was. Somehow she knew his hard masculinity would be satisfying. With trembling fingers, she undid her gown and stepped forth as naked as the day she was born to stand in front of her long mirror and examine herself. Would he find her as fair as those other women? What would he think of her, and her performance? She trembled with anticipation. That night she would find out for herself.

He was as she imagined. He was so very different from Caleb, who had the fascination of youth. This man was a seasoned courtier, who had fought at the King's side. His muscles were like steel from their hard usage, and as he stood before her, naked and unashamed, she surveyed the rippling muscles and the hard flesh under the dark hairs of his chest.

Then he closed the crimson curtains around the four-poster and the secret world was theirs alone. He taught her to love in a totally new way, to bring pleasure and anticipation to that love, to find ecstasy at the same time as he did—to prolong it, and be swept away on the wings of passion. And he was cruel. He used her roughly and she loved it. And when she thought passion was slaked, he started all over again, and the night was spent in finding new thrills. At first she was frightened and ashamed, but soon he showed her how to enjoy her body and how to enjoy his, and she reveled in his dominance. And at last, as the dawn was coming up, he slept and she lay for a while glorying in the sensation of his sweated body on hers.

And then she too slept, and it was late before she awakened. When she did, it was a low languorous awakening, and she found herself alone. He had gone! She hugged the thought of the night to herself. Timothy's love-making had been good and satisfying, and calculatingly expert. But suddenly she thought of Caleb, and somewhere inside, part of her cried out for him. She wanted the young passionate love of the boy, without the calculated effort or artifice of the night before. His passion had been warm and unpremeditated, Timothy's the lust of passion produced to order, performing like a mechanical toy . . . She lay on the bed and cried for she knew not what.

And yet she knew she was waiting for the night to fall and for Timothy's loving to begin anew. She wanted him just as much as he wanted her. And there would be no turning back . . .

In the meantime there was Charles to watch over. And now she took delight in the deference the servants showed her and her son. In her new home her every wish was gratified, and even Sarah was looked upon as special.

That morning she found Sir Timothy had left the house and gone on business of his own. She breakfasted alone except for Charles. Later she made her way to Lady Letitia's apartments, and found that lady eagerly awaiting her, Aunt Beamish at her side.

Fanny was shocked to find that m'lady did not know that she and Charles were living in the big house, and Aunt Beamish turned her head away when Fanny looked at her with a question in her eyes.

But Letitia was pleased to have her, and her talk was gay and inconsequential. To please her, Fanny had started a piece of tapestry, and now sat demurely working on it to pass the time. Then Lady Letitia seemed to tire, and alarmed, Fanny rose to go.

"Must you go, dearest Fanny? I know I tire, but truly I like you beside me. Look, there is something I want you to have. Beamish, bring me my jewel case."

Aunt Beamish brought the leather case that usually sat on the dressing chest. Lady Letitia opened it, rummaged among the contents, and found what she sought.

"I want you to have this. It is far too heavy for my neck," she said, holding up a topaz and gold necklace. "Try it on, Fanny. I think it will be far more becoming on you than me."

"But I can't take your necklace! It wouldn't be right."

"I want you to have it, because I know you are looking after my son so well. I feel guilty at my lack of motherly concern, and I want to repay you somehow."

"But what will Sir Timothy say? He might be angry."

"It is of no concern to him. The necklace belonged to my mother. The jewels he gave me are fastened away in his own secret place. Everything in this case is my own. Please, Fanny, try the necklace on. I want you to have it."

Fanny studied it and was fascinated. She had never even seen a necklace of that quality before, let alone tried one on. She gulped, and with trembling fingers struggled with the catch. And then she caught sight of herself in the mirror.

She stopped and stared. It was a new Fanny who gazed back at her. The jewels winked and glowed, and made her skin seem whiter and softer. The necklace was the choker variety and spread itself over her bosom and shoulders, making them stand out in a seductive manner. The heavy stones with their fascinating range of hues from the palest apricot to the deepest orange red gleamed in the light. Fanny could have watched them glint for hours.

"If you are sure, m'lady."

"Fanny, I want you to have them."

Fanny's heart was full to bursting. Tears pricked her eyes and she looked down at the gentle girl, her feelings battling inside her. What would Lady Letitia do if she knew that she, Fanny, had gloried in her husband's lust last night? She bit her lip in shame.

"Th-thank you, m'lady. I'll always treasure them. I cannot begin to tell you . . ."

"Please don't try, Fanny. It pleases me, if they please you."

"But how could they not? They are beautiful! Won't you please reconsider?"

"No. My mind is made up. I shall speak to Sir Timothy about them and make it clear they are a gift."

"Then I can say no more." Fanny took off the necklace and carefully placed it in her handkerchief. "Now I must go, or Aunt Beamish will be cross with me for overtiring you."

M'lady smiled softly and settled herself against her pillows.

"I am a little tired now, Fanny. I think I will have a little sleep."

Fanny tiptoed out, and then ran like a whirlwind back to her rooms. She waltzed up to her own mirror and fastened the necklace around her slim throat again, and she liked what she saw. She hummed a little tune and, holding her head high, practiced a haughty look and then a curtsy in front of the glass. She gave an excited laugh.

She was on her way up in the world!

That night, lying naked and trembling beside Sir Timothy, she showed him all the amorous skills he had taught her, and more besides. If she was going to go through life as someone's mistress, she was determined to be the best! And as she whipped up Sir Timothy's desires, she exulted in the new knowledge that she could be as masterful in bed as he . . . and that he loved her for it! Snuggling close against him, she caressed him gently and found that the art of rousing his passion came instinctively to her. So sure was she, that she succeeded *too* well, and he rounded on her, telling her irritably to learn to gauge a man . . .

He left her, her mocking laughter following him to his own room, and she found herself alone, frustrated, and wishing that Caleb and the gypsies were camping in the wood.

As the days passed, Fanny grew to know her master and his ways, and she would watch for signs which told her what the night could hold. She found he was as two men. At times he was gentle and considerate—those nights were the nearest she came to loving him. But there were also nights when he was outrageously demanding, when nothing pleased or satisfied him—and then he was a devil. There was little wonder Lady Letitia had dreaded his demands. It was as if he hated the partner to share in the perverted love-making and wanted only to hurt and hurt and hurt!

But Fanny found the gift of forgetting, and learned to take her pleasures as they came. During Sir Timothy's visits to London, she could also enjoy Charles, and pet and fondle him to her heart's content, free of the need to lie and pretend. If there was one person she genuinely loved and put before herself, it was her son.

And it was for her son's sake that she sought out Rebecca. She knew that the older woman had more experience in financial affairs than herself. So she took her problem to her.

Rebecca looked at her with interest. It was now more than four months since they had met. Rebecca had put on weight, which suited her, and the vinegary expression had disappeared from her face. Billy had obviously fallen on his feet. It appeared that he was granted everything he wanted, except the freedom to wander. Fanny wondered how long that would last. But for the moment her interest was in asking advice.

"The lawyer in the High Street in Tunbridge Wells, Mr. Somers, is the man to advise you," said Rebecca, looking at her curiously. "How much have you to invest? I know you had two thousand pounds in gold from my father, but have you much more?"

Fanny looked cunning and smiled politely.

"A little more," she said quietly. Trust the old cat to want to know everything, she thought. But her expression gave nothing away.

"Well, if I were you, I should invest in a cargo. Mr. Somers took a thousand pounds of my money five years ago, and in two years he made twice that sum for me. How does that strike you?"

"Wonderful! He's a man to be trusted? He knows what he is doing?"

"Certainly! He is a man of business of the highest quality. Would you like me to go with you and introduce you to him?"

Fanny thought fast.

"No. I shouldn't like to put you to the trouble of such a long ride. If you gave me a letter of introduction, that would suffice."

"It would be no trouble to come with you. I should welcome a day's shopping. Next week would be convenient."

"But I must go before then. Sir Timothy will be back, and . . ." She found herself coloring guiltily.

Rebecca smiled maliciously.

"So Sir Timothy doesn't know about this? And is not likely to? I quite understand. It is said that he is quite a gambler. You are wise to put something by for a rainy day. I should not like to think of my father's money going on paying Sir Timothy's gambling debts!"

"I doubt that should happen! Sir Timothy is not down

to his last cent yet by a long way. No. I am determined, as you say, to invest my own money as a nest egg for the future. A female in my position is not exactly secure . . ."

"How right you are! I have often remarked to Billy that it was a pity you did not wait and marry someone in your own station of life. I hear Ben Wilkes is hanging out for a widow with a little money. You and he would have been well suited."

Fanny felt a wave of fury rise in her. Ben Wilkes had a small holding rented from Sir Timothy. If Rebecca thought Ben Wilkes was good enough for her, she was sadly mistaken. She rose to go.

"I should think it kindly if you would furnish me with the letter."

Rebecca gave a start, which Fanny knew was false.

"Oh, how silly of me. I truly forgot. I'll write it now." She fluttered away to her rosewood writing box on the table under the window. Taking a new quill, she scratched out a missive which she sanded and sealed without letting Fanny see the contents.

"There! That will do nicely. Must you rush away so soon? I wanted to show you the improvements in the garden."

"Another time, perhaps. I'm pleased to see you looking so well. Please give my love to Billy and tell him I shall come again soon especially to see him!"

"Oh!" Rebecca sounded put out, but she still smiled. "You must tell me what sucess you have. Give my kind regards to Mr. Somers. It is a long while since I saw him last."

Fanny walked slowly back to the big house. Sir Timothy had been away for a week now, and suddenly she found herself wondering what he did in London. Would she ever visit that big noisy city? Was there some beautiful woman waiting for Sir Timothy, some great lady whom he might one day marry? Jealousy, of a kind, rose up within her. She must find out from Tom, his valet.

Until Sir Timothy returned, she resolved to keep her impatience in check. So she arranged to go shopping in

Tunbridge, taking Sarah with her. Charles was left in the company of Aunt Beamish and the cook. The reason, she said, was to add to the already considerable wardrobe provided by Sir Timothy. She was tired of her day gowns and wanted something in the latest fashion.

Sir Timothy had been as good as his word and had given her a hundred pounds for suckling Charles. And from time to time he had given her other sums, which she had prudently hidden under a floorboard. Now, it was all in an oak chest, which she and Sarah carried down to the coach. Nellings, the coachman, looked at it curiously but made no remark. It was his duty to drive Sir Timothy's mistress where she wanted to go, not to speculate on matters that did not concern him.

Fanny was cunning. She had Nellings set her down at the dressmakers, so that if Nellings should be questioned by Sir Timothy, he could only state that Mrs. Raybold had asked for a chest to be carried into the fashionable lady's establishment. With luck, Sir Timothy would not connect the chest with gold and merely assume that she had some garments to return for alterations.

Nellings was to put up at the Rose and Thorn, and to be there waiting at precisely five o'clock for the long ride home. Until then his time was his own. And as he was looking forward to a mug of ale and a gossip, he thought no more of Mrs. Raybold's affairs.

As soon as he was out of sight Fanny and Sarah crossed the road and walked the short distance to Mr. Somers' shabby office. Several steps led up to a black oaken door. Sarah rapped sharply on it, and it was opened by a small, round-shouldered, nearsighted young man wearing his own sparse hair. He looked at them inquiringly.

"Is Mr. Somers within?" Fanny could not resist speaking in a haughty manner. She had a tendency to look down on her inferiors, a fault common among low-born people. She knew it and could not help herself.

"He is. Will you come in, ma'am. Who shall I say wants him?"

"Tell him it is Mrs. Fanny Raybold, widow of the deceased Joshua Raybold."

The young man turned and, scratching a flea under his armpit, disappeared into the inner room.

Fanny walked up and down, inspecting a shelf of books, and noting that the young man's desk was covered with breadcrumbs. She must have interrupted his luncheon. Then the door opened and, with a little more respect, he asked her to step inside.

Mr. Sommers was fat, and had the sleek look of the privileged and well-fed. He held a pudgy hand out for Fanny to take. When he smiled his eyes nearly disappeared among the wrinkles of lard.

"My dear Mrs. Raybold, how good of you to come and see me. How are you, my dear lady? I understand you are now residing at Gilbourne House . . ." He coughed, and pointed to a chair. "Will you please sit down? Your young companion can sit by the door." He eyed the chest that was at Sarah's feet, and coughed again.

Fanny sat down, feeling very self-possessed.

"I have a letter here from Mrs. William Bickler, who was my husband's daughter, Rebecca Raybold. I understand you conducted some business for her."

"Ah, that I did. She had some money that came to her from her dead mother. Now, how can I help you?"

"I have three thousand pounds in gold. I want you to invest it for me, as you did for her . . . and I want this to remain a confidential matter. If you do well for me, there will be other transactions."

"How do you want the money invested? There are several ways."

"Mistress Bickler mentioned cargo. Can I invest in a ship's cargo?"

"Ah, now the returns are high, but there are dangers. At present, there are the Dutch. Ships do go down, ma'am, you realize that? And then there are the French and, I'm sorry to say, Spanish pirates. British shipping is constantly at risk. But if the cargoes get to America as intended and a return cargo is brought back, then large sums of money can be made."

"Just what are the cargoes, Mr. Somers?"

Mr. Somers looked a little uncomfortable.

"We bring back tobacco and sugar and fruits and spices, and whatever is going in the Americas, depending on where and when."

"And what is taken out?"

Mr. Somers cleared his throat nervously.

"I do not think you need worry about the cargoes. It will be sufficient to know that your money will be put to good use!"

"I want to know, Mr. Somers, or I shall take my money elsewhere."

"Very well. We take sheeps' wool from London to the continent, and from there to Algiers and different ports in Africa, where we pick up black slaves." Mr. Somers looked her straight in the eye. "Captain Hawkins is a slaver. Have you the stomach for it?"

For a moment, Fanny was shocked. She had vaguely heard of such things, but never having seen a black man or woman, she thought of them as little more than animals. And were not most poor people slaves of someone?

She nodded.

"Yes, Mr. Somers, I have a strong stomach. Will I get a good return for my money?"

"The best ever. Always providing the ship does not sink, or the crew and cargo don't die of plague or some other act of God."

"You think I am doing the right thing? What will be your charge?"

"A mere ten percent."

"Another thing. I have a topaz necklace. I want to keep it, but would like to borrow money on it and redeem it after the voyage is over. Is this possible?"

Mr. Somers looked at her with respect.

"I should have to have it valued for you and then approach the bank. Unless you want to go to the Jews—and I warn you, their rates are high."

Fanny pulled the necklace out of her handbag and held it up to the light. It twinkled enticingly even in the dull light of the room. Mr. Somers took it in his hand and examined it.

"Mmm. Offhand I should say you will get at least another two thousand for this."

"I'll not sell it," said Fanny sharply. "I only want to take advantage of this opportunity to gamble on success . . ."

"But if the venture fails?"

"Then I lose all."

"I must admire your spirit. Is there some pressing need for this money?"

"That need not concern you. Will you write out a receipt for my money and the necklace, and also make out a contract with Captain Hawkins?"

"Of course. Nothing could be simpler. I shall send a messenger to Captain Hawkins to wait on you here, in one week's time."

"Could it not be sooner? I may not be able to come next week."

"Ma'am, he is refitting his ship at Greenwich. It could be more than a week before he comes."

"Then send a messenger to my brother, William Bickler at Fellside, and bid him to come after dark, and do remember—no letter, just a message saying the lavender gown is now ready to collect. I will understand." Mr. Somers nodded. He recognized a devious woman when he saw one. This one, still young in years, was plainly a lady to be reckoned with!

And so it was that a week later, under the pretext of visiting her dressmakers, Fanny met Black Patch Hawkins, King's man, late buccaneer and now slaver. He was a giant of a man with a scarred right cheek, part of an ear missing, and wearing a black leather patch over a damaged right eye. The other eye showed bright blue against the deep tan of his face.

Her heart leaped. Instantly she saw in him the same wild freedom that Caleb had. Though young, perhaps only seven or eight years older than Caleb, he was a man who knew what he wanted, and would take it!

Fanny had the feeling that destiny had just walked into her life.

CHAPTER SEVEN

The big man looked at her appraisingly.

"So you're the woman with the man's brain! When I received this old devil's letter, I hardly thought to meet a beautiful young woman! I thought she would be some old madam with money to spare and the stomach to use it well!"

"You are right in part, sir. I have already told Mr. Somers I have the stomach. I care not for the manner in which you use my money, but only for the return I get. Can you use my money to advantage, Captain?"

"For you I shall double, nay treble your money!"

"Good, Captain. And when do you sail?" Her voice was cool, but the man's one good eye already had her under a hypnotic spell.

"I sail in three days' time on the morning tide. Will you come to Greenwich to see me off?"

Fanny gave him a severe look.

"You are too familiar, Captain. I run after no man."

One heavy black eyebrow was raised.

"Indeed, ma'am? And how was your gold come by?"

She flushed angrily.

"That is my affair. Your business is to make use of it!"

He shrugged and then turned to Mr. Somers.

"There is no more interest for me here, methinks. Bring out the gold and I shall be on my way."

Mr. Somers rang a handbell for the young clerk. With a mutter the young man bowed and left the room.

"Wait!" Fanny's voice was cool and clear. "How much did you raise on my necklace?"

"I raised three thousand pounds, Mrs. Raybold, and it will be redeemed at the end of the voyage on payment of four thousand pounds."

"As much as that?"

Fanny's tone of horror set Captain Hawkins laughing.

"You cannot beguile the usurers to lend money for nothing. They must be paid their percent."

"I ask no privileges, Captain Hawkins."

"And you will get none from me. Good day, ma'am." So saying, he hefted the chest on to his great shoulders with ease. "The papers are signed, ma'am. I now have five thousand pounds of yours here and will use it well. Adieu, until we meet again."

She watched him go, and then just as he was preparing to descend the steps, she ran to the door.

"Captain!"

He looked back.

"Until we meet again." She gave him a demure look, and then smiled. "And thank you!"

"You're welcome, ma'am." He gave back a grin, winked and was gone.

Fanny returned slowly to Mr. Somers.

"It is a deal of gold to entrust to a stranger, Mr. Somers."

"Not a stranger to me, Mrs. Raybold. He is a competent seaman and has wriggled out of many a scrape. He'll come about, and you will be the richer for it."

"Then I must be content. Thank you for all your help."

"You are welcome, Mrs. Raybold. Might I remind you that it is to my advantage, too?"

"Of course, Mr. Somers. Good day to you."

Fanny walked thoughtfully across the road to her dressmakers to collect her lavender gown. This ploy was to satisfy Sir Timothy, who, she had soon come to realize, was prone to jealousy and suspicion. Several times he had accused her of infidelity with the servants on the flimsiest of pretexts—she had found that even a pleasant smile could set off a jealous humor. But now she thought of Black Patch, as she privately called him. Had he really meant her to go to Greenwich and see him off? And if she had, what kind of a lover would he have proved? She was stirred by the thought and chafed at not being free . . . But she would meet him again—of that she was sure . . .

On her return Sir Timothy greeted her with some relief.

"Thank God you are back. Charles has cried all day. Beamish thinks his teeth are bothering him. She's given him a measure of opium and now he sleeps."

Fanny did not stay to hear any more. Neither did she offer a cheek to be kissed. Sir Timothy watched her thoughtfully as she ran lightly up the main staircase to the nursery apartments. She certainly was excessively fond of his son—a good recommendation for what he had in mind.

Sir Timothy was considering a divorce from Letitia. It would cause some scandal, especially in the Ducal household, but he was prepared to suffer that. Lady Letitia's lack of wifely consideration was extreme. She refused even to see her child, and screamed and raved when he was brought to her room. He considered he had a right to a divorce. He would marry Fanny quietly and take her to London. Once married, Fanny would take her place in society and no one would dare to challenge her. She would also be grateful to him and so be faithful, while he could continue to visit his lady friends at his leisure. Yes, he would talk to Letitia this very night!

Fanny was resting in the great bed, waiting for Sir Timothy to come. She felt guilty about her sudden feeling for Captain Hawkins and to make up for it, she was determined to be particularly loving to him tonight. She had done well to get the gold away without Sir Timothy suspecting, and was just congratulating herself when all of a sudden pandemonium broke loose.

A woman was screaming and she heard the noise of . . . was it Sir Timothy? Shouting? Fanny pulled back the silken sheets, thrust a wrapper around herself and

ran barefoot to the door. She opened it in time to see
Lady Letitia running toward her.

"Come back, you fool!" bellowed Sir Timothy behind
her, but Letitia paid him no heed. She was laughing and
staring ahead with a fixed look, and somehow Fanny
sensed that Letitia neither knew her nor even saw her.
A cold prickly feeling went down Fanny's spine.

Letitia ran into the bedroom and her laughter turned
to a low growl.

"I know your mistress sleeps here. I have listened at
night and heard the two of you! Now I mean to kill her.
You may have your woman, but divorce—*never*!" The
arm came up and something glinted in the moonlight.
With horror, Fanny saw it was a knife. It flashed up and
down three times and then dropped to the floor. Letitia
seemed drained of strength. She turned and walked
slowly from the room, looking neither to left nor right.
She passed within feet of Fanny, but did not falter. Fanny shivered. She passed Sir Timothy and paused to look
at him.

"I have wanted to do that for a long time. Divorce?
My father would never allow it."

Fanny watched her walk slowly back to her room past
an astonished group of servants huddled near the staircase. Sir Timothy spoke sharply to them and they dispersed. Only Aunt Beamish remained. She swiftly
moved to Lady Letitia.

"There, my lamb. Let me put you to bed!"

"Bed! Don't touch me! I hate the word bed!" and she
started to run.

"M'lady! Come back, come back. It's only me, Beamish."

Letitia took no heed, but laughed and ran to her balcony window. She flung back the curtains, opened one
of the double doors and, flinging her arms wide, looked
back once and then deliberately threw herself over the
wrought-iron rail. There was a horrifying scream and
then the sickening thud of a body hitting the courtyard
below.

Fanny froze in her tracks, and Sir Timothy pushed her roughly aside as he leant over the balcony to look.

"My God! Letitia! I didn't realize . . ." Then he turned, ashen-faced, to Fanny.

"This is all your fault!"

Fanny stared at him, trembling, and then turned away. The gentle girl whom she had loved with all the best in her—dead, because of *her*, Fanny. With all her heart she prayed that Letitia had never found out who the mistress was, hoping desperately that she had not added to her hurt. Letitia would haunt her for the rest of her life.

When the coaches and the black-plumed horses had all gone and the innumerable funeral guests had dispersed, and they were alone together for the first time in days, Sir Timothy looked at her and said, "Well? Are you going to marry me?"

Fanny raised her eyes to his.

"Is it not too early to think of marriage?"

"Perhaps a little, but only the Duke will object. All my friends knew how it was. What do you say? A quiet wedding in Tunbridge, and then a season in London?"

Fanny ran a hand up his chest, and held him close. Soon, this man would be different from all others. He would be her husband, not just her lover! She would be a wife, with all the securities and rights of a wife! She reached up and pulled his head down to her, and her lips gave him her answer.

That night they made love for the first time in days—wildly and passionately.

They were married quietly in Tunbridge and came home to feast with the estate workers, but because the household was still in mourning there was no bonfire or revelry. Sir Timothy gave all his men a gold sovereign in lieu, and they toasted each other with good French wine and brandy until the time came for Sir Timothy to carry the new Lady Gilbourne to bed . . .

Three days later they were packed and ready for London. Aunt Beamish was very subdued and hardly spoke to Fanny.

"Come, Aunt. Do you not wish me happy? Surely you do not still blame me for m'lady's death? I do not want to leave with anger between us."

"I do not blame you for her death," Aunt Beamish said harshly. "But to pander to Sir Timothy and not even wait a suitable time for mourning is not the act of a lady. But, there—you will never be a lady, will you?" She stared hard at Fanny.

Fanny was furious.

"I do not need you to remind me of who I am. But whether you like it or not, I *am* Lady Gilbourne, and while you work for me I demand respect!"

Aunt Beamish gave her a mock curtsy and marched out of the room, her straight back showing her disapproval.

Sarah joined her with young Charles, now nearly a year old. It was cold, and the child was well muffled against the journey. For the first time since Black Patch had reminded her of Caleb, she wondered where he was and what fine lady or gypsy harlot was keeping him warm. The gypsies had not come this year and she wondered why . . .

Soon the well-sprung coach started its tedious journey to London. The roads were bad, and the inns they stopped at to relieve their hunger were spartan in the extreme. When mother and child finally arrived at Sir Timothy's house in Curzon Street, they were both cold and weary.

But a cheerful staff had the bedchambers and the dining room warm with heaped-up wood fires. The housekeeper took charge of Charles and Sarah, and Fanny peeled off her furs in front of the glowing fire.

"Dearest, I never imagined your house to be as fine as this! I think I am going to love it here."

Sir Timothy's arms enfolded her.

"As long as you love me along with the house. I'll not be cuckolded by my friends, my dear, I warn you. And there is another thing—from now on you are to be known as "Fancy." I think Fanny is a little too bucolic. Do you not think so, my love?"

"Well, I must say I had not considered the matter. Fancy—yes, I rather like it! Yes, it pleases me, Timothy. From now on I shall think of myself as Fancy."

"Good, good. I should not like my friends to set you up to ridicule."

"Dearest, I shall make sure that it does not happen. Fancy Gilbourne will toss her head at them all."

He pulled her close and his hands were rough.

"Remember you're mine, Fancy. I'll not be made a laughingstock!"

"I do believe you really love me, Timothy." She looked at him in wonderment.

"Of course. Should I have married you otherwise?" His tone was grim.

"You might—because I'm good in bed, and because I love your child!"

"Well, that might come into it. But even then I needn't have tied myself to you for life. I could have hung out for a rich wife and still kept you!"

"I doubt I would have stomached another wife. But, still, there's Charles. Who knows? I might endure a lot for that boy of yours!" She spoke lightly and touched him on the hand with her fan. "When will dinner be ready? I am starving."

Later that night as she lay in the big gilded bed, with the firelight playing over the magnificent room, Fancy wondered how she came to deserve all this splendor. She had certainly come a long way. Once she had been Aunt Beamish's unwanted and unloved orphan niece; now she was Lady Gilbourne, mistress of this delightful mansion and all its servants! Her happiness was all but complete. Somewhere inside was a heart-cry for Caleb, but she smothered it and reached out a questing hand to her sleeping Timothy . . .

There were busy days ahead. She had heard so much about King Charles and his Court in Whitehall. About the extravagances and excesses and his love of women.

She wondered if she would see him, this tall black-visaged man who was more a Frenchman than an Englishman.

There was talk, too, of the young Frenchwoman, Louise de Keroualle, maid of honor to the King's sister, the Duchess of Orleans, and she wondered if she was as beautiful as rumor proclaimed her. It was said, too, that many of the Court beauties had been affronted when the king had given her apartments in the Palace.

Fancy insisted on sight-seeing and shopping, and Sir Timothy, amused at her gawking country ways, pandered to her whims. She drove over London Bridge and marveled at the houses built on it at each end. To pass over it was like driving through a tunnel, with slits here and there giving a view down to the river.

They went to Vauxhall and Hyde Park and to the Playhouse, where a very young Nell Gwynne was making a name for herself as Cydaria in Dryden's tragedy *The Indian Emperor.*

She watched the Court ladies taking the air in their splendid coaches and admired the easy manner in which they acknowledged the gentlemen of their acquaintance. She bowed to several of Timothy's friends and was introduced as his wife. Though delighted with her new surroundings, she found that the painted ladies—and the gentlemen, too—were not quite what she had always dreamed of. There was little friendliness in their eyes. The men were predatory wolves, and the women . . . Ah, now the women! They were ready to snatch Sir Timothy away from under her very nose! But their elaborate clothes made her gasp. Surely silk and stiff brocade were only for evening wear? She must try to emulate them—at least in their dress.

Sir Timothy indulged her, and encouraged her to buy new gowns at the very best shops, with bonnets and fans and gloves to match. She liked the scented gloves in particular and remembered Sir Timothy's love of bergamot. Nor could she resist buying the silken bedgowns and the shifts and the new whalebone corset that laced up at the front like the old-fashioned stomacher, pushing up the breasts so that they were almost bare under low-cut gowns. It was all so new and enchanting . . .

As her acquaintances grew, in came the invitations to balls, routs, soirées, and occasionally all-night sorties that finished with breakfast. Soon she was on nodding terms with Lady Castlemaine, the King's whore, and envied her aplomb, even though she was heavy with child. She was flattered by the attentions of Lord Shallmere and the infamous Sir Thomas Rigby, a man notorious for dallying with all the married ladies. Sometimes at night after Sir Timothy was asleep, she lay awake thinking about all the adulation she was receiving and wondered, would it last?

But then a strange change took place in her relations with Sir Timothy. He began to tire of taking her about. There had been some ugly scenes between them when he had accused her of flirting. He did not like the bevy of young men who naturally drifted into her orbit during the nights of revelry. They plied her with champagne, and often she had not wanted to return home with Sir Timothy so early. Of course it was her own fault, she thought uneasily.' 'ut now Sir Timothy often found an excuse to spend . evening at his club. At first he had unreasonably expected her to remain at home, but when she refused and went to functions on her own he had given in.

Sometimes, too, she slept alone. Tonight was one such time. She faced the fact squarely. He would be playing cards at White's, and then—who knows where he would go? All she knew was that he would come in noisily in the early hours of the morning and drop on the bed in a stinking heap, to snore till noon. She thought of him with disgust. Was it only cards? Or was there a woman, too? She turned on her side and punched her pillows. Really, apart from his love-making, which she candidly enjoyed, always provided he was sober, she did not miss him. She closed her eyes and slept.

But early next morning she had a thought, and rang her bell for Sarah.

"Sarah, where are my herbs? I thought the tisane rather weak yesterday. Are we running short?"

Sarah blushed and looked uncomfortable.

"One packet was moldy, m'lady. I threw it away. We've very little left."

"Nonsense! I dried the herb myself." She looked at Sarah's guilty face. "Have you been taking it, too?"

Sarah did not answer, but her face was answer enough.

"You slut! Who is it? Who's the man you've been sleeping with?"

"I . . . I . . ." Sarah's eyes swiveled from side to side as if she longed to run from the room.

"Answer me, girl. Who is it?" Then she felt a prickle of apprehension. Sarah did not see many men, and those she did see were either old men or boys. "Is it Sir Timothy?"

Sarah's further blush was enough. She nodded.

Anger at Sir Timothy, rather than at Sarah, made her want to choke. He had raised her up and wanted her to be Fancy, and encouraged her to hope for better things, only to disport himself with her maidservant here in this very house! It was intolerable. But then her innate honesty made her see the irony of the situation. After all, she was no ailing Lady Letitia. . . .

She lay back on her pillows and considered Sarah. The girl stood with eyes downcast and nothing to say in her own defense, looking the picture of guilt.

"Well, Sarah, I don't blame you. He gave you money, I hope?"

"Yes, m'lady. He threatened to turn me away if I didn't yield . . . I was loathe to do it, but I didn't want to be turned on to the streets here in London. And the money was tempting. Are you going to send me away?" The girl's eyes brimmed with tears.

"No, Sarah. You do too good a job with Charles, and I'm fond of you. I need you here."

"But, m'lady, what about Sir Timothy?"

"What about him?"

"Well . . . if he wants me again—"

"Take him! As long as I don't know. Look after yourself, Sarah, and take his money. He will never break my
heart." The iron entered her soul. "And do not miss
taking those herbs. I can see we shall have to get another
supply!"

"I can get some, m'lady. The first footman's father is
a herbalist in Chelsea."

"Good. Then get some for us both!"

Sarah smiled with relief.

"Thank you, m'lady. I can only say I'm sorry. But
what could I do? I was forced."

"I know. Now never mention it again."

She lay back on her pillows and thought of Timothy.
The swine! But it didn't matter. From now on she would
play her own little games! She thought of Mr. Somers in
Tunbridge who possessed her secret. She would make
him her chief accountant. Money was what really
mattered—and money she would have!

The next few days passed pleasantly enough. Fancy
amused herself by buying a completely new wardrobe
and presenting the bill to Sir Timothy. In spite of his
protests she went ahead and visited the King's jeweler.
She chose several fine pieces and then set them down on
the purple velvet cushion beside her. She looked the little man straight in the eye.

"Sir, I have chosen these rubies and these emeralds. I
also want some . . . er . . . slightly less expensive jewels.
But I do not want a bill for them. You understand me?"

The little man pursed his lips and then without flickering an eye said blandly. "You mean you want them
unbeknown to a benefactor?" and he coughed delicately.

"Yes, I am bringing you the goodwill. What can you
arrange?"

"If there is to be a definite arrangement, I can arrange
to add the amount to the bill of sale for the first order. It
is usual."

She was intrigued.

"This arrangement has been used successfully
before?"

"Yes, m'lady. This is not the first time such an arrangement has been made. It has always been, I might say, highly successful."

"Good. Then what can you offer me?"

A selection was made which was satisfactory to both parties. The little man rubbed his hands. It was a pleasure to do business with Lady Gilbourne! He also gave her some extra advice.

"And as for disposing of it circumspectly, I should try Joplin and Stoneway. I understand My Lady Castlemaine has had many such dealings with them."

"Thank you, I will."

Fancy's first real quarrel with Sir Timothy erupted when he received the bill. He looked at it incredulously.

"Are you mad, woman? Nearly two thousand pounds for jewels? What is this orgy of spending?"

Sir Timothy had had a bad night and his head ached. He looked every day of his age. Fancy's lip curled.

"Why quibble about *my* debt? I hear you lost more than that on one night's play last week."

"That's another matter. That was a debt of honor. The King likes us to play. A faint heart gets nowhere at Court. But your spending will have to stop. I forbid you to bring me any more such bills."

"Very well. I'll let it be known you're a skinflint who grudges his wife her rightful luxuries."

"Rightful! Madam, you take too much on yourself. Why, I picked you up out of the gutter."

"You lie! I was a respectable married woman, and you took advantage of me, as you did Sarah!"

"Ah, so it rankles that I was tempted by the fresh-faced Sarah." He tried to pull her down onto his knee. She pulled away.

"Timothy, please."

"Oh, acting the fine lady, eh? You know, you have come a long way since you came to London. Play your cards right and you could become a Lady of the Queen's bedchamber."

"And perhaps please the King?" she said maliciously, watching him.

He frowned.

"If you pleased him on my account . . ."

"And on my own too, of course."

"Fancy,"—she could detect a note of wheedling in his voice— "Fancy, what would you do for me? And to further yourself at Court?" he added hastily.

"Do you want me to please the King? Would that further your career? I do not doubt that you would let me." Her laugh tinkled like glass.

"It might help to pay for those jewels you helped yourself to," he said sulkily.

"Perhaps I should enjoy it. Charles Stuart is a fine man."

"My dear, you are supposed to endure it, not enjoy it. And it would be to help *my* career."

"Your career? What kind of man expects advancement through his wife's efforts?"

"You would be surprised. Most of the courtiers have accommodating wives. And if they happen to be pretty and please the eye of the King . . ."

"Then court life is more corrupt and vicious than I ever dreamed. Is there no end to the intrigue and the double-dealing?" For a moment she felt despair. Being a fine lady was proving a strain, and more so now that she was finding out that she could not rely on her husband.

"Fancy, you really don't mean that you admire the King? Remember you are *my* wife. I tell you who to sleep with, and why! I shall not have it otherwise." He looked at her morosely. "I care not for the idea of fathering the King's bastard. It was a mistake bringing you here. Why are you not with child by me? If that old man could get you with child, why should I not? I'm not impotent."

Laughter welled up in her throat as she saw the perplexity on his face.

"Oh, Timothy, you are so truly complex. What do you really want? You are jealous of me, yet you yourself go with other women. You expect me to sleep with others, and yet you forbid me to enjoy it. What does it mat-

ter if we have no more children. You have your heir.
Why should we want more?"

"It matters to me. A man is judged on his prowess in
bed."

"Faugh! You talk like a prize boar! You must have
plenty of bastards growing up. Tell your highborn mistresses about them if they want to know about your bedroom prowess. Or better still, send them to me. I can
give you a good recommendation!"

The slap across the face came as a shock. She knew
Timothy could be rough when roused, but never before
had he struck her. She turned and left the room.

She did not see Timothy for several days, nor did she
inquire about him. It pleased her to occupy herself with
Charles who was now growing into a sturdy child. She
watched jealously for any resemblance to herself but
saw none. But neither was he like Caleb. Even the
child's Ducal grandfather stopped her in the park one
day and congratulated her on her devotion to poor
Letitia's son. He patted the boy on the head and gave
him a gold sovereign. "It will be a great day, madam,
when you present him with a brother and sister." She
curtsied in the proper manner and thanked him for his
felicitations. He walked away, a dignified old man, and
she laughed and scooped Charles up and kissed him
soundly. She was happy with her child.

She was also well pleased with her transaction with
Messrs Joplin and Stoneway. The money was now on its
way to Mr. Somers, and it made her first profits seem
like crumbs from a rich man's table. Now she was considering buying her own ship and fitting it out herself
with the proceeds. Black Patch Hawkins would be just
the man for Captain—if he ever came back.

Then one morning Sir Timothy came to her. He
looked distraught and his hands were shaking as he
came and sat down on the edge of the bed.

"Fancy." He took her hand and played with each finger. "How much to you love me? Enough to help me out
of trouble?"

She sat up quickly.

"What is it? I thought you were wanting to make up after our quarrel."

"Quarrel? Oh that . . ." he dismissed it with a shrug. She was alarmed.

"Have you been losing at cards again? You want my jewels?" Thoughts of missing jewels smote her. What could she say had happened to them?

"It's more than that. Your jewels won't help." She sighed with relief. "I've gambled away the deeds to Gilbourne and Letitia's holdings. If the Duke finds out, we could find ourselves in Newgate."

"You fool! Why do you never think? Is there nothing to be done?"

"Yes," he replied slowly, "there is one solution. The man I owe it all to admires you very much. He suggests an alternative way to pay the debt . . ."

"Then everything is all right?" Fancy was puzzled by his hesitant air.

"He suggests taking you away for a week. It was not my idea, Fancy. I swear it!"

Fancy showed her disgust. Timothy was shaking with fear and shame. She could have spat on him.

"And you would rather I did *that* than pay your debt with honor?"

"It would only be a week—it would soon pass. Oh, Fancy, think about it, I beg of you! Think of Newgate and of what it would mean . . ."

Slowly she nodded.

"You give me no choice. Tell him I accept his invitation."

She turned away and lay with her back to him.

"Now leave me. I want to be alone."

"Fancy, I want you before . . ."

She felt him turn back the bedclothes and get in beside her, and his arm stretched out to encircle her waist. She turned savagely and brought up her knee . . . He screamed. "Now get out of my bed and stay out!"

She heard him go, and then the tears came.

CHAPTER EIGHT

The coach lurched and rocked on its slow journey to Stepney and the residence of Sir Montagu. Betsy, the plump young Cockney maid who had come instead of Sarah, sniffed miserably. Fleetingly, Fancy thought of Sarah, who had been left in charge of Charles. She and Timothy would be alone together . . . oh well, it was no use worrying what Timothy did. Besides, she no longer cared. A pox on Timothy! Had he not got her into this intolerable situation in the first place? Her stomach churned at the thought of the man she was traveling to meet.

All she could discover from Timothy was that he was large and personable and reasonably young. But his "reasonable" could mean anything from twenty-five to forty-five. She sat with nerves stretched to breaking point. Sir Timothy would have to pay for this insult to her.

"God's teeth!" she snapped at Betsy, "Why did I ever think to bring you! I would have done better on my own. Control that dreadful sniff, girl, and if you must blow . . . blow!"

Betsy obliged and for a while there was peace.

At last the coach turned through an imposing pair of wrought-iron gates, and Fancy glimpsed lights from a far distant house. Surely they were not there yet? But the coach drew up to the great stone house and stopped. Evidently they were expected. Flambeaux threw out their eerie light and lit up the front of the house.

The great front door opened and the chief butler

came to the door of the coach.

"Welcome to Hawksley, m'lady," he intoned softly. "Sir Montagu awaits you in the Red Salon." He helped her to alight. "Will you come this way?" As they proceeded into the hall, he said quietly, "My name is Meldrum, m'lady," and bowed her over the threshold.

She looked about her, noting the armor and the crossed pikes and the gloomy oak paneling. A wolfhound sniffed at her ankles and she drew back in alarm.

"Down, Rufus . . . good boy, keep back!"

The dog slunk away. Fancy turned sharply to a door on her left. She knew that voice! A tall slim figure stood there, his shoulders nearly touching each side of the doorway.

"Welcome, Lady Gilbourne . . . we meet again!"

Incredulously, she stepped forward and craned her head up to see into the face of the man standing there.

"You!"

The man stepped toward her, hands outstretched, and laughing he encircled her waist and swung her around. His strong teeth showed white and gleaming.

"La, Lady Gilbourne, I do believe you had forgotten me. Did I not say we should meet again?"

"Black Patch! Is it really you?"

Fancy was suddenly elated. This week could turn out to be better than she thought. He bent his head and kissed her swiftly, full on the mouth.

"Ah, that kiss is just as I dreamed it should be. Come into the warmth and take off your furs."

He led her into the magnificent Red Salon where a huge log burned in a marble fireplace. A table was set with decanter and glasses.

"I was prepared to your coming."

She allowed him to divest her of her cloak and felt his warm hand caress her neck. She shivered with barely suppressed excitement.

"How . . . how did you know I was Sir Timothy's wife?"

He laughed.

"I'm not a fool. I listen to all the society gossip. You are news, Fancy Gilbourne. It did not take long to connect you with the little lady I met in old Somers' office, and I've wanted you every day since we met."

"Then . . . then you deliberately played Timothy for me?"

"Aye. I want you badly, Fancy Gilbourne. I'll make this a week you will never forget," he whispered hoarsely, and kissed her bare shoulder. He pulled her down on the sofa in front of the blazing fire and proceeded to pull the combs out of her long flowing hair. She felt him tremble as he took her into his arms. His mouth met hers once more, and it was as if he already possessed her. But then, as if coming to his senses, he rang for Meldrum and she was taken to her room.

Making herself at home in the pink chintz bedroom, Fancy changed with Betsy's help, feeling a thrill of anticipation. There was something ruthless in Sir Montagu's eyes and her flesh responded to it.

They enjoyed a feast of green goose and a boiled ham smothered in brown sugar, and then a stuffed leg of lamb served with several vegetables. A cherry tart, a huge cheesecake stuffed with fruit and a syllabub followed, washed down with wine, brandy and finally coffee.

The fire grew low and the servants cleared away, and now Sir Montagu shed his brocade coat and lounged in his frilled white shirt. It was unbuttoned to the waist, and as the firelight flickered and glowed her eyes lingered on the hard brown flesh of him and the fuzz of dark hairs sent her wild with desire.

He pulled her closer, and she did not resist; no, she pressed closer and reached out with exploring fingers to caress him and feel his hard masculinity, and the feeling it aroused in her was exquisite agony. Unable to stifle a moan, she pressed herself still closer. He laughed, exultantly and, scooping her up like a bird, swept her upstairs to his bedchamber.

And there, she found another kind of lover. A man who dwarfed all others. A man whose manhood made a

mockery of other men. He took her as his right, loving
her as she had never been loved before—like a man just
out of a desert, a man whose thirst would never be
slaked. He dominated her, making her a mere instru-
ment for his pleasure. Without stopping to consider her
need, he took her again and again.

And when it was over and his passion had been spent
for the last time, he picked her up like a broken blossom,
carried her into her chamber and laid her on the bed.
And she wept long and bitterly.

The week was nearly at an end before Fancy asked
about her money. Montagu was quiet, replete, and
sober.

"I wondered when you would come round to that,"
he grinned. "You needn't worry. We've both made
money on the voyage. You're richer by seven thousand
pounds plus your capital."

Fancy did some quick mental arithmetic. She still had
plenty over after redeeming the necklace . . .

"I think you are marvelous."

Her hand came out to caress him but he pushed her
away.

"Don't you want me to love you?" Her voice was hurt
and bewildered.

"No. You're here under duress, remember? You're
paying a debt for your husband." Montagu's voice was
suddenly ugly. "I keep remembering that!"

"But that is not my fault. I did not know it was you!"

"But you came. You would have slept with the devil
himself."

"And I think I have," she said. "I gave you what you
wanted . . . and in good measure. Why can't you love
me?"

"Because I prefer you when you're angry! Love
would make us both anemic. I've never loved since I was
a callow youth. Love is for innocents, neither of us are
that."

"You tyrant!" As her arm came up to strike, his fingers tore into her wrist and he shook her. She bit back a scream, but her eyes spat fire and fury.

"That's better. I would much rather take you against your will. That way there is the spice of not knowing whether or not you will put a knife into my ribs!"

"And truly I should, if I thought of carrying a knife!"

"There you are, then. Never think of love and me in the same breath! That way you can keep me a slave forever, my little sugar spice . . ."

She struggled to free herself, but he held her as if holding a doll. He kissed her and she trembled. And just when she expected him to go further, he pushed her away and stood up.

"It is better to finish when you are wanting me. That way I can keep you hot . . ." He laughed at her discomfiture.

She lay back to control her rising anger. He was the first man she had not been able to understand. He would take her or leave her, and the knowledge was humiliating. Then she thought of her money—the money he still held. If she was his partner . . . perhaps then she would mean more to him. She looked up at him hopefully.

"Montagu, I want to go into business with you."

He laughed scornfully, but she could see he was intrigued.

"What? With your piddling little bit of money? That amount wouldn't qualify you as a partner."

"Would another few thousand on top change your mind?"

"Are you fooling me? Where would you get money like that? Or are you a heavy gambler?"

"No gambler, but I have my methods." She laughed.

"Whoring, I suppose. I didn't expect you . . ."

She looked at him with scorn and anger.

"That's all you can think about. Do you keep your brains between your legs? There's other ways of making money and I found one of them!"

Montagu watched the signs of temper and leered.

"Did I ever tell you you were most beautiful when

your blood is up? You should always be in a rage. It is most becoming." He grinned and kissed her hand.

She pulled it away pettishly. She was itching to strike the smile from his face.

"Stop trying to cajole me. I was warned against men like you. You make me sick! I may be just a woman but I'll not let you trample all over me!"

"But you would still come running if I crooked my finger for you!"

They glared at each other, but it was she who dropped her eyes.

"Well . . . perhaps. But I hate you all the same." Then a reluctant smile broke the severity of her face. "You rogue! You know how to persuade me . . ." Then her mood changed. "Well, are we partners or not?"

"With five thousand pounds, I might consider it. Split down the middle, take profit or loss as it comes. Mind, my decisions are final: I'll not take orders from a woman. You will be just a sleeping partner . . ." He laughed again, but she ignored the joke. Her mind was on the partnership.

"You really mean that? Split down the middle?"

"Yes. You've my word on it." He held out his hand and she took it in a man's grip. Then grinning, he bent forward and kissed her. "Welcome to the Slavers' Brotherhood!"

Fancy took a deep breath. Now at last she was getting somewhere. Little would Sir Timothy know what a good turn he had played her when he made her honor his gambling debt! For a fleeting moment she thought of him, but the thought was bitter and it clouded her eyes. Then she looked at Montagu. He was ruthless and a rascal, but at least he was honest. But even as she thought that, something inside her jeered in a faint voice. Who was she to judge another man's honesty? She cast the thought from her mind and called for champagne.

"A toast . . . a toast to our partnership! Surely there must be champagne in your house?"

Montagu laughed and swung her up high in his mighty arms.

"Yes, my little witching devil. By all means we will drink your toast!"

The day before she was due to go back to Sir Timothy, Fancy and Sir Montagu coached down to Tunbridge to see Mr. Somers and have a legally binding agreement drawn up between them.

On completing the document, Somers showed it to them with a flourish.

"There now, m'lady, if you would sign here and Captain Hawkins there . . ." He coughed delicately. "It makes you equal partners, owning ship and cargoes in equal shares. M'lady, you are now a shipowner. May I be the first to congratulate you."

"Thank you, Mr. Somers." She scratched her name with a squeaky quill and passed it to Sir Montagu.

"And I should also like to make a will. In the event of my death, I want everything left to my . . . my . . ."—she stopped herself just in time—". . . my stepson, Charles Gilbourne."

Sir Montagu looked at her curiously.

"Is that not a little drastic? You may have children of your own."

She shrugged.

"It will serve for the moment."

Sir Montagu's eyes narrowed.

"You seem excessively fond of that boy of Gilbourne's. If I did not know better, I should say he was *your* . . . But he's the Duke of Lanbridge's grandson, isn't he?"

She nodded, but could not meet his eyes.

"Yes, and as you say I am extremely fond of him. I suckled him as a babe, you know."

"No, I didn't know. I knew you had a son. Are you sure you didn't switch babies? I wouldn't put it past you!"

Fancy flushed scarlet.

How dare you say such a thing! What a despicable . . ."

"Hold hard! It was only a joke. I think you are doing

the right thing in making the boy secure. I admire you
for it. Especially as that husband of yours is such a fool
with cards, and a poor gambler to boot . . ."

"What do you mean, a fool? Did you cheat to get
me?"

"Of course. I was determined to have you. I was curious about you."

"Have you no conscience? How can you sleep at
night?"

He laughed.

"Easily, m'dear. Especially when I've had all I want
and am spent."

Mr. Somers looked from one to the other, fascinated,
and then coughed.

"I beg your pardon, both. But would you prefer to go
into my private chamber? The nature of your conversation . . ." He coughed again.

"Don't be embarrassed, Mr. Somers. Lady Gilbourne is as much a rogue as I, and just as thickskinned!
I'll warrant since going to London her hide has tough-
ened still more!"

Fancy laughed and shrugged.

"Is that an insult or a compliment? Mr. Somers, I do
declare, I do not know whether I want to be compared
to this man! But never fear, our quarrels can be continued later."

"Alas, my sweet, you forget the week is up and you
must go back to Sir Timothy. I am honor-bound as a
gentleman to send you back. Our love idyll is over."

"What?" Fancy could hardly believe her ears. "You
talk of honor? You are bound to send me back at the
end of the week?" Her voice rose with incredulity and
sudden fury. Surely she was more than just a parcel to
be sent back and forth!

"It grieves me beyond words, my heart's delight, but
that was the arrangement. You have paid Sir Timothy's
debt with interest. I cannot say fairer than that."

"But, but I shall see you again?"

"Not until after my next trip, and then it will be to

give you an accounting, and for that purpose alone."

"But don't you want . . . I mean . . . is it the end for us?"

"Yes. You are in danger of becoming a burden to me. A pity. But you would bore me!"

"You are as wild and untamed as those black slaves you buy and sell! No doubt you would rather take your lust out on one of them . . ."

"Oh, I don't think so. I pleased you well enough."

Fancy picked up an inkwell from Somers' desk and threw it with great force. Montagu ducked just in time. Then she spoke in a low, shamed voice.

"Don't you dare speak of me in the same breath as those poor wretches! After you tire of them you can sell them off. I've heard plenty of gossip about you!"

"And why not, pray? They bring more in the Carolinas when they are with child. Any slaver will tell you that. I only wish you had a black skin—you would have made a fortune for me!"

"You monster!"

He took her arm and shook her roughly.

"Enough of that. Don't give me any of that virtuous stuff! Do you want to dissolve the partnership? Perhaps your stomach isn't strong enough after all!" His good eye was mocking. "I don't mind you as a partner, but I'm damned if I'll have you as a permanent bedmate!"

Fancy was silent for a long time. She was humiliated, and although there were things about him she abhorred, she was woman enough to want to do the rejecting. Finally she looked up at him and said, "Very well. We'll remain business partners and nothing else."

When Montagu came to her that night, she tried to be cold and resist him. But her coldness merely acted as a spur and their loving was wild and exhilarating. Her responses, once roused, matched his, and she, a perfect Eve, made sure he had a night to remember during that long voyage to come when only memory or a shiny black body would be his bedfellow.

The next morning, as the coach started on its long, lurching drive back to Curzon Street, she wondered about her husband . . . and whether Sarah or some other wench—perhaps a highborn lady—had warmed his bed during her absence.

But then she forgot Timothy completely, remembering she was on her way home to her darling Charles. She sighed with happiness. There was a present to buy for him, and she longed to take him in her arms. He must surely have missed her.

CHAPTER NINE

Old Nellings stood at the door when Fancy arrived at the house in Curzon Street. He was white-faced and tears were in his eyes. She ran up the steps, fear gripping her heart.

"What is it, Nellings? What happened?"

The old man shook his head.

"I don't know how to tell you, m'lady."

"Come, man. Out with it. Is it Charles?" Fear dried her throat and made her feel faint. Her Charles! Something had happened to Charles! She grasped the old man and shook him cruelly. "Speak man, speak."

"It's not Charles, m'lady," and Fancy felt the knots in her stomach relax. "It's Sarah, m'lady—she's gone down with the plague!"

For a full minute Fancy could only stare at him.

"The plague? What do you mean, the plague? You all had instructions not to go near the east side and the dock area. How did she catch the plague, for God's sake?"

"It's getting worse, m'lady. People are dying like flies."

"I've been aware of it, as you know. But I didn't realize it was getting serious. How near is it now?"

"Two families wiped out three streets away—Lord Stichfield's nurse and their eldest child, and the King's baker's son."

"But they are in this area. Where is Sir Timothy?"

"He was away on business nearly all the week. When he came back yesterday and found out about Sarah, he ordered her out of the house, and took Master Charles and left for Gilbourne. He said you should follow." Fancy gave a sigh of relief. At least Charles was safe . . . or was he?

"How is Master Charles? Was he well when he left with Sir Timothy?"

"M'lady, he had a temperature. Mrs. Bunce thought he was getting another back tooth. I don't know . . ."

Panic seized Fancy and she screamed.

"Oh Lord, perhaps he's got the plague, too!" Her knees felt like jelly and she tottered inside. This is a punishment, she thought. "I must go to him."

"Not tonight, m'lady. There is a curfew. Only the dead carts are allowed to go abroad at night. I thought you would know that."

"No, I did not realize . . . The plague has only been an ugly rumor until now. I thought it would never come to this part of London. Mercy me! Where will it all end?"

Mrs. Bunce the housekeeper came hurrying out from the kitchen, her quick fat waddle showing her agitation.

"M'lady! I have just this minute been informed by one of the maids that you have arrived." She gave Nellings a sour look. "You could have sent one of the footmen." Nellings ignored her, and she turned to Fancy. "M'lady, have you heard the news?"

"Yes. Now where is Sarah? I must go to her."

"No, m'lady . . . you must not! Think of us and Sir Timothy and the young master! You could carry the disease yourself!"

"What? Not go to see Sarah? Of course I must go! Is she being well cared for?"

"She is in Lord Stichfield's house. It is deserted but for an old woman who had the plague many years ago. Lord Stichfield left for his country home last week and gave us permission to take Sarah there."

"That was very good of him. I'll not forget his kindness. Where is the footman Bell? His father is a herbalist. Perhaps he will have some safeguard for me."

"He is downstairs, my'lady. He has already told us to wash in vinegar and to carry sweet herb bouquets with us. What more can we do?"

"I don't know. I want to talk to him." She strode into the parlor, stripping off her cloak and gloves. The fire was blazing and she saw that everything was clean and sweet-smelling. At least there would be less chance of infection. She paced up and down, in a frenzy of anxiety. Charles must surely be safe! How could a child who was so well cared for get the plague? But of course, she thought distractedly, the plague was not choosy about its victims.

John Bell brought chicken breasts, finely sliced ham and a glass of wine.

"You must be faint for want of food, m'lady. I brought you this until cook can bring you some dinner."

"I couldn't eat a thing, but thank you very much."

"You must try and eat something, m'lady." The young man looked anxious. "Or you, too, could go down with the plague."

She smiled slowly.

"We all could, Bell. We are all in God's keeping." She was startled to hear herself speak about God, for it was a long time since she had set foot inside a church.

She made more inquiries about the precautions the staff had taken to combat the plague and was satisfied that all had been done that could be done. Now she must see Sarah.

Betsy wailed at her decision.

"It is madness, m'lady! Perhaps Sarah will not know you if you go to see her! You will undoubtedly become infected and pass the sickness to Master Charles. God save us all!"

"Be silent, Betsy, if you can't be helpful. Sarah is only three streets away. I must see her. I shall go alone, and you may lay out my oldest gown and shawl—everything I wear will be burned on my return. I must go! Sarah has been my friend as well as my maid. She will expect no less of me."

But when Fancy was ready to set off, John Bell was waiting at the door with a basken laden with foods for the invalid.

"I'm coming with you, m'lady. It is not right that you walk alone through the streets at this time. There are vagabonds abroad looking for women to molest and rob. I have heard of murders . . ."

"Are there such people?" Suddenly Fancy was apprehensive.

"There are always such people who feed on others. The plague brings out the wicked like maggots from under stones."

"Then you walk with me, Bell, and I shall not forget you for it!"

She muffled herself close so that no one should recognize her as a lady. They walked in silence and saw very few people, and those they did were muffled as they were. It was eerie and frightening, like walking through a dead city. Fancy shuddered at her own thoughts. Would she ever see Charles again?

At first there was no answer from Lord Stichfield's establishment. Finally John Bell gave the knocker a thunderous hammering, and a small grille at eye level opened and a voice said gruffly, "Who knocks on My Lord Stichfield's door? He is not at home."

Fancy spoke sharply.

"It is I, Lady Gilbourne, come to see my maid. Let me in."

"Go away, m'lady. Sarah is dying. Not even God can save her! Go home and pray for her soul."

"Let me in, I *must* see her. I have brought her food to give her strength."

"She's past eating, m'lady. But if you want to see her . . ." There was the sound of bolts being drawn. The door opened and they stepped inside.

The old woman stepped back and Fancy looked at her with distaste. Her gray stringy hair hung down her back uncombed and unwashed, and she stank of cheap gin.

"I've done all I can for her," she quavered, as she met Fancy's eyes. "Sir Timothy paid me to look after her. I've done what he said."

"Stop talking and lead me to her."

The old woman shrugged.

"Well, I've warned you." She moved along the stone passage, the only light coming from the evil-smelling candle flickering in her hand. They passed through a large stone-flagged kitchen and then to another narrow stairway. Here the old woman stopped and pointed.

"She's up there, in the kitchen maid's room. I only go up once a day to see if she's still alive. You can go up yourself."

Without answering, Fancy took the basket from John Bell.

"Stay here, Bell. There is no need for two of us to run the risk. Put the water on to boil, woman. Sarah will need bathing, if I know anything about the disease."

"What? You'll handle her? Even I daren't do that!"

"Boil the water, and have it ready when I come back."

"You're a fool and asking to get sick!"

"How dare you speak to me like that? Do as you are told. Sir Timothy has already paid you!"

"Aye, but not to handle her!"

"I'm not asking you to touch her. I only want you to boil water. I will do the rest."

"You? God save us. What next?"

Fancy's hand came up and caught the woman a vicious smack over the right cheek. The woman cowered back. Fancy then let fly with a word she had learned during her village days. John Bell looked at her with astonishment and respect. He stepped forward.

"I'll see to the water, m'lady. I've also brought herbs to burn to purify the air."

"Do what you have to do, Bell. I'm going up now to see Sarah."

The winding stone staircase was damp and smelled of fungus. When she stepped into the small room, she nearly choked on the smell. A small high window cast a pale light across the room, and Fanny's first act was to pry it open. It was stiff and she tore her hands in doing so.

She looked around in the light of a dim wick swimming in a saucer of lard and shuddered. The room was strewn with stale rushes that crackled as she walked over to the truckle bed where Sarah lay. Could this hollow-cheeked creature on the bed be the plump and comely laughing girl of only a week ago? The head moved slightly, and Fancy realized that Sarah was awake and looking at her. She bent down, taking the hand plucking at the sheet, and spoke quietly.

"Sarah, can you hear me? Do you know me?"

Sarah nodded slowly and tried to speak. It was a great effort.

"You should never have come, m'lady. You know I've got . . ." She stopped and swallowed.

"I know. Don't talk now. Save your strength."

Sarah shook her head with an effort.

"Too late. Save yourself. The boil . . ."

Fancy drew back the coverlet and recoiled. The stench from Sarah's open wound was beyond anything she could have imagined. She felt herself go white and struggled not to faint.

Sarah's hair was hanging around her shoulders like greasy rats' tails and her body was covered in a slimy yellow sweat. With horror, Fancy saw lice moving in her hair and jumping on the straw mattress under her.

She forced herself to pour out a cup of calf's foot jelly from the jug cook had sent, then took Sarah by the shoulders and raised her enough to drink, but the broth ran down the side of her mouth. Despairing, Fancy laid her down and proceeded to examine the wound. Somewhere in the back of her mind she remembered that if the boil was lanced and the offensive matter expelled there might be a chance of recovery.

She ran to the head of the spiral staircase and shouted for Bell.

"Bring the water up, Bell, and leave it outside the door. See if you can find some sweet water to cool it. And Bell, make that odious old woman give you some tolerably clean cloths."

She heard Bell come slowly up the stairs and deposit the bowl outside the door as directed. He also brought herbs and a bottle of vinegar, and she blessed his

thoughtfulness. Going back to Sarah, she looked at the
fetid bed which stank of stale vomit and excretia. She
had made up her mind . . .

"Bell," she called, "I want you to go back to Curzon
Street and get the coachman to bring the cart we use for
taking to market. And put in it a straw mattress that can
be burnt afterward. Go quickly. I mean to take Sarah
home!"

"But, m'lady!"

"No buts, Bell. Hurry! I've heard somewhere that if
the boil bursts there is a slight chance of recovery. Sarah
will have that chance." Not stopping to hear his reply
she hurried back to the bed and, pinning back her voluminous skirt, got down to her task.

She sponged the emaciated body and cleaned out the
huge hole in Sarah's groin. Around it was a hard yellow
mass, but already it was softening at the edges. So much
pus had oozed out that it was caked around and under
her legs.

She doused the long matted hair in vinegar to help kill
the lice, attending to her own hair at the same time—she
knew that lice were carriers of the infection. She covered her again and waited.

She tried Sarah with some watered wine. This time
there was a better response. Sarah opened her weary
eyes and smiled faintly, and Fancy dared to hope.

Then she bundled all the dirty, reeking rags together
and shouted for the old woman to take them away and
burn them.

The old woman, protesting and coming part of the
way up the stairs, shouted, "I'm not touching those
filthy rags. She'll die and that's the end of it."

"Sarah's not dead and I'm taking her home. I think
she might live."

"Never! She'll die for sure. She has death written on
her face. I've seen 'em before!"

"Well, you're wrong this time. You've never tried to
save anyone! You've only panicked and left them to die!
I've heard of your sort. You make a living pretending to
nurse the unfortunates for money, but you don't lift a

finger to help. You *hope* they die so you can go on to the next. You're a parasite, feeding on corpses! God's curse on you—you'll suffer some day!''

The old woman sidled away and quickly made the sign of the Cross.

"Don't curse me, m'lady. I should starve if I didn't look after the sick. No one else will do it. Even Lord Stichfield trusted me with his servants.''

"And where are they now? In the death cart, I warrant.''

"'Twas the will of God. I helped their passing. I was there. 'Twas better than dying alone, with no one there at all. I did me best,'' she whined.

"Well, do as I tell you. Lord Stichfield will think more of you if you disinfect his house against his return.''

Fancy went back to Sarah and saw that there was no change. She sponged her face and waited. And then there was a noise below. Thank God, Bell had returned with the cart. But when he came to her she found that the coachman had refused to help, so it was left to the two of them to carry Sarah down the narrow stairs to the cart below.

Back in Curzon Street, Sarah was carried to her old room. As the staff stood back and watched, Fancy realized that she herself would have to nurse the poor girl. A blanket soaked in vinegar was hung up at the door, and Fancy burned every stitch of clothing on herself and Sarah. She wore only a cotton shift in the sickroom, and each time she left it she sponged herself down with vinegar and herbs.

All thoughts of Gilbourne had been put aside now. It was better to keep away, although it nearly broke her heart to do so. John Bell called in the family doctor but he, poor fellow, overworked and despairing, only stood in the doorway while Fancy told him what she had done for Sarah.

"I only wish other people had your sense. Cleanliness is the only way to fight it. But as long as the weather remains hot, the deaths will continue. Only the frosts will kill the infection.''

"Can nothing be done? What precautions can be taken by the dock side?"

"The bubonic plague is carried by the rats that come from the ships in the harbor. Some ships are suspected slavers, diseased from end to end. All slaving ships should be burned to the water line, but with such money at stake there's little chance the captains will ever allow it."

"You mean, they carry the plague?"

"Yes, but not only slavers—convict ships, pirates and even man-o'-war have been known. If ever you got down wind of a slaver you would know it! You can smell them ten miles off." Fancy went white and felt sick. Could her own ship—hers and Sir Montagu's—be one of those bringing the disease to these shores?

During the next few days, Sarah was the only person she saw, for the other servants would not come near the sickroom. Their food was left outside the door. Then one morning Sarah sat up and smiled. Gone was the sickly odor surrounding her, and the hole in the boil was healing and become smaller. It still suppurated, but now, the cloths were coming away cleanly. And her appetite had returned!

She had Sarah removed to another room, while she herself cleaned and disinfected the sickroom. Windows were opened and Fancy made the entire household wash everywhere with either vinegar or Sir Timothy's best wine, for she knew alcohol to be a disinfectant.

She thanked John Bell for his loyal help and support, and promised that when all was well again he would be rewarded with promotion.

There had been no messages from Sir Timothy and now that she once more had time to breathe, she worried about Charles. In a couple of days she would be able to travel and take Sarah and John Bell with her. Her heart leapt and her arms ached to hold her boy . . .

And then Nellings came to her, his eyes downcast.

"Nellings, what is it? Is there a message from Gilbourne? Is it Charles?"

"M'lady, I don't know how to tell you . . ."

"For God's sake, is it Charles?"

Nellings shook his head, and she felt a surge of relief.

"It's Bell, m'lady. The silly young fool was getting too bold. He's been sneaking out to see some wench from the tavern near the docks. I warned him, but he only laughed. Said he was immune . . ."

"You mean . . .?" She looked at Nellings with horror.

"Yes, m'lady. His father sent a message early this morning. John Bell is dead of the plague!"

CHAPTER TEN

Fancy would never forget the agonies of that journey back to Gilbourne. First, the shock and misery of hearing of John Bell's death . . . and then as they came closer to Gilbourne, her concern for Charles. Would the child be well, or had the plague been lurking in his veins? Sarah, silent and withdrawn, was a living reminder of the risk Charles had run. Had Sarah kissed him after the fatal contact? She looked at Sarah, but the maid remained unresponsive.

Nor would Fancy forget the rush of emotion she felt for Timothy at her arrival at Gilbourne. Never before had she wanted the security of his arms or his name. She threw herself into his arms, sobbing with relief that at last there was someone to share the responsibility.

Sir Timothy, misinterpreting her emotion as relief at returning from the tryst with Sir Montagu, tried awkwardly to calm her.

"There, there. It is all over now. I admire your spirit in honoring my debt. Was it so very terrible, my love?"

She looked at him without comprehension, and then remembered. It seemed such a long time since she had parted from Sir Montagu. She had even forgotten he existed!

Looking back, it amazed her that she could greet her husband after all he had done, and share his bed without rancor. But she had found a new strength. Now she could use him, just as he used her, to satisfy her own healthy lust, and her heart would not be touched. It was a satisfying arrangement to both, and as long as Charles was between them, nothing would spoil the relationship.

For when Fancy hastened to the nursery and saw the small plump figure of her son and his smile of recognition, she felt such a surge of joy that she could have slept with a dozen men and cast her reputation to the winds! The small arms about her neck and the quick shy cuddle made her drunk with relief.

She celebrated her return in the only way she knew how, with a delighted Sir Timothy, and once again they reached heights of passion they had nearly forgotten. Fancy was generous in her giving, and Sir Timothy took full measure . . .

So the rest of that summer they spent together at Gilbourne, shunning London while the plague grew to epidemic proportions and the death toll soared. Charles grew and thrived in the fresh country air, and Fancy delighted in doing small things for him. Sometimes she would see Sir Timothy watching her with a strange look on his face, and for a while she would be uneasy. But the feeling would pass.

There was not much visiting at this time. Society was at a standstill, with everyone fearful of contact with the plague. The odd case in Tunbridge was blamed on the wandering gypsies, whose nomadic ways made them natural scapegoats.

Fancy listened to the gossip of the village, but at no time were the gypsies mentioned, until one day, by chance, Aunt Beamish mentioned a gypsy had mended a black iron kettle. He had done a good job and the woman had given him a shilling, which showed up in the household accounts.

That day Fancy went walking alone. She passed by the old campsite, but it was overgrown with brambles and no fires had been lit there for a very long time. She turned away, half disappointed, half relieved—for what could she say to Caleb Neyn if she met him again?

As she walked pensively by way of the paddocks, she smelled smoke. Someone was nearby, preparing a meal, no doubt. She climbed over a ditch and into the small copse, and there, under a tree was a rag of a tent.

She crept closer and waited. No one seemed to be about. And then there was a rustle in the undergrowth, and an old bent woman appeared with a dead rabbit in one hand and an old rusty snare in the other. Fancy started. She knew that old figure. She had seen her about the village years ago. She stepped forward, and the old woman stopped and peered into her face. And then her old lined walnut-colored face cracked into a professional smile.

"Can I tell your fortune, lady? Cross my palm and I'll tell you all you want to know. I can see you have a lucky face . . ." and the patter went on.

Fancy waited until she drew breath.

"You're Mrs. Neyn, aren't you?"

"Who wants to know?"

"Never mind. If you were as clever as you say you are, you would know! Where is Caleb Neyn?"

"Caleb?" The old crone laughed a high-pitched laugh.

"It's a long time since anyone asked for Caleb." She came closer and her dark eyes took in Fancy's fine gown and embroidered shawl.

"Eh, I know you! You're the wench who made a fool of my son! The *gaujé* wench whose life is mixed up with my boy. How is the boy Charles?" She smiled knowingly.

"You did not answer my question. Where is Caleb?"

"Away—and his brother with him. Both wanted for sheep stealing. I don't know whether they are dead or alive. Why do you want to know?"

"Because . . ."

"You want to return to the past? It can't be done. You are both different people now. The shy untried wench and the young hopeful boy are dead. Only their bodies are alive! Don't try to go back. Look forward. That way you may find your heart's desire—at the end of the road, not at the beginning."

"I don't understand you . . ."

"Why should you? I hardly understand myself. Caleb may be dead. Perhaps you will only find what you are looking for when all hope is gone. Give Charles my love." She turned away to move behind her lonely tent.

"Wait. Don't go. I want to give you something . . ."

"I don't take money from the mother of a *posh-rat*!"

Fancy started. She felt a cold finger of fear run down her spine.

"What do you mean, *posh-rat*?"

The old woman shook her head.

"The Neyns would never recognize a *posh-rat*. We've kept our tribe pure. Let this be a secret between us."

"But . . . how did you know?"

"I saw it in the crystal. I was puzzled at first, and Caleb wondered who Charles was, but then I knew! When the crystal showed me the link between you two people and the link was called Charles, I knew! He never guessed. He went away without ever knowing."

Fancy turned to go. Would the old woman ever see her sons again?

The months passed and as the cold weather came, the plague abated. The death toll went down and at last Sir Timothy decided that it would be safe to go back to London.

They found the city much changed. Shops were boarded up, and the refuse in the streets was piled high for lack of men to remove it. Nellings was dead, and one of the other footmen and a kitchen maid. Old Mrs. Bunce, looking thinner and more careworn, managed the house with the help of a young woman who had come looking for shelter with a child of six months at the breast. She offered to work for nothing if she could have food and shelter, and Mrs. Bunce took advantage of the offer and worked her all hours.

At once Sir Timothy let it be known they were back in town. Invitations came from those who had braved the metropolis again, though many friends and acquaintances were missing, presumed dead during the height of the epidemic.

Charles was now four years old and growing fast. Fancy delighted in taking him with her on her rides in the park. He loved to sit up with the coachman and be indulged, and sometimes he would try to wield the mighty whip, with dire results to the horses on several occasions.

He was becoming spoiled and precocious. Fancy could not bear to see him chastised or spoken sharply to, and often she and Sarah exchanged hot words on the subject. The boy was turning more like Caleb, and though proud of him, Fancy worried about Sir Timothy's reactions if he ever found out. He had the dark slumbering look of the gypsy—with a gold ring through his right ear, and his hair long and unruly, he might have been Caleb over again.

But there were differences, for which Fancy was thankful. His skin was not as coarse or swarthy, and his features were more refined. His voice, too, was cultured and his mannerisms those of the monied class. In his first boyish suit he looked very much the son of Sir Timothy Gilbourne . . . or so Fancy hoped.

One day in the park, he had stepped down from the carriage to play ball and she had followed him while the coachman waited a little further along the road. They played in fine style, and Fancy delighted in the way he could run and jump. And then the ball rolled farther away and, as he ran for it, Fancy was startled to see a shabby figure step out from behind a tree and stop the ball with his foot. He spoke to the boy, who smiled up at him.

Fancy's first thought was that it was some sinister person who might kidnap the boy. She had heard of such things happening. But another look at the man stirred a memory within her. Those shoulders, that stance—she caught her breath and started to run.

The man turned and watched her approach.

"Hello, Fanny. It's been a long time."

The boy looked from one to the other.

"Mama, this man stopped my ball from running away . . ." His childish treble faltered, for neither of them were listening.

Fancy experienced the strangest sensation of being transported back in time. *Fanny!* It was so long since anyone had called her that!

"What are you doing here in England? I thought you were a wanted man!" She could only stand there and look at him, feeling once more the old stirring of her blood and fighting against it as she always had done. He looked older, and there were gray streaks in his shaggy hair.

"I am. I've traveled a long way since those innocent days at Gilbourne. Can we talk somewhere?"

She looked hastily around. Charles had wandered away to watch another child play.

"Perhaps we could walk a little." She wanted badly to reach out a hand to him, but willed herself to appear cold and distant. "Did you have a bad time? I spoke to your mother and she told me about you and your brother."

He laughed bitterly and shook his head.

"It was bad, but I do not dwell on it. I'm alive, and that is all that matters. You seem to have done well for yourself." He looked her up and down. "I heard you married Sir Timothy. How did you manage to persuade him? As if I didn't know." He laughed and the color whipped into Fancy's cheek.

"Caleb, I had to do the best for myself," she said sullenly. "I married old Joshua Raybold first."

Caleb's eyes followed the boy.

"And you had a child—but was he Raybold's or was he mine?" He turned round to face her. She drew in her breath.

"Now don't lie, Fanny, m'dear. The old man was never capable of fathering a child."

The guilt on Fancy's face said it all.

"So who is Charles? Don't tell me he is Sir Timothy's son . . ."

"He is . . . he *is* . . . I married Sir Timothy after Lady Letitia died."

"That boy is never Lady Letitia's son. She was a sweet and gentle lady. She could never mother a son like him. How did you do it, Fanny? How did you pass off your *posh-rat* son as a son of the aristocracy?"

Fancy licked dry lips. Was it safe to admit to Caleb that the child was his? Did he want him, or . . .? Then she remembered. He would have been ashamed of a half-breed son! She raised her chin and looked him in the eye.

"It wasn't what you think. I loved Lady Letitia and her child died. I wet-nursed both boys."

"And you let the poor little devil die . . ."

"No! I did all I could. He was a sickly child. I tried my best. He would never suckle right from the first, so to give our son a chance, Caleb, I took him to the big house and passed him off as the son of Sir Timothy."

"Are you telling me that Lady Letitia didn't know her own child?"

"She didn't want her own child! She rejected him, and after Joshua died I went up to the big house . . ."

"And became Sir Timothy's mistress . . ."

"And what if I did? You didn't want me. You married Savina."

"I told you why. And much good it did me. After she came back to me, forced to by the Fingos, she gave me two more daughters. Your Charles is my only son." He laughed, but it was not a happy sound. "What a joke! My son the heir to a baronet!"

Fancy hardly heard him. She was thinking of Savina and of Caleb's three daughters.

"Do you love her, Caleb?"

He threw back his head and laughed.

"Not love . . . lust! She is a fine woman and a fit wife to bear gypsy children. But love, now that is something different . . ." His eyes softened, taking in every bit of her. "When will I see you again?"

"We are going to Gilbourne for the summer. The

plague makes it necessary. It has already broken out again near the docks."

"Because of those pestilential slavers coming up the Thames. How dare they anchor so near land. Surely the port authorities must know—they are thinly enough disguised!"

"But they bring goods to England."

"The smell remains. Anyone who has ever been windward of a slaver knows the stench. I know!" He rubbed his wrists. Fancy started and her hand went out to him.

"You were a slave?" She felt the rough skin of manacle scars on his wrists.

"Aye. I was pulled out of the sea with my brother by a Captain Black—Black Patch, to those in the know. An English blackguard, and one of the gentry by the sound of his tongue. I should like to meet the bastard again . . ." His voice sank to a whisper.

"Captain Black?" Fancy's astonishment gave her away.

"You know him?"

"Yes, but he is not important. What is important is us. Kiss me, Caleb."

"Not here, mad-brained fool! I'll come to you at Gilbourne . . ."

With that, he turned and ran into the bushes, just as the carriage arrived.

CHAPTER ELEVEN

Fancy could hardly believe that the meeting had really taken place! She pinched herself to make sure it had not all been a dream. Seeing Caleb again had brought back her yearning. There was something about him that wrung her heart. With no other man had her feelings burned so fiercely. She wanted him, not just because of his prowess as a lover—indeed, Sir Montagu had been a more accomplished lover—but because their minds were so attuned. She knew he was her man, despite Savina, despite the years of separation, and despite all the other partners they had loved.

She felt shame that she had enjoyed others, and a fierce jealousy of all the unknown women Caleb had loved. But she hugged their secret to herself. Charles was the link between them. Caleb would return to the village some time in April, and she knew in her bones that he would come to claim her . . .

But now as she enjoyed her child, she often found that Timothy watched her strangely. He said nothing, but she feared that her love for Charles was betraying her. She tried to turn the child away from her, but the boy was hurt and she could not bear him to cry.

Then Sir Timothy broached the subject of finding a tutor for Charles.

"He is with you too much, my dear. It is not healthy in a boy of his age. He wants to be taught to be a man."

"But he is still only a baby," Fancy said fearfully. "Give him time to play and enjoy his childhood while it lasts. I know how strict a tutor can be."

"You show him too much attention, Fancy. Indeed, you act as if you were his mother."

"And would you call that my fault, Timothy? I loved his mother and can only help her now by looking after her son."

"It is time you were thinking of children of your own. You talk as if this child was your own. Why, Fancy? Why?"

Fancy shrugged.

"I have no mind to bear another child. Charles takes the place of any I might have. I am content."

"But I am not." Sir Timothy spoke harshly. "Since the plague, I have been thinking. What if anything should happen to Charles? He is the only heir I have. You love me, do you not, Fancy? I raised you up. I made you what you are now. Have you no gratitude?"

"Of course, Timothy, I have a certain regard for you. But if I must speak honestly, I would have to say I do not respect you . . ."

"You have not forgiven me for making you pay my debt. I appreciate what you did, Fancy."

"Not enough for you to give up your women! But make no mistake about it, Timothy, I don't mind . . . as long as you don't come home with the pox!"

"Is that why you refuse to have my children? I assure you I am most careful with whom I indulge. You need have no fear."

"I have told you I don't mind. As for children, perhaps I shall have a baby next spring, who knows?"

With that Sir Timothy had to be satisfied. But there were times when he fired her as a lover, when the night was spent recapturing their early rapture, when he would look at her, naked and wanton, and then kiss her breasts and murmur in her ear that surely she was at last with child . . .

But at that she only smiled and went on taking her herbs twice a day. If she was going to have a child it would be when she was good and ready—and not before.

Sometimes she thought of Joshua and the life she

would have led if he had lived. If he had not gone celebrating with his friends at the village inn and fallen drunk into the ditch, she might have been condemned to live with him for years and years! And what of Caleb then? Would he have allowed her to live forever with that dirty smelly old man? What did the new Caleb think of her? Would the taint of her *gaujo* blood ever be washed away?

She would often lie in bed and picture him with her, and feel the manliness of him. Surely he would come to her soon. And then the ache for him had to be assuaged with Timothy and she would turn away from him and cry into her pillow . . .

So she started to walk alone to the outskirts of the village, waiting for his return. She watched the young buds open on bare branches and her thoughts were all of Caleb. *Would he return?*

One day her steps led her to her brother Billy and his wife Rebecca. Billy looked older and thinner than on her last visit. She found him cleaning out the barn, and he smelled of cow muck and sweat, but his eyes lit up when he saw her.

"Fanny! Is it really you? You look a proper lady!"

"Don't call me Fanny. I'm Fancy Gilbourne now," she said. Billy's look of pleasure vanished and the old surly expression was back.

"Oh, too good for us now, eh? I wonder you bothered to call . . ."

"Billy, I'm pleased to see you, only I've got used to my new name. Timothy likes it and . . . well . . . I suppose I do, too. Fanny reminded me of the bad times."

"I'm sorry. I spoke hastily. I'm afraid I do it all the time now. Come on up to the house and see Rebecca."

"Wait, Billy. How are you? Are you happy with Rebecca? Has everything turned out the way you wanted it?"

Billy pulled a face.

"Does anything turn out the way you want it? I'm better off married than I was scratching a living from Sir

Timothy, though. I've money in an old black sock and a bonny bairn, and another on the way . . ."

"But . . . there *is* a 'but,' isn't there, Billy?"

Billy scratched his head.

"She's too old, Fanny. It's like sleeping with my mother! I sleep with her because she insists. God, how she insists! She turns it into a duty. And I hate doing my duty . . ."

"And then?"

"We quarrel, and she screams at me, and then begs, and I hate that more than the screaming, and I go down to the inn and I stop there until only my legs know the way home . . ."

"Oh, Billy!" He had been the only person she had looked up to and loved when they were children. His hurt was her hurt. She wanted to cry.

"Now then, don't you take on. I'm used to it now. Besides, I got the land, didn't I? That was what it was all for. If we have a son, he'll be Bickler of Fellside. He'll be somebody. Even young Susan will have a decent dowry. My kids will have a better start than we had, m'girl!"

"If that's what you want, Billy—if you want to sacrifice yourself for land. But is it worth it?"

"Aye, it *has* to be worth it! Else I'd be a man of straw."

"Come up to the house with me, Billy. There's so much to talk about."

"You look as if you've fallen on your feet. Are you happy?"

"Yes, I think so. Like you, my life has its drawbacks, but none I can't surmount! I wouldn't have it any different."

Billy smiled at her, and they left the barn and walked up to the house. Fancy noticed the improvements: a new fence and a neat well-dug garden. But Fellside still reminded her of her life there with Joshua: it all seemed like something that had happened in another world.

Rebecca seemed to expect her. She smiled a plump

smile, and Fancy saw that she was heavy with child. She fussed over Fancy and dusted a chair before inviting her to sit down.

"I knew you had come to the big house. The vicar told me of your return."

"The vicar?" Rebecca turned scarlet.

"The curate. You remember him? He is now our vicar."

Fancy nodded her head.

"Of course! I had forgotten him. He's the one . . ."

"Yes," replied Rebecca hurriedly. "A saintly man. Too good to think of marriage, but a friend to the village. Will you have tea? Or would you prefer a glass of elderberry wine? I do keep a supply for special occasions."

"Elderberry wine would be nice. Where is little Susan?"

"She is with Nelly, hanging out the washing. she will come in like a little gust of wind. She is a healthy noisy child," she said proudly.

"Billy tells me you are increasing?"

Rebecca laughed and patted her stomach.

"No need for Billy to tell you. He is a very devoted husband, are you not, Billy? *Billy!*"

Billy raised his head wearily.

"I heard you. Yes, I'm a devoted husband . . ." He looked at Fancy as he spoke, then dropped his head again.

"What is the matter, Billy?" Fancy asked.

"There's nothing wrong with Billy," said Rebecca sharply. "He always acts this way after a night down at the inn! Drink is his trouble. I am always lecturing him on the evils of drink. But the devil gets into him! Why he does it, I do not know. I pride myself on being a good wife to him."

Billy sighed.

"Perhaps too good!" said Fancy half to herself.

"One can't be too good a wife! I've done the best I can, but Billy is a hard man to please! I sacrificed myself

. . . even to bearing him children! And he is still not grateful."

"Stop it, woman! You go on as if I never did you any favor! You were a sour man-starved spinster when I married you! Where else would you have found a husband who would bed you?"

Rebecca's face turned an unbecoming red.

"That is no way to talk in front of your sister—"

"She's no fool! She will have to know sooner or later . . ."

"Billy!" It was a cry from the heart.

"Who are you trying to fool? Nobody but yourself would think that we were a matched pair," he snarled. "You might as well know now as later, Fancy. The woman's like a leech! She bucks like a rabbit and looks as if she'll breed like one too. But not for the love of me! If she had her way she would possess me! Have you ever heard of a man dominated by a woman? She's the man in this household. I'm only a means to an end . . ."

"Billy! You can't mean what you say . . ." Fancy bit her lip. Billy gave her a long look, then dashed out of the door, but not before Fancy saw the poisonous glance he shot at his wife.

There was silence for a short while, and Fancy fiddled with her wineglass. Rebecca looked at Fancy and her lips twisted.

"Billy's right, you know. But I love him, Fancy. Do you believe that?"

"Yes . . . I suppose so, or you wouldn't have married him."

"It's not just a spinster wanting a man! When he makes love, he makes me feel like a young girl again—and having babies is living proof that I can match him. I love him and I want him . . . After all those wasted years I suppose I feel I must make the most of what time remains. I know Billy will tire of me. Already he feels trapped. Oh, I know it! I can see by the way he smiles and looks at the maids!"

"But you are his wife. If you are ready and waiting, he

will always come home to you. Billy just feels . . ."

"Don't you see? I *must* keep him with me! I do all I can. I play the wanton even when it goes against my nature . . ."

"And you think he doesn't realize that? Perhaps that is the trouble, Rebecca. Perhaps you try too hard."

"Perhaps, perhaps! That can be a terrible word. Help me, Fanny, if you can. I love him for himself. He can be kind and gentle on occasion, and he is a good father. Yet he thinks I have trapped him."

"But why? He has got the best of the bargain. Maybe he feels guilty."

"You mean because he married me for the farm? Don't look surprised. I know it, you know. Who would marry an ugly woman like me for love?"

"And when you are angry, do you let him know this?"

"There have been times when I have reminded him."

"Then you're a fool! A very old woman who had much experience in affairs of the heart once told me that the way to keep a marriage good was to garnish with patience and sweeten with smiles—to wrap in a mantle of charity and always keep warm with a steady fire of devotion. Follow that advice and you could keep your husband for years."

"Oh, if only that was true!"

Fancy shook her hand.

"My dear Rebecca, a marriage must be worked at. It doesn't just happen! My own . . ." A pained look crossed her face. "Well, mine is not perfect, far from it, but Timothy and I have found a compromise. We deal well together."

"I wondered. Oh if we only knew how life was going to turn out!"

"You are lucky, Rebecca. After years of waiting you found a good man, you bore one healthy child and now you hope for another. This time you may have a son. It is up to you to show gentleness and make your home a haven for Billy. That way, if he does stray, he will always come back to you."

"And you think I should just forget his affairs with the village girls?"

"Of course! They are sure to be trivial. At your age you cannot afford to be too particular." Fancy was brutal, but felt sure that it was the best approach. "Give him comfort and a full belly, and you can fight any little piece he fancies! And when the wind blows cold and the rain lashes down you will find he will get his ease in your bed! What more do you want?"

"Oh, you've grown so very wise. I never thought when you came to Fellside as a servant . . ."

Fancy flushed and looked wounded, and Rebecca instantly regretted the words.

"I'm sorry. I should never have said that . . ."

"I'm Fancy Gilbourne now, Rebecca. The little orphan girl is dead, and Fancy Gilbourne grew out of her ashes."

"I'm sorry if I offended you."

Rebecca poured out another glass each of the elderberry wine, and held hers up to the light.

"I think this calls for a toast! To the family, and to Fancy Gilbourne!"

They smiled at each other, and Fancy said mildly, "I like this wine. You must give me the recipe!"

So Fancy got into the habit of calling at Fellside two or three times a week, and always she watched for signs of the coming caravans. Sometimes she took Charles with her, and he played with Susan as she and Rebecca enjoyed their cozy chats.

Billy still brooded and regarded Fancy with some suspicion since she was evidently on Rebecca's side. Fancy, for her part, worried about his morose condition. He appeared so changed from the boy she remembered.

But then one morning as she made her way alone to Fellside, she saw smoke lazily rising above the campsite.

Her heart beat more quickly as she neared the curling black plume. There was the scent of burning wood on the still air, and the smell of fresh vegetation after a night's rain, and suddenly Fancy was aware that her pulse was racing at a fever pitch. Sight, sound and smell were accentuated and suddenly she started to run. Then at the edge of the clearing she paused, shocked. There were children playing near the three caravans, and a group of women looked up at the sound of her coming.

Her heartbeats threatened to overwhelm her. Holding her side, she watched the women, fascinated. One of them, tall with the stately bearing of a queen, left the group and came toward her. Her head was high and the light in the fierce eyes arrogant.

"Well? What do you want? Are we worth staring at?" The tone was haughty and the accent certainly not of the south country. The gypsy woman looked back over her shoulder and said something to the others, and they laughed. Fancy could just understand the word *gaujo*. She gritted her teeth.

"I might be a *gaujo,* but I'm not quite a fool!"

"Ah, so you know the Romany? Why do you come here?"

"I am looking for Mrs. Neyn, mother of Caleb Neyn," she lied.

"She is dead. I am Caleb Neyn's wife. What did you want with her?"

Fancy considered the woman. She reminded her of some proud bird of prey with gorgeous plumes, ready to attack.

"It is none of your business. Tell Caleb Neyn I am sorry his mother is dead."

"You lie! It is Caleb you wanted to see! Well, he is not here. He is running horses at Tunbridge Fair." She came to stand in front of Fancy, hands on hips. "So you are the woman who comes between me and my man. I spit on you, *Gaujo!*"

They glared at each other and Fancy's hands curled. She wanted to tear at the woman's face.

"And you are Savina Fingo. The woman who left her child with her husband and went back to her own folk!"

"Ah, so you know about that! But I came back, and I've twin daughters to prove it! Get back to your fine house and leave my man alone, before you find yourself surrounded by fire!" She peered close into Fancy's eyes, then backed away. "I mentioned the word 'fire' and the flames leap up in your eyes! Leave my man alone, or else the fire will have you. I warn you!" She moved away and then shouted over her shoulder, "Don't come back here. I rule this piece of ground. Next time you come, you may get a knife in your ribs!"

Fancy shivered, for never had she seen such menace in a woman's eyes before. She stumbled along the narrow path and out on to the winding road to Fellside.

Rebecca was making butter when Fancy hurried up the front path. She had just instructed Nelly to scrub the churn out with soda, and leave it clean and rinsed to dry in the sun. She washed and dried her hands, then left the golden mass of butter to rinse in sweet water before starting to pat it.

"Come along in. You look as if you've seen a ghost. What ails you Fancy? Are you with child at last?"

Fancy shook her head and sank down in the window seat in the kitchen. It was untidy and smelled of baking bread, and a wooden doll and cradle was taking up much of the space before the huge open fire.

"I'll make a pot of tea. That will revive you. Drat the child! She leaves all her toys laid about. Susan, where are you? Come and say hello to your Aunt Fancy, there's a good child!"

A small girl peeped around the back door and looked shyly at Fancy before sticking a grubby thumb into her mouth. Rebecca bustled about with the black iron kettle and brown earthenware teapot and soon they were sipping the precious tea.

"Susan, don't stand there with your thumb in your mouth. How often have I to tell you it is a dirty habit? Now, Fancy, what is the matter?"

Fancy shivered again and then looked across at Rebecca.

"It was the gypsies—I quarreled with one of them," she said in a low voice.

"Why on earth go near them? An arrogant lot, they are. I won't have them on the place, even though I've been threatened with bad luck."

"Do you think they can really curse you?"

Now it was Rebecca who laughed scornfully.

"Only if you let them! I don't worry about them, so their threats don't touch me. Forget them, Fancy, and remember they are just an ignorant lot! What happened? Did you refuse to buy their pegs?"

"No. I don't want to talk about it. It was unpleasant, but it will not happen again."

"You should make Sir Timothy lay a complaint and have them shifted!"

"Oh, I couldn't do that!"

Rebecca looked at her curiously.

"Why not? It strikes me you don't know what you want!"

"Just leave it, Rebecca. It's all over now, so forget it. Where's Billy working today?"

"In the Smiddy field, getting the land ready to sow. It's been a late spring and the first sowing failed, so Billy's been bad to live with these last few days . . . But I minded what you said. I've fed him and cheered him when things went wrong, and mothered him when he was discouraged and tired, and tried to be a comfort to him in bed." She laughed gently and patted her heavy stomach. "He's not had too much of that kind of comfort, lately, but I'll make up for it soon enough."

"Mind you don't get with child again too soon. There are things you can take . . ."

"I'll take nothing! If the good God wills me to become a mother again, I'll suffer it cheerfully! I'll not harm God's gift!"

"It wouldn't be God's gift, it would be Billy's! I only want you to recover properly from this coming lying-in. You know how weary women can get, having a baby every year. Think of Emmy Rider with eight of them and dying before she was thirty with her ninth, and Tom left with all the brood to look after! And you are a lot older than . . ." She stopped at the glare from Rebecca. "I'm sorry. I always say the wrong thing. I only wanted you to know that I worry about you."

It was three days later, when Fancy was walking slowly home after another visit to Fellside that a blackbird's whistle made her look around. There he was laughing and beckoning to her as if they had never been parted!

Fancy's heart was in her mouth. She ran over to the hedge where Caleb was standing and his hands came out to her. She allowed him to help her over a gap and then panting with exertion, she sank into his arms. He cradled her gently to him and his broken words of love were balm to her spirit. They kissed, and it was as if she had taken wing. Her head reeled and she clung to him in an ecstasy of feeling. Nothing mattered but that she was in his arms once again.

As his kiss seared her lips, it was as if they were welded to him, and that her very soul was being drawn from her mouth. The world dwindled to the shelter of his arms and all feeling was fused into her mouth. All her mind could register was that at last they were together.

He laughed exultantly and swung her up, shoulder-high, then carried her to their tree where he drew her down with him and held her to his heart.

"Remember? I taught you to love here, in the shelter of the old oak." His hands fondled her and became intimate. She thrilled to his touch and her arms went out to him, locking their bodies together.

Tenderly he loosed the laces of her bodice and his hand fondled her breast. She closed her eyes and arched her back, and his questing hands caressed her and drew long-forgotten feelings from her. She wanted him; ached for him, and then with heavy, half-slumbering eyes, she sought him and found him.

Now she was pressed beneath him, his heavy body pinning her down. She was his, and her whole body sang, her breath came in gasps and she could feel his mouth on her breast, her neck and then again seeking her mouth. The delicious moment hung on the air, fulfillment came, and she felt his grasping arms relax. She lay in his arms, content, and for a long while nothing was said. They were slaked of passion, like two rag dolls entwined together, he frightened that she would get up and leave him, and she hoping he would want her again.

Then he leaned up on one elbow and spoke, and the world swung into place again.

"You came to the campsite, Savina told me."

"Yes, and she warned me off."

"It was a silly thing to do."

"I did not think. I saw the smoke and thought only of you." Her arm crept around his neck, and she gently pulled at the curls on the back of his neck. "Do you want to bathe? Do you remember telling me to wash first?"

"Yes, but then you were a dirty little heathen. Now you smell wonderful."

He took her roughly in his arms again, and his kiss was as passionate as the first. Then he tucked her head onto his shoulder and sighed. "I'm not as young as I was . . ." She laughed, delightedly.

"But you wanted to, I could tell." He nipped her lovingly.

"Wretch! You would kill me with love! I never knew such a girl." He rolled over. "Are you coming tomorrow?"

"If you want me . . ."

"*Want* you! You know I want you!"

She nibbled his ear, and then kissed him on the neck.

"God's teeth! Must you do that?"

He grabbed her by the hair, and she felt his hand shaking. She smiled. She knew that soon he would be lusting after her again. And she wanted it so.

Now she knew how Rebecca felt. She wanted to exhaust this man, to prevent him from ever looking at another woman. How she hated Savina! Vague thoughts of having another child by him plagued her. Her natural desire was to do so, but she choked the thought down. It would be another *posh-rat*, a half-blood, to be rejected and spurned by him.

But he was aroused once more, and this time was not so easy to please. Now it was Fancy who was exhausted, Fancy who had taken the initiative. But at the end she knew that for tonight at least, Savina would sleep alone . . .

And so they met each day, and for Fancy it was like starting all over again. She sang as she played with Charles and was especially loving to Timothy. Timothy continued to watch her suspiciously, but as she had started taking Charles with her to Fellside to play with Susan, he did not question her visits.

Rebecca had her own ideas about Fancy's mysterious excursions, but held her peace. It was no affair of hers who Fancy was dallying with. Fancy's presents to her, ostensibly in return for watching Charles, insured that! And Aunt Beamish, who occasionally visited Fellside to see Billy, also kept a disapproving silence.

So Fancy was in her own Heaven at this time, and looking back later on the summer's idyll knew it for the happiest of her life. Her whole mind was on Caleb and how she could please him. The time spent apart had to be endured, but by now Fancy had become a good actress and put a brave face on it.

One afternoon she met him under their tree as usual. It was August, and already the summer showed a ripeness that heralded autumn. She was pensive.

"I must go to Tunbridge tomorrow," she told him. "I have had word from my man of business—one of my ships is moored in the Thames."

"So the story you told me was no fairy tale after all? You really are Black Patch's partner?"

"Of course. Would I lie to you?"

"You might, if it pleased you. Do you ever go aboard?"

"Never. I have never even seen one of the ships."

"Good, because while the weather remains hot, the plague is still a danger."

"You seem to know a lot about it?"

"I should. I was aboard one of Black Patch's ships for a year, remember?"

"Yes, I remember. Was he such a very bad captain?"

"Not the worst, but bad enough. Unscrupulous and cruel on occasion, but fair. No slaver captain can afford to have scruples, or he wouldn't survive long in the business. But he did not torture for pleasure. Nonetheless, I would kill him if I ever met him face to face."

"Why? What did he do to you?"

"He made me a slave and sold me to an Arab, me and my brother Benji. And he had Benji castrated. Is that not reason enough?"

Fanny listened with horror.

"I thought you were just a slave on his ship. I didn't know he sold you!" She put protective arms about him. "Oh Caleb, I might never have seen you again!"

He pushed her away impatiently.

"Must you always think about what you might have done or not done? I'm not worried about myself. It's Benji I worry over! You've not said one word about what Black Patch did to him!"

"But I don't know Benji! How can I worry about him? You are the one I worry over! Caleb, let's run away together, just you and I! I could take Charles with me and we could make a fresh start somewhere, alone! Oh Caleb, it would be Heaven!"

Her arms went around him clingingly, and her mouth sought his. He pushed her from him and stood up.

"Don't be a fool! Would you take Charles away from the only life he knows? And lose him the birthright you bought for him? You could never do such a thing! And besides, he's no child of mine."

"But he *is* yours, Caleb! He looks like you . . ."

"I spawned him, I'm quite aware of that. But his outlook and his upbringing make him no child of mine! And something, the most important—he is a *posh-rat!*"

"You say that as if it is something to be ashamed of! How can you talk that way about your son?"

"I don't regard him as my son. How many times have I spoken with him? Twice or thrice, and he stood behind you and held on to your skirt. He was frightened by the big clumsy gypsy! No doubt his nurse frightens him to sleep at night with tales of naughty boys being taken away by Romanies!" He moved away and leaned up against a tree, head down. He turned and stared at Fancy. "You know it's impossible. We should never get away from gypsy vengeance. The Fingos and the Kalderash would seek us out wherever we went. No matter what country we tried to escape to, there would be gypsies who would send word. This is our only way of meeting, can't you see that?"

A great lump rose up in Fancy's throat, and then the tears came.

Caleb took her into his arms and smoothed the loosened hair, kissing her white throat and murmuring endearments. The large roughened hands were surprisingly gentle, but Fancy was too upset to notice.

"Then—then all our loving is wasted? It will get us nowhere?"

"You were content to meet me here, and to love me. What is changed?"

"But—but I want you all the time. Not just for a summer idyll and then to lose you when you move on—with *her!*"

"Savina is my wife," Caleb said quietly. "She is well-respected in our community and is already a wise woman and sits in during our law-giving. A wife must have her rights. I am her husband and therefore must protect her and our children. There is no question of my leaving her. She has already given me three daughters. Someday she may give me a son—and he will be a true gypsy."

"So you *are* ashamed of your posh-rat son! You are an unnatural father. I never thought that of you! I thought if you had the chance of looking after the boy . . ."

"Stop it!" Now Caleb was angry. "There is no difference between our son and the sons Black Patch begets on his slaves! They're all half-breeds!"

"But they're black women and slaves! Your son's neither."

"They're still half-breeds, just as our child is a half-breed. Can't you see that?"

Fanny struggled to her feet, white-faced. Her stomach heaved and she wanted to be sick. She swayed drunkenly.

"Then it's all over. I'll not see you again. There'll be no question of you begetting another half-breed bastard! I'm not coming here again to pander to your lust."

"And your own . . ."

"Very well—mine, too. This is the last time."

Suddenly there came the sound of someone rushing toward them at a furious pace and breaking the branches of bushes in his path. They both turned in the direction of the sound. Fancy's heart froze. Timothy, disheveled and holding Charles by the hand, confronted them. In the background were two of Sir Timothy's farmworkers.

"So this is why you sing and seem so happy in the country. I've suspected for a while something was wrong. You common little whore!" He marched straight up to Fancy, pushing Charles to one side, and struck her across the cheek, knocking her to the ground. Charles started to cry and crouched down beside his mother, who lay confused and half-conscious, listening to the sounds of a furious scuffle above her head.

Charles crouched low over her and held her hand.

"Mama, Mama, wake up. Papa is fighting . . ."

But Fancy, dazed and feeling the sting of the blow, lay still. Wearily, she knew there was plenty of time to put Sir Timothy straight.

Then she heard Sir Timothy's voice say, "Have at him, men."

She struggled up in time to see the two men holding Caleb and Sir Timothy punching him in the stomach. Caleb doubled up and groaned, but the men pulled him to his feet again. A second time Sir Timothy's fist lashed out.

"And this is for looking as you do!"

Sir Timothy's cryptic remark made Fancy catch her breath. She looked swiftly at the two farmworkers, but they were impassive, unaware of the significance of his remark.

"Stop!" she shouted. "Let him go. It is not as you think!" She looked at Caleb, his eyes steadfast on hers as the blood poured from his nose and a cut over his right eye. He smiled faintly, a mocking smile. "This, I think, takes care of our problem," it seemed to say. And as the two men pulled away, she watched him go, his wrists fastened behind him. The light was going out of her life.

She wanted to run after him, but Sir Timothy held her back.

"And where do you think you're going?"

"I must say goodbye to him. What are you going to do with him?"

"His Majesty is giving criminals a chance to enlist for the new war with France, Sweden and Holland."

"You mean kidnapping them," she said bitterly.

He shrugged.

"Very well if you prefer! But if he lives, his life is taken care of for the next seven years!"

"You monster! You didn't care when you promised me to Sir Montagu. Why vent your spleen on Caleb Neyn, a man who has done you no harm?"

"No harm? You must be mad. Do you imagine I don't realize who he is? Caleb Neyn is the father of my son—I knew as soon as I laid eyes on him. I would have killed the bastard, but the scandal must never come out. I want him dead, but the war will see to that."

"Why? What do you mean? Sooner or later the scandal *must* come out and when it does you will be the laughing stock of the Court. Can you stand that?"

"I will not, madam. For I shall simply go on as before. Charles is my son and as such, will take his place in society. And you madam, will stay at Gilbourne as my invalid wife. You will be cared for, but confined to your room. I'll not have you wandering the countryside and sleeping with every common gypsy you happen to take a liking to!"

Fancy could only stare at him, and then as his cruel fingers bit into her arm, she tried to pull away.

"You mean that, Timothy? You seriously mean to lock me away?"

"Quite correct, madam. All inquiries after you will be answered with a statement as to your health from your loving grieving husband. The world will hear no more of Fancy Gilbourne. As far as it is concerned, you are dead!"

CHAPTER TWELVE

Fancy was aghast.

"Timothy, you cannot mean this? Caleb is gone now. We must talk this over."

"There is nothing to talk over," he said grimly. "Perhaps if it had only been a brief affair things might have been different. But to substitute his child for mine . . ."

"You don't understand. I did it simply to spare Lady Letitia pain and cruelty if her baby died."

"But you deliberately let him die!"

"No! I loved him as my own. I gave him more love and attention than my own son, just because he was so weak and feeble. You were not concerned then with your own child. Why should it concern you now—now that you have a fine healthy child? He is a boy to be proud of!"

"He's a gypsy half-breed! Must the Gilbourne line disappear and gypsy blood take its place?"

"Then let me take him and disappear. I'll never trouble you again!"

"No! You are to be locked up. This way I do not lose face. I'll have no man or woman laugh behind my back and say I was cuckolded by a gypsy! Charles will take his place as my son. Now get along with you!" Dragging her roughly behind him, they followed the fast disappearing farmworkers. "And I must remember to pay those two off and see that they leave the village," he muttered, half to himself.

His fingers bit into her wrist, and it took all her will not to cry out. Charles, who had wandered away to watch a bird searching for grubs, ran to her.

"Mama, why is your face pale? Are you going to cry?

Papa, look at her. You are hurting her!"

Sir Timothy strode on, pulling Fancy by the wrist and taking no notice of Charles.

"Papa, wait for me!" The child tried to catch up, and he stretched out his hand to his father, but Sir Timothy turned, anger twisting his features. "Don't touch me, you little bastard!" he snarled and struck him across the face.

The boy fell backward, astonished and fearful, and burst into tears. Fancy was beside herself with alarm and terror.

"Charles! Are you hurt?" She tried to twist herself around, but Sir Timothy dragged her on mercilessly.

"You unspeakable devil," shouted Fancy, "to take your vengeance on a child! Hit me if you like, spit on me, but leave Charles out of this!"

Sir Timothy gave an ugly, heartless laugh.

"He'll pay for your whoring, never fear! You'll hear him scream in that room of yours, and you will not be able to do a thing about it!" Fancy managed to wrench one of her arms free and clawed his face, drawing a thin trickle of blood which dripped slowly down his cheek.

"You're mad. No sane man could think of doing such a thing to the child he brought up and loved as his own! Let him go away with Sarah and I'll remain as your whore, or your servant—anything! But let him go, I beg you . . ."

Sir Timothy shook her brutally.

"There's nothing you can say will change my mind, so be silent, woman. You are in no position to bargain. If I want you, I'll take you—willing or unwilling."

And so Fancy found herself locked away in an attic room with only a small skylight to give her sight of the outside world—a square patch of sky and scudding clouds. The attic was comfortably furnished—Aunt Beamish had seen to that, watched by the suspicious eye of Sir Timothy. Reluctantly the old woman had gone about her tasks, but had refused to meet Fancy's eye.

Once Fancy heard Sarah wailing outside the door, but her shriek and the sound of a body thrown roughly to the floor made it plain that Sir Timothy meant business.

There followed a time of misery. The days were long and Aunt Beamish was banned from seeing her, since Sir Timothy hired a woman to "nurse" her. An expert in the care of mad people in Bedlam, Mrs. Snell was tall and strong as a man, and her trap of a mouth never showed a trace of sympathy. For all Fancy knew, the woman might truly have believed her to be a lunatic.

The only time her bed and clothing were changed was when Sir Timothy was due to come to her. She became accustomed to his visits, and both hoped for and dreaded them—hoped, because she was allowed to wash, and dreaded because each time he came he devised new ways to humiliate her.

And now there was another dread. The supply of dried herbs she had treasured was running out.

Before she was installed in the attic, Sir Timothy had allowed her to visit her bedroom to collect various personal belongings, such as clothing and brushes and combs. Unseen, she had snatched up the box containing the herbs and hidden it under a pile of undergarments. Now she watched it anxiously. If she did not escape soon, there would be a real danger of having to bear another child. And if it was a son, Fancy feared for Charles' life. She must get away!

She made plans by the hour. There was nothing else to do. Her efforts to converse with Mrs. Snell brought forth only grunts. She was too handsomely paid to become friendly with her "patient." In desperation Fancy thought of hitting the woman over the head with her water pitcher, but Mrs. Snell was always on the lookout for trouble. She carried a small leather whip on a thong on her wrist, and whenever Fancy walked towards her she would smile and run the whip through her hands.

And then one night as she lay restlessly watching the moon's glow through the small cobwebbed skylight, there came a scratching at the door panel. Fancy held her breath, and the sound came again. She threw back the bedclothes of the hard trundle bed and ran to the door. Crouching down, she whispered through the keyhole. "Who is it?"

"It's me, Sarah. Shh! Keep quiet, m'lady. I've come to tell you the master's gone to London and taken Charles. He's sending him away to school. The excuse is that you are too ill to cope with him, and that you tried to kill him. God's curse on him for it!"

"Oh, Sarah, how is he? Is he well?"

"He's changed, m'lady. He hardly ever speaks. It fair breaks my heart to see him. He's clung to me so much he's even been sleeping with me because he has such nightmares. God knows what he'll be like at school. They do say it is a tough school. The master says they will make a man of him!"

"Oh, my poor Charles! Can you get me out of here, Sarah?"

"I don't know, m'lady." Sarah's voice was frightened.

"What is the date, Sarah? Are we into September yet?"

"Not yet, m'lady. It is the twenty-fifth of August, I think."

"Thank God. Listen, Sarah. Captain Black Patch Hawkins is moored in the Thames until the beginning of the second week in September. I was to meet him, remember? Can you send a message to Mr. Somers to bring a coach? How long will Sir Timothy be away?"

"He said more than a week, m'lady, all depending on how he finds the roads. There has been quite a lot of rain lately. It could be heavy going."

"What about Mrs. Snell? What does she do when Sir Timothy is away?"

"Huh! That one!" Sarah's voice was contemptuous. "She is foxed on gin most of the time."

"Then you go now Sarah, and send that message. I'll be ready any night you can arrange it." Suddenly hope swept her depression away, and her mind became active.

"I'll go now to your brother Billy. He's been fair worried about you. Both he and Mistress Rebecca have called to see you in your sickness, but Sir Timothy refused to let them see you. Once Sir Timothy knocked Billy down . . ."

"And he never told me they had come! Poor Billy—

and I thought they had forsaken me."

"Never that, m'lady. I'll go now, before that woman comes round. I can be back before I'm missed."

"Sarah, I'll never forget you for this. You have all my gratitude."

"You gave me my life. What else can I do?" said Sarah simply. Then she was gone.

Two anxious days went by. Mrs. Snell came and went with her meal tray, and Fancy noticed she was not so well fed as when Sir Timothy was at home. There was no sign that she was drinking heavily, until one night Fanny smelled gin on her breath. Mrs. Snell was drinking again! Her heart leaped.

That night the scratching at her door came again. She was ready and waiting, her pitiful bundle of belongings under the bed. She was taking only essentials, except for the topaz necklace Lady Letitia had given her.

"M'lady, are you awake?" Sarah's voice was trembling with emotion.

"Yes, Sarah, awake and ready. Can you get me out?"

"We can't find the key of the room. Billy's hunting through Mrs. Snell's room now."

"There must be another key! Ask Aunt Beamish. She may have one."

"Billy didn't want her to know. That way she can't get into any trouble. You know how the master is . . ."

"Oh! I never thought about that. What about you?"

"I'm coming with you. I'm all packed and ready."

"Oh, Sarah, you wonderful, wonderful girl. I don't know what will happen to us."

"I don't care. I won't stop here without you or the young master. I would rather starve first!"

"Then find Billy and tell him to break down the door."

But there was no need. Fancy heard the sound of a key in the lock and then the door opened to reveal a grinning Billy. He had found the key on a chain around Mrs. Snell's neck, and had gently twisted it loose while she snored. Fancy flung herself around her brother's neck.

"Thank God," she sobbed. "Oh, Billy, how can I thank you . . ."

"There, there, it's all over. The coach is waiting down near the gate. You can leave Gilbourne forever."

"But Charles—I must find him!"

"Aye, that will be more difficult. I'll watch out for him at this end. But they do say he's not coming home for holidays."

"I must find him, if it takes the rest of my life."

"Come then, let's away. I want no one to see me here. I'll not be knowing about this night's work . . ."

"Don't worry, Billy, Sarah's coming with me, so she will take the blame."

Sarah followed, carrying Fancy's bundle.

"Aye, I'll be blamed. Not that I care! I should like to see Sir Timothy's face when he knows we are gone!"

Mr. Somers' coach was waiting. The black horses were pawing the earth, impatient to get back to their stable. Billy saw that the two women were well-wrapped against the chill air, and then before the coach started on its way he clasped Fancy in his arms.

"Take care of yourself, sis, and here's a few guineas to help you on your way. 'Tis all I have to spare, but me and Rebecca will pray for you."

"Oh, Billy!" Fancy flung her arms about him." Keep the money. You need it more than I. I've got money with Mr. Somers. I'll be fine. If ever you hear of Charles, send a message to Mr. Somers. He will keep in touch with me."

They kissed, and she felt hot tears on Billy's cheek.

"And, Billy, be kind to Rebecca. She means well—and you may yet have a son!"

He nodded, and then gave the signal to the coachman. . . .

It was nearly dawn when the coach arrived outside Mr. Somers' modest house. The solicitor was there waiting and Fancy found to her grateful surprise that a huge fire had been lit in the spare room and a young maid was waiting with hot water to help her with a sponge-bath. Afterward both she and Sarah ate a hearty supper of cold beef, ham and pickles, washed down with small beer. And then they curled up together in the massive four-poster and slept well into the morning.

The sun was high before Fancy was ready to go down-stairs to meet her benefactor. He was waiting in his library, his face anxious and tired. He bid her welcome and pulled forward a chair.

"You slept well? I trust my housekeeper looked after you?"

"Yes, thank you. The bed was comfortable, and your housekeeper and your little maid served me well."

"Good. Now we can get down to business. I sent a message to you more than two weeks ago telling you that Captain Hawkins is now in London."

"Yes. I was trying to arrange to meet you when I was . . . was . . ." She stopped, unable to go on. Mr. Somers nodded his head.

"I know, I know. A terrible business. I would never have thought it of Sir Timothy."

"He had his reasons, Mr. Somers. Much of the blame was mine."

"Well, that is your business. Now as to your financial state . . ."

"Yes, Mr. Somers?"

"I am happy to tell you that Captain Hawkins has had two successful trips since seeing you last. I'll not go into details now, but I can assure you, you are a very wealthy woman!" In his manner and smile Fancy saw a keen desire to please, so her wealth was considerable! Fancy's heart jumped in her bosom. Perhaps now she could find Caleb!

"Mr. Somers, could I ask another favor?"

"Anything, Lady Gilbourne. Just name it."

"I want you to find out what happened to the gypsy, Caleb Neyn. I want him found and set free."

Mr. Somers looked at her with some curiosity. M'lady's interest in a common gypsy was indeed strange. But then, she did not come from highborn stock herself, although her manner disguised it perfectly. So m'lady had been whoring with a gypsy, had she? He smiled at Fancy.

"No need to seek very far, m'lady. Caleb Neyn was tried last week at the Assizes and sentenced to ten years' hard labour for the rape of a woman of quality. He was given the choice of Dartmoor or serving on one of the King's ships. He chose the ship."

"Then will he be still in England?"

"That I do not know. But no power on earth will get him out of the Navy! Unless he is killed in action, he will serve out his term."

"So I must disappear and wait . . . And my son Charles?"

"M'lady, I am sorry. Your stepson is with his rightful parent. You cannot take him."

Fancy bit her lip and sat thoughtfully for the space of a few minutes, and then she sighed.

"What I tell you is to be confidential. I understand you respect a client's wishes?"

"Of course. That is the only course for a good lawyer. I know many secrets."

"Then what I have to tell you will be a surprise but not a shock. Charles Gilbourne is my son, and his father is Caleb Neyn, the gypsy! Are you shocked, Mr. Somers?"

"Surprised, perhaps. I often wondered why you wished to leave all your fortune to a mere stepson. Now I understand it. You were providing for an emergency."

She inclined her head.

"It was in my mind. But I could hardly have foreseen this precise situation. I fully expected to remain Fancy Gilbourne. It was to furnish my son with funds if ever Sir Timothy lost everything at cards. He is an inveterate gambler, as you know."

Mr. Somers nodded slowly.

"A common fault among gentlemen. But perhaps Sir Timothy is more prone to it than most."

"Yes, indeed. And now, I think, he will care less about his son's patrimony. So my will still stands."

"You need not worry about it. The provisions of your will are quite unambiguous. And I will watch out for the boy."

"But I want to find him and take him away."

"I think you will find that difficult, Lady Gilbourne. In the eyes of the world you are his stepmother. Besides, Sir Timothy is proud. Perhaps he will not report your disappearance. He may simply go on as if nothing had happened. He has already given it out that you were confined to your room with an illness. Even I heard that, and was mighty worried for you, I can tell you."

"You mean he could guard an empty room?"

"Yes. So I advise you to lay low for a while. A client of mine, a gentlewoman in low circumstances, will give you a home temporarily. I can arrange it for a small sum. I think it would be best in this instance."

"But I should feel like a prisoner again!"

"You will be free to come and go, within reason."

"Very well, Mr. Somers, speak to your lady. I'll do as you say."

And so Sarah and Fancy moved in with Miss Henrietta Mumble of the Hollys, a small stone-built house with a door set between two small diamond-paned windows. They occupied one with drawing room and Miss Mumble the other. Not that the arrangement was a strict one. Miss Mumble was more often to be found in their room, talking and drinking rhubarb wine, and regaling their bored ears with the story of her life. Miss Mumble's life-long infatuation with the local curate was the single most exciting feature of her life, but it had kept her a Christian and a virginal spinster—the curate had married another.

The third morning, Sarah came back from the market with staring eyes and fear in her heart.

"M'lady! I've just read a notice by the posting-house. I'm wanted for the murder of Nurse Snell!"

"What are you talking about? What devil's work is this?"

"Oh, m'lady, if they catch me, I'll be hanged!" Sarah was hysterical with fear and panic.

"Stop it, Sarah. Here, have a glass of French brandy. You are talking like a fool! Now pull yourself together and tell me what's happened." She poured out a generous measure and stood over Sarah while she drank it. "Now tell me about the poster. What did it say?"

"I didn't read it myself—the writing was too much for

me. But I listened to a big old fellow dressed in black. He was reading it aloud to a crowd . . .''

"Yes, yes. Get on with it, Sarah. What did it say?''

Sarah looked hurt at the interruption.

"It said . . . it said I attacked Lady Gilbourne's nurse, and that I killed her, and that you collapsed with shock and that your mind was unhinged!'' She faltered, and then whispered, ''m'lady, I'm frightened. I never thought he would do such a . . .''

Fancy interrupted her.

"Curse him for the dog he is! Mr. Somers had the measure of him. We must get away from this place. If he should find either of us, we could both disappear for ever.''

"M'lady, what shall we do?''

Fancy paced the floor, sometimes exploding into unladylike oaths against Sir Timothy, while Sarah sat and wept quietly. Fancy looked despondently at her. Plainly the little fool was going to be a liability and, although Fancy loved her, she wondered whether it would be wiser to find somewhere or someone she could hide with. Then her imagination took over. If Sarah was found . . . ! No, she must keep Sarah with her, and protect her. It was her fault Sarah was in danger from Sir Timothy, and it was up to her to make amends. She would see Sarah was comfortable if it was the last thing she did!

Her mind was made up. She would venture forth to visit Mr. Somers and make arrangements to meet Captain Hawkins. She could never show her face in society again, so she must disappear. And where better than on her own ship? She and Sarah would go to sea.

They stole out like two fugitives. Fancy was wearing one of Sarah's gray homespun gowns, and both were well swathed in shawls, to look like two servant girls going about their business.

Fancy knew full well that Sir Timothy would be paying his spies to look out for her. If he could find her and once more incarcerate her in that attic . . . She shuddered at the thought. No. They must get away!

Mr. Somers was worried. He, too, had read the announcement and looked gravely at Fancy.

"Are you so sure Mrs. Snell was still alive when you locked her in that garret?"

"As far as I was aware. According to Billy she was stupid with gin and in a disgusting state. But she was snoring, I swear."

"Then something must have happened when Sir Timothy or one of his men let her out. I understand Sir Timothy returned the following day at noon."

"He would most likely come straight upstairs to me. He usually did so, to gloat and remind me that I was a prisoner and that he was free to go to his women at any time."

"Just so. M'lady, I think you must leave." He stopped. There was a commotion outside the window. Mr. Somers left his desk and went to look. He frowned and then turned to Fancy." It appears I am to have the honor of a visit from your husband." He rang his little brass bell, and his clerk came in from the outer room. "Quickly, Thomas. Take these two ladies to my bedchamber, and then return to whatever task you were doing. No one has been here this morning. You understand?" The thin white-faced man nodded. Without a word he led the way through a side door to Mr. Somers' private apartments.

"Wait in there, ma'am, until called for. You may even get under the bed if you wish." He grinned and looked younger. "I don't know what all this is about. But I'll not let anyone come snooping, and that's a promise." The door shut quietly behind him and they heard him running down the stairs, and then there was a long silence.

Sarah crouched down on Mr. Somers' easy chair, but Fancy could only peer nervously out of the window, where she could see the familiar coach of her husband. The two women stayed there some twenty minutes, until Fancy saw Sir Timothy run across the pavement to the coach and shout something to the coachman. He was scowling. Fancy shivered. So it had been the coachman who had led Sir Timothy to Mr. Somers! Why else should he call here, of all places? The coachman had noticed more than Fancy had realized!

After another ten minutes or so, Thomas came up and beckoned them out.

"Mr. Somers says it is safe for you to come down now. Would you care for some wine?"

"Thank you, I do feel a little faint, and so does my maid."

"Then please go straight to the drawing room. Mr. Somers will be with you in a few minutes."

Mr. Somers came bustling in, angered by Sir Timothy's haughtiness and rudeness.

"He actually doubted my word when I told him I did not know where you were! He made threats!" He sat down and waited for his clerk to bring the wine. "And pour yourself one," he said irritably to Thomas. "There's no formality here. I trust Thomas like a son."

Thomas bowed, and, taking a glass, sat down beside Sarah. Mr. Somers sipped his wine and then looked at them all.

"Well now, has anyone any suggestions as to how m'lady is to make her way to London?" He looked at Thomas as being the one with most ideas.

"Mail coach, Mr. Somers? Two booked seats and then catch it just before it moves out?"

Mr. Somers shook his head. "They'll be watching the stage. Sir Timothy will have his men stationed everywhere. Two women traveling together will be suspected. No, we shall have to use more guile than that. Sir Timothy is determined to find you, m'lady. I don't want to frighten you, but . . ."

"Mr. Somers, you need not tell me what kind of man he is. I know. Can we borrow Thomas? Perhaps if Sarah and he travel as man and wife, we may get away."

"And what about yourself, m'lady?"

"If Sarah and Thomas travel in your dog cart for part of the way, they could catch the stage at Sevenoaks and, if you are willing, Thomas could escort us to London."

"But I repeat—what about yourself?"

"I could catch the stage from Tunbridge dressed as a newly bereaved widow. A black veil and a handkerchief will keep all respectable passengers at bay. Do you have an old carpetbag, Mr. Somers? I think I could bluff my way through."

"And Thomas and Sarah would meet you at Sevenoaks?"

"Yes, Mr. Somers. I think we could manage that."

"And then you would seek out Captain Hawkins?"

"Yes. I think I know where to find him."

"Very well, m'lady. I have misgivings about the whole sorry venture, but I don't doubt that Sir Timothy means business. I do not fancy your chances if you stay here—"

"We must go as soon as possible. I understand the plague is abating a little. Do you think the coaches will travel into London?"

"Ah! That is a further problem. I understand the Tunbridge coach is pulling in at the King's Head at Greenwich. The coaches are not going into the heart of London . . ."

"Greenwich would do well for us. I will seek out Captain Hawkins—he is sure to have lodgings somewhere about there. There are not all that many good inns for a man of his kind to stay at. If he is ready to embark I doubt if he will stay in London and risk meeting some of his Court friends. Captain Hawkins and Sir Montagu Hawkins keep their lives well apart. It would not be well if the King's friends knew he traded with the enemy and dealt in slaves!" She laughed a gay reckless laugh. "I wonder what my friends and enemies would say if they knew that Fancy Gilbourne was considering going to sea with a slaver!"

CHAPTER THIRTEEN

And so on the first of September, the stagecoach from Tunbridge brought in three well-disguised passengers. Sarah and Thomas had not wasted their journey together. They were holding hands as the coach trundled into Greenwich. Fancy, well aware that there was an attraction between them, pretended to be asleep. She had no desire to watch a budding romance. It hurt to see someone else palpitating with happiness, and she knew by the look in Sarah's eyes that she cared for Thomas.

Thomas was gentle but forthright. Fancy wondered if he would indeed look after Sarah, even marry her. She sighed. It was too early for them to think of marriage, and soon Sarah would be on board ship, perhaps never to see England again. Besides, Thomas was plainly not a man of sudden action. It would never occur to him to do anything on impulse. That would be his lawyer's training . . .

Nonethless, Thomas was visibly disturbed when he said goodbye at the inn they chose to stay at. Sarah's eyes brimmed, but she did not lose control. Fancy thanked him for his help and thrust a guinea into his hand. He flushed but accepted the money, and then she left the two alone to take their leave of one another.

Her mind now returned to how she would locate Captain Hawkins. They must find someone who could direct them to his lodging. She slipped into the taproom of the inn, which was foggy with smoke. The floor was sanded, and it was with difficulty that she passed between the customers. One man grinned up at her and caught her arm.

"Hey! A new wench, I see. Come, fill up my friends' tankards and my own, and then tell us your name. Is it Nell or Sue . . . or Moll? You would make a sweet Moll!"

Fancy shook herself free from him.

"Take your hands off me, you big oaf!" Her eyes flashed sparks at him.

"Oho! The wench has spirit. Do you know who you are talking to?"

"No, and I don't care. Out of my way, rinse-pot, I want to see the landlord."

The man sprang to his feet, face twisting.

"Who are you to call me rinse-pot? No woman talks to me that way. I'll have you know that anyone who falls foul of Pete the Pimp bears the scars for life!" He grabbed Fancy by the hair and swung her around. She screamed, and Sarah and Thomas ran in through the door. Thomas made a great effort to wrest her from the sweaty drunken man, but suddenly Pete the Pimp had a knife in his hand and Thomas fell back bleeding with a cut in the arm.

Fancy's hand clawed out behind her and struggling to free herself, grabbed a bottle by the neck. Pete never knew what hit him . . .

Fancy stood and faced the suddenly quiet crowd, eyes blazing.

"Now, you drunken swabs, who can tell me where I can find Black Patch Hawkins?"

The men froze and then someone let out a long gasp.

"Caw! She's Black Patch's woman!"

Everyone stared at her in silence. Fancy felt as if she was being stripped naked.

"Well? A shilling for the man who will take us there!"

A man stepped forward.

"I'll take you, but it's a long walk through roundabout narrow lanes. The plague is still raging on the waterfront. It will cost you a guinea."

"A guinea? I'll not pay that!"

"Please yourself!" The man shrugged and made to turn away.

"Wait a minute. How do I know I can trust you?"

"You don't. But a guinea is a lot of money . . . and I don't care for Pete."

"Very well, I'll give you a guinea. What's your name?"

The black eyes danced.

"Why? I'm only doing you a service. You don't need to know my name for that."

"All the same I would like to know who I'm trusting myself to."

She faced him and liked what she saw. This dark tanned man of medium height looked all muscle. She liked the hint of dark curly hair growing in a tuft under his Adam's apple. She smiled, and he smiled back. He took her hand in his.

"First you'd best attend to your friend." She started. She had clean forgotten poor Thomas. She hurried to the corner of the room where he was. Sarah was on her knees staunching the blood.

"Is he badly hurt, Sarah?"

Sarah looked up at Fancy. Suddenly she had grown haggard.

"A ragged flesh wound, m'l . . ." and then she stopped and looked guilty. "Sorry, ma'am . . ."

"I'm Mrs. Gill," Fancy whispered angrily, "and don't forget it. How is he?"

"The landlord is finding something that will do as a stretcher. He will have him carried upstairs to a spare room. He will not be able to travel tonight. Oh, ma'am, we cannot leave him to journey back alone." Sarah looked quite distraught. Fancy considered her carefully.

"Do you want to go back with him? Have you the courage to stay with him and risk being caught by Sir Timothy?"

"Oh, ma'am, I don't want to leave you . . . but I think we love each other! Thomas has already asked me to stay. I refused him, but my heart is heavy."

"Then stay . . . and go back to Tunbridge with him. And, Sarah, remember. I'll be praying for you."

"You talk as if you will not be returning here. You'll come back tonight?"

"Perhaps. Perhaps not. It all depends on Captain Hawkins."

"Then, then this could be goodbye?" Sarah looked as if she was on the brink of tears.

"Yes, Sarah. It could be goodbye. But I'll be back someday. If you have any messages for me, go to Mr. Somers. He will get in touch with us, somehow. And, Sarah, watch out for Charles. I may not be able to find him. If I do not, keep in touch with him until my return."

"But what of Sir Timothy?"

"Keep out of his way, but stay in touch with my aunt. She will tell you how he is. And be sure and send me a message now and again."

The dark man who had been standing in the background cleared his throat.

"If you're wanting to find Captain Hawkins, you'd best come now, or he'll be too drunk to know what he's doing. He has a way with women, and when he's foxed he's not particular . . ."

Fancy followed him out into the night. The alley he turned into smelled of decayed refuse and human excreta, and Fancy had to be careful not to put a foot into the overflowing channel, or trail her skirt in the mud. The journey seemed endless, and it was as if the man deliberately took her by the most winding route in order to confuse her sense of direction. She began to feel alarm.

"How much longer is it? I thought you said it wasn't very far?"

"We are keeping out of the way of Pete and his friends. If he catches you—or me—we could both end up in the river." They walked on in silence.

At last they arrived at a narrow wooden house, tumbledown and without light of any kind.

"This is it. Now give me the guinea."

"Not so fast. How do I know it is the right house?"

"Ring the bell pull and see."

She did so, and the dull sinister sound of an iron bell

rang faintly inside. For a while nothing happened, and then the bolts were pulled back and the door opened a crack.

"Who's there? Who would disturb a poor body at night?"

"Is this Captain Hawkins' house?"

"Aye, he lodges with me now and then."

"Then tell him he's got a visitor and I want to see him now, at once!"

The old woman laughed.

"I'll not be telling him tonight. He's gone aboard his ship."

"He's not sailing tonight?" Consternation made her shake.

"No. He's supervising his cargo. He's been commissioned by the King, all because of this war . . ."

"Then I'll find him on board? How do I find the ship?"

"You'll not get aboard this night! He'll have his women with him and won't take kindly to visitors."

Fancy turned back to her guide, sick at heart.

"I must go back to the inn."

"It will cost you another guinea."

Fancy rounded on the man furiously.

"Curse you! Wait until I tell Black Patch how you have treated me!"

The man shrugged.

"What will you tell him? You do not know my name. And if you go back to the inn, Pete will be waiting for you." He grinned unpleasantly. "So I would not advise you to quarrel with me. Is there anywhere else I can take you?" His teeth appeared very white against the tanned skin. Fancy saw in him a sudden resemblance to a wolf, and shivered. Then she had an idea.

"Will you take me to a house in Curzon Street?"

The man looked at her in disbelief.

"Are you mad, or are you some fine gentleman's doxie? In any case I'll not take you. It is much too far."

"Five guineas if you take me!"

The man hesitated.

"How is it you have so much money? Been robbing some poor devil?"

"Mind your own business," said Fancy coldly. "Do you want to earn the money or don't you?"

"Well. . ." the man considered and then shrugged. "I might as well. 'Tis easily earned and you'll not take off and leave me, I'll see to that." He grinned wolfishly into her face. "Any quaint ideas about running off in the dark and I'll make sure you regret it!" His hand ran suggestively up and down her arm.

"Take your hand off me. If you want to earn good money you can help me. You could have ten women for the price I will pay you."

"If you have the money."

"Listen to this if you don't believe me," Fancy jingled the leather bag deep inside her skirt pocket.

"It sounds like gold . . ."

"It is. Now lead the way."

They seemed to travel for hours, picking their way through winding streets and narrow passages, but as they walked Fancy was busy formulating her plan. If she could get inside the house in Curzon Street the servants would be sure to tell her where Sir Timothy had taken Charles. It was her only chance and she was willing to take it, for tomorrow she must find Black Patch and persuade him to take her to sea with him. If she could find Charles—the thought made her pulse leap—she would take him with her.

At last, she seemed to recognize certain landmarks. They were not so very far away from her old home. The night would soon be over. Even now there was light in the sky. She heard the stranger swear and then watched him stop and gaze long and earnestly towards the glow in the sky.

"What is it?" Fancy spoke fearfully.

"I don't know, but I smell wood smoke. I'm damned if I'll take a step further. You give me the money you promised me, and then I'm for getting back to the docks."

"But you promised to escort me all the way!"

"Damn you, woman! You're near enough to make no odds. You can run the rest of the way yourself. I tell you I smell wood smoke, and the wind is coming from that direction. There is a fire somewhere this night and I'll not be caught in it. I've been press-ganged before in fighting fire. Those army bastards can put out their own damned fires! Give me the money!" He caught her wrist and twisted.

Fancy gave a little scream and then thrust her free hand into her skirt pocket.

"Very well, damn you. I told you I had the money. Here, take what is yours," and she thrust the purse under his nose. He laughed and let go of her wrist.

"So you were telling the truth! I'll just take the five guineas and be off. Thank you, my pretty miss. I hope we meet again sometime." With that he flung the purse back at her and turning on his heels loped off in the direction they had come.

For a moment Fancy was daunted. She had never before been all on her own in the city. But taking comfort in the fact that she was so near, she set off with a will.

The house was in darkness when she finally reached it. For a moment, emotion overwhelmed her. So much had happened since she had lived there with Timothy . . . She used the knocker with resolution. Someone must hear her!

But it was quite some time before shuffling footsteps opened the grille and asked who was there. The old butler opened the door fast enough when she made herself known.

"M'lady, whatever are you doing here like this? Sir Timothy told us you were ill at Gilbourne."

"Yes, yes. Just let me in. I must speak with you."

As she stepped inside, relief flooded over her and she took no notice of the strange looks the butler gave her as he noted the poor gown and shawl. Remembering the talk he had heard of Lady Gilbourne's madness, he moved away from her, suddenly frightened.

"M'lady, if you would but come upstairs to your bed-chamber, I could find refreshment for you. Sir Timothy is at Gilbourne, but young Master Charles . . ."

"Master Charles?" Fancy broke in. "What about Master Charles? Is he here?"

"Yes, m'lady. A Mrs. Emma Judd brought him here. I understand there has been a fire at the school, and Mrs. Judd is by way of being the school ma'am," he said quickly, catching Fancy's questioning look. "She was very shocked and upset, for part of her establishment has burned to the ground. All the children, I understand, were taken to safety."

"Then I must go to him. He is quite well?"

"Yes, m'lady, although he cried a little and seemed very frightened of the good lady. Not a person who should have charge of children, I opine."

Fancy listened no further, but ran through the hall and up the stairs to the nursery suite. There, she hovered over the little trundle bed where Charles lay sleeping and took in every detail of his face. Seeing the traces of tears, she was filled with a slow burning anger against Sir Timothy. Dear Charles, she wanted to kiss him and smooth the slight furrow on his brow. The little sleeping maid who shared the young master's room stirred and opened her eyes, but Fancy put a finger to her lip and the maid lay back and watched as Fancy stole out of the room.

She went to her room, which was nearby, and lay down on the huge bed, too tired to undress. An instinct told her to be alert and ready. The glare in the sky was unsettling, and she wanted to be prepared to move at a moment's notice.

Cook brought food, and she ate and felt better. Then she sent for one of Sir Timothy's coveted bottles of Madeira, thinking she might as well avail herself of some of the good things of life while she had the chance.

As she lay back on the bed, she plotted the next step. She wanted to be on the dockside well before dawn. She must get aboard before the business of the day began . . . and after those women had gone. Then she would see Black Patch, and she would take Charles with her! They would make a new life together, a good life

Had she not her own fortune to fall back on?

Only one uneasy thought went through her mind. Sir Timothy would leave no stone unturned to find the boy. But she shrugged the thought away and lay dreaming of a golden future . . .

Suddenly she was aware of someone shaking her by the shoulder. Realizing she must have dozed, she opened her eyes and saw a frightened butler.

"What is it?" She was confused and could hardly gather her senses.

"M'lady, there is much shouting and the fire is nearer. It seems that the whole of this side of London burns."

Suddenly Fancy was very wide awake. Throwing back the cover, she raced to the tall window and looked to the east. The whole of the horizon was a flickering orange glare. She could see the clouds of smoke hanging in the air and there was a strange hungry licking sound intermingled with screams and yells, as if some mad dog was on the loose. She turned away from the window, her face drained white.

"Mother of God! The whole world is going up in flames! What on earth is that noise?"

"George, the youngest footman, has just come in, m'lady. He says the rabble are out looting. Many houses are burning, and they say the militia are out blowing up buildings in the path of the fire. M'lady, I think we should leave the house."

They stared at one another.

"Oh my God! Will I get to the dock? I must get to the dock!"

"It would be madness, m'lady. It would be better to go out of town to the heath. I have taken the liberty of ordering the coachman to pack the valuables."

"Good. But I must go to the dock." She took two or three steps up and down the room, distracted and uncertain. "I must run and waken Charles . . ."

"He is already being dressed by Rosie. The other servants have gone, m'lady. I couldn't hold them back. I can't blame them. I want to go myself."

"Then do so, and thank you for what you have done. Do you think the coachman will be able to take me to the dock?"

The old man shook his head.

"I'm sure I don't know, m'lady. George says the roads are jammed with broken-down coaches overloaded with furniture and valuables. Horses have been cut free and the common people are fighting for possession of them. There have been many foul deeds done this night, m'lady and there will be many more deaths before this fire abates."

But Fancy's resolution had returned. She pulled on her cloak and ran to the nursery where Charles was just finishing a bowl of bread and milk. He was sobbing quietly, but when he saw Fancy he held out fat little arms and clung to her as if he would never let her go.

"There, there, my little man. We are going for a ride in the coach. Now don't be frightened. Mama will look after you."

Rosie looked at her, twisting her apron in her hands.

"M'lady, I want to go to my mother. She has three small bairns to look after, and I'm afraid the house might be in the path of the fire. I want to go . . ."

"Then go, Rosie. Thank you for looking after Master Charles. And Rosie . . ." She delved down into her pocket and came up with two gold coins. "Here. I hope you find your family safe."

The girl pocketed the coins. There were tears in her eyes.

"Thank you, m'lady, and I hope you . . ." She bit her lip and then burst out. "We did hear rumors. They said you were ill, but I knew different. God go with you, m'lady, and the young master." She swooped down and kissed the staring Charles on the cheek. Tears sprang to her eyes, and then she ran from the room.

For a moment Fancy felt deserted. Then she picked up the heel of the loaf left on the nursery table and tucked it into her shawl. Then picking up Charles, she made her way swiftly down the stairs, only stopping when she passed her bedchamber to take what was left of the bottle of Madeira. It could come in useful.

The coach was waiting and the horses snorted and pawed the ground nervously, as if they were aware of fire. Casting a hasty look around, Fancy was just in time to hear a muffled roar and see a cascade of sparks flung high in the air. The smell of wood smoke was unmistakable now, and with alarm she saw that the fire was much nearer. At times, when the blaze was fanned by the rising wind, she could see figures silhouetted in the flames. The fire was swiftly eating everything in its path. It was time to be off!

They wasted no time in moving away from the house. Fancy did not look back. She had no regrets at losing her home. Her mind now was solely on escape.

"As fast as you can, Billings. How long will it take to get to the docks?"

The coachman shook his head.

"I'll do my best, m'lady, but you might have to get down and walk. There's no knowing what we'll find. Everyone is going the other way. I daren't even trust these horses . . ."

"Do what you can, Billings. It is most important."

But it was to no avail. The streets became meaner and narrower, and howling dark figures frightened the horses. Men, women and even children were heaving great loads on their backs and struggling with smaller children or animals.

And then a figure ran through the crowds tearing off his clothes, eyes staring with madness. "Confess your sins, confess your sins, all ye sinners. This is the might of the Lord and he shall smite . . ." The dreadful words died on the wind as he wove his way nearly naked through the crowds. But the shrieking and the commotion upset the horses, and the coachman cursed and strove to quieten the animals. Charles cried out and clung to Fancy, and she screamed up to the coachman. "What is to do up there? What is the matter? Can we not proceed?"

The coachman gasped and swore and gripped the reins.

"We're jammed in the pack, m'lady, and there's every chance of the coach being turned over by this mob . . ."

Fear hit Fancy. Already she could see dark sweaty creatures looking greedily at the coach and its precious load. One man tried to claw his way in and grab her carpetbag. She knocked his hand viciously with the wine bottle, and he yelped and dropped back amongst the crowd.

"How far are we from the docks?" she yelled above the hubbub.

"Just half a dozen streets away, m'lady. If we could but get an even passage through."

"Then I shall take Master Charles and walk. You take the coach and go to your home. You come from the country, I take it?"

"Yes, m'lady, in Chelsea. But you cannot go alone."

"Yes, I can. Everyone is going the other way. You take charge of the horses and the coach, and do not stop for anyone. Now if you would but let us down."

The coach stopped at a cross roads and Fancy peered into the gloom. The coachman pointed with his whip.

That way lies the docks. God go with you, m'lady."

"And you, too." She clutched the frightened Charles to her. "Come on, my brave little man, and I'll show you a fine ship that will take us away from the fire." She started to walk, pulling Charles behind her. They moved along easily enough. Most of those rushing the other way stared ahead in a dazed fashion, hardly seeing her and the child. Only the looters gave them a second glance and passed on. But then, Fancy stopped. Somehow she had wandered into a square—she must have missed the turning to the dockside. Dazed, she tried to take her bearings, and it was then she saw a party of sailors led by an officer. There was a rattle of muskets and, above the din, the sound of orders being given. Perhaps one of the men would show her the way to the dock . . .

But the sailors were too busy. They were trying to counteract the fire by clearing a windbreak, and were furiously tearing down the old, shaky houses along the sides of the square. This was one of the oldest parts of the city, and the wooden houses were dry as tinder from the summer's drought.

She heard the crash of a falling wall and knew she was in danger if she stayed a moment longer. She hurried on, and then someone took her by the arm. She stopped, and there was Caleb watching her. A strange new Caleb with an unruly black beard and an oiled pigtail. But they were still Caleb's eyes piercing her through and through.

"Fanny! What are you doing here?" She looked at him with incredulity. Was she dreaming? But it was Caleb!

She fell into his arms, and Caleb held them both. His eyes took in Charles and he understood.

"Caleb," she sobbed. "I must get to the dock, and find the *Emma-Jane*. If I can get aboard, I can get away from Sir Timothy. He wants to keep Charles . . ."

Caleb looked about him. His officer was nowhere to be seen.

"I know where the old tub is. Hide in this doorway for a moment while I see what is going on. I'll be back."

For a few agonizing minutes Fancy thought Caleb had deserted her, but soon he returned, grinning.

"That bastard will not trouble us! I've just hit him over the head with a pole. I owed him that. Come on, let's get away from here." He picked up Charles, and Fancy clung to him while he used his free arm to clear a path.

They turned into a lane too narrow for coaches, and the sound of fire became louder. Fancy gasped as sudden flames seemed to shoot to the sky a short way ahead.

"It's too late, we're not going to make it. We're going to be burned alive!"

"Shut up and save your wind for running. This lane leads directly on to the wharf. I know an old sailorman with a boat. I guarantee he'll not leave his mooring until he has to, and then only if someone will pay him. Come on . . . run!"

He seized her arm, and they staggered and stumbled their way to the dockside. The air was thick with smoke and caught their throats. Fancy's eyes felt gritty, and she could taste the smoke. Charles' face was grimy with soot and she knew she too was streaked with black grime and stank of wood smoke.

But here the press of people was worse. Families clamored to be taken on board the small boats and ferried out to the middle of the Thames. Men were holding up watches, jewelry and leather purses to bribe the boatmen. Here and there women were shrieking to be allowed to join their families, but the boats were already overcrowded and loaded down to the water line.

Caleb pulled Fancy along to where the big ships were moored. Some of His Majesty's ships were already taking passengers aboard.

"The King is out there somewhere, directing operations," he yelled into Fancy's ear. "And I hear the Duke of York's regiments are in the city to stop looting. They are shooting looters on sight! Come on, I think old Ben Gear's boat is down there!"

Fancy stumbled to her knees.

"I can't go on! I haven't got the breath."

"Get up, you whining bitch! he said savagely. "You're not giving in now!" and she felt a vicious blow to the cheek. She gasped, and struggled to her feet, blind rage giving her new strength.

"You brute! I'm not finished yet! Go on, and I'll follow. I'll show you which of us is the stronger! You're no better than a—"

Caleb gave a great peal of laughter.

"That's the Fanny I used to know! Fighting mad and loving it! Come on, if Ben's not about we'll take his boat." But Ben was there, blind drunk in the boat, his hand holding an empty stone demijohn. Caleb kicked him with his foot, but he lay still.

"The old fool has been looting some inn. God knows what has been going on in these parts. Come on, get in the boat and we'll stand out in the river."

"Can you not row out to the *Emma-Jane* now?"

"What? And put myself into the hands of Captain Hawkins? You must think I'm mad!"

"But what shall we do? We cannot stay in an open boat all night."

"Why not? You know you will be safe with me . . ." and laughing, he shot her a look that made her stomach turn to water. His hand came out and touched her ankle, and she smiled, wetting her bottom lip with a soft pink tongue. How long it had been since she'd had a man!

CHAPTER FOURTEEN

Old Ben had been looting on a grand scale. In the bottom of his boat they found a small keg of French brandy, and another demijohn of beer, several flat bread-cakes and half a boiled ham.

"What are we going to do with him?" Fancy asked cautiously. "He'll hardly be the guest I should like on this little trip."

Caleb eyed her suggestively.

"I'll kick him overboard if you like."

"We'll put him ashore where he'll come to no hurt, farther along the riverbank. There's no risk of the fire down there."

"Poor old devil deserves a chance. He's stocked up the boat for us."

Quietly, Caleb pushed the boat out into the river and weaving in and out of other craft, made for the higher reaches of the river where they anchored among the reeds.

It took Caleb, strong man as he was, quite a long time to lift Ben over the side and carry him to the grassy bank. Grinning, he left him half a demijohn of ale and a bread-cake.

"That's more than the old devil deserves," he muttered as he jumped aboard and steered the boat into midstream.

Meanwhile Fancy fed the drooping Charles, who leaned heavily against her. His eyes were already tightly shut when she laid him down to sleep, covering him with her gray cloak to protect him from the night wind sweeping up the river.

And then she turned to Caleb, and gave him all her attention. They had supped well on the ham and sampled the brandy, and now she was feeling reckless. Grateful for the lull in the storm, she snuggled up to him and together they watched the flames leaping along the skyline.

"How long do you think the fire will last now?" she whispered.

He shrugged.

"It could burn all tomorrow and the next day. There doesn't seem to be much of London left. The fire's swept a long way since I found you. I wonder what happened to your coach?"

"You mean you saw me leave the coach?"

"Of course. I was with the rest of the sailors on picket duty. I followed when I could get away, but I knew my officer was coming after me. That was why I went back." For a moment his mouth was drawn back to show his strong white teeth, and Fancy was reminded of some vicious beast of prey. She recoiled. Caleb would be an unforgiving enemy. But quickly the vicious mask dissolved into his ordinary self, and he laughed. "He'll not torture any more young boys, I've seen to that!"

"Do you think you killed him?" Fancy's breath caught in her throat.

"I don't think—I know! It will be put down to timber falling during the fire. I'm not going back. I'm going to find my kinfolk . . ."

He pulled her to him, and taking her long black hair, he twisted it in his hands and held her head so he could kiss her mouth.

"Why talk about the future when you are sitting so close? The last time we met you were finished with me, but I have a distinct feeling . . ." His hand ran around her breasts, pressing and kneading. She quivered under his touch. "God! I haven't had a woman since they clapped me in jail! I'll get Sir Timothy for that someday! But enough of grievances. Let's live for the present. Kiss me, Fanny, and let me see you still want me."

Heart thumping, Fancy obeyed. She tried to hold herself back, but her nature betrayed her, and when she felt his warm lips on hers she thrust herself into his arms and pulled him close.

The kiss seemed to last for an eternity, and Fancy thought she was drowning in his sensuality. Then he raised his head and her mouth reached out for his, grudging the moments spent apart.

"Hey! Not so fast. Do you want me to spend myself before we've even touched? I said I hadn't had a woman . . ." But Fancy did not listen. She only groaned, conscious of her own need . . .

It was one of the strangest, eeriest nights of her life. While the boat rocked gently at its moorings, and Charles slept the sleep of the dead, they drank freely from the keg of brandy and loved each other to excess. Time and time again Fancy begged for mercy. She was replete and satisfied, her hunger abated for a time, but Caleb was insatiable, his manhood impossible to appease.

When dawn broke, Caleb lay asleep in her arms, and she, bruised and spent, smiled in the thin light of dawn. This dirty sweaty man was hers, her mate. Unscrupulous and cruel as he undoubtedly was, he was her other half—even though she knew their destiny was to be apart.

Somehow she knew it did not matter. One night of perfect love with him was worth a hundred with any other man. Others only pleased her body, but Caleb pleased her body and soul. This passion was something she had only ever known with him, and yet—and yet, something told her he was not the man she was looking for. She looked down at his sleeping form, and something deep inside her rejected him.

And then he was awake and reaching out for her, and she lived only in the present. Destiny and puzzling premonitions were thrust to the back of her mind, and her body thrilled again to him as they lay closely entwined.

But later, when the sun had come up and they could see the desolation over the smoking ruins of the city, everything changed between them. They were two fugitives again, planning their own escape, he to his family and she to the ship that was half hers.

She awakened Charles, who for a while looked bewildered at finding himself in an open boat.

"Mama, I want to go home!"

"There now. Eat your bread and meat and take some of this nice ale and you will feel better."

"Mama, I don't like boats."

"We'll be out of it soon. Have patience, Charles."

"I don't like being dirty. And you are dirty, too. You smell of smoke!"

"We'll soon have you bathed and clean, my love. Just eat your breakfast and soon we shall be on board that big ship yonder."

"Why the big ship, Mama? Can't we go back to our house?"

"Be quiet, my love, and eat your breakfast."

"But, mama, I don't like . . ."

"Do as your mother tells you!" Caleb's voice broke in on the altercation, and Charles drew back, frightened.

"I don't like him, Mama. He is too rough . . ."

Caleb's hand shot out and caught Charles on the side of the head. The boy's mouth trembled but he sat still, too shocked even to cry.

"Quiet, little coxcomb! And do as I tell you."

Charles sat silent and still.

Fanny watched and listened, and did not like what she saw. Caleb did not particularly care for Charles, and Charles certainly did not like him. Even if Caleb was willing to go away with her, Charles would still be a problem.

Caleb rowed to the *Emma-Jane* and, catching a rope, hailed her.

"Hey! You on the watch up there, is Captain Hawkins aboard?"

A bleary face wearing a wooly cap peered overboard.

"Who wants to know?"

"I've brought a lady with a child to see him."

"Not another woman! He had three aboard last night, and some rare junketings there were."

"Is he still aboard?"

"No. He had himself rowed down river to the Mermaid."

"The *what* did you say?"

"The Mermaid. Haven't you heard of the Mermaid Inn? The fire passed it by and the Cap'n's gone looking for his mate and some of his men. We've got to have a full crew to sail day after tomorrow. Do you want to sign on?"

"Not me, mate. I know the conditions on Captain Black Patch Hawkins' ships."

"We're sailing under the King's orders this time. It will be better pay!"

"So *you* say. I beg to differ. Everyone knows the King is scraping the barrel to find money for this war!"

"You sound smarter than the usual run of sailor. I'd keep clear, if I was you. Cap'n was talking about kidnapping men if he can't get 'em by other means."

"How do you come to stay with him?"

"Because I know which side the bread's buttered. Besides, I'm wanted ashore."

Caleb laughed and waved a friendly hand.

"I'll make for the Mermaid, mate. Good luck to you."

"And you, too, mate," called back the sailor.

The boat turned downstream and Caleb rowed easily, while Fancy watched his brawny shoulders at work. No doubt tomorrow or the next day the memory of them would cause a pulsing and she would ache for him, but now she was at peace.

She shaded her eyes from the morning sun and looked at the devastation. Black smoke still rose lazily to the sky, and in the far distance she could see the fire still raging. With a start, she realized that the blaze must have reached Sir Timothy's town house by now. It was probably burned to the ground . . . but she did not care. She and the boy were safe.

A short while later Caleb was mooring the boat to the small quay that ran down to the river from the Mermaid Inn. It was a waterman's inn for sure, and someone was bound to know where Captain Hawkins was.

The taproom was full of sailors and their women. Even a fire such as had never been seen before had not deterred the land-thirsty sailors. Many had watched the swift licking flames with indifference. It was not their problem. Others, the looters and despoilers of women, had disappeared into the throng and come back with mysterious bundles.

When Caleb asked for Captain Hawkins, the landlord's eyes narrowed and he jerked a thumb toward his parlor.

"But he's got a visitor. You'll have to wait. Can I get anything for you and the woman?"

"Is there anywhere this lady can wait? I must be going. I have business of my own to see to."

"Aye. She and the child can wait in the kitchen. This way, mistress." He opened a door for Fancy, but she clutched Caleb's arm.

"So soon, Caleb? Can you not wait until I see Black Patch?"

"No. 'Tis better this way. I have no love for him or he for me, and if a quarrel broke out here I wouldn't stand a chance."

"Then it's goodbye again, Caleb. I hope you find your family." Their eyes locked.

"Hurry up, lady," scowled the landlord. "I've got to get back to my customers!"

Caleb turned on him.

"Get the hell back to them, then!" he snarled.

"All right, mate. There's no need for that! Go in the kitchen when you're ready," and he sidled away.

Fancy held up a trembling hand and stroked Caleb's bushy beard.

"I like the beard, Caleb. And I liked your loving. Thank you for last night."

"And thank you, Fanny Gilbourne. It was like old times. You never forgot all those tricks I showed you. You're good, Fanny, you'll get on in this world!" He touched her lips lightly, and then laughed and squeezed her breasts, and then he was off back to the boat.

Fancy watched him go with mixed feelings, as Charles clutched her hand. She sighed. It had been good to be plain Fanny again for a little while.

"Mama, I've seen that man before. Who is he, Mama? I don't like him and I'm glad he has gone."

"Only an old friend, my love. I don't think you will see him again." Something in her heart echoed the words. She did not want to see him again.

Fancy paced the old kitchen, watched by a gawking serving wench in a torn dimity gown. Her hands were red from washing clothes in hot soda water. Now she was peeling turnips into a huge black pot slung over the open fire. Charles watched her intently and Fancy brooded on the thought that she too could have spent her days thus!

She smiled at the girl and looked around the black-beamed kitchen. A dog occupied the cage by the fire, ready to walk his wheel if a joint of meat was spitting over the fire for roasting. It was the dog's job to turn the spit mechanism. As reward he was given the tibits and leftovers.

Fancy walked toward him to tickle him behind the ears, but as she moved her hand he growled. This was no kitchen pet! Charles followed her and watched.

"Mama, why are we here? I like our kitchen at home better. I wish I was at Gilbourne . . ."

Fancy smiled apologetically at the girl.

"My son is young. He is not used to unfamiliar places."

"He's right, ma'am. Sometimes I can fair be sick in this place. And the flies—they cover everything. I think the little boy can smell a pig's head we had hanging. We cut it down yesterday, covered in fat juicy maggots. It made you sick to see it!"

Fancy closed her eyes at the thought. She had nearly asked for a pot of small beer for herself and Charles, but the smell made her change her mind. Surely they would soon be out of this terrible place?

"Can we walk in your garden a while? I see through the window that you grow vegetables there."

"Aye, that should be all right. 'Tis not my garden. I only work for the mistress. But she'll not complain if you walk there. It smells better than this kitchen." She grinned and opened a ponderous old door that creaked on old wrought-iron hinges. "It be a mite stiff so rap hard on it when you want to come back in and I'll pull it open from this side. There now, mind the step down. Many's the time the master's fallen down there in his cups. There's a seat under the apple tree yonder if you want to rest."

"Thank you. You are very kind."

The girl blushed and gave a quick bob.

"What is your name?"

"Betsy, ma'am."

"Then thank you again, Betsy, and here's a sixpence for you." Fanny delved into the deep pocket let into her skirt and pulled out one of her remaining coins.

"Coo, sixpence for me! Thank you, ma'am. It's you who are kind. I don't often have money in my hand, the master sees to that. I'll hide this with some more that he doesn't know about. Thank you again."

"Where do you live, Betsy? Is your home safe?"

"My home? Lawks, ma'am, I got no home! The master found me when I was about six and gave me jobs to do around the garden and house, and I lived under the arches of yon bridge. And then when I became old enough, he set me on here. I sleep in the loft above the stable."

"But—but are you never molested? Don't the men . . .?"

"Aye, they try a bit of the old how's-your-father once in a while, but I've a pitchfork handy, and if they try climbing the ladder . . . I stuck a man once and he fell back screaming and broke his bloody neck! That's kept 'em away most-wise since."

"How terrible! Did you get into trouble over it?"

"No. He was a sailor and not of these parts. The master flung him into the river, and when the officers came looking for him, he'd already been found under the pilings of the wharf. The rats had made a mess of him, so nobody was the wiser."

Fancy shuddered. "I think I'll just take Charles for a walk around the garden."

The girl grinned and went back to her turnips.

The garden was long and narrow, and just outside the flagged porch was a small herb garden, lush and overgrown, where sage and thyme plants were now showing yellow. They had passed their best, but the huge borage plants still held the tiny blue blooms used in the making of spiced ale. There were other herbs she recognized— marjoram, lovage, lemon balm, mint and horehound . . . The landlord's good wife must be adept in medicinal herbs, as well as a good cook! Fancy herself could make a good cough mixture from horehound. She looked around for the herb that she took regularly, but there was none to be seen.

And then a thought occurred to her. It had been quite a while since she had made her tisane, and last night— her eyes went black as she remembered their passion. Would she be carrying Caleb's seed once again?

They strolled the paths and Charles, forgetting the ordeal of the previous evening, ran and shouted and played hide-and-seek behind the old gnarled apple trees. Fancy shrugged away her problems. Had she not found Black Patch? Her immediate problem solved, she ran down the paths like a child and gave herself up to the game of tag with her little boy, delighting in his shrieks of joy.

At last they sat down on the old wooden seat flanked by rough hand-cut grass. It had been newly scythed and a sundial covered in green moss stood in the center of it. Fanny held Charles up to explain how it worked, and Charles put out an exploratory finger to trace the sun's shadow. There was a motto cut out in the stone: *Time And Tide Wait For No Man*. Fanny set Charles down slowly, and while he ran off to investigate a forsaken sparrow's nest in the hedgerow, she seated herself and thought about the future.

Suddenly she was disturbed. She had never thought beyond fleeing from Sir Timothy and finding refuge on

Black Patch's ship. But once out to sea, what would happen? She remembered the black slaves. She was putting herself at the mercy of Black Patch. Would he expect her . . . She sighed. Despite her riches, her body was her only true asset . . .

But if she changed her mind and took Charles and left this place before Black Patch came looking for her, where could she go? Sir Timothy loomed like a great black cloud. Wherever she was in England, she would never feel safe with her husband's spies seeking her. No, she must get away!

The day was warm, and while Charles played she dozed in the sun, thinking of Caleb and their night of love. A blackbird trilled and several cheeky sparrows hopped close, seeking crumbs. It was a peaceful interlude, and she enjoyed every minute of it. It was so long since she could while away a morning with her son beside her, careless of time and responsibility.

But then her peace was shattered. The creaking old door opened, and she sighed. It would be Betsy to say she was wanted in the parlor. Captain Hawkins' visitor must have gone. But no—it was Black Patch himself, there on the step, watching her and laughing. He held out his hands and strode forward.

"Fancy Gilbourne! My beautiful sleeping partner!" With a wolfish grin he took her in his arms, kissing her on the mouth before she could struggle to free herself.

"Take your hands off me! How dare you handle me like that before we have even spoken?"

Black Patch laughed so heartily at Fancy's protests that Charles came running and stood open-mouthed at the rough man who was holding his mama.

"You haven't changed. Still the little spitfire! Why should I not kiss you when you come running so eagerly to me. What else do you expect?"

"You could have waited to find out my wants."

"I know you and your wants. Come on, kiss me and show me you are pleased to see me. Well?"

She pulled away from him and stood back adjusting her gown.

"I shall kiss you if I want to! Not because you command it!"

He frowned, and she went on.

"I came because I am in trouble. I want to come aboard the *Emma-Jane* and sail with you."

He raised his eyebrows.

"Do you understand what you are saying?"

Fancy bit her lip.

"I am your partner. I have the right!"

"But you will be the only woman aboard! Have you thought of the mood of the men?"

"I can keep out of their way!"

"And my way? I'll be more of a danger than they. Have you thought of that?"

"I will take that risk. We dealt well enough before."

"But that was different. You were paying a debt for your husband."

"Well? Why should that make a difference?"

"Because my visitor this morning was Sir Timothy. I have just entered into a gentleman's agreement to find and return his son! Sir Timothy suspected you might contact me . . ."

Fancy stared at him aghast.

"But you would never betray me? You would never hand over Charles?"

"Why not? He is Sir Timothy's son, not yours. He wants his son, and you can go to hell!"

"I'll never let Charles go! He's my son!"

Black Patch shrugged.

"He's also Sir Timothy's heir. He wants him back."

Fancy stared at him.

"But—but . . ." Suddenly she was more frightened than she had ever been in her life. "You are not going to take him from me?" Her voice rose to a shriek.

"I'm afraid so, Fancy. And I know you are going to hate me for it."

"Hate you? I'll see you rot in hell before I let you touch one hair on that child's head. You wouldn't dare!"

Charles sensed something was wrong. He whimpered and nestled into Fancy's arms, and she could feel the frightened beat of his heart. She was choked with anger fiercer than any she had ever felt in her life. And she could see in his eyes that Hawkins intended to carry out his pledge.

They glared at each other. The child cowered between them when the door opened again and Fancy was aghast to see Sir Timothy standing on the steps. She looked wildly around for some means of escape, but apart from one tall hedge of hawthorn and brambles, the rest was brick wall. There was no way out.

Sir Timothy stepped leisurely toward her, deliberately pulling off his gauntlets, observing her like a cat watching a mouse.

"So—I was right! You sought him out, just as I said you would. Though I must say, even I never thought you would find him so quickly! Well, madam? What have you to say for yourself?"

Fancy glared at him, and then spat at him. He flushed and made as if to strike her. She gazed back fiercely as if daring him to touch her, and then turned her back, holding Charles tightly.

"Charles is mine! You know he's mine, and I am taking him with me, so please, please, Timothy, have mercy on us and let us disappear from your life! I'll make no demands. I am going away from England forever, so you can marry again and have another heir. Please, let us go!"

"You forget something. Charles, as my official heir, is also heir to part of the Lanbridge estate. His official mother's portion comes to him. The Gilbourne estate could do with a boost! I'll not let him go. Come, Charles, come home to Gilbourne with your father. There's a new puppy waiting for you in the stables."

Charles raised his head and looked with some interest at his father.

"What is its name, Papa? What color is it?"

"He has no name, Charles. He's waiting for you to

give him one. You will like him. He's a red and white spaniel like the King's own spaniels. He's waiting to play with you . . ."

Charles looked up at Fancy and pulled at her hand.

"Come on, mama, let's go home. I like being at Gilbourne. I'll let you play with the puppy, I promise."

Fancy's eyes filled as she looked down at him, and she pulled him to her in a frenzy of heartbreak. He struggled free himself.

"Mama, I'm a big boy now. Please don't cry over me." He looked uncomfortable.

Sir Timothy smiled sardonically at Fancy.

"See! He wants to be rid of the petticoat brigade already! As he says, he's a big boy now, and ready for his first pony. How about it, Charles?"

"A pony, too! Will it be a black one? I'd love a black pony."

"Black it will be . . ."

"Then I'll come. Mama, what are you crying for? You'll come to?"

"No, my love. I'm not coming back to Gilbourne. I'm going away on a big ship . . ."

Charles mouth trembled, and he looked uncertainly from one to another.

"But I *want* you to come . . ."

"No, Charles," Sir Timothy's voice was harsh. "Your mother is not coming to Gilbourne. You are coming alone."

"But I want mama. She promised I could stay with her!" He started to cry. "I don't want your pony or your puppy if I can't have mama!"

Sir Timothy took a step forward and took hold of the child.

"You are coming with me!"

Charles struggled and kicked Sir Timothy's shins, and was soundly cuffed in return. Fancy struggled vainly to wrest him from Sir Timothy, but Captain Hawkins pinned her arms behind her, and she kicked and struggled until she was exhausted.

"You loathsome pig!" she yelled. "How could you do

such a thing? Let me go, I tell you!" But the captain only laughed and held her more tightly. They watched while Sir Timothy subdued the crying boy with a well-aimed blow, but not before Charles had drawn blood on Sir Timothy's face.

"Well, I've got the boy, Hawkins, and you've got the woman. It seems our bargain's complete. Take her and keep her, but don't bring her back to England! When you've tired of her, sell her. You'll get a better price for her than those black bitches you traffic in."

Fancy shuddered at the cold hate in his voice. She stood with face averted, still held by the captain.

"I'll take her, never fear, Gilbourne. I know what I'm going to do with her, and she'll not escape me as easily as she did you!"

"Good. Then I can keep up the pretense that she's out of her mind and safely under lock and key at Gilbourne. When the time's ripe, there'll be a funeral. I hope to marry again!"

Captain Hawkins laughed wolfishly and showed his strong white teeth.

"I like a man who can make decisions! You go your way and I'll go mine. Perhaps we shall never meet again, Sir Timothy, so good luck to you!"

"And to you. With that bitch for company you'll need all the luck in the world! And remember, this meeting never happened! If we should meet again, it will be as strangers, nothing more."

"As you wish. But what of the child?"

"He will forget in time. His studies and his dog and pony will fill his mind. Soon even his mother will be forgotten."

Fancy gave a low cry from the heart. "Charles, don't ever let them make you forget!"

The child struggled to reach out to her.

"Mama, mama . . ."

Sir Timothy shook him and he subsided into sobs, and Captain Hawkins slapped Fancy's face. It was a light blow, and only jarred her enough to stop the rising hysteria.

"Stop it! Do you want to upset the boy? Let him go in comparative peace. He's got to go, Fancy, so make the best of it."

"Oh, I hate you—hate you! You'll never know a moment's peace with me. Someday, I'll take my revenge on you both!"

Sir Timothy looked over his shoulder and laughed. He picked up the boy and walked up the steps, and as he moved into the kitchen he shouted over his shoulder, "If it is any consolation to you, I have got Sarah back to look after him. They are fond of each other, Fancy. Think of Sarah looking after him . . ."

"And what of Thomas, whom she wanted to marry?"

"When he is better of his wound he is coming to me as my bailiff, and they are going to marry soon."

"Then give her my love and tell her—tell her . . ." she stopped and broke down. "Tell her she's got the one person I love in this world."

And then the door closed and she was left facing Captain Black Patch Hawkins, who now seemed bigger and broader than ever. He looked down at her with a ruthless gleam in his one good eye.

"Now then, are you coming quietly, or do I have to fling you over my shoulder and carry you abroad?"

CHAPTER FIFTEEN

Fancy leaned against the deck rail and looked out over a devasted London. Great columns of smoke drifted skyward, blotting out the sun. The air smelt of wood ash and charred timbers, and in the distance flickered the dull glow of fires still raging. On shore she could see people scrabbling among the embers, trying to scratch out any undamaged goods. Others wept and walked about, dazed and unable to believe that their homes had once stood on this desolate ground.

There were soldiers and sailors, too, trying to bring order to the chaos, demolishing houses that the fire had licked and then left smoldering. Occasionally the wind would change and fan the flames into life again. Frequently she could hear the distant roar of a house collapsing in smoke and ashes.

Very few houses had escaped. Some, built of brick and with extensive grounds, still stood, but even the churches and public buildings had been swallowed into the inferno.

Frozen with the shock of her own loss, Fancy could hardly take it all in. With lackluster eyes she stared across the water. It was as if the end of the world had come. She had not slept all night, but stood there, willing herself to the spot where Charles would be lying. Her heart was bitter and she railed against her fate, brooding on Black Patch's treachery. All the hate of her passionate nature was centered on him. He would suffer one day as she had suffered! Whatever she could do to hurt Black Patch she would do. She hated him even more fiercely than Sir Timothy. At least Timothy had known and loved Charles, thinking he was his own son, and some of that love must still be there. But Black Patch had sold him for his own ends, betraying his partner, cornering her and leaving her at his mercy . . .

She turned as she heard Black Patch coming toward her. He stopped and looked around, breathing deeply of the smoky air.

"Ugh!" he gasped. "Have you stood there all night taking in that foulness? You should have come to bed!" He louged towards her, unperturbed at her scornful glance. "Still sulking?" He twisted her toward him, took her chin in his strong fingers and gave a low laugh. "That's my woman! All spunk and guts! There'll be time enough to break you in. Meanwhile, you get below and eat some breakfast and then sleep. I don't want a haggard woman on my hands for the rest of the voyage."

"Leave me alone! Your touch disgusts me!"

His hands dropped from her, and she staggered back against the rail.

"Very well. Get below, eat and sleep. That's an order!" She looked up at him, ready to defy him again, but the sight of the leather thong that he ran suggestively through his fingers made her snap her mouth shut. Gritting her teeth she went below without a word.

She followed the smell of food down the ladder. Below decks in the captain's stateroom there were deviled kidneys and thick slices of bacon waiting for her in a chafing dish on a huge polished table, that would have seated a dozen men. A grinning negro dressed in white waited for her to be seated.

She felt alarmed for she had never come in contact with blacks before, but the man's huge grin and flashing white teeth soon made her feel at ease.

"White ma'am want coffee? We finest coffee, much best! Or Sam can give you brandy. Master say woman have anything she like . . ."

"Coffee would be very nice—Sam?"

Sam nodded.

"Yes'm, me Sam. Me work for captain's woman. Tell me, me get!"

"Thank you, Sam, but I'm not captain's woman. I am Mistress Gill."

"Captain said you his woman, captain always right!" Grinning widely, he left the cabin, and after swearing some unladylike oaths Fancy attacked her breakfast as if the fork was spearing Black Patch himself.

The stateroom led to a corridor and two sleeping cabins, and walking beyond them Fancy found the small galley where Sam worked. This was his domain. He showed her to her own cabin, which was fitted out in mahogany and gold. The bunk was narrow but adequate, and there were drawers for the clothes she did not possess.

Suddenly she was no longer interested in her new surroundings. She was mentally and physically exhausted, and a dull headache forced her to lie down. She slept for three hours.

When she awakened, it was to find Black Patch sitting quietly by the bunk in the cabin's only easy chair. He was dozing, and she leaned up on one elbow to examine him.

In repose his features were fine, much finer than when he went about his daily duties, when his mouth twisted into a permanent sneer as if he fought all the world. Now his mouth was soft and gentle, and he was smiling in his sleep. He must be dreaming about all the black beauties he had slept with, she thought spitefully.

He stirred in his sleep and muttered something which she could not catch. It was more of a moan than words. But his face changed, and once more he was the Black Patch she knew. He stretched up, and sat up smiling.

"So, you are awake at last! You certainly look better for it. You and I must have a talk."

Fancy watched him suspiciously, then thrust out her chin agressively.

"What is there for you and I to talk about? You give the orders. I obey them!"

Black Patch bent over her and kissed her lightly on the nose.

"So you still intend to fight me?"

"Yes. Do you expect anything else?" Her scorn showed in the turn of her lips.

"I am not easily angered, Fancy. If I want you, I'll take you! But before you puff yourself up like a pouter pigeon, let me tell you that I still regard you as my partner, and as such you will come in for the profits—and the losses—incurred on this voyage. I am a man of my word. As we stand at present, we are both rich in our own right. A pity Sir Timothy did not know of our alliance. Possibly he would have thought twice before he let me have you. Would you have preferred him to me?"

"I-I don't know! I doubt if there is a hair to choose between you!"

Black Patch laughed.

"I flatter myself I am twice the man he is! I know I can please you, and I know you can please me! So what about an amicable agreement while you are aboard my ship!"

"Our ship!"

Black Patch frowned slightly.

"Well, all right, then—our ship."

"If by "an amicable agreement" you mean I should warm your bed, can you give me one reason why I should? After all, I am just as much master of this ship as you!"

"I can give you one good reason, my cocky little madam. If the crew realizes you are *not* my woman—and Sam would surely talk, because he has no guile—then you would be prey to any man who could win you. I fear you would have very little say in the matter!"

"But you would never allow that to happen!"

"Why not? If I can't enjoy you, why should I fight to hold off the other men? I would hate to be accused of being a dog in the manger, but they are a very simple lot of men and that would undoubtedly be their opinion of me."

"I think you are all animals! You leave me little choice."

"Madam, all men—and many women—are animals when love is in short supply. Have you never felt the need?"

Fancy stared at him, confused. And then a memory smote her of how she had felt at times with Caleb, and she dropped her eyes so that Black Patch could not see.

The captain smiled and took a turn up and down the small cabin, noting the lack of baggage.

"You need clothes. I think I can help you there."

He rang the bell and Sam came in, grinning wide as usual. His prompt appearance led Fancy to wonder if he had been listening at the door.

"Sam, go to my stores and bring the ironbound chest with the letters A and P stamped on them . . . and look sharp!"

"Yessir!"

While he was gone, Black Patch looked down at Fancy, and touched her hair.

"You may thank your stars I had my share of loving while ashore. I'll not trouble you tonight. I have more on my mind than wenching! So I'll leave you now and see my first mate about the rest of the cargo." He went to the door and then turned. "Oh, and all that's in the chest is yours. The woman it was destined for went off with another man. I came back too late!"

Somehow Fancy was piqued. She wondered who A and P might be. When Sam returned, she got him to open the chest and then she spent a pleasant hour trying on all the shifts and gowns, and matching them up with shawls and fans and shoes, all the time feeling curiously jealous of her unknown benefactor.

She found hairpins, a silver brush and comb, and a mirror backed with tortoise shell, all of which she set out on the dressing chest. Then she selected a gown of lilac silk embroidered in pink and blue and green, with a deep-scooped neckline trimmed with a scalloped edge of heavy lace. The skirt, too, was scooped up and caught with lace knots and a matching lace shawl set off the whole.

She brushed her hair until it shone, twisting it into loops and ringlets at each side of a center parting, and was quite pleased with the result. Vaguely she had a plan. She wanted Black Patch's love—desire alone was not enough. Love would make him suffer, and she wanted him to suffer—for Charles' sake. As for herself, how could she think of him other than with hate? Had he not been the means of her losing her son?

The time dragged interminably. She climbed the wooden stairs to the top deck and looked out again over the desolate waste. The fires were fewer now, and at the end of the third day, with the wind dropping, it seemed as if there was nothing left to burn.

Now that the air was fresher, Fancy resolved to walk around the deck for exercise. The *Emma-Jane* showed signs of wear and tear after her many round trips to the Americas. As Fancy walked farther away from the captain's quarters she noticed an unidentifiable smell, musky and unpleasant, lingering in the air, and mixed with it the odor of vinegar and lime-wash. Quickly she realized what it was—it was the tangy smell of slaves! However much a slaving ship was washed down and scrubbed, the bitter reek hung in its timbers.

As she walked she watched out for signs of slave decks which would have been dismantled before the ship docked in an English port, the holes where the chains and anklets would be fastened . . .

So it was all true! The *Emma-Jane* went out as an ordinary cargo ship—this time there was to be a cargo of raw wool and plowshares—and the money gained from the cargo was used to buy slaves in Havana or off the African coast. From there the ship would make a run to the Carolinas, where slaves fetched big prices, and then home with sugar and spices—and a profit which doubled and trebled in the process. No wonder her share had grown so fast!

The smell of slaves was like a reproach and made her feel sick. She hurried back to the captain's quarters to escape it, but already the whole ship stank in her nostrils.

She found perfume in the chest and liberally splashed herself with it to mask the smell. And when Sam came to announce supper, she went with some trepidation to the saloon.

Black Patch was already drinking brandy. He had with him his first mate, a man with a harelip whose speech was hard to follow. Fancy was shocked when she first saw him and had difficulty in not staring at him.

"This is Ned Gamble, my right-hand man—a good man in a fight."

Ned grinned and showed yellow teeth.

"Ma'am, your servant . . ."

Fancy inclined her head while Ned touched his forelock and stood back.

"No need for that, Ned. Sit in with us. She will have to get used to you eating with us. We'll not be making any other arrangements. We shall carry on as before."

The man mumbled something which she could not understand.

"Nonsense, man," said Black Patch easily. "My friends are her friends. You'll sit with us. No woman of mine will keep my friends from my table!"

Fancy cast him a look, and he, mocking, clasped her in his arms and kissed her full on the mouth for Ned to see.

Ned grinned.

"You'll be wanting more'n your victuals, cap'n. I'll come back when Sam sets out the meat."

"You'll stay where you are and drink your brandy. She can wait for her dessert until afterward!" He winked at Ned, and Ned looked slyly at Fancy and chortled. Forgetting himself, he dug her sharply in the ribs. Fancy was furious but remained silent.

The meal passed quietly enough. Black Patch talked to Ned about the cargo and how it was being stowed, about bills of lading and ship's stores, and reminded him to get an extra cask of vinegar. On the last voyage, which had been prolonged by bad weather, the supplies of vinegar had run out and there had been attacks of scurvy among the crew.

Fancy yawned. All this talk bored her. She wanted to go to bed.

Black Patch noticed the yawn and stood up punctiliously.

"You would like to retire?"

"If you would not think it rude?"

"Certainly not. Ned will not mind. He will probably be able to concentrate better when you are gone."

Ned laughed, and bowed.

Fancy gave a quick bob and then left the room. She ran up the companionway to the top deck. On impulse she considered leaving the ship, but her mad rush came to a halt when she saw a sailor standing by the gang plank. Arms folded, he stood his ground when she approached.

"May I pass, please? I want to go ashore."

"No one is allowed to go ashore tonight, ma'am. Orders is orders!"

"But I'm not a sailor, surely I can go ashore?" Now she was growing angry.

"Not tonight, ma'am. You can ask the cap'n yourself, ma'am."

"But . . ."

"Having trouble, Fancy?"

Fancy whirled about. Black Patch was standing nonchalantly behind her.

"This man won't let me go ashore. I wanted to walk awhile," she lied.

"Oh, so you want to walk on dry land. Then you won't mind if I join you, Fancy. I could do with a walk."

"But I shouldn't like to trouble you. You seem so busy."

"Not now. Ned and I have decided on our course. I am at your disposal."

"But—"

He took her arm.

"Come along. No one will recognize you. We'll walk along the towpath for a while and look at the moon. They tell me it has quite an effect on lovers."

Fancy kept her head down, for she felt a spark of triumph steal through her.

"Very well. If you say so."

She allowed him to hold her as they moved down the gangway together. Her heart was beating fast. It was dark and the path rough and stony, forcing her to cling to his arm.

"By God, Fancy, you smell like a brothelkeeper! Have you changed your mind about me? Do you want me tonight?"

She turned indignantly to him.

"I've told you. I want none of you. You'll never take me willingly. *Never!*"

"Never is a long time," he said softly. "I could make you come to me—willingly and without asking, if I had a mind!"

"Never! You must be out of your mind!"

"Is that a challenge? I never say no to a challenge, whether it be by kiss or sword!"

"There's no challenge about it! Please, can we go back now? I'm tired."

"Certainly. It was your idea to go walking."

They turned back, and when they came once again to the gangplank, Black Patch motioned her to go first and did not offer to help her. In her fright she had to beg for his support. His mocking smile made her want to smack his face.

"So you still need my help, even though you want to appear cold."

"Damn you, I can manage." But as she stormed ahead up the gangplank, she caught her foot in her gown and, before she knew it, had landed with a splash in the muddy Thames!

She sank down and down and down until her lungs were bursting. Her gown felt like a millstone about her and she wanted to scream, but when she instinctively opened her mouth, thick oily water gushed in. She choked and it was then she felt a relentless hand grab her hair and pull her through the water. A strong arm lifted her clear of the water and heaved her over the side of the ship. She fell on deck, black water oozing from her garments. The taste in her mouth was foul. She retched and was sick on the boards.

Black Patch climbed over the side, and he too was dripping, but now he let fly a string of curses that made Fancy want to blush. He picked her up and set her on her feet.

"Now I expect you will be satisfied. The next time you fall in, I might not be there to pull you out!"

Fancy did not answer, but went down to her cabin, where she stripped and threw what had been her pretty new gown and clean undershift into the passage. The white lace shawl had floated away on the river, and now all she was left with was the linen belt, around her waist, containing the precious topaz necklace.

She wound her long hair into a knot. It stank of river mud and would have to be washed. She tried to remove the traces of mud from her limbs . . . and suddenly she felt eyes on her back. She turned, and Black Patch was lounging against the door, he too drying his hair.

He had removed his black leather patch, and his face looked subtly different without it. Apart from the puckering of the saber wound, the scar was not offensive. Suddenly he looked more of a gentleman and less of a pirate.

Her eyes slid from his face to his body. His tight-fitting seaman's breeches accentuated the bare chest above. Her eyes lingered on the broad shoulders and hairy black mat that was his chest. Seeing his hard muscular form, Fancy was reminded of that week they had spent together. She shivered slightly, and he frowned, his attention taken with her rounded beauty.

"Are you cold? What you need is a hot toddy. Sam!"

Sam put his head around the cabin door.

"Yessir, cap'n?"

"Mix a good large jug of that hot toddy of yours. And make it the strength you bring me after a Force 9 gale!"

"Yessir!"

Black Patch moved inside the alcove which housed the bunk. He sat down and surveyed her dispassionately.

"You are a little fatter than when you last came to me, but I like it. A ripe woman is a joy to hold!"

Fancy snatched up her counterpane and covered herself.

"I'm your partner, remember? I'm not a slave to crawl into your bed at your bidding! And you said yourself that the week you refer to was to be forgotten. You told me it was all over . . ."

"And that rankled, did it?"

His mocking smile roused her to fresh fury.

"Why should it? I was glad to get away."

"Liar. You wanted to meet me again. In fact you expected it!"

"I-I did no such thing. I hate you as Black Patch, and I hate you as Sir Montague!"

"Very amusing. It is quite a strange situation, isn't it? You are my partner, to whom I am in honor bound to make an accounting; in doing so, I will make you a rich independent woman. And yet here we are alone, crossing swords with each other, knowing the delights of each other's body—and he made a swoop and encircled her with his arms, pulling her so close that she had difficulty in breathing." What kind of game are you playing?"

"It's no game," she gasped, but it was a lie. "I'm not a whore who can go with any man. I've got to fancy a man."

"Aye, well named—Fancy! And you are saying you don't fancy me?"

"Not at all. You forget Charles has come between us! I could never fancy a man who separated me from my son."

"Even though it was for his own good?"

"How can you say that? A child should be with his mother!"

"Charles is better off with Sarah than on board this ship. God knows what atrocities you will witness before you leave it. Do you want him to witness such things?"

"But-but . . ."

"You never thought of that, eh? Well think well on it!" And he loosed her and pushed her onto the bunk.

"And while we are on the subject, I think you lie about not fancying me! You shiver like an untried virgin when you see me stripped! I watched your eyes and I saw desire leap into them!"

"You lie! It's not true. I loathe the very sight of you."

"We shall see about that."

There was a discreet knock at the door and Black Patch opened it to Sam, who stood there with a tray bearing a huge jug of steaming spiced toddy and two tankards. Black Patch took the tray without a word and kicked the door to with a booted foot still wet from the river.

"Get into the bunk, wrap yourself about and drink this." He poured out two full tankards, gave her one and then, raising his in a silent toast, took two or three great gulps. Then he sighed and set the tankard down on the dressing chest.

"Thank you. What is it?" Fancy looked at her steaming tankard. It smelled delicious. She took a careful sip.

"Don't sip it, drink it like the good partner you are! Hot toddy needs to be gulped, to warm the belly and thaw out feet and hands! It's rum laced with Jamaican brown sugar, with molasses, lemon peel, hot ale, and a dash of cinnamon. We have it often, and you'll come to appreciate it."

"I like it. It's warming me already." She lay back against the hard pillow and let the pleasant warm glow rush around her body. She smiled at Black Patch and to her alarm, felt her antagonism vanish. She tried to concentrate on his betrayal of Charles, but her body weakened her resolution. She sighed langorously, and Black Patch watched her calculatingly.

"Another fill up?" He did not wait for an answer but refilled the half-empty tankard.

Fancy hiccupped. "Here's to a fruitful voyage . . ." and she waved her tankard, slopping some of its contents onto the counterpane.

"Come on now, drink up like a good sailor," said Black Patch. Fancy took a good swig.

The counterpane slipped from her shoulders and Black Patch's good eye fixed itself on the smooth skin of her arms. His sensitive hands played up and down her body, and Fancy made no protest. Slowly and lightly he caressed her and she, eyes glazed slightly from the potent drink, nestled closer to him until he could feel the whole length of her body.

And then all her resistance gave way. Her free hand came up and explored his chest, feeling his powerful heart beat. His skin, warm and still smelling faintly of the river, excited her and she craved his body on hers. She groaned, and his caressing hands moved to her breasts, and then she was in his arms.

She lay there, palpitating in her nakedness, and closed her eyes the better to enjoy his wooing. Then, supine and eager for him, she felt him fumble with his clothing and in a moment he was on the bunk beside her, mastering her. She felt his nakedness and his naked manhood, and took him like a woman hungered.

They lay in each other's arms all night, and again and again he had his way until, sated, he slept at last, his arms tight-clasped about her waist. But she, after a fitful doze, lay in a drunken half stupor, confusing Caleb and Timothy and Black Patch until all three became one.

With the dawn came remorse and anger. Fancy, head aching, awakened and found she was alone. Gritting her teeth, she cursed Black Patch and thought with horror of how her body had betrayed her. Now the very thought of that scarred male body dominating her filled her with revulsion. She wanted to hide herself away from him. He had reduced her by trickery to a willing slave!

But there was nothing of this in his eyes when he came into the cabin. He was newly bathed and his hair curled in wet rings. His linen was immaculate and Fancy could find no fault with him. So she lashed out about the night before.

"That was a low trick you played last night! Making me drunk and taking advantage! It shows what a monstrous rogue you are! I could kill you for it!"

"Taking advantage! You make me laugh! If ever a man was nearly raped, I was!"

Fancy's hand shot out, catching Black Patch a smart wallop on the jaw that made him stagger. He grabbed her wrist.

"I could have you flogged for that!" He glared down at her and she glared back, and then a reluctant look of admiration came into his eyes.

"God's teeth! You make a pretty mate for a red-blooded man! A pity I didn't meet you before you married Sir Timothy!"

"What's that got to do with it?"

"I think I should have married you, Fancy Gilbourne!"

"Liar! You don't deceive me. I'm no fool! You would have taken me, and left me the moment you found somebody else."

He smiled curiously and then turned away, but she noticed he did not contradict her. Her lips curled. All men were the same. Please them in bed, and they forgot all about you until the next time. But for a woman there had to be some kind of love, even if it was only the love of the body. A man was never simply a means of release.

Black Patch rummaged in the chest and pulled out a cherry silk gown.

"Wear this. Red is one of my favorite colors. If you please me, I shall give you something to match it." And he turned and left the cabin.

Fancy considered the gown. It was vulgar, and she did not greatly care for it; the bodice was picked out in black lace and showed nearly all her breasts through the fine black mesh.

Instead, she chose a pale blue gown, cut high with a ruff coming up to her ears, which made her look fresh and virginal. Sam found her some coarse yellow soap, and she washed her hair and coiled it in shining ringlets. She was pleased with the result.

When she ventured to the main stateroom, she found Black Patch poring over maps and tracing out a possible route. He raised his eyes for a moment and something flickered at the back of his eyes, but he made no comment. He motioned her to a chair and went on with his calculations. She sat quietly studying him. She wished they had met under less extraordinary conditions. She could have respected him, given the right opportunity. Now she despised him.

He looked up and caught her eye. One eyebrow was raised, as if he knew what was going on in her mind, and he deliberately moved a silk kerchief that was laid on the table.

Fancy's eyes widened, but she said nothing. Her eyes flicked to his, then back to the exquisite ruby and diamond necklace on the bed of black velvet. Beside it was a pair of long drop earrings. And still he said nothing. Then he flung down his quill and sat back, crossing one leg over the other.

"Well, I must say you look beautiful. What about some hot chocolate or some such thing? I understand the ladies like chocolate."

Fancy pulled a face.

"Not chocolate, thank you. I could take a cup of coffee."

Black Patch rang the bell and Sam shot into the room.

"Hot coffee, Sam," he said before the black man could speak, "and bring the best Jamaican sugar. Mistress Gill likes it sweet!"

"Yessir!"

There was a long silence while they waited for the coffee. Fancy moved nervously and coughed, conscious of the war of nerves between them.

The coffee came, and Fancy muttered her thanks to Sam. He fussed around, pouring out the strong black liquid and placing the fine china cup and saucer at her elbow. There was a look in his eyes like that of a sheepdog that had once belonged to her brother. A trusting, worshipping look. She knew she had a friend in Sam.

"That will do," cracked Black Patch, and Sam disappeared without a word or glance at Fancy.

"Drink your coffee and listen."

She picked up the delicate cup and saucer and sipped,

as if in a formal drawing room. Black Patch's fingers drummed on the table. He was keeping his temper in check, but only with a great effort.

When Fancy replaced her empty cup and saucer on the table, he sat forward and pointed a finger at her.

"In the future you will do as you are told! I want no mutiny on my ship either from my crew or my woman. And I shall not allow you to undermine my authority on board. You may not realize this, but once at sea all the men will be aware of what goes on between us. They will know by instinct. A captain who cannot control his woman can hardly be expected to control his crew. Is that clear?"

She nodded, not daring to speak.

"Then remember it. Because if ever you displease me and the crew get to know it, I shall have you flogged publicly. It won't be the first time a woman has been flogged on this ship."

"You make me sick in my belly!" Fancy turned away in disgust. So much for her dreams of his being a gentleman. He leaned over the table and caught her wrist. His eyes were blazing with fury.

"This is for your own good—and for the good of my position. Can you imagine what could happen to you if I was hurt or killed? You would be shared among twenty men, who are more like beasts in their lusts, including the officers! Make no mistake about it, your life would be a misery."

"How do you know it isn't a misery already?"

"Because of last night! If you were miserable last night, you must be a better actress than Moll Davis or Nell Gwynne!"

She dropped her eyes, and he smiled grimly, picking up the earrings and dropping them nonchalantly into one of his capacious pockets. The necklace he swung before her bemused eyes.

"These were intended for an obedient little lady from a grateful lover. But still, they'll keep!" He dropped the necklace in the same pocket with the earrings, and Fancy, unable to keep still any longer, stood up and left the cabin, banging the door savagely behind her.

Out on the main deck she watched the men preparing the ship for the beginning of the voyage. She felt as if they eyed her with a kind of sick satisfaction, studying her shape, weighing up her bodily charms. One dark oily-haired sailor thrust out his tongue at her in a lewd gesture and Fancy ran back to the comparative safety of the captain's quarters, knowing he had told the truth about the passions of these men.

Taking refuge in her own cabin, she sorted out her garments, then sat, hour after hour, gazing out on the desolation that was the waterfront of London. Now she could see more of the populace returning to survey their own personal disasters. There was a scraping and a digging, and sometimes sparks from seemingly dead embers sprung to life again on the slight breeze. And then she saw Betsy, a bundle in her hand, walking up and down on the towpath beside the ship. On impulse, she ran up the gangway to the deck rail and leaned over and waved.

"Hey! You there! Are you looking for me?"

The girl's face brightened.

"I thought you might want a maid," she shouted back.

Fancy considered, and then nodded her head. She had made a swift decision.

"Come up the gangplank and watch yourself. I fell in last night and I can still smell the muck of the river."

Betsy ran like a gazelle up the narrow swaying plank and Fancy helped her aboard. They surveyed one another and then both laughed, and Fancy took her by the shoulders.

"Welcome aboard. I'll take you down to my cabin."

But at the head of the teak staircase stood Black Patch. He looked down at them both from his great height.

"What is this? What is she doing here?"

"She's come aboard to be my maid. She'll be company for me."

"You don't need any company other than mine. I can

maid you, too! We don't want another woman aboard.
She'll send the men crazy!"

"But I have nowhere to go!" Betsy's face crumpled.
"I've left the Mermaid. The landlord's lost all his customers and he can't afford to feed me any longer. I must
find somewhere—"

"Please, please let her stay. I want her with me." Fancy looked up anxiously at him.

He laughed.

"I would have been better pleased if you had pandered to my request." Fancy flushed with some confu-
sion, but he went on." I suppose if you want her you
may keep her aboard. But remember—I am the one
pandering to your whims!"

"Thank you, Black Patch." She offered him her
mouth, but he only chucked her under the chin.

"Call me Monty, and try to look happier in my pres-
ence. I can't abide sulky women!"

And so the next day, the fifth of September, the *Emma-
Jane* slipped her moorings and nosed out of the Thames
and into the North Sea on her way to the Straits of
Dover, and then on to a port in France where war or no
war, a merchant was awaiting his cargo. From there the
ship sped on past the Bay of Biscay and on to North
Africa to Tangier, where a caravan of black slaves culled
from the surrounding countryside was held in a barra-
coon, against the coming of the first trader willing to pay
the right price. And then followed the long haul over the
Atlantic to the Carolinas, where the slave trade was the
most brisk . . .

Fancy had not bargained for the long delay near
Tangier. The small bay in which the ship anchored was
desolate except for brown scrub that grew precariously
among the sand and rocks. Here the ship was being
refitted to take the slaves. Black Patch reckoned on taking aboard some four hundred, provided they were
shackled back to back with no more than twenty inches
of board per man. The staging was placed so that the up-

per slave deck gave the man underneath just enough room to turn. The hammering of chains and shackles went on, day after day, and the rough carpentry work seemed never to cease. Fancy could have screamed at the monotony of it. A part of the deck had been enclosed with tarpaulin for Fancy's and Betsy's private use and now their walking was restricted to a small area aft. Black Patch explained that Fancy must never get windward of the slave quarters, since the stench would be difficult to control later on in the voyage. He laughed and showed his teeth.

"It is time you knew how we make our money. Until now you took your share without thought. Only I knew how hard it was come by. Now you will see for yourself!"

Fancy had no notion of what conditions were like below decks, but she discovered soon enough. Already the heavily-laden ship was wallowing low in the water and the stench was building up. She remembered the feeling of horror when she saw the slaves shuffle aboard the ship, ten at a time, shackled to a long chain. The great cavernous hold was like a giant mouth, swallowing the blacks whole. She thought the long black column would never end. And there were fifty women. Some heavily swollen with child, whom Black Patch surveyed with great satisfaction. They would no doubt bear several new little slaves before the journey ended, to take the place of any who died in transit.

"Do you mean to say some of them die?" Fancy was astonished.

"Of course! You cannot stop dysentery and fever breaking out! We douse them with sea water twice a day and put vinegar in the drinking water, but there are always casalties. You will get used to it. They're only savages after all."

"But you've slept with their women . . ."

"Aye, and passionate little whores they are too! They know nothing else."

"And you gave them babies. You might have sons and daughters working as slaves on the sugar plantations. Does that not worry you?"

"Why should it? If I didn't give them babies some other fellow would. Besides, they like half-caste babies. It gives them prestige."

"I think it is disgusting. I know they are strange and black and ugly and they frighten me, but they should be allowed to keep their dignity."

"Dignity?" Monty gave a great bellow of laughter.

"They wouldn't know what the word means! If we were kindly disposed to them, the men would take advantage of our softness. They are just animals. Fancy, make no mistake. If one of them cornered you in your cabin, do you think he would consider your dignity? He would have you down on your back and raped before you could flick an eyelid. And you would stay raped! Have you ever seen a black man's pizzle?"

Fancy gasped and recoiled at the picture he conjured up.

"That . . . that could never happen!"

"It might, if we did not put the fear of God in 'em and make sure their manacles were all shipshape."

"But what of the women? Are you not worried about getting a knife in your ribs?"

"Not a bit of it. They like a white man's handling, it makes them feel good."

Fancy felt a sudden fury and her hand come up to strike his cheek. He laughed and caught her wrist.

"Jealous?" His laughter was a growl in his throat. She lashed out and freed herself.

Breathing deeply she said huskily, "Not a bit of it. I was merely wondering how you could take a woman like that. A black woman straight out of the jungle. I think it is monstrous!"

"Why? They all look alike in the dark! You want to worry about yourself. At least your child won't be half-caste!"

Startled, Fancy looked at him.

"How, how did you guess?"

"I've seen too many women with child not to know. You've been sick a lot lately. But I have a strange feeling about it." He pulled her to him and held her by her pretty throat, staring into her eyes and making her feel as if her soul was being drawn out. "It happened before you came aboard. The timing was wrong. How did you come to find me in the first place? Who brought you to me? Answer me!"

"Caleb Neyn the gypsy brought me. You knew him and his brother Benji."

"Caleb!" He gave a great shout of laughter. "The old devil slipped you a length, did he? Poetic justice! I once took a woman away from him. I wonder if he thought of that . . . Well, I'll not hold it against you this once. It happened before you came to me. But if you have another child," his voice sunk to a menacing whisper, "it will be mine—or I'll kill you for it!"

He pushed her away, and she watched him wide-eyed. He was a puzzle of a man. But he was right. She had been sick every morning, and her sickness had nothing to do with the rolling motion of the ship, or the stink on board. At first she had hidden the fact from Betsy but one morning Betsy had found her in her shift lying across the bed and groaning. Betsy had cradled her in her arms until the retching had passed. Then she had slipped off the soiled shift and looked at Fancy's slightly swollen belly and put a hand tenderly on it.

"There's a baby there, Mistress Gill!" And Fancy had looked down at her own slim outline, marred by the slight thickening. Wordlessly she had looked at Betsy and then her face had puckered.

"Dear God, Betsy. What are we going to do? Two women on board a slaver and a baby coming . . . and the risk of infection! Betsy, what are we going to do?"

CHAPTER SIXTEEN

Fancy looked across the wide dinner table in the stateroom at the man lounging and peeling an orange opposite her. His deft fingers covered with fine black down fascinated her. She had seen their cruelty on many luckless sailors, and felt their gentle roughness herself, but now they reminded her of surgeon's hands, quick and decisive and altogether in contrast with the nature of the man.

"Monty, will you stop peeling that orange and attend to me?" Her voice, impatient and imperious, only caused him to raise a quizzical eyebrow. He continued with the delicate operation. "Monty! I am your partner. I have a right to know!"

"Be quiet, woman! You sound like a nagging wife! Let me remind you that I am the captain here and that you are the sleeping partner!" He grinned.

Fancy wanted to smack his face but knew that violence on her part was useless. Their struggles always ended the same way—he would pinion her arms to her sides and carry her off to his cabin, and the grinning Sam would play watchdog and keep the crew away for as long as it took for him to take his fill of her. And Monty was not a man who liked to be hurried.

So now she sat still and patient. In the month they had been at sea since taking on the slaves, she had seen much—and a lot of it had disgusted her. Monty had been a revelation. With her, he was gentle and ruthless by turns. But with crew or the slaves, he was merciless. If a fight broke out between decks—as it often did, for

232

the crew quarrelled violently over the few young slavegirls—Monty would take the leather bullwhip loaded with lead at the tip, and Fancy would cower in her cabin at the screams of agony it drew from the men.

When she expostulated at his cruelty, he would shrug his shoulders.

"You might thank me for having that whip some day. It could be the means of keeping you from the rabble. If anything happened to me," and he gave a low reckless laugh, "they would be like dogs after a bitch in heat."

So she watched and waited. For although she hated him, he was her lifeline, and being bedded by him was, after all, a far more pleasant fate than being used again and again like those poor black girls below. She sighed, and tapped her long fingers on the table.

"Pour me another brandy if you want something to do? And stop that infernal tapping," he growled. Silently she did as he bid. He bit into the segments of the orange and then, finishing, he delicately rinsed his fingers in the bowl of water provided.

"Very nice. I shall have to remember to take on board a supply of oranges on each trip. I think they benefit the men." He took a gulp of the brandy and then looked at Fancy. "Now then, what do you want to know."

"You know very well. I want to know about the King's commission. I understood you were to organize the breaking of the blockade, and that you were under the King's orders."

"Indeed I am, my love. I am doing exactly as the King ordered!"

"But—but we're taking a cargo of slaves!"

"Quite right! Our other ship is plying the Channel under my orders, while we are plying the slave trade to find money for His Majesty's wars!"

"I don't understand."

"You will. King Charles is a shrewd ruler—and a first-class business man. He knows that he can only extract a certain amount of money from the Government. So he turns a blind eye when his captains do a little pirating on the side for him. In return for a tax on our overall profit, we can do as we like!"

"Then as long as he is guaranteed a certain sum of money, we can forget the war?"

"Not forget it, just ignore it—pay our dues and go on making our own fortune. Very neat, isn't it?"

"I did not think the King approved of the slave trade . . ."

"Officially, he doesn't. But since he's always short of funds, he can't afford to object to it. As long as each voyage brings in some money for his depleted coffers, he doesn't mind how it is earned."

"I've never wondered how the King comes by his money. Of course I know about the taxes paid in the villages, but beyond that . ."

"No, I don't suppose you ever thought of the colossal bills he runs up with Lady Castlemaine and all his other women, either. His financial commitments to his women are a scandal, and the Queen, too, is extravagant."

"Yes, but poor Queen Catherine is to be pitied. Openly humiliated at Court and so far from her home in Portugal. I don't blame her for her excesses!"

"There is no need to pity her! She has her lovers, uncomely as she is!"

"Well, why not, when her husband is so brazenly open in his affairs!"

"Oho! You sound mightly righteous all of a sudden! Don't tell me you are becoming a fount of moral wisdom in your old age! Increasing must slow you down!"

"It has nothing to do with my increasing! I have always thought that husbands and wives should bear each other a certain loyalty. . . ."

"Like the loyalty you showed to your husband?"

Fancy blushed with annoyance.

"Sir Timothy showed no loyalty to me! And when I came to you, I only did as I was bid!"

"You needed no persuasion. I do not remember you screaming for help!" His lip curled. "You are no better than any of those fine ladies at Court! A lift of a finger and a dozen would come running."

"I am not like that! I don't give my body to anyone!"

"No?" Monty raised his eyebrow in polite disbelief. "Then what about . . . .?" and his eyes wandered to Fancy's still slim stomach. She put up a hand and touched herself in a kind of defense.

"This was different. I knew Caleb long before I knew you. I love him!" A curious, implacable look came over Monty's face. He took a gulp of brandy and then lowered his eyes so that she could not read his thoughts. Then he said quietly, "I should have killed him when I had the chance. He took a woman away from me. I was entitled to kill him and I let him go."

"And he's threatened to kill you, too, if he ever meets you again," said Fancy breathlessly.

"Good. Then it will be no holds barred, and the best man will win you!"

The sudden glance from his good eye was like a rapier thrust. Fancy drew a deep breath. Did this man love her after all? He had all the signs of jealousy, yet he could be still cold and callous towards her.

She stood up to leave the table and, as the ship lurched, she staggered and would have fallen if his arms had not shot out and gathered her to him.

"You little devil. Was that deliberate, or haven't you got your sea legs yet?" She felt the usual tiny tingling of her flesh when he held her, yet knew that her response to him was absurd. Caleb was the love of her life—or was he? Doubts about herself showed in her face. She didn't know who, or what she wanted.

Monty gave her a slight shake.

"What's the matter with you? I like my women full of fire. If you settle down to domesticity, I'll swap you for Betsy . . . or one of those black wenches. There is quite a comely creature down there, though I don't like her tribal markings!"

"You wouldn't dare take Betsy or one of those smelly women while I'm aboard!" She raised her fist, suddenly furious.

He grabbed her wrist and laughed.

"That's more like it! I like a woman who needs taming and never gives in! You're the one for me—for the moment anyway! Come on, give me a kiss, and I'll come to you just as soon as I've checked my charts, or we'll miss Charleston by a hundred miles.''

She tried to evade him, but he caught her in a kiss that was long and strangely satisfying. But once again he had aroused her slumbering hatred, and when he came to her later, it was to find her cabin door locked. He rattled the knob.

"Fancy! Stop playing tricks and let me in!" She huddled down under the bedcovers.

"Go away! I'm tired tonight. I want to sleep."

There was silence for a few moments and then came a terrifying barrage on the door.

"Open the door, or I'll break it down! You little bitch, I'll teach you to defy me!"

"That's what you wanted, isn't it? Someone who defies you? Go away, and come in the morning," she shouted.

"I want you now—this minute. So get your lazy bottom out of that bed and open up! I'm warning you, Fancy."

Fancy's heart beat fast. This situation had never arisen before. But had he not said he liked his women untamed? She could be as untamed as he wished! Betsy came out from her little cubbyhole and crouched down by the bed.

"You'd better open the door, ma'am," she said carefully. "God knows what he'll do to you otherwise . . . and me too. He might even have us flogged!"

"Not he. He can rant and rave, but I know Black Patch! While I am increasing, he'll not harm me. Perhaps afterward . . ." She shuddered. Betsy looked at her in some astonishment.

"I do believe you love him! You always find a gentleness in him that no one else can. It must be love!"

"Betsy! Don't be a fool! I could never love a man like him. He parted me from Charles, remember? I hate him, don't you understand?"

"Oh, yes. I understand." She nodded and then looked at the door. "What is he up to now, do you think? He can't have just gone away?"

There was a silence on the other side of the door.

"Go back to bed, Betsy. He's probably so drunk he's dropped down somewhere and won't remember any of this in the morning."

"It's not like him to give in so easy, ma'am," she said uneasily.

"Go on now, go back to bed. I shall be all right."

And now, Fancy lay, ears stretched and body quivering. Would he leave her alone? Had she underestimated him or overestimated him? Somewhere inside was a feeling of anticlimax. If it had not been for Charles, she could have found the thing she was looking for in this giant of a man. But now that elusive something was fast disappearing.

Suddenly the door suffered an onslaught so loud and long that she feared the timbers would splinter. But the door was stout and made of oak, and she lay with the bedclothes stuffed around her ears to block out the sound.

At each moment she expected to be taken in rough arms and to feel the cruel passion of him, whipped to fevert pitch by her rejection, but the door resisted all his efforts.

Then she heard the chink of liquid being poured into glass and she knew he was still drinking. She smiled into the darkness. The brandy would prove her friend tonight! She heard him fall and swear, and then he was rattling the door again.

"Are you going to open the door, Fancy? The joke's gone far enough."

"It's no joke, Monty," she rapped back smartly. "I'm not your slave, remember?"

"Then if you won't have me, I'll set the men loose on you!"

"You wouldn't dare."

He laughed drunkenly.

"Try me and see."

"You said you wanted an untamed woman!"

"Aye, but not on the other side of a thick oak door.

Come on, open up, I say!"

"Go to Hell! I'm stopping on this side tonight."

There was silence for so long that Fancy sat up on one elbow to listen better. What could he be up to now?

Soon she had the answer. To her horror she heard voices! Surely he wouldn't do as he threatened? Then there was a new sound, as of a battering-ram being hoisted into position. Dear God, he had organized a battering party!

"Right, lads!" She heard him shout. "*One . . . two . . . three . . . away!*" And the door, sadly damaged as it was from the early onslaught, gave way and crashed against the wall. Black Patch, bigger and blacker than ever, stepped inside, and with legs well apart and arms akimbo, towered over her. She crouched down in the bed and stared up at him.

"What are you going to do?"

"What I promised to do if you did not open this damned door."

"But—"

"No buts, Fancy, my love!" He turned to the men. "Well, who's to be the first?"

Fancy gave a squeal.

"Not—not these men?" Her heart thumped in fear as she looked at the four of them. One she knew—Ned Gamble of the harelip. But the other three . . . She shuddered and wanted to be sick.

"I hate you! God, how I hate you."

He smiled.

"Well? Come on, which one of you brave men is to be the first?"

They grinned and crowded around the bed to look at Fancy, but she gave them very little to see, for only her face was visible.

"Have a good look, fellows! See what you are going to fight for!" Black Patch stripped the bed of its coverings and left Fanny shivering in her long white shift. She curled herself into a small tight ball, and waited.

One man, whom Fancy had never seen before, stepped forward, licking his lips.

"I would fight the whole ship for her, cap'n."

"You would? Even though it means keeping awake twenty-four hours a day to fend the others off? You would have little enough time left for loving the woman—and, believe me, she likes her loving!"

Anger at Black Patch's words nearly overcame her fear, but she lay still. She was still too frightened of a concerted attack from all the men to scream or resist. Even Black Patch would be no match for the four of them, *if* he chose to help her—and in this drunken mood, he probably would only stand by and watch the men slaughter each other. She held her breath.

The man stepped back, and then looked at Black Patch.

"But if I take on these men and win, surely I should have the right to her? I thought . . ."

"No, Jake. What I don't want, the whole ship shares, right? You would have to fight each other for her. Isn't that right, lads?" The others nodded their heads. "Well? Who's going to start the ball rolling?" The men looked at each other and shuffled to their feet. The first man went to the door.

"Count me out, cap'n. I'm damned if I'm going to fight a whole ship for her—I'd probably be too wacked even to think of tackling her! I'll stick to the blacks!" He walked out of the cabin, and the rest sidled after him.

Black Patch leaned against the open door.

"Well, Fancy? How about that? It seems there's no takers for you. You've only got me to fall back on!"

With that he pounced on her, and his kisses were so fiercely passionate that she was in fear of suffocating. She pounded his chest, but it was as if he could not feel. She felt his hands caressing her breasts and thighs and then suddenly her shift was torn clean off her. He stopped and sat up to gaze on her new loveliness. The baby she was carrying had added an alluring roundness to her figure. Then he kissed her breasts and his warm wet mouth traveled down to her navel, and she felt the familiar surge of desire. Her arms came out to him and her fingers became claws as she pulled him to her. She

wanted him, and her body was pulsing and craving his
loving. She moaned in a sudden need and arched herself
to his body, expecting him to take her and dominate
their love-making as usual. But to her surprise he
stopped what he was doing, and by the light of the tropi-
cal moon streaming through the window, studied her eager face and gave a low laugh.

"So! You're feeling very differently now, eh? You
wouldn't want to keep me out of your cabin now? So
much for your vaunted hell-raising! Well, keep your
body to yourself! I am just in the mood to try one of the
blacks!"

Fancy gasped as if he had thrown a bucket of water
over her. She put out a hand to stop him.

"Monty, what are you saying? Monty . . ." But she
felt him lurch to his feet and then he looked down at her

"A proper bitch in heat! You didn't want me before
so now to Hell with you!" He banged the damaged door
behind him, and it crashed to the floor, hinges snapped
and broken beyond repair. She lay, huddled and frightened. Black Patch had never shown this mood before.

Betsy crept out of her cubbyhole and helped to re-
make the bed.

"Should I find Sam and see if he can make you some
coffee?"

"No. I would rather have a rum or brandy. Go along
to the stateroom and see what is there."

Fancy lay back and tried to calm her jumping nerves.
Would he really go down to the slave deck and pick
out a woman? To her surprise, the thought stung and
wounded her. She sighed and tried to muffle her
thoughts with dreams of Caleb, but somehow his face
remained vague and featureless tonight.

Betsy returned with a decanter and two glasses.

"I found his best brandy, ma'am, and I took the liberty of bringing a glass for myself. I could certainly do with
a drink!"

"Then fill up both glasses, Betsy, and enjoy yourself.
I feel like getting roaring drunk myself!" Silently the

both sipped, and when Betsy choked on the throat-searing drink, she laughed recklessly.

"You know what they say about brandy, Betsy? It makes you randy. Who do you fancy tonight?"

"Ma'am!" Betsy was shocked. "I'm not given that way, ma'am. Nobody's touched me, and unless I find a man to love, none shall!"

"But what if some man waylays you? Sometimes you have to move about the ship doing what you have to do. What then?"

"I've got my trusty little knife!" and Betsy whipped back her shift and showed Fancy her bare leg, where strapped to a garter just above her knee was a sheath from which she pulled out a wickedly sharp-looking knife, honed nearly to a point. "I used it once, just after we came on board. I pricked a man and he never came near me again. I am careful where I go and usually take Sam with me. Nothing has happened so far."

"But what if you fancy a man? What then?"

"Never having been with a man, I cannot imagine . . ."

"Oh Betsy! Don't tell me you have never looked at a strange man and admired his wide shoulders and wondered what the feel of his muscled arms would be like around you? Nor felt a surge in your belly at the sight of a hairy chest?"

"No, ma'am, I haven't . . . and what's more, I don't like the idea!"

Fancy sighed.

"You lucky, lucky girl! I wish I could start all over again! I should dearly love to find one man, a strong man who would satisfy me and whom I could trust. I would thrill and satisfy him so much that he would never look at anyone else—such a man would get all my passion and loyalty. So much so that I should never again look at another man with yearning, always wondering if the next man is the man I am looking for." Fancy's eyes had taken on a dreamy, half-drunken look.

"You have found such a man, ma'am. You don't see

what's under your nose."

"What do you mean?" Fancy's tone was sharp and belligerent.

"The captain, ma'am—*he* loves you!"

Fancy gave out a great peal of laughter.

"That bastard? He no more loves me than he does the woman he's gone looking for! I'm just another slave to him!"

"He loves you, ma'am, I'm sure of it." Betsy's voice sounded stubborn and positive.

"Here, fill our glasses up again and tell me why you think that."

Betsy slopped the brandy into the two glasses and hiccupped. She was not used to the strong drink. She giggled a little and gave Fancy her glass, slopping some more of the liquid over the sheets.

"Well?" Fancy leaned forward, hugging the bedclothes. Suddenly she wanted badly to know.

"It shows in his face, for one thing. Don't you recognize love when you see it?"

"Nonsense! You're foxed and don't know what you're saying. He's never told me he loves me!"

"No, he wouldn't. And you know why?" Betsy did not wait for an answer. "Because you would squeeze all the love out of him, and he would be helpless! You would have no mercy on him if you once found his weakness!"

Fancy stared at her in the moonlight and hiccupped softly.

"By God, you're right! I should milk every emotion out of him! Make him suffer, like he made me suffer. But I should flog you for knowing it! Do you hear, Betsy? I should flog you for knowing me so well." Her head flopped on to her pillow and the glass slid with a crash onto the floor. When Betsy, swaying and lurching, looked at her, she was sleeping like a baby. Giggling a little, Betsy slid down beside the bed and stretched out on to the floor. There was silence, except for the heaving and creaking of the ship . . .

When Fancy awakened, she felt as if her head was going to fall off her shoulders. She groaned. Trying to raise herself, she felt a searing pain go through her eyes. She lay back and ran her dry tongue around her foul-tasting mouth, wishing she was dead. She was lying in a damp patch, and had the horrible suspicion that she had wet herself, but on raising her arms she found herself merely bathed in a heavy sweat. Her body stank of stale sweat and brandy. A groan nearby made her turn her head carefully, and if she had not felt so wretched she could have laughed out loud. Betsy was still lying at the side of the bed and she looked a queer shade of green.

For a long while Fancy lay, rolling with the movement of the ship. She too, felt sick and wished for nothing better than to feel land under her feet once again. She groaned and this time Betsy managed to get to her knees.

"Are you all right, ma'am? I feel terrible bad myself."

"You look it. Have you strength to shout for Sam? He will bring us some coffee. It is a wonder he hasn't come near us already. The sun is high." Betsy groaned and managed to stagger to her feet, clutching the bed.

"Oh, never again! I'll never drink brandy again. Oh, my head!" And she stood, swaying slightly and holding her head.

Fancy tried to look up at her and failed.

"What happened? We only had two glasses?"

Betsy held up her own and Fancy's broken glass, and said nothing. Fancy gave them a quick look and then shut her eyes.

"Ale glasses, you fool! We must have drunk most of the decanter . . ."

"We did," Betsy held up the empty decanter," and I don't think the captain is going to be pleased."

"Black Patch!" Fancy sat up with a little scream and then moaned, her head dropping back to the pillow. "God! I wonder what happened last night?" The earlier events flooded back into her mind. "If that swine . . ." She stopped. There was a figure standing in the doorway.

"Which swine would that be, Fancy?" Black Patch

stood before her, looking suspiciously healthy and fit after his drunken debauch of the night before.

"Get out of here—you smell of black woman!"

He grinned and stretched and took a deep breath.

"It's a fine morning and the sun's hot. You want to get up and out on to your deck. But watch the wind. The holds are beginning to reek."

"You don't deny being with a black woman?"

"Why should I? It is my business."

"You devil!" Fancy snatched the hairbrush that was lying within reach and let fly. Black Patch ducked, and then everything whirled around her and she sank back on the bed, eyes shut, head spinning. Black Patch frowned, and his good eye glittered.

"What's been going on here?" He looked at Betsy and around the cabin, then lit on the decanter. He swore.

"My best brandy! You two drunken sluts! So you are trying to take your revenge by drinking my brandy! Well, let me tell you, from now on you can both shift for yourselves! I've already warned Sam not to wait on you any longer, and as for you," turning to Fancy, "you can eat in here! I'll not have you at my table!" With that he walked arrogantly out of the cabin.

Betsy stared after him, while Fancy, pushing the tumbled hair out of her eyes, tried to sit up.

"By God, ma'am, I wonder what made me think he loved you? He means what he says. The rest of this voyage is going to be very unpleasant!" They stared at one another, and silently Fancy agreed. She wished now that she had not asserted herself but her mind was not on the uncomfortable time ahead. She was thinking of the smooth black glistening body in Monty's arms the night before. She could have killed him!

Betsy brought the coffee, which was simmering in the galley. Sam had rolled his eyes and looked fearfully in the direction of the captain's apartments, but he had shown her where the food was and promised to prepare something for Betsy whenever she asked.

Fancy sipped the brew thoughtfully. What was she

upposed to do now? Did he intend her to crawl to him?
Her pride made that unthinkable. To crawl would be to
admit that she was his woman to do as he liked with.
Never! She would be flogged first!

And so the day came and went, and she saw no sign of
him. Twice she heard him call out and Sam answer, but
he did not come to her cabin. Betsy and she found that
they had taken for granted many of the jobs that Sam
had done for them. Carrying water for washing and
emptying their slops were tedious. Betsy grumbled and
Fancy began to grow impatient.

"For goodness sake! Try to be a little more cheerful.
Here, give me the slop bucket and I'll carry it up to the
deck." She grabbed it from Betsy and made her way up
the companion-ladder. The ship swayed and she narrowly missed being drenched with the slopping mess.
Staggering slightly, she tried to lift it over the wood-
work.

Betsy screamed after her, "Watch the wind, ma'am.
Watch the wind!" But too late! Fancy caught the slops
full in the face. There was a loud raucous laugh, and she
looked up to the bridge to see Black Patch watching
with Ned Gamble behind him, grinning openly.

Streaming and stinking, she stamped her foot and
hurtled the wooden bucket the length of the tarpaulined
part of the deck. She swore at him, and then made her
way down to her cabin again.

After that, Fancy made certain that he was not on the
bridge when she came up for air and exercise.

When the wind dropped, the stench was so great that
she and Betsy could not remain for any length of time
above deck. Sometimes, they could hear the slaves
mustering in a long shuffling line to be doused with sea
water and then deloused. Then the bullwhip would
crack and a general cleaning-out of the holds would begin. When the slaves were finally reshackled and
washed, they would sing their tribal songs and beat out
the time on the timbered sides of the ship. The rhythm
would go on and on until Fancy could have dashed her
head against the wooden bulwarks, and then it would

suddenly cease, as if someone had silenced them all at
the same moment, and her ears would ache at the awful
stillness, expecting any minute for the chanting to break
out afresh.

One day when she knew the fifty women were on
deck, she peeped around her tarpaulin. She knew the
women were there because the crew whistled and cat
called and she could hear giggling. Several small chil
dren raced around the deck and there were shrill cries
from their mothers to keep away from the sides of the
ship.

She watched, marveling at their ugliness. Their fuzzy
matted hair plastered into high peaks, their ornament
and lack of dress intrigued her. She noted the lean
flanks and firm bosoms of the young girls and wondered
which one had pleased Black Patch, making a note of
those who were evidently with child or feeding babies.
Some of the children were much lighter in color than
their mothers.

But the greatest shock came when she realized they
were all like children, with no memory for wrongs or
ability to bear grudges. They laughed and played
amongst themselves, and when they were full and well
fed, they accepted whatever happened to them. They
were not frightened of the crew. In fact, certain of the
young girls flaunted themselves to the men, and she
watched them being taken away.

A strange thing was happening to her. These same
ugly black women were becoming more acceptable to
her, and now that she saw them as human beings she was
beginning to feel ashamed—ashamed that she should be
Monty's partner and stand to gain from the sale of their
black flesh.

With nothing better to occupy her time, she came to
watch them more. Betsy, too, would peep and exclaim.

"Nasty smelly-looking lot! I don't know how the cap
tain . . ." and then she stopped and bit her lip.

Fancy said nothing. As the captain had said, it was
none of her business. But it had been more than a week
since her little rebellion and Fancy found herself con

antly on the lookout for him.

In her own mind she had decided which girl was
sharing his bed. She was small and neatly made, with
narrow waist and well-rounded buttocks and her breasts
were high and smooth and pointed upward. She walked
with the air of a queen, and when Fancy pulled aside the
tarpaulin to get a better view of the women, the girl
stared back at her proudly, her black eyes never flinch-
ing, and then turned insolently away. This was Umboo,
the girl the others deferred to. She was their leader and
she alone had the right to sleep with the captain.

She wore copper bracelets on her forearms and anklets of the same metal and Fancy noted that her
earlobes were stretched to take ivory hoops. The only
things to mar her animal beauty were the tribal marks
on her cheeks.

Now Fancy had found someone to hate. All the re-
sentment she felt at her treatment from Black Patch
poured out on that girl. If she had dared to climb into
their compound, she would have killed her.

But soon Black Patch sought her out again. She had
been hanging out her own and Betsy's things. Betsy had
done the washing and while she busied herself preparing
them some food, Fancy had offered to string out the
white shifts and cotton hose. When she had finished, she
turned swiftly, with the feeling that someone was
watching her—and there was Black Patch leaning over
the rail, a strange smile curving his lips.

"Hello there, partner! How are you making out?"

"Very well, thank you," she said coolly, her heart
hammering inside. She picked up the laundry basket
and turned away.

"Wait! I want to talk to you. Come up to the bridge."

"We have nothing to talk about! I am going down to
my cabin."

"I should throw you overboard," he said furiously,
"but you are still my partner. I want to talk business
with you."

"Then you can talk now. I am not stopping you!"

"I said the bridge, Fancy. I have things to do. Sailing

this ship is one of them."

"Very well," she said reluctantly. "If you say so, suppose I must."

She climbed the short enclosed stairway to the bridg She had never been there before, and as she climbed sl looked around at the great expanse of sea. Was that smudge of land over there? When she reached tl bridge, she shaded her eyes and pointed.

"Is that land? Have we actually reached America?"

"Aye. A day's sail and we'll be in Charleston, ar we'll be rid of this batch of savages. You look a litt hag-ridden Fancy. You've not enjoyed the voyag then?"

Fancy clenched her fists but did not rise to the ba She stood quietly by his side. For a few minutes l buised himself with map and compass and then straigh ened his back, as if he was weary. She looked at hi with surprise. He was never a man to suffer from il health. Then the explanation came to her, and sl curled her lips contemptuously. He was suffering afte his excesses with his black mistress! And yet when sl saw his drawn look, she was seized with an unexpecte pain in her heart. *Fool!* To be affected by this horrib man!

At last he turned to her, and his face was devoid expression.

"Well? Did you not at least enjoy part of it?" F looked at her and she flushed with annoyance. Tl beast could only think of his own coarse desires. The was no need to remind her of her own appetites! No tr gentleman would have reminded a lady about suc things. But then, she thought drearily, perhaps she w no lady.

She turned away to the sea and contemplated tl smudge of brown on the horizon. What would Americ be like? Could she make a new life for herself Charleston? But the thought of Charles left behind England drew her thoughts back home. No. She cou never settle so far away from her son. It would be ha to go back to England but life without Charles and tl

prospect of never seeing him again appalled her. Rather
go back and become a servant than to know she would
never see him again.

She felt cruel fingers dig into her shoulders and spin
her round.

"Well? I asked you a question?" His good eye raked
her face for an answer. What did he want to know? Bewildered, she looked up at him.

"You know the answers. You know there were moments when both our baser selves were satisfied! But
then you can get the same pleasure with Umboo, can't
you?"

He let go of her as if her flesh scorched him.

"Is that all you can say?"

"What more is there? You took me against my will.
You knew I hated you for what you did before we sailed.
Charles will always come between us!"

"Charles, Charles!" he snarled. "It is always Charles
with you. Do you care for him because he is your son?
Or is it the father you care for—the gypsy who fathered
that brat you're carrying now?"

Fanny moved away from him. She had never seen him
so moved by the thought of the child she was carrying.

"So you are jealous of Caleb. Dear God! I don't expect to see him again. But I did love him! He was my
first love! But he did not want me as a wife. Do you
hear? I wasn't good enough to be his wife!"

"Why?" The word was a bark.

"Because I was a *gaujo,* not gypsy. My two children
are half-bred gypsies, *posh-rats,* he called them, and he
would never have recognized them." Her voice sank to
a whisper. "He did not want me as a wife."

Then she flung her head high. "But if I met him again
and he wanted me, I should go with him!"

Black Patch turned away.

"Fool," he muttered to himself, and Fancy was hard
put to hear the words.

"He refused his Heaven on earth. If I had that
chance."

He stood gazing out to the land-smudge on the hori-

zon. "We must talk about your future. Do you want to
remain in Charleston, when we land? I can give you
your share of the voyage up to the time we touch
Charleston and then on a later voyage I can bring your
share from Mr. Somers. You can trust me, Fancy." His
back was stiff and straight, and he stood unnaturally still
as he waited for her answer.

Fancy felt the tension in the air as she watched him,
head bent in thought, eyes fixed on the swell of the sea.
She shivered and felt somehow she had come to a cross
roads. At that moment, for the first time, she felt the
child leap in her womb. She took it as a sign. It reminded
her of Caleb and the possibility of seeing him again.

"I want to go back to England and Charles."

"You mean you want to find Caleb," he said furi
ously.

"Yes, if you like. But it is really Charles I want."

"How can it be? No child could be more important
than the man."

"What's got into you, Monty? It has never mattered
to you before. Why bring all this up now? You used me
and I used you—It is as simple as that, and no regrets on
either side." Fancy knew that it was a lie as soon as the
words were out of her mouth. There was regret, at least
on her side, a regret she hardly liked to face, but which
existed nonetheless.

The hard saturnine face turned to her and he did not
smile.

"You are hard, Fancy, and uncompromising, I
thought you might have come to love me a little."

"Love!" She went into peals of laughter. "*Love!* You
don't know the meaning of the word! Why should you
have the satisfaction of owning a woman and using her
for your lust, and then asking for her soul as well? Men!
You're all the same. You're greedy and grasping and
want blood out of a stone. Is it not enough that you used
me?"

"Fancy, I . . ." He made to take her in his arms. She
pulled herself free.

"Don't touch me. Not after Umboo! I might have

ondoned your conduct before, for I too, used you, but
ot now, not after . . ."

Black Patch's face darkened.

"Don't malign Umboo. She's an innocent savage who
njoys doing the thing she knows best. She's given me
vhat you never gave."

"And what is that, pray?"

"Love and gratitude. Oh yes, she loves me in her way.
've been kind to her."

"And you think that is enough? You're kind, and you
vant her to lick your hand like a dog you have fed and
patted! You make me sick, Sir Montagu Hawkins,
night and gentleman of England! You want the impos-
ible! A white woman with the savage instincts of a
black slave. Someone who will lie there and take all
our lust, and love you into the bargain. Do you never
hink that you too could love in return?"

Black Patch clenched his fists and laughed bitterly.

"Women turn men into mice if they know they're
oved! Would you respect a man who crawled to you and
vas turned weak by love? Bah! You would put your foot
on my neck. I pity the man who loved you and let you
now it."

"Thank you. Now we both know how we stand."

"So you want a passage to England on this ship. What
f I refuse you?"

"You can't do that. I own half of it."

"True. But what if I say I want a woman? Do I take
Umboo with me, or will *you* oblige?"

"Take who you like, as long as I get back to
England."

"And you'll risk being caught by Sir Timothy? What if
I tell him you have returned?"

"I'll just have to disappear then, won't I? I would
quite expect you to play a dirty trick like that."

"Then it is settled. You leave Charleston with me,
nd I shall make my own arrangements."

"Thank you. You have been very obliging," she said,
vith biting sarcasm.

And so the next day, Fancy watched the coastline

getting nearer and nearer and more distinct until, wit
some dexterity, the ship anchored just a little down th
coast from Charleston.

Here the slaves were led, chained in tens, into th
longboats and rowed ashore to a palisaded baracoon
ready for the market.

She felt pity and guilt at the sight of the shufflin
mass, some with running sores and manacle burns. Bu
what could she do as a mere woman to alleviate thei
wretchedness? Monty would have laughed at her weak
ness and reminded her of what she stood to gain. Sh
closed her eyes in unaccustomed despair and concentra
ted her thoughts on Charles. Shaken by her thoughts
she turned her attention to the women clustering aroun
Umboo, who stood straight and unafraid.

She saw the girl's eyes wander to Black Patch who wa
standing on the bridge supervising operations, and a
feelings of remorse left her. The hated Umboo! Bu
Black Patch did not once look in her direction. Fanc
smiled to herself. Umboo had done her duty and wa
now to be discarded.

It was strange to walk down the narrow gangplank t
dry land after so long at sea. She took a deep breath an
set her shoulders back. So this was America, the ne
land. What would it hold for her?

CHAPTER
SEVENTEEN

Fancy enjoyed her stay in Charleston. She found the people strange at first, but they were all friendly and welcomed a new face. Indeed, if it had not been for Charles, she might have been tempted to stay.

She found the men foreign and exciting, their boldness and free manner so very different from the more stilted English. These men and women were pioneers, and came from many different countries, yet there they had an ease of manner which united all the different nationalities. Fancy sensed that emotions ran hot in this country. Men worked hard and played hard, and when not carving out careers and fortunes from this alien soil, proudly showed and boasted of their amorous exploits.

She had two proposals of marriage within a week of arriving, despite being large with child. Laughingly she had refused both offers, hardly crediting the sincerity of the men. Both scowled and soon showed the other side of their charming exterior.

The women, too, were strange to Fancy, and their ways amazed her. She was used to Court ladies having their little affairs, but usually they were conducted discreetly and after a certain pattern; even if a lady was as keen as her lover, she managed an air of coy reluctance. But these women showed their likes and dislikes openly, and often quarreled and fought in public over some lucky man.

She and Betsy were staying with Señor Pedro del Fernandez, a portly Spaniard who had drifted into Charleston in a longboat after a storm eleven years before. With quiet determination and an unscrupulous mind he had prospered, and was now the Governor of Charleston and South Carolina. He owned two estates and took the pick of the new slaves before they were put on the market. He was married to a creole, a beautiful girl of about twenty whom he kept busy each year with a new baby. She and Fancy became good friends, even though Paola knew little English. They would mime to each other and teach each other words, and their conversations usually ended in gales of laughter.

It became quite a game for them to pat each other's stomach and say, "how well?," and soon Fancy found out that Paola's child was due in six weeks. They would sit together during the heat of the day and talk together, with Betsy joining in, all three engaged in sewing tiny baby clothes. While quietly resting between voyages, Fancy planned to take advantage of the time to buy materials for baby garments and her own and Betsy's wardrobe.

She and Betsy had just completed a ballgown for their last night before sailing. They had been nearly three months in Charleston and it was almost like preparing to leave home. She had seen very little of Black Patch, who had been kept busy seeing to the sale of the slaves, the dismantling of the slave decks and the preparations to take on another cargo to take back to England.

Now, in her pretty blue and silver ball gown, Fancy felt at her very best again. Expecting a child had made her more beautiful. Her hair was glossy and had grown considerably, and she now wore it high and puffed, curled and held with Spanish combs. It suited her.

Except for the bulge, which was becoming an encumbrance, she was pleased with the effect, the adding of a special tier to the gown's dropped waistline made it less apparent. She twirled in front of the cheval mirror.

"It looks as well as any of Mademoiselle Annette's expensive gowns. No one in London would believe we made it ourselves! You are a clever girl, Betsy. I had no idea you were so capable."

Betsy blushed with pleasure.

"I always wanted to be a seamstress, ma'am, and I love running rich materials through my fingers."

"Then I promise that you will have your own business when we get back to England! And I'll bring all my friends . . ." She stopped abruptly, and bit her lip. "That is . . . if I dare show myself in London again!" But quickly she cheered. "There are always other towns where you can set up a business. Women everywhere will always patronize a good dressmaker."

"Oh, ma'am, if only I could!"

Happily, Betsy went on with her work. She did not always approve of Fancy, but she adored her, and was content to be where she was, knowing she was the warmest person she had ever met.

Fancy stood with her host and hostess to receive the guests in the great hall of Pedro's huge white mansion. The black and white expanse of marble floor was already crowded. Black slaves thrust into unaccustomed shoes and European livery were offering trays of drinks, the rum and fine wines were flowing freely, and the noisy chatter was fast becoming a roar. In the distance was the sound of music, and already the young unattached couples were dancing, chaperoned by the elderly ladies of the town.

And then Fancy caught her breath. The fine dandified figure of Black Patch was coming toward them. Pedro smiled and held out his hand.

"Ah, my friend, so you managed to make it! Where is the ragged captain tonight? You look the perfect gentleman, doesn't he, my dear?" he said, turning to his wife.

She nodded, saying little but putting her hand out to be kissed.

Then he turned to Fancy and they stood looking at one another. Seeing his distinguished air and fine clothes, and the strange look in his eye, Fancy was disturbed. A thrill ran from her fingers and up into her head as he gave her palm a lingering kiss. It had been so long . . .

"You look beautiful tonight. I didn't remember just how beautiful. Are you well?"

"Very well—and you?" She did not realize how radiant her smile was.

"Better for seeing you. Are you going to dance with me?"

"Perhaps." Fancy was trying to still her fast-beating heart, but she could not resist adding, "And Umboo, how is she?"

Black Patch scowled.

"Umboo? Who is she?"

"You know damn well who she is," Fancy hissed furiously.

Black Patch gave a wide smile which showed his strong white teeth.

"Still the same old Fancy! Forget Umboo. I sold her as soon as we reached Charleston. I already had a buyer for her." He nodded slightly in Pedro's direction, and Fancy's eyes opened wide.

"You mean . . ."

"Yes, and keep quiet about it, or else . . ."

Fancy meekly cast down her eyes.

"Just as you say, Monty."

"Oho! We're on Monty terms again, eh? Come away from this dais. I want to talk to you in private."

"But I am supposed . . ."

"Damn what you are supposed to do. Señor Pedro, may we be excused? Fancy and I have much to talk about."

Pedro smiled benignly and waved his fat cigar in their direction.

"Of course. I kept her by my side for your sake, my friend! She has many other suitors sniffing round her skirts." He smiled and winked at Fancy.

Black Patch turned to her, and her heart leapt. Was he jealous? Then she chided herself. Fool to think that a self-sufficient man like him could be jealous!

But it was a grim Black Patch who took her hand and led her in a stately fashion through the hall, smiling stiffly at his acquaintances as he went. Suddenly he whisked her into a small anteroom and shut the door firmly behind him.

"Now, Fancy, what is all this I hear about suitors? Even I have heard the rumors. Are you thinking of staying in Charleston?"

"There's no man who could tempt me to stay in Charleston," she said truthfully.

"Charles again I suppose!" His mouth curled. "Have you got a stone for a heart, Fancy? Can no one tempt you to fall in love?"

"Why bring love up again? Are you obsessed with the word? It all depends what you call love, in any case. I pleased you once. Isn't that enough?"

"I wasn't talking about pleasing me, I was talking about love—that emotion that lives even when the recipient does not deserve it . . . that survives disasters and treachery . . . that will not die even when stretched to the limit!"

"You talk of love as if it was a miracle . . . a miracle of endurance! Could either of us hope for that kind of love?" But Fancy's heart beat fast. Was he . . .? Did he . . .? But Black Patch turned away and the emotion-charged moment dwindled and died.

Suddenly Fancy was in a fog of despair. What did she want of this man whom she hated, who disappointed her in some way that she could not fathom? Half-formed feelings engulfed her. It was as if her body and her mind were pushing her in opposite directions. She was confused—and he appeared no better.

"Are you taking me back to England then?" Her voice was harsh and sharp, yet there was a lump in her throat. He *must* not know how near to tears she was.

"Yes, after the child is born. I'll not have you aboard beforehand."

"Then you will have to wait another four weeks. Do you mind?"

"Not in the least. Tomorrow we sail for the Bahamas. With good weather, and luck with us, we should be there in good time for your lying-in. We deliver a cargo for Señor Pedro and take on a cargo of spices. It should make us a good profit. King Charles will be well satisfied with his share of the enterprise."

"How long will it be before we start for England?"

"Three, perhaps four months. Plenty of time for you to recover."

"I was not thinking of that." Fancy's mind seethed with possibilities. Such a long time at sea with Black Patch. Could it be a fresh start for them? Something inside made it seem possible—or was he planning something different? A woman with a small baby at the breast could be distasteful to a man like Black Patch. Would there be another woman to take her place? Was he planning to humiliate her again? She pursed her lips to a stubborn line. Why should she care? He wasn't the man she was looking for.

Black Patch noted the stubborn look.

"You do not like the idea? I see. My company is abhorrent to you now. Very well, madam, I can make other arrangements!" He turned to leave the anteroom, but Fancy took his arm.

"Wait. I did not say so! Why is it that we quarrel whenever we meet? You are very touchy, my friend. Is it to be so all the way to England?" She looked up at him pleadingly. "Monty, be my friend. I need a friend badly. When we get back to England, I know not what will happen. If I am still supposed to be imprisoned for my so-called madness, and Sir Timothy hears I am back, he will leave no stone unturned. . . ."

"You must remember he placed you in my care."

"What does that mean?"

"It means I can dispose of you as I see fit!"

"But that is absurd. You will not want me a burden around your neck forever! I am not your ward, or a piece of baggage to be disposed of!"

"You heard what he said yourself! It was a gentleman's agreement."

"But—but . . ."

"He said I could enjoy you . . . and sell you when I was tired of you."

"But you would never do that! I am your partner!"

"Aye, and you will continue to be! But to be my partner you must sail with me again. Is that clear?"

Fancy's eyes filled with tears.

"But I don't *want* to sail again! I want to have my baby nd settle down somewhere quietly in the country with etsy. I want to smell England after the rain and walk he woodland paths and see the green, green grass!"

"And wait for that blasted gypsy, no doubt!" Black atch's voice was a snarl, and suddenly he pulled Fancy lose to him. She could feel his heart thundering in his hest. "If you think I'm going to take you to England nd leave you free to cavort in the woods with your gyp- y lover, you are mistaken! You're mine, and I've pan- ered to your whims long enough. If it had not been for he baby, I should never have let you sleep alone! And vhen you've dropped it—" he smiled—"we shall go on s before!"

"Never! Not after Umboo! I'll not follow that lack . . ."

He kissed her savagely.

"Never?" His mouth lingered over hers, causing her o shiver. She fought her sudden emotion and stiffened. Ie laughed.

"Stop it!" she stormed. "I'm going to England . . ."

"To look for Caleb?"

"No. Caleb will not be in England, his tribe was lipping out to France. It's Charles I want to see gain . . ."

"And then?"

"Then—I don't know . . ."

"If he is content and happy, will you bring unhappi- ess to him? Or strip him of the birthright he thinks he is ntitled to? Fancy, Fancy, you're in a world of your wn! What will you do?"

"I'll think of something."

"You want to wait for Caleb! He'll be back. Those ypsies come and go from one country to another as free s birds. You have a dream about that man, but it won't vork, Fancy. He would only break your heart if you ver let yourself love him. No. You and I belong togeth- r. We deserve each other. I know your faults, and you now mine. I've been honest with you. What more can

we hope for? I am not giving you a choice, Fancy, I am
telling you: you *are* mine, and that is the end of it! Now
come and enjoy yourself in the ballroom. This party is
being laid on for us." He took her arm and gently but
firmly led her back to where the music was playing.
"Smile, damn you! We don't want to look as if we've
been quarreling!"

Back on the ballroom floor, he smiled brilliantly to a
fat matron who had a hopeful daughter. She fluttered
and smiled back, twirling her fan coquettishly. Fancy set
her teeth and gave a tall dandy with protruding teeth an
encouraging smile.

Black Patch held out his arms and Fancy melted into
them for the gavotte, and as they twirled and parted she
watched him flirt outrageously, not only with her but
with all the other ladies. She had an urge to bite
him. . . .

Thoughts of England and the past flared within her, and
as the days passed, she found herself thinking of Caleb.
He was a tantalizing mystic figure who came to her in
dreams but always turned into Monty when she reached
out to touch him. But most of all, she yearned for
Charles. She remembered Lady Letitia, the gentle creature whom she had loved, who had spurned her baby as
if she had known it was not her own. She wondered how
the boy looked now. Would he be tall and strong like his
father? And was he happy? Or had Sir Timothy succeeded in destroying any affection the boy had for her.
Bitterly she wondered when they would visit England
again.

But now they were aboard the *Emma-Jane* again and
heading for the Bahamas. The wind was hot, and Fancy
was forced to leave off her stiffened stays and let out her
gowns. The first night out after asking discreet questions
of Sam, she learned that there were neither slaves nor
other women aboard except Betsy and herself. Black
Patch slept alone.

She and Betsy spent the time quietly sewing and

dozing on their own part of the deck. But soon Fancy became uncomfortably aware that she was not going to reach the islands—her child was in a hurry to be born.

She spent an uneasy night. The pains were niggly and would desist suddenly, as if they had settled down again. But the swaying and rocking of the ship did nothing to help matters, and by morning she felt distinctly unwell.

Betsy came to her, frightened and white-faced.

"What are we going to do, ma'am? I've never delivered a baby before. What can I do for you?"

Fancy groaned. The pains around the pit of her belly were fiercer now.

"Go to the captain and find out if there is a doctor aboard. I understood there was a doctor of sorts for the slaves. If there is, bring him." And then she tensed as another pain came to a crescendo and died away again. Sweat had streamed down her face and neck, and ran in a river between her breasts. She bit back a groan. It was too early to shout. She must save her strength.

Black Patch came down to see her. His face was expressionless.

"Are you sure? The baby is really coming?"

"Of course I'm sure! Don't talk like a fool!" she said sharply. "Is there a doctor aboard?"

"Of a kind. He's rough and it has been many years since he delivered a child. But still . . . I suppose he knows how it is done. I'll fetch him." He turned to go, and then came back to the bed and grasped her hand. "Hang on Fancy. Everything will be fine, you'll see!" He went out, and Fancy bit her lip. His unaccustomed gentle tone had made her want to cry.

He returned a short while later with Betsy and an old, wizened little man who smelled strongly of rum. His rheumy eyes and dirty fingernails filled Fancy with apprehension.

"This is Doctor Theobold, Fancy. Will you let him examine you?" She remained silent, in the throes of a pain.

The old man bent over her and his hands mercilessly pressed and pushed.

"Hmm, I think she will go some hours yet. There's nothing to be done now. Nature must take its course. It will be a big baby." He turned to Betsy. "Watch her well, and give her slops, and tell me if and when she gets her bearing-down pains. I'll be back." Betsy nodded and the old man left the cabin. "I'll go and see about boiling some water and finding fresh linen."

"And get out those baby clothes," said Fancy weakly, waiting for the next onslaught of pain.

Black Patch watched her for a moment and then silently sat down at the side of the bed. He took a cloth and wiped away the sweat from her brow, and then held her hand.

"Do you want me to stay?" His voice was gentle.

"Will you mind? I must look a dreadful sight!"

"I don't mind. But do you want me to stay? Will it help you?"

Fancy smiled faintly.

"It would be a comfort. I feel very alone. It will all depend on my own efforts from now on."

"And the baby's efforts too, Fancy."

"Yes. Funny, I haven't thought about it much. It's been only a lump until now. I wonder what it will be?"

"You'll love it, whatever it will be. You're a true mother." He smiled down at her encouragingly. "Just see, it will be as easy as shelling peas!"

She tried to laugh but the pain came again. She gripped his hand until her nails drew blood, but he did not wince. And then she felt the damp cloth move firmly but lightly over her forehead and neck. It was refreshing.

"A drink?" he said, holding out a glass of fresh water in which a lime had been squeezed. She drank gratefully, then gasped as the pain started again . . .

The long hours passed slowly, and Black Patch stayed with her, talking little. Somehow, his silent sympathy was a comfort. Betsy came and went, ready to lend a hand if necessary, but Black Patch would wave her away, keeping private vigil by her bed.

Fancy was now reduced to an exhausted, sweat-drenched, quivering mass. This birth seemed a lot more difficult than the last . . . Suddenly the first bearing-down pains brought a groan, long and shuddering, from her lips.

"Betsy!" called Black Patch sharply. "Fetch Doctor Theobold at the double!" and he turned Fancy sharply over on her back. "Bring up your knees and pull, like you never pulled before." Gasping, Fancy tried to do what he said, but her strength was ebbing.

"I can't," she sobbed.

"Come on, Fancy my girl, the blacks push 'em out like peas! Don't tell me you have less courage than they!"

She tried to raise her head and glare at him, but she only managed to gasp instead.

Betsy came back at a run.

"I can't find the doctor anywhere! Sam thinks he's gone off with a bottle somewhere and could be hiding down in the hold!"

"Is he, by God! I'll have his skin off in strips, if he is! Send Sam to look for him—and, Betsy, bring that water." Betsy sped off again, crying into her apron.

Fancy set her teeth. The pains were long now and practically continuous.

"Come on, Fancy, another one gone. It can't be long now. Again, girl . . . that's good . . ." To her surprise, Fancy felt his hands gently examining her. "It's nearly here, girl! Another strong pain, and it'll come. Now gently, gently, no tearing . . . and now . . . now!"— and Fancy felt a pain that nearly tore her body in two.

"*Aaaah* . . ." She screamed and felt a wet slither and a gush, and warm water flowing. Then, somehow, Black Patch was holding a squirming snuffling scrap, that opened its mouth and gave a huge wail. It was over!

For a moment, she lay in dazed exhaustion, vaguely aware of Black Patch moving about beside her. She was too tired to wonder about the child or what sex it was. She was at peace now, and there seemed to be a hollow where the great lump had been.

Then she heard Black Patch's voice close to her ear.

"Push again, Fancy. You must get rid of the afterbirth."

She had the feeling of slithery fish coming away from her, and then it was over, and she lay drowsily while he fussed over her, making her comfortable. Betsy leaned over her and placed the baby in her arms.

"What is it?" she said sleepily.

"A girl, and her skin is pink and smooth as the petals of a camellia," said Black Patch gently.

"Then I'll call her Camille," she said, on the verge of sleep . . .

After that, life took on a dream-like quality. She slept and awakened and fed the hungry child, and found herself disinclined to get out of bed. She would lie half–awake to try to recall those hours when Black Patch had encouraged and helped her, but the memory of it all became confused. Black Patch became another man altogether, not his usual rough grumpy self but some vague, dream-like lover . . .

And then one morning the Black Patch she knew burst into the cabin and yanked the bedclothes off her. Standing over her and looking grim he said.

"Now isn't it about time you got up out of that stinking bed and started to live again? The baby is more than two weeks old. You cannot hide here forever."

Fancy turned lackluster eyes on him.

"What does it matter? The baby is well-fed. I have plenty of milk. She is not suffering."

"No, but Betsy is overworked. She is looking after the baby and you as well, and the wench looks all in. Get your backside out of there, and look after your child yourself." Fancy took a deep breath and sat up.

"Very well, I suppose I must do as you say . . ."

"Damn right you must! Are you afraid I'll want you again? If so, let me put your mind at rest. I'm not an animal, and I know when a woman needs to be on her own. Get up and help look after Camille. She's a lovely child and needs her mother's love." He looked at her accusingly. "Betsy says you rarely hold her except when you feed her. What's the matter with you? Did you want another son, to take Charles' place?"

Fancy flushed. It was true she had hoped for another boy. Shamefaced, she turned to him.

"I wanted another boy, but not to take Charles' place. No baby could do that. I simply never thought of having a girl."

"Well, think of her now—and don't make me ashamed of you!"

But there was something else bothering Fancy. She had never felt shy of the great rough Captain before, but now she somehow feared facing him. He knew her so intimately that she began to fear that she might no longer be attractive to him, and found herself dreading that he might never again desire her in the same eager and demanding way.

So it was that she found herself suddenly and reluctantly faced with the truth that her hate was turning into a red-blooded love after all! For who could ever hate the man whose comfort and help had given her courage to give birth?

So she dragged herself out of the bed and made her way to his stateroom, to observe him and watch for his reactions. Would she be obnoxious to him? This was the fear that had kept her in her bed. She watched his face for a sign. There was none. His face was dispassionate as he looked her up and down. Then he poured out a glass of wine for her.

"There! You look better. I see you have washed your hair. You will soon be your old self again. I have arranged for Sam to carry the cot up on deck on the days the wind is in the right quarter."

"But will it not be too hot for her?"

"Of course not. We shall rig up a shelter. It will be better than sitting in that stuffy cabin. Betsy is all for it. She is thriving now, so good fresh air will not hurt her. You've got a bonny baby, Fancy, so cherish her!"

"I think you really like her, Monty!" The name slipped out unconsciously.

He grinned.

"Of course I love her, you little fool. Didn't I help to

bring her into the world? You and I, Fancy, did a great job! Of course I love her!"

"And you don't—don't hate me, for what you saw when I was helpless?"

"Fancy! What's got into you? Of course I don't hate you. Why should I?"

"Well I wasn't at my best . . . I was a sight to put any man off . . ."

"Nothing you did would shock me, Fancy. You and I are kindred spirits! We hate each other, look down on each other and have no illusions about our bad qualities. You're no saint and neither am I—and yet . . ." He stopped and Fancy's heart began its familiar thumping.

"And yet . . ." she whispered.

"Aw, come on, Fancy. It's not like you to be frightened of the effect on me . . ."

Disappointment washed over her and she flung her wineglass at the porthole. It shattered, and he looked at her with amusement.

"What in Hell's—" and then he laughed. "That's more like my girl!" He swung her around and kissed her. "I was getting worried. I thought you were sickening for something!"

And for some unknown reason, Fancy's heart sang. She had not been so happy for a long time. The quality of the kiss was the same as before. He might not love her, but he still wanted her—that was enough for now!

CHAPTER EIGHTEEN

Great Bahama Island lay shimmering in the heat. Fancy shaded her eyes and watched the vast expanse from the bridge of the *Emma-Jane*. The heat was sweltering and she was wearing as little as possible under her low-cut cotton gown. Now she could understand why all natives went naked. Already her gown was uncomfortably sticky. She glanced down into the cot beside her. Camille was sleeping peacefully and her little curled hands lay above her head. She too wore very little, and Fancy smiled to herself when she thought how shocked the ladies of England would be at the sight of her . . .

Camille was comfortable and growing rapidly. Her skin was still like a camellia and now, in the heat, her fine black hair curled on her slightly damp forehead. It squeezed Fancy's heart to see the child's resemblance to Caleb, but now it was more because she wished her father had been Monty . . .

For Monty seemed to be no more. It was the bad-tempered Black Patch who had sailed the ship to the Bahamas. He had never once come into her cabin at night. She sighed. It was as if she could not get near to him. He was polite and kind, rough and bad-tempered by turns—but never loving. It was as if he kept a tight rein on his emotions. The only time a hint of that tenderness she knew existed in him came to the surface was when he picked Camille out of her crib and cradled her to him. And then for a few magical moments she saw him as Monty, her man.

But those moments were few and far between. Other

nights he drank and sang with Ned Gamble and the other officers. And then when the dawn was coming up, he would stagger to his bunk, and at last there would be silence . . .

But now, with the island within reach, Fancy had a new interest. She anticipated her trip ashore with pleasure. They needed fresh fruit and vegetables and sweet water, and as part of the cargo had to be unloaded and another taken on, it would be some days, perhaps weeks before they departed.

She scanned the coastline and the hills in the background, hoping it would be possible to walk and explore. She would ask Black Patch about a picnic . . .

But when Black Patch came back from his first excursion ashore, his face was as black as thunder.

"What is it?" she asked fearfully. "Are we not welcome? Señor Pedro said . . ."

"It's nothing to do with Juarez. It's something else . . . or rather someone else."

Fancy stared at him, puzzled. Who could it be?

"What do you mean? You can't know anyone in the Bahamas?"

For a few minutes Black Patch strode up and down the stateroom, his hand on his chin. Then he stood glaring out of the porthole. There was a long silence.

"Monty, you frighten me. What is it?"

He laughed and turned swiftly and caught her to him and lifted her high in the air.

"Monty . . . are you mad?"

He set her down gently, but did not let her go. He held her by the shoulders and then kissed her. For a moment his brow cleared, and she smiled timidly at him. She did not understand his mood. And then he spoke.

"You are going to have your wish granted, Fancy!" She stared up at him uncomprehending. "You know who I bumped into on the wharf?"

"Of course not! Don't tease me, Monty. Who did you meet?"

"Your gypsy friend, Caleb Neyn!"

Fancy froze. It could not possibly be true! When he

had left her that night of the fire, he had been setting out to look for his family . . .

"It can't be true! Are you making some kind of a joke?"

"No joke, Fancy. He drifted into the Bahamas six months ago and has carved himself a nice little niche right here."

"But I can't understand it . . ."

"He's working for Juarez, and doing very well. He tells me that after he left you, he was on the run two days, and then was caught and sent back to his ship. For a while his ship, the *Royal Cygnet*, patroled the Channel and then became embroiled with the rest of the Fleet with the French and Dutch. They were wrecked out in the Atlantic, and he and several other men survived a week at sea in an open boat until they drifted near to the island of Bermuda. Then he and two others worked their passage here."

"And you talked together? You did not fight?"

"No. Why should we? He is Juarez's assistant. He does not know you are aboard."

"Then—then, you don't want me to see him?"

He turned away and looked out of the porthole at the busy wharf. She held her breath, waiting for his answer. He shrugged.

"It is up to you."

Fancy's hopes sank. He did not care after all! She was just another woman to him.

"Then I'll see him. I want to see him again, and show him Camille."

"Is that wise? You know he will regard her as another *posh-rat*?"

She stopped in her tracks.

"But now he has no wife with him, perhaps he will think differently."

"It is your decision, Fancy. You must do as you think best."

"But what do *you* want me to do?" Her cry came from the heart. He looked at her strangely.

"I want *you* to decide your future. I'll not cause you to

hate me more. If I kept you hidden from him, you would
never forgive me for it! No. It is right for you to decide
for yourself."

"You don't care if I decide to leave you and remain
here in the Bahamas?"

Again he turned his back.

"Of course I should care! I should miss quarreling
with you, for a start!"

"Is that all?" Fancy's voice broke.

"What more could I miss, as things are? Charles and
Umboo are between us."

"Oh, Monty . . ." She made to go to him, but he
spoke roughly over his shoulder.

"Get out of here, and go and find your gypsy lover
. . . See if he measures up to your girlish dreams! And
while you're about it, stay with him and get him out of
your system! We sail in ten days from now, with you or
without you."

"You're not serious?"

"Fancy, I've never been more serious in my life!"

She stared at his back and then turned to leave the
cabin.

"Goodbye then, Monty . . . and thank you for what
you did for me." When he did not answer she went to
her own cabin and, to Betsy's great surprise, burst into
floods of tears.

"Ma'am . . . ma'am, whatever's the matter? Has that
brute been ill-using you? I'll go and give him a piece of
my mind! The very idea . . ."

"No, no, wait! Betsy, it's not him at all. It's Caleb . . .
he's on the island and I'm going to him. So pack and
we'll take everything with us."

"Everything, ma'am? What about England and
Charles? Your only thought was to get back."

"Oh, Betsy, I don't know what I want! But I must see
Caleb. Monty was right. I must find out about him, or
lay his ghost to rest forever."

So Fancy, carrying Camille and followed by a
disapproving Betsy, was helped down the gangway by
Ned Gamble. There was no sign of Black Patch, and she

stopped and gave the ship a long look. It could be the last time she saw it . . .

She made for the great factory built of pilings on the wharf. Beside it was an office that served duty as a house. She guessed Caleb might be there. Now hope and fear warred inside her. Would he be as she remembered him—the young virile gypsy with the guileless face, the man who had loved her so openly and well?

Giving the baby to Betsy, she motioned for her to sit on the cool verandah. And then she pushed open the door and walked into the dim interior. She blinked, blinded by the sudden gloom. And then she looked around, and there was Caleb, watching her as if he had seen a ghost. A bolt of cotton material dropped unheeded to the floor, then he smiled and pulled himself together.

"Fanny! The cunning bastard didn't tell me you were with him! Who told you I was here?"

"He did. He told me to come to you."

"Did he now? Sick of you, is he?" Suddenly his face changed to one of suspicion. "You haven't got the pox, have you?"

Fancy flinched as if she had been struck and flushed hotly.

"How dare you say such a thing?"

"I'm sorry, Fanny. But it would be just like him to give me a woman like that . . . especially after I took that copper-colored wench from him before!" He chuckled.

"I don't think he ever gave that a thought. He gave me the choice of coming, if you want to know. But I see you've changed, Caleb, grown away from me."

"Aw, come now, I don't know what you are talking about. Come on and give me a kiss. I'm glad to see you." She held up her face for his kiss and, grinning, he took her in a bear hug. She noticed he had lost two teeth, and the gaps altered his face.

He dropped her abruptly.

"You're different, too. Not so . . . giving! You aren't putting much feeling into it, are you?"

"Give me time, Caleb. What have you been doing with yourself?"

"Come along to the other side of this place. I have my own quarters there. Luala!"

A young girl with narrow fluid hips appeared from behind a curtain. She looked up hopefully at him. Fancy pursed her lips. So Caleb was nicely settled in.

"Luala, me go now. You look after store. Understand?" He waved his hands around the office. "Luala watch!"

The girl nodded, looking at Fancy with some speculation in her black eyes . . .

Caleb led the way to a roughly furnished room with a bed in one corner. She wrinkled her nose in distaste. The air was foul and smelled of stale spirits, among other things. Fanny thought of the girl, Luala. She sat down while Caleb poured two drinks and noticed that his hands trembled slightly. Was it because of her, or was he drinking too much? She watched him carefully. In the merciless light of the window she saw the changes in him. There were lines around his mouth that had not been there before. And had that chin always been weak? Or was it just in comparison with Black Patch? She felt disturbed. Somewhere inside her the image she had carefully built up of Caleb was crumbling . . .

Uneasily she took the wine and sipped. Caleb tossed his off at a gulp and refilled his glass. He leaned back in his chair.

"So you want to come to me on a permanent basis? What will Black Patch say to that?"

"As I said, it is up to me."

"And do you want to stay?" He put down his glass and stood up. He looked down at her and licked his lips. "*I* want you to stay . . ." His hand, which Fancy noted with surprise was hot and clammy, rested on her shoulder. He bent down and looked into her eyes. "Remember that night on the boat? God, I wished afterward I had kept you with me! I wanted you for weeks afterward . . ." Fancy found herself in his arms. "I want you now," he said thickly. His kiss was demanding and rough, and she felt his hands caressing her in the old familiar way . . . but now they did not arouse her: she felt revolted.

"What about Luala? Will she not object?"

"Oh, I've got Luala well-trained. She's used to my pecadilloes." His voice was low and he was too busy kissing Fancy's shoulder to note the effect his speech was having on her. She stiffened.

"You have *other* women then, Caleb?"

"You never expected me to turn against women, did you? We have slaves here, too, you know. Don't tell me you are fussy about slaves, after being on Black Patch's ship? I'll not believe it!"

"I'm not very proud of my part in the slave trade." She moved out of his arms. "How many women do you have, Caleb?"

"Oh, I don't know—ten or twenty, sometimes more, sometimes less."

"And Luala?"

"She's permanent. She's my number one girl."

"What about children, Caleb? You don't mind them being *posh-rats*?"

He grinned.

"I was young in those days—it meant more to me then. Now it doesn't matter so much! I expect I've left a few *posh-rats* around . . . How's Charles by the way? Still heir to the Gilbourne estates, I take it? You managed very well there . . ."

"I've got another baby now, Caleb, a daughter. Do you want to know about her?"

"So Black Patch got you with child! Ah well, it was to be expected. No. I was never one for children. They come, whether you want them or not. I never could understand Savina wanting . . ."

"Savina? How is she?"

"I don't know. I never found her again. Oh, someday I'll go back . . . when I have made my pile. And then it will be silk and velvet for Savina and the girls. I might even buy them a new *vardo*. The old one was a wreck . . ."

"So you expect her to wait for you?"

"Of course. Even if I never go back I know she wi
wait. That is what being a gypsy is all about. We're fam
ly people, you know. The Neyns and Fingos will loo
after them. I'm not worried about her . . . Now com
on, another kiss—the bed's comfortable." He grabbe
her again, but she twisted from him.

"No. I'm going back to the ship. I've got Betsy an
the baby outside. I'll take them back."

He narrowed his eyes.

"You mean you *were* going to stay? And you change
your mind?"

"I haven't changed my mind. I want time t
think . . ."

"Then bring them in here while you think. I shoul
like to see this child of yours."

Without more ado he strode through the outer offic
and beckoned for Betsy to come in. She came slowly
clutching the baby to her. Without a word, he took th
child in his arms and uncovered the shawl from abou
her face. For a long moment he looked at her and the
handed her back to Betsy.

"For a moment I thought . . . but never mind that!"
He gave Betsy an appraising look. "I like the look o
you, too. A man gets sick of native girls all the time."

Fancy overheard him. She looked sharply at him an
then at Betsy, noting Betsy's look of disapproval.

"You will leave Betsy alone! She's particular."

He laughed.

"Jealous, are you? I like to keep my women jealous."
Not deigning to reply, Fancy took the newly awak
ened child from Betsy.

"Is there anywhere where I can take her to feed her?"

"Feed her here. I'm used to seeing women sucklin
babies. It doesn't bother me!"

"But it bothers me. Where can I go?"

"In there, if you want to," he said grudgingly, an
Fancy moved through another door and found herself i
Luala's room, a dark chamber strewn with the nativ

rl's ornaments and heavy with her unmistakable
usky scent . . .

As she fed Camille, her mind was not on her baby but
a Caleb. Was the boy she knew still there, under the
rd, coarsened exterior? She doubted very much if
ey could ever reach that feeling of mutual love
ain . . .

But she *must* try to find some semblance of love. She
uld not go back to Black Patch, who obviously did not
ind her going with her gypsy lover . . .

Betsy stormed in with a carpetbag in each hand, high-
indignant.

"That man's no gentleman! He did not so much as of-
r to help me with the bags . . . and while I was holding
em and helpless he put his arm about my waist and
ssed me! You would do well to go back to the ship!"

"I can't," said Fancy flatly. "I told Black Patch I was
aving. He ordered me off the ship to find him—"

"Not this uncouth fellow?" gasped Betsy. Fancy
dded her head, unable to speak.

"Well, you're a fool, ma'am, and no mistake. To ex-
ange the captain for this—this—" She choked on the
rds she would have used. "You must be out of your
ind!"

"Oh, Betsy . . . what am I going to do?"

"Go back to Black Patch—what else?"

"But he doesn't want me! He doesn't care whether I
or stay!"

"Fiddlesticks! You talk like one of those birdbrained
nnyhammers one sees in London. Where's your cour-
e, ma'am? Why don't we just go back?"

"Go back where?" Fancy and Betsy looked at each
her, and then both turned to the door. Caleb had been
inking and now, straddling the entrance, he looked
gressive and tough. He hiccupped and threw the bot-
e he was holding through the open window. "Neither
you are going anywhere. I'm going to have you both.
u first," he pointed to Betsy, who stood mesmerized,
ust to whet my appetite for white women!"

Betsy's mouth dropped open in surprise. He move
to take hold of her and then she was galvanized into ac
tion. With a practiced swoop, her hand dropped to he
leg and Fancy saw the glint of a knife.

"You bitch!" snarled Caleb and made a lunge at he
Instantly, Betsy stabbed and drew blood. Caleb put h
hand up to his cheek and looked at his fingers.

"I'll flog you for that, then give you to Juarez to sell t
the highest bidder!"

"Leave her alone," screamed Fancy. "What's be
come of you. You're no more than a whoring monster.

Caleb's eyes lit on the baby and he smiled.

"You'll both do as I say! Luala!" he shouted. The gi
appeared at his side. "Take the brat, and get out o
here." The girl looked from him to Fancy and gave
slow smile. She seemed to coil herself, and then, befor
Fancy was aware of what she intended, she felt a blo
and dropped to the floor. As she fell, Luala snatched th
baby. Fancy screamed.

"Stop her, Betsy! She's got Camille!"

But Betsy was too late. Luala dodged to the door an
Caleb blocked Betsy's path. He lunged for her, bu
Betsy kicked him smartly on the shins. Fancy manage
to get on her feet again and, as Caleb groaned with pai
tried to make for the door after Luala.

"Oh, no you don't," growled Caleb, maddened wit
pain and a desire to master the two wild women. He wa
past thinking of Fancy as the girl he had once loved bac
in England. Now she was just a woman to be taken . .

He grabbed her about the waist and threw her dow
on the bed. Then he turned his attention on Betsy
"You wild bitch! I'll have some fun taming you!" and h
right hand came up and hit her on the point of the jav
She went down like a stone.

"You've killed her! You've killed Betsy!" screame
Fancy, and she made to get off the bed to go to her. Bu
Caleb pushed her back.

"Get back there. She's only knocked out. Forget he
and think about me!"

Fancy gave a dispairing look at the motionless figure lying on the ground.

"Get away from me! You're not the man I remember . . ."

But her struggles only inflamed him more.

"No? But we'll soon alter all that . . ." He pressed her back to the bed and she felt his full weight on her. With familiar, practiced hands he caressed her, but now her response was to fight. She kicked and bit, and gasping, he seized her with hard fingers on her shoulders. She moaned as he satisfied his cruel lusts, and for the first time ever, Fancy knew the sensation of a rape. She felt besmirched, dirty, and bewildered—bewildered that the man she had loved for years could treat her so brutally.

Suddenly, after lying with eyes tight shut while he tried to rouse her to some kind of passion, she felt him being bodily torn away from her. She opened her eyes and found herself staring into the blazing countenance of Black Patch. Everything became a whirl. Caleb flew into a corner, and Black Patch seized her by the throat.

"So you couldn't even wait until I sailed! I should have known you better. I told you to go with him, but I never thought you would! By God, I should kill you both!"

"Monty! Monty, wait! It isn't like you thought . . ." But Black Patch was deaf to her. He threw her down and turned to Caleb. Caleb was just regaining his feet when Black Patch sprang. Somehow Caleb had a knife in his hand.

Crouching on the bed, Fancy looked around for Betsy. Some time during the rape, she must have come to and crawled away . . . Then, with a shock, Fancy remembered Camille. What would that savage Luala do with her?

Her heart was in her mouth as she watched the two men fight. Quietly she inched herself off the bed and rushed through the door into the other room. She thought she would collapse with relief! Betsy was sitting on the prostrate form of Luala and holding the baby. There was blood from a small cut on Betsy's forehead, but Luala looked as if she had walked into a door.

Fancy turned back to the scene of battle, and was just in time to see Caleb smashed against the wall and slither down like a broken ragdoll. Staggering and gasping, Black Patch stood before her. His face was a hideous mass of sweat and blood. He had lost his patch and the puckered scar about his empty eyesocket was red and livid. Fancy felt fear of him that she had never experienced before. He was looking at her with loathing.

"So I was wrong about you. You're a whore after all! You'll go with any man who wants you. You don't care that Caleb's a downright rogue! You went to him like a cow to a bull! Well, you can have him, and share him with all his other women. I'm finished. You are not what you seemed." He turned away, and then Fancy recovered from his onslaught and found her voice.

"It's not what you think. Monty. He raped me. I didn't want him . . ."

"Raped you? *Raped* you! Don't make me laugh! Fancy—Fancy—no one could rape *you*! You are too eager for love-making for anyone to rape you—I know!"

"But I *was* raped, Monty! Believe me—I felt nothing. That is, nothing pleasurable. He was obnoxious to me . . ."

"What? You with two children of his? Don't try and fool me, Fancy. You've always been honest in the past . . ."

Suddenly she was angry, and the feeling sprang from the bottom of her belly and rushed to the top of her head.

"Very well, think what you like! I've told you the truth and, to my mind, you're simply jealous. You have a nasty feeling that he's a better lover than you! Well, if it will give you any satisfaction, I'll stay on the island— but it won't be with him! There's not a toss between you! I'll be glad to be rid of you both!" She got up to adjust her clothing. "And as for men . . . it will be a long time before I let another man into my bed!"

"Fancy . . ." He moved toward her.

"Get away from me. I'm a whore—remember? I said don't touch me!"

As they glared at each other, Betsy burst into the room, holding Camille and looking agitated.

"I cannot bear to listen any longer, ma'am. He must be told! Captain Hawkins, sir, the mistress was telling the truth! She implored him to leave her alone and she fought him. I know because I was laid dazed on the floor. And when he finally pinned her down . . ."—she stopped and looked pleadingly at Black Patch—"he—he—*took* her—and she lay like one dead. I know because I watched . . ."

He turned to Fancy, who bit her lip and turned her back so that he could not see how near she was to tears.

"I'm a brute, Fancy. A jealous unthinking animal. You are right—I'm not fit to touch you. Will you forgive me, Fancy?"

She stiffened.

"You change your tune when someone else testifies for me, but you would not take my word . . ."

"Now you're being proud and awkward. I said I was sorry!"

"Well perhaps now you feel better. I don't!"

"What do you want me to do then? Go on my knees?"

Fancy's lips twitched at the thought. She spun around.

"Oh, Monty, I only want you to love me! I'm not a whore, really. You don't believe those awful things you said?"

He pulled her into his arms savagely and he kissed her fiercely, mindless of the blood on his face.

"I did when I said them! But now . . . never!"

Fancy looked up at him wonderingly.

"Do you really love me?"

He laughed.

"Of course I do, witch. You must have always known it!"

"But I didn't. What fools we have both been." Then a thought struck her. "How did you happen to come here?" Then she noted his red-rimmed eye. "You've been drinking!" Her voice was a reproach.

"And a good thing for you I had! I wanted you, Fancy, and couldn't bear the thought of you being here with that carrion. I came to take you back."

"And you found me with him . . . and not struggling?"

He nodded.

"And then I went mad. I don't really know what I said. I wanted to hurt you like you hurt me . . ."

Fancy shuddered at the memory of his accusing face.

"And you did hurt me, Monty. I had just realized what Caleb was. I knew I wanted to be with you, and Caleb knew it too. That was why he made me . . ."

Monty's arms closed about her protectively.

"It's over now and we'll forget it . . . and if you're with child, we'll get over that, too. From now on you're mine."

"There'll be no baby, Monty—not unless I have yours."

"Oh! Why do you say that?"

"Because—" She stopped to laugh. "I never thought Caleb would ever fail in his lust, but this time . . ."

"Then—then—he didn't?"

She shook her head.

"Nearly, but not quite."

"And you would have had me believe . . ."

"But that was your fault, Monty. You *wanted* to believe that I was a willing partner! Your jealousy deceived you!"

He put a finger on her mouth.

"But you always made it clear that you only used me. How should I know you loved me? You were a little naughty, too, my love!"

"Only because I didn't know myself! I thought my love was hate. I could not understand my own feelings."

"Then you are coming home to England . . . and Charles?"

"Yes, if you really want me . . ."

"Want you . . .? Oh, Fancy!" He kissed her again

and then, stroking her hair out of her eyes, he said,

"You know what it means, don't you, Fancy?"

"No. What does it mean, Monty?"

"That you're my woman now. There'll be no hankering after other men."

"Monty!"

"And I have the right to beat you on occasion, to remind you who is the master . . ."

"How could you . . .?"

"And your other children will be all mine! There'll be no more gypsy lovers or sleeping anywhere except in my bed . . ." He swung her high in his arms. "How will you like that? Answer me woman?"

"If you really love me, I'll like it very well. Monty, I had made up my mind about Caleb long before you came. I knew I was wrong about him . . ."

"Poor Fancy, fighting for your honor . . ."

"And Betsy's," she said, very dignified.

"And will you fight for your honor again tonight?"

"Oh, Monty," she sighed, and put her head on his chest. "It has been so long . . ."

"Too long, my heart." His gentle tone told her she had found the thing she had been looking for all her life.

That night they lay in each other's arms aboard the *Emma-Jane*, and Fancy thrilled to his love-making. Now her passion had a special thrill to it—she knew he loved her, not only desired her, and it made her giving more intense. He too, sensed the difference, and as he knew he had the one woman in his arms who mattered, he too let down the barriers. He was as she had never known him before. . . .

Then, happy in her giving, she lay quietly beside him, thinking of the future. She felt his questing hand around her waist.

"You are quiet. Are you asleep?"

Drowsily she shuffled, to let him know she had heard the question.

"Are you happy now?"

She smiled in the dark at his anxious tone.

"I had nearly forgotten what loving was like . . . Are *you* happy?"

He squeezed her to him.

"Of course. You smell wonderful—what is that scent?"

"Just myself, Monty. No doubt I smell very different from . . ."

He rapped her smartly on the buttocks, and she yelped with pain.

"None of that now. That's all over. You are my woman now, and I want no other. Do you really love me, Fancy?"

"I'm sure so. And I love fighting with you . . ."

"Even though I'm ugly and lost an eye?"

"Oh my love, I never think about it! You're you, my dearly beloved. Do you really love me?"

"What a silly question to ask a man!"

"But do you, Monty? Do you?"

He laughed.

"What do you think? I've told you I am a one-woman man."

"But a woman likes her man to tell her, and keep on telling her . . ."

"All right, you witch! I love you! Now are you satisfied?"

She snuggled into him, and he smiled into the darkness.

"Careful now, or we'll be at it again . . . and we must get some sleep!"

Suddenly Fancy sat up with a jerk.

"Now what is it, Fancy? Can't you rest?"

"Monty, what about Charles?"

"What about him?" said Monty drowsily.

"I want him with me in England. He must be with us!"

Monty sighed and pulled her down beside him.

"Don't worry your pretty little head about him. We'll have him for visits."

"Visits! I want him with us all the time!"

"That cannot be, Fancy. You made him the heir to Gilbourne yourself! If Sir Timothy gives you up quietly, you can hardly turn round and make a fool of him publicly. You will have to make the best of it."

"But will Timothy divorce me, Monty?"

"Of course. The King will see to that, especially after he finds out what we have in the coffers. And you need not worry—even if you were never free of Gilbourne, you would still be my woman! I don't care how I have you—married or not. You're still mine!"

She hugged him close.

"I think I should rather be Black Patch's woman than Sir Montagu Hawkins' wife! It can be very boring at Court: one never knows who is sleeping with whom. And it can be most frustrating when one wants to gossip about someone, and they happen to be friendly with the person you hate!"

"No danger of that with you. You will never turn into one of the royal whores! You are coming with me on all my voyages, babies and all. I shall not leave you behind to be tempted . . ."

"Monty!" she squealed, and gave him a great buffet on the head. He ducked.

"Now stop behaving like a common strumpet or a nagging wife . . ."

Indignantly Fancy opened her mouth to argue, but he firmly closed it by pressing his mouth over hers. And suddenly she had other things on her mind.

It was much later that her mind turned again to Charles. There was an ache in her heart for him, which would never be assuaged while they remained apart. And then there was Camille . . . Were brother and sister destined never to know and love each other? She sighed, and, being practical, concentrated on that that was most important to her at the moment. . . .

"Monty. My love . . . wake up. I still have a fancy . . ."